NOT
QUITE
DEAD
YET

NOT QUITE DEAD YET

A NOVEL

HOLLY JACKSON

BANTAM
New York

Bantam Books
An imprint of Random House
A division of Penguin Random House LLC
1745 Broadway, New York, NY 10019
randomhousebooks.com
penguinrandomhouse.com

LIBRARY OF CONGRESS CATALOGING-IN-PUBLICATION DATA
Names: Jackson, Holly, author
Title: Not quite dead yet : a novel / Holly Jackson.
Description: New York : Bantam, 2025.
Identifiers: LCCN 2025014936 (print) | LCCN 2025014937 (ebook) |
ISBN 9780593977057 hardcover | ISBN 9798217091591 international edition |
ISBN 9780593977064 ebook
Subjects: LCGFT: Thrillers (Fiction) | Novels
Classification: LCC PS3610.A35174 N68 2025 (print) | LCC PS3610.A35174 (ebook) |
DDC 813/.6—dc23/eng/20250423
LC record available at https://lccn.loc.gov/2025014936
LC ebook record available at https://lccn.loc.gov/2025014937

Printed in the United States of America on acid-free paper

2 4 6 8 9 7 5 3 1

First Edition

Book design by Debbie Glasserman

The authorized representative in the EU for product safety and
compliance is Penguin Random House Ireland, Morrison Chambers,
32 Nassau Street, Dublin D02 YH68, Ireland. https://eu-contact.penguin.ie.

For Jet

Friday
October 31

ONE

Dead gray skin, rotted away to show off the stringy sinews of muscle below. Sunken, rubbery sockets around sparkling hazel eyes. Those were actually hers, though; they moved as she studied herself. Decaying corn-on-the-cob teeth with gore stuck in the spaces between. What did zombies eat again? Just brains, or they weren't fussy about the other guts too? Probably didn't enjoy the candy apple she'd had earlier.

Jet watched her reflection in the funhouse mirror, her dead face—sorry—her undead face. OK, she'd worn the mask for three whole minutes, so Mom couldn't complain and now Jet couldn't breathe; hot toffee air that turned wet against the rubber, sticking it to her skin. She pulled the mask off. Still pale, slightly less gray, though, but the mirror elongated her round face, distorting her thick brows and upturned nose. Her short blond hair was sticking up now; static buzzed against her hand as she flattened it.

"Jet?"

"—Damn." She flinched. The mirror warped his face behind her, squashed his muscular frame into accordion ripples, but Jet knew his voice. Of fucking course. JJ Lim. But not with his usual black swept-back hair and clear tawny skin. He wore a garish red wig and denim overalls over a striped shirt, train-track gashes drawn on his face. Chucky. They'd watched that movie together on their third date.

"Didn't mean to scare you," he sniffed, awkward.

"It's Halloween, that's the point." More awkward. Jet walked away without looking at the unwarped him, past a stall of pumpkin pies and apple bread. *Just $5!!!* yelled the chalkboard sign.

"It's . . ." JJ slipped off his wig and stumbled after her, through a group of freshly face-painted kids. Why was he following her? She'd given them both an easy out. *Again.* "Sorry," he continued, "I was wondering. I just . . ."

Well, this was fun. Jet was super glad she'd come to the Halloween Fair now. The whole of Woodstock, Vermont, swarming The Green in the middle of town, and she'd managed to run into the one person she didn't want to see.

"Trick-or-treat!" a small vampire yelled up at her.

Jet hoped he'd choke on his slobbery fangs. Were kids always this annoying, or did the sugar rush bring it out of them? It was past ten now; when did parents put children to bed these days? Not fucking early enough.

She picked up her pace, but JJ didn't give up.

"Jet, please." He reached out for her arm. "I need to talk to you about something."

Jet stopped, sighed. *Something* meant *them,* didn't it? And they weren't a *them* anymore, not for months. "I can't right now." Lie. "I'm helping my parents run the fundraising booth." Bigger lie. "Did Henry draw those scars for you?" Change the subject.

JJ narrowed his sharp eyes. "Please, Jet, it's important."

"Oh, *important,*" Jet snorted, "like when you said I was the best you could hope for . . . in Woodstock. Such a poet, J."

"You know I didn't mean it like that. And it's not about *us,* it's—"

"—Hey buddy, think you dropped this," a voice said over JJ's shoulder, saving her. It was her brother, Luke, bending to retrieve the crumpled red wig from the grass. Pinpricks of string lights reflected in his matching hazel eyes as he straightened up and squared up, passing JJ the wig.

JJ took it, and finally took the hint too, losing himself in the crowd.

"Saved you," Luke said.

Jet would never admit it. She was about to tell Luke so when he punched her in the shoulder, aiming for the dead-arm spot. He missed. But—also—he was fucking thirty and a dad now. When would the punching stop?

Jet didn't react, a lesson all sisters learned one way or another. It annoyed them more.

Luke grinned, sharpening his jaw. Actually, his whole head somehow—he'd had his honey-brown hair cut too short again; no honey, just fuzz. But Sophia liked it that way, apparently. And—great—here she was now, holding baby Cameron dressed as an unhappy pumpkin.

"Was that JJ?" Sophia asked, slotting in beside Luke, hip to hip, claiming her husband back. She was dressed as Catwoman, tall and lithe in a tight leather suit that would be unforgiving on Jet's shorter, curvier frame. Remember when they used to share clothes, when they were teenagers? Back when they were the ones joined at the hip. Until Sophia got tall and Jet got boobs.

"Didn't JJ get the message?" Luke surveyed the bustle of the fair, finally starting to die down, thank god. "How clear can you make it when a guy gets down on one knee and you say no?"

"Literally," Sophia added, unhelpfully.

"That's not how it happened," Jet said.

"So, Marge," Luke said, looking for another reaction. "What did you come dressed as this year?"

"Oh." Jet gestured down her black turtleneck sweater and sleeveless denim jacket, black pants and boots. Yes, the boots were also black. "I thought it was super obvious. I came as a law school dropout who still lives at home with her parents at twenty-seven." Made the joke before someone else could.

Luke hissed. "Scariest costume here."

Sophia nudged him.

Something stirred in Jet's gut, burned in her cheeks.

"You're also not wearing a costume," she reminded her brother.

Luke cleared his throat. "No, 'cause I'm here representing our family, representing Mason Construction. This is our fair, important to look professional and approachable."

"With that hair?" Jet laughed, still smarting. Maybe she'd feel better if she took Luke down with her. Just a little. "Company's not yours yet, Luke."

A muscle ticked in his jaw.

"Next year." Sophia squeezed Luke's arm, a red-lipped smile spreading across her face. *Next year,* when Dad retired. No, sorry, *if.* He'd been "about to retire" three times already. They weren't supposed to talk about that and Jet knew it; she shot him an empty grin, too many teeth.

"Cameron's first Halloween," Sophia said quickly, switching to something they *were* allowed to talk about. Her baby. All she ever wanted to talk about, actually. "He's a pumpkin." She jiggled him on her hip.

"Oh shit, really?" Jet said. "I thought he was a butternut squash."

"Jet." Sophia turned on her. "Can you not swear in front of the baby, please."

"Fuck, sorry." Jet clapped her hands to her mouth.

"Seriously?"

"It slipped out." It hadn't.

"You still writing that . . . what was it?" Sophia asked. "That screenplay?"

Jet shuffled, digging the toe of her boot into a fallen leaf. Didn't want to talk about that but Sophia and Luke were staring, and she had no choice. "No, I'm not doing that anymore."

Luke tucked his hands into his front pockets. Here we go. "Given up already?" he said, and clearly enjoyed saying it. "That must be a new record."

"I'm working on something else, actually." Jet kept her voice level, walls up, teeth together. "A new idea."

"It's not that dog-walking app business thing, is it?" he said.

That feeling burned brighter, churning in her gut. Jet hardened her eyes, an unsaid question.

"Dad told me."

"Well," she said, like she didn't care at all. "I wish you'd all stop talking about me."

"Well," he replied, "I wish we didn't need to."

"Fuck off, Luke."

"Jet!"

"He can't talk yet, Sophia."

"That's the difference between me and you," Luke said. "When I have goals, I actually see them through."

Jet laughed. A dark, husky sound that didn't match her face, people said. An old man's laugh, like she'd smoked a pack a day when she'd never smoked one.

"I've got all the time in the world," she said, same thing she told herself every Monday morning when her parents went to work and she didn't. Repeated the words until they stuck. Anyway, she shouldn't let Luke get under her skin like this. "And I think you're forgetting that I won that district spelling bee when I was just ten."

Luke bowed his head. "I remember." Of course he remembered, because that wasn't the only thing that had happened that day.

"Well," Sophia said, unaware of the dark memory she was trampling over with her singsong voice. "We're heading off. This little guy is getting grouchy."

"Aw, Luke, haven't had enough protein today?"

Damn, he wasn't even listening, craning his neck to look over the heads of witches and superheroes, toward the stall their parents were manning.

"I gotta go rescue Dad now," he said, no goodbye.

"Good little CFO," Jet muttered.

He heard, turning back, a flash behind his eyes.

"At least I'm chief financial officer and not chief fuck-up."

"That doesn't even match."

"Jet!"

"That was Luke who swore, not me!"

Cameron fussed and Sophia sighed, watching Luke through the crowd.

"I wish you two wouldn't fight," she said.

Jet shook her head. "That wasn't a fight. Just a normal conversation. You wouldn't know."

"He's under a lot of stress."

"He's Luke," Jet said, "he's always stressed. And I bet he managed to find time to play golf with Jack Finney and David Dale at least twice this week. *Stressed.* I knew him first, remember. Knew you first too."

Because that was the real thing, that cold, barbed thing between Jet and Sophia. You go away to college and your best friend who stopped calling and stopped replying—and stopped caring—sets her sights on your brother instead. Anything to be in with the Masons. Jet didn't know how to talk to her anymore, and she'd never say it, but she thought the baby was boring as fuck.

"Well, I'm going to . . ." She didn't finish, didn't really need to; Sophia looked just as relieved when Jet left her behind, disappearing into the thinning crowd.

People were starting to leave now, werewolves and serial killers jostling her. A ginormous cat costume headed her way, a mismatched human head bursting from its white-and-ginger-furred shoulders, cat head tucked under one arm. Jet recognized the human part: bald head and dark brown skin, eyes magnified by circular glasses. It was Gerry Clay. He was on the board of village trustees with Mom. Actually, Gerry was chair and Mom was vice, and Mom said she didn't mind that when she was elected, but Mom was a bad liar.

Cat-Gerry was walking between two police officers. Not costumes this time, uniforms. Shields on their chests and guns in their belts. Lou Jankowski, their newish chief of police, and Jack Finney, who lived opposite the Masons, always had.

"Hello Jet." Jack gave her a familiar smile, tall and broad shouldered, the gray in his dark hair creeping into his stubble. Sophia used to call him a silver fox when they were teenagers, even though the silver part was pretty new.

"Hi Mr. Finney." She was supposed to call him Sergeant or something, but it had never stuck. Mr. Finney was an improvement on *Billy's dad* at least, and that's what Jet had called him for most of her life.

"Billy was looking for you," he said, like he'd read her mind.

Wow, Jet was Miss Fucking Popular tonight.

"Sorry, Lou," Jack added. "This is Jet. Scott and Dianne's daughter. Don't know if you've met?"

"Don't know if we have," Lou said. His face looked mean, hard eyes, but his voice didn't match, too soft. Yellowy-gray hair, close to mustard, and ketchup-ruddy cheeks. Clearly the man had never heard of retinol. "It's been a pleasure working with your mom, and Gerry of course. Oh, that's my wife, that scarecrow waving at me. Excuse me a minute."

"A pleasure?" Jet said, watching the chief go. "He must have the wrong Dianne Mason."

"Ha!" Gerry shouted it, not really a laugh. "You're a funny one."

Jet already knew she was a funny one. Sometimes that was all she had.

"What do you think of your new boss, Jack?" the half-cat half-Gerry asked, his attention on the retreating chief. "Don't tell anyone I said this, Jack, but it should have been you. Made so much more sense to have a chief who's lived here for decades, not some out-of-towner who doesn't know anyone. Of course I voted for you. I don't know why the other trustees— shit, don't tell anyone I said that. But . . . it should have been you."

Jack's shoulders dropped. He glanced away awkwardly, probably for somewhere else to look, finding a perfect distraction in the stall behind them, where Jet's parents were selling bags of candy corn, fundraising for the town's *Green Spaces*. All sponsored by your friendly local home construction business, of course. The ones who built mansions next to those *Green Spaces*.

Jack coughed, coming back to them. "I'm sure you picked the right man for the job."

How had Jet found herself in yet another conversation she didn't want to be in?

"Cool," she said, trying to break the tension. "If you want to arrest someone to cheer yourself up, Mr. Finney, I nominate my brother. Think we both know he deserves it."

Jack didn't smile at that, clearly still lost in what Gerry had said.

"Oh," Gerry piped up. "There's my kid, Owen, the one taking the photos. He's starting a photography course soon. Let's get a picture, Jack."

Gerry looped one thick cat arm through Jack's and dragged the poor man away.

"Hey, Jet."

For fuck's sake, could she just get one minute?

"Billy Finney." She turned to face him, her fakest smile. "You found me. Thank god, because I've hardly spoken to anyone tonight."

"Really?" he said.

"No. I'm sick of people."

"Am I people?"

"You sure look like one."

A tall one, with dark brown curls that skimmed his wide-set watery blue eyes. A mouth that was always open and always slightly crooked, even when he wasn't smiling. He raised his eyebrows at her. She knew that look; Billy hadn't changed much since he was ten years old.

"What?" Jet asked.

"I just spoke to your mom, and she asked me my name."

Jet snorted.

"I literally grew up next door, spent more time at your house than I did my own." Billy shrank somehow, even though he towered over Jet. "She was joking, right? She hasn't forgotten who I am?"

Poor, sweet Billy.

"Don't take it personally, bud." Jet clapped him on the arm. "I never do." Which was, maybe, her biggest lie tonight. "Is that why you wanted to find me . . . sorry, what's your name again?"

"I'm not ready to joke about it." Billy frowned. "Actually, I was going to ask if you wanted to come to the bar on Tuesday. We're doing another live music night. It's me, actually, I'm the one who's playing, I—I think I told you before, a few times. Guitar, singing some songs, some I wrote." Why was he talking so fast? And—was he sweating? "Just wondering if you could make it this time. N-no—no worries if not."

Jet sucked in a breath. She couldn't, not the last time he asked, not now. Because what if he was terrible and she laughed and then it became this whole thing? "Sorry," she said. "I can't this week. Really busy. Maybe next time?"

He shrank again. "Yeah, cool." Billy nodded, his turn to fake smile. "There'll be a next time, don't worry."

Jet wasn't worried but didn't get a chance to say so because a clown was bounding toward them, slipping and stumbling on the grass. A drunk clown, beer bottle in hand.

"You OK?" Jet asked.

Now she recognized him, only a clown from the neck up, a half-assed red nose and wig. Underneath that, it was just Andrew Smith. He rocked on his feet, his eyes unfocused, setting on fire when they found her.

"You," he slurred, pointing the empty beer at her. "Where's your brother? I need to speak to him."

"Luke?" Jet shrugged. "I think he left." Lucky prick.

Andrew laughed, a dark, whistling sound. "Your fucking family. Think throwing this fucking party every year makes up for any of it?"

Billy stepped closer to Jet, into the line of fire. Well, beer.

"All of you. Destroy everything you touch!" Andrew spat.

"I—I think you've had a little too much to drink, huh, Andrew?" Billy said, raising his hands, palms exposed. "That's OK. How about I get you some water?"

"Don't tell me what to do, boy! Always telling me what to do!"

Andrew half charged, half fell into Billy, shoving him backward. Billy didn't fight back, let himself get pushed.

"It's OK, Mr. Smith," he strained to say, the clown throwing weak drunken punches at his chest.

Why wasn't Billy doing anything?

"Hey," Jet yelled, doing something, but it was done before she could reach the scuffle. Billy's dad—shit, old habit, try again—*Jack* had appeared out of the thinning crowd, Chief Lou on his heels. Jack grabbed Andrew, wrenched him away from Billy. Andrew tripped over his own feet, into Chief Lou, who held him in a barrel grip.

"Calm down, sir!" Lou barked into his ear, the softness gone from his voice. Not super calming.

"I've got this, Chief." Jack gripped one of Andrew's arms. The clown's head lolled onto Jack's shoulder. "You OK, Billy?" Jack asked his son, over Andrew's head.

"Yeah, fine, Dad," Billy answered. "Just a misunderstanding. He needs to go home, sleep it off. Please don't arrest him."

"You know this man?" Chief Lou asked Billy's dad.

Jack nodded.

"Know where he lives?"

Jack nodded again. "He lives in the apartment next to Billy's."

"All right." The chief righted his uniform. "Can you escort him home, Sergeant? Make sure he gets a drink of water."

"Yes, Chief."

"Next time," Lou spoke down to the clown, "it'll be a night in the cell and a charge of disorderly conduct."

"Come on, Andrew," Jack said, leading the man away, toward the road and the streetlamps, holding the clown upright, the man too.

The chief turned to speak to Billy, and Jet slipped away. She was done talking to people and done with this Halloween Fair. Maybe she'd pretend she was sick next year. Actually, it didn't matter: next year she wouldn't even be here anymore. She'd be in Boston again, maybe back in law school, or maybe running her new company. There was time for that. She had time.

"What was that about?" Dad asked when she finally reached their stall.

"Andrew Smith." Jet dropped her zombie mask on the table. "Drunk and sad again."

"About his house?" Mom said, distracted, counting cash into a lock-box, her sharp haircut swinging around her neck.

"No, probably about his only daughter killing herself last year."

Dianne hissed, an intake of breath. "Jet, I wish you wouldn't."

"Wouldn't what, Mom? Speak? Exist?" Her mom gave her a look, those fierce green-brown eyes magnified by her glasses, but not softened.

"Ah," Dad groaned suddenly, bending double, his hand pressed to his side.

"Bad again?" Mom turned, a wad of twenties in her hand. "Take some painkillers when we get home. And don't say no, Scott; you're going in for another checkup."

Dad could only grunt. He was sweating, his thinning hair stuck down to his temple, new lines etched in his face, pain bracketing the wrinkles.

"A heating pad and a whole bunch of water," Jet said with a sad smile. "That works best for me. You can borrow mine."

She understood the pain. In fact, she was the only one in the family who could. Mom and Luke had never spent weeks at a time pissing blood, or unable to walk because of the pain in their side. Them and their normal kidneys.

"Well." Jet clapped her hands. "It's been a pleasure, but I'm going home."

"You can't," Dianne snapped. "You said you'd stay till the end and help us clear up. People are leaving now. You can make yourself useful and take the chairs back to the hotel."

Jet had never agreed to that, and she hated when her mom told her to make herself useful. It didn't make her feel useful; it made her feel small.

"I'll do it tomorrow," she said.

"Your catchphrase, Jet," her mom sighed.

"That's not the catchphrase," Dad said, but there was warmth in his voice. "It's: 'I'll do it *later.*'"

"*Later* is a great word," Jet said, voice rising as she turned away from her parents. "Means I never have to be *useful.* See you at home."

Mom was distracted again anyway: Gerry Clay was back, a full cat this time.

"Boo!" He jumped out from behind the stall. "Dianne, I know your deepest, darkest secret," he said, low and diabolical.

"You're having too much fun, Gerry," Dianne clipped back.

Jet walked across The Green, onto the street beyond. It was dark, but not yet late enough to worry about it. The town was still thrumming and shrieking, with departing cars and the undead. A gaggle of teenagers outside the little church, too loud and giggly for just sugar. Found Mom and Dad's liquor cabinet, she'd bet.

Past the houses beyond, jack-o'-lanterns still glowing outside, mean triangle eyes glaring back at her. Someone hadn't bothered carving theirs; just a bunch of naked pumpkins and gourds lining the steps up to their front door.

Jet turned up College Hill Road, saluting the skeleton hanging outside the Romanos' at number 1, its limbs creaking and flailing in the fall breeze. Up the hill to number 10.

Home.

This big obnoxious house that Dad had renovated and extended, and extended again. It stuck out against the normal houses on the street, against the Finneys' directly opposite at number 7. Jet might just hate the Masons too, you know.

She jogged up the large ringed driveway, past her truck, giving it an affectionate pat on the cargo bed. A Ford F-150 in powder blue. Mom thought Jet had bought it just to piss her off. Mom wasn't totally wrong.

Just one jack-o'-lantern outside their red front door, but its eyes had blown out, gone dark. A bucket on the front step with a sign: *Please help yourself. One candy per person.* What world did her mom live in? Damn, the bucket was empty. Fuckers.

Jet searched her jacket pocket for her house keys, the Ring doorbell camera eyeing her, so she eyed it back, stuck out her tongue.

She unlocked the front door, and Reggie was at her feet in a rush of red fur and a helicopter tail, the happy squeaks he only made for her. He jumped up and pawed her knees.

"Hello, hello, handsome. Who's a good boy, huh?"

Jet bent to tickle him behind the ears. Those silly, long, English cocker spaniel ears.

The dog ran off, skittering around the corner and back two seconds later.

"Oh, did you bring me some dirty socks?" Jet said, thumbing his muzzle, the proud wiggle of his little body at the sacred offering. "Thank you so much, my absolute favorite."

Jet closed the front door and moved through the hall, crisp white walls and Moroccan rugs, too neat, too styled, like a show home, and—man—was Jet in trouble every time she dared to treat it like a home, dropping crumbs or leaving her boots out. Through to the kitchen at the back of the house, Reggie trotting in behind her.

There was a plate of cookies on the kitchen island. Sophia had baked them, dropped them off earlier, black iced bats and orange pumpkins. Sophia did things like that. Baked. Jet picked up a bat, bit off its head. Damn, they were actually good. She finished it off, wiping her sticky fingers on one of the dish towels by the stove, a matching set of three: little marching lemons and oranges and avocados, because everything had to match in this house. Jet turned and passed the cookies again. Fuck it, actually; she took one of the pumpkins too, wandering through the wide, corniced archway into the living room.

Cookie in mouth, she reached into her pocket for her phone. Unlocked. Thumb finding Instagram before her eyes did. She bit off half the pumpkin, the sweet orange icing cloying against her tongue. Girls from school or college who were now married, having anniversaries and babies. Or no weddings and babies, but fancy dinners and sipping glasses of champagne to celebrate new jobs. That could have been Jet too, a humble-brag post about a big promotion at a firm with an acronym everyone pretended to recognize. If she hadn't quit and left Boston overnight.

Jet finished off the cookie, sticky fingers against the screen. It didn't matter. Jet had time to find the right thing; she had all the time in the world, remember? And then life would really begin, and when it did, you better believe she'd be shoving it down all of their throats in return. Just you wait.

Reggie stood in front of her, started to whine.

"Sorry bud. Human cookies."

The whine lowered, sinking into a growl.

"Wh—"

A rush of feet behind.

A fast crack to the back of her head, the wet of splitting skin, crunch of skull.

The phone slips from her hands. No growl anymore but a scream. Jet should scream too but—

Another explosion, harder. The feel of blood, the sound of things breaking inside her head.

Someone's killing her.

Jet can still think that, but she blinks and the light doesn't come back and—

Woodstock Police Department, Woodstock, Vermont
Emergency call log
Date: 10/31/2025
Time: 11:09 p.m.

DISPATCHER: This is 911, how can I help?

CALLER: Oh my god, oh my god, help! Send help!

DISPATCHER: Sir, please calm down. What service do you
             require?

CALLER: Fuck. Ambulance. Get an ambulance here.
             Police. She's not moving, oh my god. No!

        [screams in background]

DISPATCHER: Can you give me an address, sir?

CALLER: Yeah, fuck. It's number 10, College Hill
             Road.

             Oh my god, Jet. No, please don't be dead,
             please. Is she dead?

DISPATCHER: What's happening over there?

CALLER: Someone's attacked her. There's blood
             everywhere. Her head. No, no, no.

        [screams in background]

DISPATCHER: Is there anyone else with you at the scene?

CALLER: No, no, it's just me and her. I found her,
             she wasn't—

DISPATCHER: Who's screaming?

CALLER: That's the dog. This can't be happening, no.
             Jet! Jet! Please don't be dead, I'm begging
             you.

DISPATCHER: Can you check if she's breathing?

CALLER: No, no, no. Jet, please.

DISPATCHER: Sir, what's your name?

CALLER: Billy. Billy Finney.

DISPATCHER: Jack's kid?

CALLER: Yeah.

DISPATCHER: OK, Billy. It's me, Debbie, from the station. I need you to stop crying and stay calm for me, please. The ambulance is on its way. Help is coming. But I need you to check if she's breathing, if there's a pulse.

CALLER: There's so much blood, I don't . . . I can't. Oh my god, Jet, no. Please god, no. She's dead. Someone killed her. She's dead. She's dead.

NOT QUITE . . .

SUNDAY
NOVEMBER 2

TWO

J et blinked. Something beeped. Someone gasped.

"She's awake! Doctor, she's awake!"

Who's *she*? Talking about her? The room was fuzzy, too white, too bright. It hurt Jet's eyes and the hidden places beneath. She blinked again, smudges of flesh and hair and teeth looming above her.

"Luke. Get the doctor, now. Go!"

Her mom's voice, raw and unfamiliar.

"Mom?" Jet croaked, croakier than usual. She tried to sit up, her body sleep-locked, trapped by thin, rough sheets tucked over her elbows. A white gown, patterns of pale yellow and blue.

"Let me help." Dad's voice now. Must belong to that smudge there, beside her. Warm hands on her shoulders, she sat up, something stuck to her head, crinkling against the pillows behind her, and a shooting jolt of pain.

She rubbed her eyes, got tangled in the tube sticking out the back of her hand.

"Water?" Mom said, and it was already by her lips. Jet couldn't get the angle. She slurped and she knew Mom hated that, but maybe Mom could forgive her this one time because Jet was in the hospital.

And she knew why. She remembered. The room was fuzzy but her mind was not.

Someone had tried to kill her. Smashed in her head. The crunch of the pumpkin cookie and her skull, and the strange scream of the dog. But Jet was still here, she was breathing—gulped one in just to check. This was real—another blink to be sure, her body laid out before her, two hands, two legs that moved when she asked. And she must have a head because she was seeing and hearing and breathing out of it.

She was alive.

She'd survived.

Fuck.

Thank you, thank you, thank you.

"Jet." Mom's face was clearer now, inches from hers. "The doctor is coming now. She's going to explain to you, and you need to listen, OK? It's very important. They won't do it unless it's your choice. You'll know the right choice, sweetie."

Mom reached out to stroke Jet's hair, but her fingers stalled. "Sorry, I forgot."

"Got her!" Luke's voice, charging into the room, breathless, like he'd run all the way. "Hey, Marge," he said softly, not like Luke at all. "You OK?"

"Got a bit of a headache." Jet smiled. None of them would look at her. Come on, she was just trying to lighten the mood. She was alive.

The door swung open again, a small woman with dark skin and braided hair, a file clutched in her hand. She didn't smile either.

She cleared her throat, eyes alighting on the bed. "Good to see you awake. Your family said you like to be called Jet," she said. "I'm Dr. Lee."

Jet didn't know what to say. *Nice to meet you?* Why did everyone look so fucking miserable? She was alive, she was awake.

"Can I just . . ." Dr. Lee said, coming close, drawing a penlight from the pocket of her white jacket. And, yes, she could just, because she was already doing it, shining the light in Jet's eyes. One and the other. Light off. "How much have you told her?" The doctor turned to Jet's mom.

"Nothing," Dianne said, backing off. "We were waiting for you."

"Guys, it's OK," Jet sniffed. "I already know. I remember everything. Someone hit me in the back of the head. Tried to kill me."

Silence.

"Didn't do a very good job of it," Jet said. Jazz hands, for effect.

Dad cupped his fingers to his mouth, holding back a sob. A silent tear rolling down his knuckles.

"Mr. Mason, please," Dr. Lee said, pulling up a chair to sit beside the bed. "Jet. I'm a neurosurgeon. You're in Dartmouth Hitchcock Medical Center."

"How long have I been here?" Jet asked. "What day is it today?" What day, or what year? Fuck—had she been asleep a lot longer than she thought? Oh fuck, had she been in a coma for years—is that why everyone was being so weird? She hadn't turned thirty already, had she? All that lost time.

"It's Sunday," Dr. Lee said, voice calming, reacting to Jet's panicked eyes, "at 2 p.m. You've been here about thirty-six hours."

"Fucking phew," she said. "That's a relief. I thought I was old."

Dad turned away, faced the wall.

"Jet, you were in a bad way when you arrived at the ER," Dr. Lee said, fiddling the edges of the file. "You were an eight on the GCS on arrival, which means you were comatose, had to be intubated. Suffered cardiac arrest from blood loss shortly after. We were able to stabilize you, get you into surgery. You had a subdural hematoma, here on the left side of your head, under that bandage. That means a buildup of blood on the surface of the brain. We evacuated the blood and there didn't appear to be any significant brain trauma. But we believe you were hit three times. Once on the left side of your head there, and twice on the back of your head, near the base of your skull."

Those were the ones Jet remembered.

Dr. Lee swallowed.

"Your skull was fractured. A longitudinal fracture across the occipital bone. The first blow would have caused the fracture, the second would have depressed the bone farther into your brain." She paused, looked down. "Considering the site of the injury, the violence of the attack, it's a miracle there isn't significant damage to the vital tissues and vascular structures of the brain, that you're able to move and think and function as you are. I've never seen anything like it. But."

Jet knew there had to be a *but* coming. Because if it was a miracle, her family wouldn't be looking at her like this. Like she hadn't woken up at all.

Her head was throbbing, the base and the left side; now she knew where to pinpoint the pain. Hot and sharp, an imitation, a ghost of how it had felt at the time. When her head had exploded open.

Dr. Lee flipped the file in her lap.

"The fracture was successfully mended during surgery. We've reconnected the skull pieces with screws and wire mesh. Stitched up your scalp."

It flared and itched as she mentioned it.

"And after surgery, you were sent for another CT scan."

She pulled out a scan from the file, the plastic quivering with an almost comic *wub-wub* sound, not reading the room. Dr. Lee held the scan up, against the afternoon light streaming through the window. A black background. White writing glowed at the very top: *Margaret Mason, Age: 27, 11/01/2025,* more numbers Jet didn't understand. Below was a grid of pictures. Different angles of her brain, dissected this way and that, rendered in a strange pale blue.

"There is a bone at the base of the skull, at the deepest part, right in the middle of your brain, called the clivus. The trauma to the back of your head has resulted in a fracture to the clivus." The scan trembled in Dr. Lee's hand, threatening that noise again. "A clivus fracture is an incredibly rare event, seen in less than 0.5 percent of traumatic head injuries. And if you look here"—she pointed to the scan, to an image taken through the top of Jet's head—"you can see there is a small piece of bone fragment separated from the clivus."

Dr. Lee's finger pressed against a tiny pale white orb, floating there in the middle of Jet's brain. She pointed it out in the side view too, checking that Jet could see. Not even an orb, just a speck really.

"OK," Jet said. "But it's tiny, right? And I'm fine. Look, I'm fine."

Luke pulled out the chair on the other side, made Mom sit down.

"Jet," Dr. Lee said, her teeth holding on to the *t,* chewing on it, so she didn't have to continue. "That tiny bone fragment is leaning against the wall of your basilar artery."

Jet breathed out. "That sounds important."

"One of the major arteries supplying blood to your brain."

Yep. Important.

"A surgery to remove the fragment would normally be considered impossible. It's so deep, so hard to access without damaging other parts of the brain. Too easy to accidentally nick the artery and cause a catastrophic bleed. Chances of mortality far too high. Better to leave it and, in time, the fragment may migrate to the outer edges of the brain, where it could be more easily accessed and removed. But."

Another *but*.

The throbbing was a drumbeat in Jet's head now, mirroring her heart, answering fear with fear.

"You have polycystic kidney disease, Jet."

"I'm well aware." Jet sniffed. Again, those weeks of pissing blood, pain so bad it doubled you over, the phantom bruises, quitting her job and moving home because it all got too much, the high-blood-pressure pills she took every day, never smoked, not too much salt, even though she'd once loved fries. "What does that have to do with my brain?"

Dad was standing behind Mom now, hands on her shoulders, lips in a tight white line to stop him from crying.

Dr. Lee swallowed.

"A complication of PKD is that patients have much weaker arterial walls, in the heart and . . . and in the brain."

"Right."

"I'm sorry, Jet, there's no easy way to tell you this. With the fragment's position, putting extra pressure on an already weak arterial wall, an aneurysm will form at the site. A large one. And when it ruptures, the resulting hemorrhage, the bleeding, it . . . it would be fatal."

"O-K," Jet said, nodding, stopping when she realized that hurt. "And how likely is it that an aneurysm would form?"

"It's a certainty, Jet. And it would be fast."

"How fast?"

"It's impossible to accurately predict, especially before the aneurysm has formed."

"Give it your best guess, doc."

"Jet," Mom sniffed.

Dr. Lee straightened, looked at the floor instead of Jet. "Given the particular circumstances of your case, I would say we have just days. Maybe a week until it ruptures."

Jet clicked her tongue, to hide the thrum of her heart, fight-or-flight fast. This couldn't be happening. Was this really happening? "So . . . you're saying that I'd be dead in about a week?"

No one answered.

Dad couldn't hold it any longer, burying his face in the crook of his elbow as he sobbed.

"Dad, it's OK," Jet said, shifting in her bed. She'd only seen him cry once before like this. A guttural, primal sound. She hoped she'd never have to hear that sound again; seventeen years wasn't long enough.

"It's my fault," he cried.

"Dad, it's not your fault. It's hereditary. There was a fifty percent chance that me or Luke or Emily could have inherited PKD." That made Jet the unlucky one. She already knew that, because the other two had normal names and she was the one who got stuck with Margaret. "So, the surgery, then. Right?" Jet looked from Dr. Lee to her family.

Mom nodded, wiped her swollen eyes. None of them looked like they'd slept much, in the time Jet had slept too much. "It's the only choice, Jet."

"Please, Mrs. Mason," Dr. Lee's voice hardened. "I need to make something clear to you, Jet, before you make any decision. Like I said, under other circumstances, this surgery wouldn't even be considered. The risk of mortality is high. I have to be honest with you: it was my colleague, Dr. Fuller, who performed the initial surgery on you. After the second CT scan, once the situation became clear, Dr. Fuller refused to even consider performing surgery to attempt to remove the bone fragment. I said that I would only do it if you had all the information—if you chose this, understanding the risk."

The drumming in her head quickened, unnatural, like it was counting down to something, racing her heart.

"What is the risk?" Jet asked. "Can you give me a percentage or something?"

Dr. Lee hesitated, her tongue moving around inside her mouth, bulging through her cheek. "Less than ten percent chance of survival."

The drumming stopped.

"So, more than a ninety percent chance that I'd die on the table?" Numb, detached, like she wasn't here in this body, in this bed. Sometimes minds did that, didn't they, to save you from the pain? Or was this a result of the brain trauma, the kind of broken that didn't show up on CT scans? "I'm not a betting girl, but those don't sound like good odds."

Jet wasn't good with chance. She'd already lost that game with polycystic kidney disease. And that was with fifty percent. Not ten. Less than ten.

"There's nothing else you can do?"

"I'm sorry, Jet," Dr. Lee said, a tremble in her voice that she coughed to cover. How many times had she had to tell someone they were going to die? Could you get used to a thing like that?

Jet looked at her family. Luke, gray and silent, a muscle ticking in his jaw. Dad crying, a quieter, more unsettling kind of cry. Mom leaning forward in her chair, taking Jet's hand in her own, giving it a squeeze.

"So." Jet hesitated, trying to stick her mind back together, to fix what the doctor couldn't. "My choice is I can die now, or I can die in seven days?"

THREE

The room was silent, but the world was not. It carried on; a high-pitched beep from a machine, a low-pitched scream down the corridor, the fall sun beaming through the window because it didn't care about her and her little problems.

What kind of choice was that? Jet couldn't even decide what to have for breakfast most days. Die now, or die in a week? Toast or cereal? Both?

There was a humming too, but that wasn't down the corridor; it was in Jet's head, behind her eyes, playing with her heart. A symphony of the damned. Her throat constricted; she wouldn't let the others hear it.

"Damn," Jet said. "You sure there isn't a door number three?"

Her mom replied before the doctor could.

"Everything's going to be OK, sweetie. It's obvious which choice to make," she sniffed, her grip tightening until it hurt. "One of them has a chance, the other doesn't. I can't lose you. You have to choose the surgery, Jet. Quickly. The doctor said every minute counts."

"Mrs. Mason—"

"—Not much of a chance." Jet looked at her. "Less than ten percent chance of survival. I know it's been a while since high school for you, but that's not great math, Mom."

"Don't make this a competition, Jet."

"How was I making it a—"

"—You have to have the surgery." Mom's eyes filled but they didn't spill. "I can't lose another daughter. You can't do that to me."

The humming became a roar of thunder. Jet could normally leash it, back down and walk away, but maybe that had gotten broken too.

"I didn't bash my own fucking brain in, Mom. *I'm* not doing this. Not everything is my fault."

Dad stepped forward. "Jet, your mom didn't mean it like that. She only wants what's best for you. We all do, baby girl."

He hadn't called her that in years.

"Yeah," Luke said, gruffly, like that added anything.

"But you're going to choose the surgery," Mom said, tears released, chasing each other down her cheeks. "You know that's the right decision, don't you? Scott, help me."

Dr. Lee cut in, rising from her chair. "This really has to be Jet's decision." Her voice softened. "You don't have to make it right this moment. The police are outside. They've been waiting for you to wake up. They need to ask you some questions about your assault, before you decide."

"In case I choose the surgery and don't make it," Jet said, seeing through the doctor's words. "They're here, now, to i-i-in . . ." What was the word? Ah, fuck, you know the word she meant. What you do to get a job, same thing when the police ask you questions. Sounds like . . . Jet couldn't remember what it sounded like. "I-in . . ." What was that fucking word?

"Interview?" Luke offered.

"Yes. Interview." Jet smacked her hand down on the bed. "What was I saying?"

Dr. Lee's eyes narrowed. "Jet, are you having trouble finding your words?"

"No."

Yes. Not some of them. Like *Fuck, fuck, I'm going to die, fuck.* But she couldn't find the word for that thing resting around Dr. Lee's shoulders. That long thing with earbuds and a metal disc, for listening to hearts. Jet didn't need one; her heart was too loud already.

Dr. Lee nodded, like she could read minds, even if she couldn't fix this one.

"One of the blows was to the side of your head here." Dr. Lee gestured to the stick-on bandage. "The left hemisphere, where the brain's language center is. Sometimes trauma to this area can cause problems with understanding or producing language, called an aphasia. Your comprehension and speech seem mostly unaffected, so it's likely anomic aphasia, the mildest kind." She paused. "You may have trouble retrieving certain words, specifically ones you don't use too often. It can be temporary, may only last a few weeks or months, and can be treated with speech therapy."

Jet shrugged. "I don't have weeks or months, though, do I?" Not really a question.

"If you have the surgery, Jet—" Mom began.

"—I think we need to let Jet speak to the police now." Dr. Lee gestured with Jet's medical file, sweeping Dianne to her feet.

Luke lingered by the door.

"Who was it, Jet?" he asked, mouth in a grim line, hiding his teeth. "Who did this to you?"

She exhaled. Three words she definitely knew how to find: "I don't know."

"Come on, Luke." Dad patted him gently on the back. "Let's let the cops ask their questions. There's not much time."

Mom pressed her hand to the lump of Jet's foot, beneath the sheet. "I'll be right outside, sweetie."

The doctor was the last to leave, looking back at Jet, a sad half-smile. The smile of an execu-exec—fuck, what was that word? You know: the people who wore hoods in movies, swung the ax or dropped the platform?

"She's ready for you," Jet heard Dr. Lee say outside, muffled by the door swinging shut. "Please don't press her too hard. I've just broken the news."

The news.

Ha.

Extra, extra, read all about it. Jet Mason's got a time bomb in her head.

The door was going to open any second now. Was that enough time to scream?

The hinges creaked. No. Not enough time. To scream. To live.

A man in a suit was the first in, a file clutched in his white-knuckle hands. All this paperwork; lucky her.

"Margaret Mason?" he said gently, overenunciating. "My name is George Ecker. I'm a detective with the Vermont State Police."

"It's Jet," said another voice, one she recognized. Billy's dad—sorry—Jack Finney walked into the room, his badge glinting at her. "She likes to be called Jet." His face was wrung out, sleep deprived, but at least it was familiar under all of that.

Chief Lou Jankowski was the last in, shutting the door behind him with a click. He nodded. "Hello again, Jet."

George Ecker cleared his throat. "The chief said you might want Sergeant Finney in here. That you know each other."

"All my life," Jet said.

Jack bowed his head, like it hurt to hold her gaze. Mourning her before she even had the good grace to really be gone. Pre-dead. Un-dead. Fuck sake, a *zombie*, that's what she was. Talk about foreshadowing. And Jet was surprised she *could* talk about it—shouldn't that be a word lost to the black hole in her head? So many syllables.

The three of them stood around her bed, like silent sentries, Jet's neck craning to look up at them.

"I didn't see who it was," she said. "Before you ask. They attacked me from behind. I didn't get a chance to turn around."

Detective Ecker clicked and unclicked a pen, scribbled something in his file. "Did you hear or see anything that might help us identify them?"

Jet swallowed. "So you don't know who it was either? Isn't there evidence or something?"

"The scene is still being processed," the detective said. "Anything at all?"

"Footsteps," Jet answered. "Coming up behind me."

"Did they sound heavy?"

"I don't know."

"Could you tell what kind of shoes? Boots? Sneakers?"

"I don't know, it was just footsteps. It was so fast."

"One set or more?"

"One. It was one person."

Detective Ecker flicked to a previous page. "Do you know what was used to hit you?"

"No." She paused. "Wait, so you don't have the murder weapon either?"

She didn't even realize until she'd just said it. *The murder weapon.* That's what it was, though, wasn't it? Because Jet hadn't just been attacked, or assaulted—those paler, one-size-fits-all words. She'd been . . . murdered. Someone had killed her. More than ninety percent killed her, unless Jet was due another miracle and the surgery actually worked.

"The weapon was not recovered at the scene," Ecker said, omitting the vital word that made them all uncomfortable.

Jack removed his cap, held it by his side.

"Who found me?" Jet asked him, not this stranger with her file. "Was it Mom and Dad?"

Jack coughed. "Billy found you."

"Is he OK?" she asked. A strange thing to ask, for someone who was much less than OK. But Jet was tough, everyone said so. Billy was soft. Used to cry when Jet stomped on spiders.

Jack didn't answer.

"Margaret—sorry—Jet." The detective pressed closer, bringing her attention back. "Can you think of any reason, any reason at all, that someone might want to hurt you?"

She wanted to make a joke, to trick that drumbeat in her head, cobbled together with wire mesh and screws. *Who, me? I'm fucking delightful.* But she couldn't this time, couldn't drown out the dread.

"No," she said, voice almost failing her. "I can't think of any reason someone would want to kill me."

But someone had had a reason. You didn't smack someone three times in the skull if you didn't. The *why* almost as confusing as the *who.* Would Jet ever know the answers? Not if she chose the surgery and the percentage played out as percentages tended to do.

The detective clicked his tongue and Jet wanted to rip it out.

"Can you tell us where your ex-boyfriend is?" He paused to read out the name from his notes, finding it with his finger. "JJ Lim. Know where he is?"

Jet clicked her tongue too. "I dunno if anyone's told you, but I've kind of been unconscious in the hospital."

Ecker raised his eyebrows.

"No, I don't know where he is, Detective. Why?"

"We've been unable to reach him. He's not answering his phone. We've spoken to his brother—Henry—who doesn't know where he is either. Says he left town suddenly on Friday night, on Halloween. Didn't say where he was going."

Jet straightened up, peeling away from the pillows.

"You don't think he's a suspect, do you?"

But by the looks on their faces, they clearly did.

"How long were you together?" the detective asked.

Why was that relevant?

"Almost two years," she answered. "Look, JJ didn't do this."

"But you didn't see your attacker?" the chief chimed in now.

"No. I didn't. But . . ." Jet didn't know where that was going, left it dangling in the stale room.

"One last thing we need to ask you," Ecker said, turning another page. "Your cell phone is missing. Do you know what model it is?"

"They took my phone?"

"It wasn't on you and it's not at the scene."

"iPhone. A 14, I think."

"That's what your father guessed." Ecker made a note. "And—finally—you were wearing an Apple Watch during the attack. We have it now. Can you tell us the passcode, so we can access the data? It would help speed the process along, so we're not waiting on telephone records."

Jet glanced at her bare wrist. "Yeah. It's 0709."

"You sure?" Ecker eyed her.

"Yes, I'm sure. My passwords didn't get knocked out of my head."

The detective sniffed awkwardly, and that's when Jet knew, realized why he was double-checking. If she chose to have the surgery—if she died on the table like chance said she would—then this was their final chance to speak to her. That's why they had to be sure. Because they were talking to a dead woman.

"0709," she said again.

He wrote it down, Jet's eyes following the swish of his pen. He nodded, glancing over at Chief Lou and Jack, closing the file.

"I think that's everything we need from you now, Jet," he said.

"No, wait." She sat up, brought her knees closer to her chest. They couldn't be done, because if they were, that meant it was time for Jet to decide, to make her choice. And maybe, maybe she could put it off just a few minutes more. Not right now. Later. Later. Let her choose later.

"It's OK, Jet," Jack said, voice gruff and raw, like it had been overused since she last saw him. But his eyes were kind, glittering with the threat of tears. "I promise you, kiddo. We will get the person who did this to you. I promise. I will do that for you."

Jet locked onto his eyes, blinked. Didn't he know? She couldn't let people do things for her, because what did that prove? That her mom was right; that Jet was born useless and would die that way too? Now she had no time to prove anything at all. This wasn't fair, it couldn't be happening.

Jack wiped his eyes, following the other officers to the door. He thought she was going to choose the surgery, didn't he? That this was goodbye.

"Goodbye, Jet," Detective Ecker said, leaving no room for doubt.

The door swung shut, taking them away, Jet's last hope with them.

She was out of time.

Alone for less than four seconds before the handle twitched again, Mom in first, followed by Dad and Dr. Lee.

"Luke, come on," Mom barked, beckoning him into the room too.

Dr. Lee stood there, holding her own hands, arms crossed in front of her, watching the family assemble around Jet's bedside. Luke was breathing so heavy that Jet couldn't think, and she needed to think, they were here for her choice, and she needed to think.

"Luke, shut up," she snapped.

"I didn't say anything."

"It's time, Jet," Dr. Lee said, quiet and serious. "We would need to get you prepped for surgery right away. Do you know what your choice is?"

"Of course she does," Mom said, running her hand over Jet's shoulder, gripping on. "The surgery. She's choosing the surgery. It's the only choice, the only hope."

"Jet?" Dr. Lee pushed.

Jet looked up at her mom, that drumbeat doubling in her head, tripling, her heart throwing itself against the cage of her ribs. The song building to its end.

Mom looked down at her, eyes unwavering.

Jet blinked.

"Come on, sweetie."

"I don't . . ."

"She's choosing the surgery. We all are."

"Mrs. Mason, please." Dr. Lee raised her voice. "Jet. What do *you* want?"

What did she want? She wanted her life back. She wanted to go back two days and unbreak her head, make sure none of this ever happened. She wanted what she'd always wanted. To *do* something, achieve something big, something undeniably great, to prove that she could. So that life could *finally* begin. Jet had played the waiting game too long, and now she was out of time.

She'd run out of road, and she'd run out of *later*.

Someone had taken them from her.

But not all of it.

Die now or die in seven days.

Jet didn't have hope, but she could have that week.

To do what?

Jet swallowed, stared straight ahead, turning her mom's face into a blur.

"I'm not choosing the surgery."

Dr. Lee looked almost relieved. Mom did not.

Her face cracked open.

"What are you talking about?" Voice grating against her throat, against her teeth. "Doctor, she doesn't know what she's saying. She must be confused. We're doing the surgery."

"No, Mom, we're not."

"Yes, Jet. We are." Her eyes were wet but full of fire. "I just knew you would try to pull something like this. Scott, tell her!"

Dad didn't move.

"Luke." Mom tried again. "Tell your sister. Tell her she can't do this to us."

"I'll die in the surgery, Mom." Jet fired up at her. "Everyone else knows that."

Dr. Lee had known it, the way her shoulders had slumped, the weight of Jet's death gone from them.

"There is no hope. And if it's die now or die later, I choose later." Jet kicked off the sheets, baring her legs.

"Jet, no!"

"It's my catchphrase, isn't it?" She swung her legs out, toes dropping to the cold floor. "That's what you always say, huh? *I'll do it later.* Why change a habit of a lifetime? I'll die later."

"Jet, you can't do this! Scott?!"

Jet stood up, unsteady on her feet, taking one step, legs firing up.

"Luke." Jet pointed. "Go catch the cops. Tell them to wait up."

"No, Luke!" Mom shouted at him instead, snapping her fingers.

"Luke, I'm the one that's dying. Do me a favor, huh?"

Luke didn't say anything, slipped out the door before anyone else could yell at him.

"Stop it, Jet. You've made your point. Get back into bed."

Jet ignored her.

"Doc, my skull is all stitched back together, right? Brain's not gonna fall out if I walk out the door right now?"

Dr. Lee nodded, a glint in her eye, ignoring Dianne too. "Just change the dressings every day."

"Where are my clothes?" Jet looked at her dad.

"Evidence," he coughed, almost too scared to speak.

"Jet, stop!" Mom screamed. "Please stop!"

"I can't, Mom. I don't want to die now." She was listening to her head and her heart, and they both said the same thing, throbbing in tight, panicked couplets: *Not now, not now, not now.* "I choose the seven days. I want that time. I need it."

"For what, Jet?" Mom snapped, and it wasn't the words that hurt; it was the spaces between them: what Mom really meant. That Jet had had twenty-seven years of time and done nothing significant with it; what difference would a week make?

All the difference.

"I'm finally going to *do* something, Mom. Something important. And I'm going to see it through to the end. This time will be different. It has to be different, because it's my last chance."

"Do something?" Mom cried. "What do you mean? Do what?"

Something great.

Something no one had ever done before.

"I'm going to solve my own murder."

FOUR

Yellow and black and striped—angry wasp colors—from one hedge to the other, blocking off the driveway, only a glimpse of the house beyond.

CRIME SCENE—DO NOT ENTER.

A cop was posted in front of the tape, screwing his eyes to stare at the approaching cars.

The chief and Jack Finney pulled up ahead, lowering a window to speak to the cop. He nodded, unhooking one side of the tape, letting it fly free, slithering against the road before he rolled it up.

Jack stuck his arm out the open window, beckoned them to follow.

Luke did, releasing the handbrake and rolling forward. Silent. Silent the whole way. Jet had ridden with him from the hospital, couldn't face the way Mom wept and the way Dad stared, carrying a guilt that wasn't his. Luke was never the better option, but today he was, and Jet met his silence with her own. He *could* learn to breathe quieter, though.

Their parents were following behind, too close, pulling up and parking beside them. A driveway this big and there was hardly any space, white vans and dark vans and police squad cars all boxed around Jet's blue truck, trapping it there.

The red-and-white front door was wide open, a rectangular mouth mid-scream, burping human shapes in white plastic suits, blue gloves and blue masks and blue shoe coverings, only a band of flesh around their eyes to prove they were people at all. In and out. Paper and plastic bags marked up with thick pen that Jet couldn't read from here, passing them over to disembodied gloved hands waiting inside the vans.

Jack Finney stepped out of the squad car, so Jet did the same, avoiding her parents' eyes as they emerged too, the twin slams of the car doors burrowing into her chest. She looked ahead. The house Dad had built with love and hard work and a fuck load of money, and now another daughter had died here too. Could it ever be a home again, now that it had been a murder scene?

Jack sidestepped the narrow pathways between vehicles, walking back over to Jet. She pulled the toggle tighter on her gray sweatpants, the cuffs rolled up but still dragging on the ground. Luke's. The spare gym stuff he kept in his car: sweatpants and a hoodie that swamped Jet. Smelled a little stale too.

"The crime scene techs will be finished soon," Jack said, looking down the line of Masons all the way to Luke, back to Jet. "About an hour or so. Then we can get the cleaners in. They've already been called, waiting down the street until we're ready. Get your house back."

Mom sniffed, her eyes red raw.

Jack looked at her, opened his mouth, but nothing came out, just a glimpse of his bottom teeth. He turned back to Jet.

"You said you wanted to see it? You sure?"

Jet nodded, jaw tight and creaking.

"It's . . ." Jack hesitated. "There's a lot of blood. Even some of the officers can't—"

"—I want to see it," Jet said, rolling up her sleeves to uncover her hands. "Please."

Someone was walking over to them. A person with a face not made of white-and-blue plastic. Detective Ecker, already here, pulling off his shoe coverings.

"Jet. They said you wanted to see the scene before it's cleared. I really would advise against that, but if you want, I can take you around now."

"I want Billy's da—Sergeant Finney to," Jet said, standing taller, still the shortest person here. Jack knew her and she knew him, so maybe he'd tell her more than this stranger would, protocol forgotten because he'd known her since she was in diapers. He couldn't even escape the crime scene when he went home, his front windows facing it. Maybe that's why he looked so tired.

The detective studied Jack for a moment. "OK, Sergeant," he said. "No need for full PPE, everything's bagged. They're just taking the last photos now. Shoe coverings only. And don't touch anything until the scene is released."

"Detective." Jack bowed his head once. "Come on, Jet."

"Luke." Detective Ecker turned to her brother. "I know you must be tired, but I didn't get a chance to take your statement at the hospital. Can I talk to you now?"

Luke coughed but didn't catch it, something Mom hated. "Sure," he said, burying his hands in his pockets.

Jet followed Jack, winding around the vans and cars, up to the front door. The tallest trees in the backyard swayed over the house, leaves jeweled in amber and ruby, the colors that brought the tourists and leaf peepers to Vermont every year. Forests of fire. And Jet's final time seeing them.

"Here." Jack pulled out two fresh shoe coverings and Jet slipped them on over Luke's gym socks, staring back at the pumpkin on the front step—a mean grin. Jet lost the staring contest, eyes trailing to the front door, to the splintered wood around the lock, catching on the plastic box mounted above.

"The doorbell cam," she said suddenly, grabbing Jack's arm. "Did they check? Does it show who—"

Jack shook his head, cutting her off. "We've checked. It doesn't show. Just you coming home, then later Billy finding you, kicking the door in. Whoever attacked you, they got in the house another way. Come on."

Jack stepped over the threshold and Jet followed. It didn't smell any different, still smelled like home. She thought it wouldn't. That it would smell like decay and dead things somehow. But there wasn't a body rotting inside. Nope, she was rotting right here, on the *Welcome* mat.

A white-and-blue man passed them in the hall, out of place against the Moroccan runner rug. Jack veered left, through the door into the living room. Jet followed, her covered feet shushing against the pale polished oak. She looked down to take a breath, before entering the room, before seeing . . . everything. But she saw something worse instead.

A trail of blood. Shaped into little paw prints.

Jet gasped, leaned back against the door to catch herself. "Reggie?" she said, her heart crawling into her throat. "No. Is he OK? Is he—"

"He's fine." Jack steadied her, arm under her elbow. "The dog is fine."

Jet still couldn't swallow, not past her roving heart.

"Billy brought him in the ambulance, refused to leave him behind," Jack said. "The dog is with your sister-in-law now, at their house. He's fine." Jack's eyes narrowed. "Are you sure you want to see this?"

She had to. How could she work out who killed her if she couldn't even stomach seeing the place where they'd done it?

Jet nodded.

Blinked and held on to it, then stepped out and opened her eyes.

Not her living room. Not the place where she cuddled Reggie and watched Netflix too late. Not where she once dropped spaghetti and stained the rug and begged Dad not to tell Mom. Not the extra-long couch, one corner that belonged to teenage Luke, the other to Jet. It used to be Emily's, until Emily hadn't needed it anymore. Jet had left it a few years, just to be safe. The TV was now just an empty black mirror, trapping Jet inside it. This was a different room, no longer living. It wasn't even the red she saw first; it was the yellow.

Little crime scene markers, black numbers printed on them, placed around the room, counting up and up.

The red was next.

More paw prints in panicked circles.

Jet's eyes followed Reggie's ghost feet to a pool of blood, drying but not yet dry, winking the afternoon light back at them. Thick and spread out, half on the wood, half soaked into the corner of the rug. Well, forget spaghetti sauce—*that* stain was never coming out.

It was more blood than Jet thought a person could lose.

Hers.

Instinct moved her hand to the bandage at the back of her head. She stopped it before her fingers touched the dressing. So much blood it needed four markers of its own: *6, 8, 9,* and *11.*

"You OK?" Jack asked. "We can stop anytime."

Jet took a breath, looked up at the ceiling for air that wasn't tainted by blood. That was a mistake too. Two more yellow markers, stuck there on the white ceiling. Numbers *31* and *32.* Droplets of red dashed in a strange pattern up there, across one of the LED lights, caking the glass.

"What's that?" she sniffed.

Jack joined her, looked up. "It's a cast-off pattern," he said quietly. "From the weapon . . . between hits."

"And they don't know what the weapon was?"

"It has not been recovered."

Cop speak for *no.*

Two voices moved through the hallway then, a snatched view of her mom and Chief Lou as they passed, bumping shoulders, Lou's hand hovering behind Dianne's back as they headed for the stairs. Shoes covered in blue.

"We already did a walk-through with Scott yesterday," Lou was saying to her, voice butter-soft again, "but it would be really helpful if you can check for us too. Might have a better eye. See if you think anything is missing or out of place. Anything at all."

Their footsteps disappeared upstairs.

Jet moved closer to the bloodstain, seeking permission in Jack's eyes. She passed behind the couch, cushions fluffed, their top corners pointy, so neat and out of place in this room of horror.

Jet stopped. Right where her feet must have lain while her head was making all that blood.

"The doctor said I was hit three times," she said, bending it up into a question.

"Yes," he said. "That's what the evidence shows."

"What else does it show?"

Jack chewed his tongue, checked over his shoulder.

"Please, Mr. Finney. I need to know."

Jack sighed, lowering his voice. "The blood-spatter evidence, there." He pointed to the fireplace in front of the pool of blood, markers *13, 14,*

15. "Suggests that you were hit twice while you were still standing, in the back of the head."

Jet could have told them that. She heard it again: the crunch of her skull, an echo that reverberated inside her head. She should take more painkillers soon.

"And the third hit? This one?" She gestured to the dressing on the side of her head, above her ear. The blow that had stolen her words.

Jack pointed to another set of markers—*7* and *10*—almost subsumed by the hungry pool of blood. Jet squinted, could make out small dashes of red just beyond its boundaries.

"The blood spatter there suggests you were on the floor when you received the final blow, the one to the left side of your head. The attacker leaning over you."

Jet swallowed, picturing it, because she'd already been gone by then, couldn't remember the third crack. "Definitely wanted me dead, then."

Jack rubbed his eyebrow, nodding to a forensic tech who'd just strolled into the room, a camera in his hand. Jet waited for him to leave, out toward the kitchen.

"Does the blood spatter tell you anything else?" she asked. "I've watched some *Dexter,* you know. Shit ending."

Jack's eyes shifted.

"No one's listening," she pressed. "Please."

He spoke low and fast. "Trajectory of the spatter and the cast-off suggests that the attacker was using downward strokes. Which tells us that they are taller than you."

Jet sighed. "I'm five foot three—it's not hard. Anything else?"

"Right-handed," he said. "The blow was only to the left side of your head because that's the way you were facing when you fell. The attacker is right-handed."

"So, right-handed and taller than me?" Jet said. "Doesn't really narrow it down. Like, at all."

"I'm sorry," he said.

"Anything else I should know?"

Jack looked around the room. "We don't have all the findings from the search yet. Hairs have been collected. Fibers. Fingerprints. But, as

this is a room with a lot of visitors, and there was a lot of activity after—
from the first responders, the paramedics, Billy finding the scene—it's
hard to know if any of it will be relevant."

"Do you know what time it happened?"

Jack pulled a small notebook from the chest pocket of his uniform,
flicked through the pages. "We don't know the exact time of the attack.
But we have a range, from canvassing the neighbors, asking witnesses."

"Witnesses," Jet said. "They saw something?"

"No. They heard something. The dog. Screaming."

Jet's heart inched a little higher, reaching for her mouth. She'd heard
the scream too, right before she'd heard nothing at all. She never knew
dogs could scream.

"Did you hear?" she asked Jack. He was their closest neighbor.

"I wasn't home," he said. "Was still out after escorting Andrew Smith
back to his apartment. I was in the car when the call came through the
radio. I can't tell you what that felt like, when I heard it was this address."
He paused to clear his throat, to rub his nose. "Anyway. The doorbell
cam shows Billy approaching the door at 11:05 p.m., drawn by the sound
of the dog, so we know it was before then. The Thomases in number 6
think they heard the dog from about 10:40. But Mrs. Elliott in number
12 believes it was later than that, more like 10:55 p.m. So, the attack happened sometime roughly between 10:40 and 11:00 p.m."

Jet nodded, raking over his words again, committing those times to
memory. She'd write them down later. "So, the killer probably didn't
hang around much after, knowing that the sound was going to draw at-
t-at . . ." Fuck. What was that word? The word for when people noticed
something. Fuck it, she'd go around it. "That people were going to notice
the sound. So, the killer would have panicked, right? They left Reggie
alone, but must have taken my phone and the weapon and ran?" Jet's
eyes left the living room, darting into the hallway beyond. But she
stopped herself, corrected herself. "But not through the front door, because they would have shown up on the doorbell camera, and they
didn't. Which means they must have known we had one. So how did
they get out? And in?"

"This way," Jack said, turning his back to the bloody scene. Jet followed him, taking their morbid tour through the open archway into the kitchen.

Sophia's Halloween cookies were still out on the counter, untouched, unmoved. Probably still good—it had only been a couple of days, right? No, shouldn't eat the crime scene. But she should probably eat something soon, her legs felt weak, a little lightheaded, but maybe that was because someone had spilled all the blood out of it.

"Here," Jack said, walking into the laundry room off the far side of the kitchen.

The back door was open, the crime scene tech standing outside, taking photos of the muddy grass right outside the door. More markers: *49, 50, 51, 52.*

"You seen the size of their pool?" the tech said, not looking up, thinking they were somebody else.

The whine and hiss of the camera, a blinding flash. Another. Imprinted in the back of Jet's eyelids. She cupped one hand over her eyes.

"Sorry." The tech looked up now, a slow blink when he realized. "Sorry. I'm done." He dipped his plastic head awkwardly, disappearing around the side of the house.

"This door was shut, but it was unlocked," Jack said. "We think this is how they got in. A lot of shoe impressions. We've taken casts. But it looks like this door gets used a lot."

Jet nodded. "I come in this way when I take Reggie for a walk. Mom makes the cleaners use it too. Dad when he's gardening."

"Your parents seem to think it was possible the door was left unlocked on Friday night?"

More than possible. Jet never remembered to lock it. But neither did Mom or Dad. That doorbell camera at the front was all the security they thought they'd needed. A show. A deterrent, Dad once said. But it had deterred nothing, and the killer had known to avoid it, to come around to the side door instead.

"It's possible, yes," Jet said. "Likely. Seventy-five percent chance it was left unlocked." Because she spoke in percentages now.

"Got it," Jack said, making a note in his little book.

A phone buzzed. Jet patted her pockets, forgetting that the killer had taken hers. She felt naked, incomplete, without one.

Jack glanced at her apologetically and pulled the phone from his pocket, checking the screen.

"That's Billy again. He'll be asking after you."

"Does he know?" Jet asked, but Jack didn't have a chance to answer.

Detective Ecker's voice sailed through the open-plan house.

"OK, that's it. The scene is released. Let's get those cleaners in here ASAP. Move this poor family back in. Oh, sorry, Jet. Didn't see you were still in here."

Didn't see her. Because she was small? Or because she was dead in a week and didn't matter as much as the other people here, the ones who didn't have a countdown hanging over them. Halfway between the living and the not, her edges less defined somehow. No . . . probably just the small thing.

FIVE

They carried the rug out, rolled up, the browning blood soaked through the underside. There was no saving it, apparently. Even though they were *#1 in Forensic Cleanup and Decontamination of Crime Scenes*, or so said the vans.

More plastic people, in and out the front door. And now Dad too, heading toward Jet on the drive, carrying a plate with a sandwich.

He handed it over. "Made this for you. Found a loaf in the freezer," he said, as though that made the bread safe, separate from the murder somehow, behind the freezer door.

Jet's stomach growled, a new song, now her head had gone quiet. She took a bite.

"It's the good cheese," Dad said with a small smile. "Not the low-sodium stuff. Figured you were allowed that now."

Jet matched his smile. "Won't be my kidneys that kill me after all." She took another bite. He'd been liberal with the mayonnaise too.

"I bet that's good."

He was right, Jet already on to the second half.

"You warm enough?"

She nodded. She'd put a coat on over Luke's sweats. Finally found some shoes too, the Birkenstocks from the closet.

Another two non-plastic people emerged from the front door: the chief of police and Mom. A look passed between them before they broke apart, Mom walking briskly toward Jet and Dad.

"You eating now?" she said before Jet could ask her anything.

"I was hungry."

"Dinnertime soon," she sniffed.

"Yeah, Mom. I think it's probably OK if I don't stick to standard mealtimes. I'll be dead in a week."

Mom flinched, closing her eyes. "Jet, please. Please. I'm going to ask you one last time."

"You already asked me *one last time* in the hospital parking lot."

"It's not too late to change your mind. We can go back and Dr. Lee can—"

"—I made my decision, Mom. There is no going back."

"Jet, please." Eyes wide and begging, a cliff edge of more tears.

Jet couldn't see her mother cry again, and she couldn't keep saying the same thing. So she said something else instead, wanted to know what that look between her mom and the chief had meant.

"Was anything missing?" she asked, gesturing toward the house. "Or out of place?"

Mom shook her head. "No, don't think so. Everything looks normal."

Jet chewed the air and chewed her thoughts, now she was finished chewing her sandwich.

"So they weren't in the house to steal something," she thought aloud. "Or maybe they were, and I came home early and surprised them. But they hit me three times. Just once would have been enough for a thief to get away, if that was the motive. And why take my phone?"

"Let the police worry about all that," Mom said. "It's their job."

Jet looked over at the cops: at Jack Finney and Chief Lou speaking to Detective Ecker, standing around an unmarked car.

"It's their job," she said. "But it's my life. I have to do this. It has to be me."

"Jet, don't you—"

Jet wasn't listening, spoke over her mom.

"—And they didn't just hit me until I was in-inca-in—" Fuck, another hole in her head.

"Incapacitated?" Dad offered.

"Right." Jet blinked her thanks. "I was down and out after the first two hits. But the blood spatter shows that they then leaned over me, hit me a third time. Which doesn't seem like they were just trying to get away. Seems like they wanted to make sure. That they wanted me dead."

"Excuse me." Mom covered her mouth, stumbling away around the side of the house, toward the backyard.

"I'll go after her," Dad said, taking the empty plate from Jet.

"Wait, Dad. You also thought nothing was missing from the house, right? Checked everything?"

"Yes."

Jet took a long breath, allowed the thought time to grow, winding through all the broken parts.

"If nothing is missing, that means they didn't find the weapon at our house, that it wasn't op-op—"

"—Opportunistic."

Jet nodded. "Doesn't that mean it was something they brought with them?"

Dad studied his feet.

"And if they brought the murder weapon with them"—Jet paused, not long enough to lose the budding thought—"that means they came here with one purpose. It wasn't a stranger. It wasn't a robbery gone wrong. It was someone I know. And they came here to kill me."

Dad ran one hand over his stubble, pulling his mouth open, a silent scream.

"Who would want to kill me, Dad?"

His eyes filled. "I don't know, baby girl."

A car door slammed, breaking the moment, and an engine turned over.

Detective Ecker was pulling away.

"Wait!" Jet waved her hands, running ahead to cut him off, rapping her fist against his hood.

The engine cut out, car door opened again. Detective Ecker's face, a new crease between his brow.

"What?" he asked, stepping out.

"Where are you going?"

"I'm working . . . on your case."

"So am I," Jet said. "And I'd say I'm slightly more motivated to find the killer. Seeing as they—well—killed me."

The detective stared at her, waiting for more.

"Help me, and I can help you." She folded her arms. "How many murders have you solved?"

"A fair few," he grunted, crease deepening.

"This is my first," she said, hands up. "First time being murdered also. Newbie. But I'm a quick learner. Adaptable skill set. Almost got a law degree, by the way." Jet clapped. "So, if you've solved a *fair few* murders, then you've already worked out that if nothing is missing from the house, then this wasn't a— Dad," she yelled suddenly, "what's that word again?!"

"Opportunistic!" he called.

"An opportunistic murder. It wasn't a stranger robbing the house and I interrupted them. The killer brought the murder weapon with them. They came here with the intent to kill me. Someone who knows me."

Detective Ecker screwed his mouth.

"We aren't ruling out any possibilities just yet."

Cop speak for: *You're right, Jet, and you're amazing at this.*

"OK, well, I am," she said. "I'm on a pretty tight deadline here, bud."

Jack had wandered over; the chief too, listening in.

"My Apple Watch," Jet said. "You haven't looked through it yet, I only just gave you the code. Do you have it?"

Detective Ecker hesitated. "It's in the car."

"Can I look through it with you?" she asked. "I mean, it is mine?"

Ecker looked back at Chief Jankowski and Sergeant Finney.

"Then you can take it and do whatever cop things you want to do with it, I promise," Jet said. "I just need to see." She glanced down at his wrist. A gold expensive-looking thing. "Looks like you don't own one.

I'm Gen-Z—n-no offense. But I know my way around an Apple Watch pretty well. I'll find you the good stuff. Let me help you. Please."

The detective checked with the other two cops.

Chief Lou shrugged. "Can't see the harm in it. We'd tell her anything we find anyway."

The detective sighed. He circled around and popped the trunk, coming back a few moments later with a small black device in his hands. Jet's watch. He handed it to her, drawing close to look over her shoulder.

"Don't delete anything," he breathed in her ear.

"I won't," Jet replied. The device asked for her passcode and she typed it in: *0709.*

"So," she said, "I was thinking, you have an estimated twenty-minute range for the time of the attack from those witnesses."

The detective looked over at Jack. Oops, might have gotten him in trouble there.

"But if we're going to be asking for alibis, shouldn't we know the exact time it happened, the very minute? This thing tracks my heart rate when I wear it. Won't it show us the exact moment I . . ."

Jet trailed off, swiping a notification away: Yep, she was aware she hadn't closed her activity rings the past couple of days, give her a break. She thumbed onto the small gray square with a red outline of a heart.

It brought up today's data: no heartbeats, *Resting Rate* at 0 beats per minute. Only because she hadn't worn the watch, but it felt pointed somehow, mocking.

Jet swiped to yesterday's data, starting the day at midnight. Nothing. No beats. Was that because they'd taken the watch off her when she arrived at the ER? Or was some of it true: had she been in cardiac arrest as Friday turned into Saturday? She'd almost died, right here, somewhere in this blank data.

Jet swiped again, back to Friday, to Halloween, and the graph filled with white lines, the daily dance of her heart.

"The doorbell camera shows you getting home at 10:39 p.m.," the detective said, leaning closer. "So it's after th—"

"—It's here," Jet said, cutting him off. Tracing the white line with her finger. A peak out of nowhere, a white tower rising above the rest of the day, 158 beats per minute. And then a drop. Sharp. All the way down that tower, to 56 bpm. "My heart rate rose, maybe when I heard the foot-steps. The first blow. The second, when I realized what was happening. Then I must have lost consciousness here." Jet thumbed the line to bring up the exact time.

"10:46," Ecker read it over her shoulder.

Jack removed his notebook, scribbled something down.

"10:46," Jet repeated. "That's when it happened."

"Any messages?" Jack piped up now, his pen ready and waiting. "That thing shows your texts, doesn't it?"

Jet didn't wait for permission from Ecker, searching for the green message app. "I think it would've only picked up any messages I got while I was still here, on the WiFi. Anything after that, the watch would have been out of range from my iPhone, wouldn't receive. Yep, just two texts. One from my mom at 10:48 p.m." Jet sniffed, eyes running ahead of her. "You wanna do the honors, Detective?"

He cleared his throat, read aloud: "*We will be back later now. Have to take the chairs back to the hotel because you wouldn't do it.*"

Jet looked up at the cops. "I don't think that's a strong enough motive for murder, do you? The chair thing?"

None of them smiled. Come on, she was the one dying; they could at least pity-laugh.

"The other text?" Ecker asked as Jet backed out into the menu of messages.

A blue dot next to the contact name.

Ecker stiffened beside her, leaning closer still. "Who's that? Who's *Don't Pick Up*?"

Jet bit down on her lip. "That's . . . my ex-boyfriend. JJ. I changed his name in my contacts after we broke up." They were all looking at her, eyes narrowed, Jack's going farther than that, more like troubled. "Look, it's a thing, OK? People do it. Young people. Never mind, not a big deal."

Jet pressed the notification and their message thread jumped up.

Weeks of silence. Then, on Halloween, just one word from JJ:

Sorry.

"What time did he send that?" Ecker asked, voice picking up speed.

Jet swiped the message to see.

"10:58 p.m."

"After you were attacked." It wasn't a question. "Why is he apologizing to you?"

Jet shrugged.

"You can't think of any reason?" Ecker sidestepped to face her, to study her eyes.

"No. Not really," Jet said, meeting his gaze. "We've been broken up a while, since July. He didn't want to, but it's fine. It's been fine. I bumped into him at the fair—"

"—Did you speak? What did he say to you? What time?"

"Nothing. I think it was around ten. He asked to talk to me, about something *important,* which I knew meant he wanted to talk about us, so I blew him off."

"Are you sure that's all?"

Now Jet's eyes were troubled. "I have no reason to withhold anything from you. I want to solve this more than you do. I didn't give JJ a chance to talk to me at the fair—I don't know what he wanted. And I don't know why he sent *Sorry* to me. Or why he's left town, not answering his phone."

"I can think of a reason," Jack said quietly.

"Sergeant," Ecker snapped in his direction, sharpening the consonants to a point.

"You think he tried to kill me, then texted me *Sorry* twelve minutes later?" Jet asked, not to any of them in particular: collective cop. "The timing is weird; I give you that. But the killer took my phone. Why would JJ text the phone he knew he had?"

"Well, it came up on your watch, didn't it?" Ecker said.

"Could have been symbolic," added the chief.

"But if the killer has my phone . . . wait," Jet stalled, her heart picking up on it the same time as her head. "The killer *has* my phone, I'm so stupid." But she wasn't; the cops were. Why had they wasted time looking at heart rate data and messages? "Find My Phone," Jet explained, turning back to the watch, scrolling through the home screen until she found the little green app. Pressed it.

Three devices were listed.

Jet's Apple Watch. Battery half full. *With you now,* it said.

Jet's MacBook Air. Low battery. *At home.* Upstairs in her room.

Jet's iPhone 14.

Jet clicked the final option and it expanded.

Jet's iPhone 14. Woodstock, VT. Last connected Friday, 10:56 p.m.

A map appeared on the little screen. Small white roads, gray background, and a blue flashing dot. The location of her phone.

Ecker pointed at the screen. "Where is that?"

Jet zoomed in until the road names appeared, and the bend in the Ottauquechee River.

"River Street," she said. "Near the corner of North Street. Just beyond Elm Street Bridge. That's less than five minutes away."

Most of Woodstock was less than five minutes away.

The blue dot didn't look like it was sitting in any of the houses, out there in the middle of the road.

"Last connected Friday at 10:56 p.m.," Jet read out. "So that's when they turned it off, hasn't been on since. But it was there, right there, when they turned it off."

"River Street," Ecker sounded it out. "Does that mean anything to you? Know anyone who lives there?"

Jet searched her mind, memories intact, even if not all her words were. "Nope, I don't know anyone who lives there."

The detective swapped a look with the other two, then up at the darkening evening sky. "All right. I'll go speak to the people in these houses. See if they saw anything that night. Chief, you coming?"

"Coming," Lou said, screwing on his cap.

The detective held out his hand, gesturing for Jet's watch.

Jet looked down at it: 6:49 p.m., it told her, still trying to be useful. She placed it in his open palm but didn't quite let go.

"You'll tell me? When you learn anything more?"

"I'll let you know what you need to know," he said, closing his hand around the watch.

Cop speak for: *Maybe.*

Ecker got back into his car, the chief climbing into the passenger seat. Jet and Jack backed away as he started the engine, driving off with a wave, fingers tapping the glass.

"Can I borrow your pen, please, Mr. Finney?"

She smiled up at him. He offered it over without a word.

"And maybe a couple of pages from your notebook?"

A bigger ask. But he still did it, without a word, ripping out two fresh sheets.

"Thanks." Jet grabbed them, leaning against the roof of Jack's squad car.

10:46—Time of murder, she wrote, before she forgot any of it. Didn't know how much she could trust her condemned brain.

10:56—Phone turned off. Last known location: River Street, near corner of North Street. Is that where killer lives? Or they turned it off on their way home? Didn't throw it in the river?

10:58—"Sorry" text from JJ.

"I'll just go say goodbye to your parents," Jack said when she finally looked up from her scribbles. "The cleaners should be finished soon, then you can get back in, get back to—" He stopped abruptly.

"Normal?" Jet guessed. They both knew it was the wrong choice, *sorry* written all over his creased eyes.

Then he blinked and they softened, the flicker of a smile. "Someone's here to see you," he said, pointing, then turning away toward the backyard.

Jet spun around.

The crime scene tape lay trampled across the drive now, forgotten in the wind, pinned down by a pair of boots. And four paws.

"Reggie!" Jet yelled, stuffing the paper in her pocket, darting forward.

Billy smiled, letting go of the leash.

Reggie launched toward Jet, his back half almost leaving his front half behind, legs a tangled blur, yipping as he collided with her.

Jet dropped to her knees, screwed her face as he jumped up to lick it.

"Hello handsome boy," she said, rubbing his belly. "Hello. Hello. I'm here. I'm here. Careful of that bandage. No, you can't have it, silly. I'm sorry you had to see that, boy. I'm sorry, I'm sorry. I'd kill them if they touched you."

She tried to hold him, but he wouldn't stay still, lurching in manic circles around her.

"Dad said you were back from the hospital," Billy said, his turn to approach. "Knew Reggie was staying with Luke and Sophia. Picked him up on my way. Thought you'd want to see him."

"He's clever, isn't he? Our friend Billy," Jet said to the dog, straightening up, knees clicking.

Billy glanced at the vans behind her, the plastic people.

"Crime scene cleaners," Jet explained. "They'll be done soon."

"I can't believe you're out of the hospital already."

"Why would I waste any more time in there?"

Billy didn't answer. He did something else: stepped forward and buried her in a hug, Jet's nose pressed up against his chest.

The first person to actually hug her.

It almost brought her blockades down, the ones made of screws and wire mesh in her head. But if they came down now, how would Jet ever bring them back up? She coughed into the fabric of Billy's shirt.

"I'm so glad you're OK," he said, his breath warm against her hair, against the bandages.

"Don't be too glad." She pulled back out of the hug, Reggie settling by her leg, dusting the drive with his tail.

"I can't believe it." He sniffed, catching a tear that fell to the groove of his chin.

Jet shrugged. "I'm only a few hours ahead of you there."

Billy's eyes settled on his dad's squad car. "They don't know who . . . ?"

"Not yet," Jet replied. "I'm going to work out who did it. I guess you're the only person I can trust *not* to be the killer, right? I mean, who would come back a few minutes later to *discover* their own crime, on camera, and leave their DNA all over the scene, call the cops and the ambulance? And we grew up together, and I know you can't even kill a bug, so it's a pretty safe bet that it wasn't you, Billy Finney. I did want to ask, though. Why were you here? You live in the center of town."

"Dad's wallet," he said. "Someone found it on The Green, handed it to me as I was leaving the fair. Think he must have dropped it during the scuffle with Andrew Smith. I walked here to bring it back, put it through the mail slot. Didn't even get to his front door before I heard Reggie screaming, knew something was wrong over here."

They both looked down at the dog. Jet might not have survived at all if Billy hadn't found her when he did. Did she owe these final seven days to this man and this dog?

"I'm going to do it, Billy. Always told you I'd do something big, didn't I? OK, I thought I was going to be president or an astronaut back then, but this is just as big: solving my own murder."

Billy dipped his head, eyes darkening. "Why do you keep saying it like that?"

Jet shrugged. "If you've gotta die, might as well be funny about it."

No one else seemed quite ready for it.

Another tear: Billy didn't catch this one in time, soaking into his checked collar.

"I was so scared when I found you. I thought you were dead. I really thought you were dead. I don't know what I'd do if . . . but you're alive, you're OK, you survived. It's all going to be OK."

"Not *that* OK," Jet said, confused by the sincerity in his face, the hope in his eyes alongside the blue, where hope absolutely did not belong. Wait a minute. "Billy . . . has no one told you?"

He sniffed.

"Told me what?"

Ah, fuck. This wasn't going to be fun.

Jet pulled her coat tighter, night settling in, claiming her exposed skin. "Billy. It's . . . the thing is . . . I'm . . . well . . ." Just rip off the Band-Aid, it would hurt him the same whether it was fast or slow. "I'll be dead in a week."

His face changed, one second to the next. Mouth cracked open, eyes faraway and spinning, a quake in his knees that made him stumble back.

Poor, sweet Billy.

SIX

J et watched it again.

The third time.

Motion Detected 10:39 p.m. 10/31/2025.

Herself, walking up the drive toward the front door, dressed all in black, hair a little mussed from the walk, from the wind, from the zombie mask.

Jet slid her knees up and her MacBook closer, resting against the lump of her thighs, padded by the comforter. Lights off, dark except for the screen, except for the video of *that* Jet, looking into the bucket of Halloween candy, realizing it was empty.

The world was dark behind her, but she glowed from the lights mounted by the front door. Then Jet turned, looking right into the camera, through the screen, staring at this Jet, the one tucked up in bed now. She stuck out her tongue and Jet stuck hers back.

"Don't go in," Jet muttered darkly, warning her past self as she pulled out her keys and slotted them in the door. The Jet who was still alive, the one who had everything: all the time and all the *laters* she could ever want. Jet envied her, hated her a little. "Don't go in."

She didn't listen.

The door opened and swallowed Jet whole, and it took less than a minute to do it.

The frame froze and the video ended.

Was the killer already inside when Jet had opened the door? Or did they come in later, when Jet was distracted by her phone and a fucking cookie? The footage had no answers for her, not the first time she'd watched it, or the second or the third. The killer never crossed the frame, never set off the motion detector.

Jet turned to the notebook spread open on the pillow beside her. The writing on the left-hand page was crossed out: ~~Ideas for dog walking app in Boston/other cities.~~ Many ideas crossed out before that one, half a notebook of them. On the top of the fresh right-hand page she'd written: *Who murdered me?* Underlined. She'd transferred the times and data they'd found on her Apple Watch, and below that she'd asked: *Ring doorbell camera—was the killer already inside when I got home?* Now she answered: *I don't know.* Dropped the pen.

Outside her door, she heard her parents creeping past on the way to their bedroom. Saw them too, the gloom from their passing feet. One set faltered, two shadows that lingered, blocking the glow under the door. A boundary, between here and there, the living and the dead.

"Keep going, Mom," Jet whispered, not loud enough to be heard. "I'm asleep."

"She's asleep, Dianne," her dad hissed. "Let her sleep."

The shadows moved on.

Mom had asked her *one last time* three times since they got back in the house. So Jet told them she was tired, going to bed. Because she didn't want to sit at the dining table and eat lasagna with her parents in the bleach-cleaned air; she wanted a bar of chocolate and she wanted to be alone: to do this. Log in to her parents' Ring.com account—got the password from Dad—and see it for herself. The moment she goes in alive and comes out dead.

Jet skipped ahead to the next video, the next time the motion detector, well, detected motion: 11:05 p.m.

Third time watching this one too.

Billy, hurrying toward the door, pulling his hands out of his pockets, an awful screeching sound that buzzed against Jet's speakers. Reggie. Screaming.

Reggie from now stirred at the sound, sleeping by Jet's feet, or trying to.

"Sorry bud," Jet said, turning the volume down, dimming his distress.

The dog wasn't allowed upstairs, and definitely not on the beds, but this wasn't the first time Jet had ignored those rules.

"Hello?" Billy called on-screen, before he even got close. "Mr. and Mrs. Mason? Jet?"

He reached the front door, knocked his fist against it, the camera fish-bowling his face, distorting his panicked eyes. "Hello? Are you OK in there? I—I can hear the dog. Is everything . . ." He stopped, cupped his hands to his eyes, peered through the crinkled stained glass of the front door. He drew back, bent down to the mail slot. "Reggie," he called through it. "Reggie, boy, what's wrong? Come here. Reggie!"

The howling didn't stop.

Billy ran his hands through his hair, fingers trapped in the curls.

"I don't know what to do," he muttered to himself, looking around. He spotted the doorbell camera, looked right into the lens, into Jet's eyes, forty-eight hours in the future. He pressed the button, that annoying chime—*doo-di-dooo*, you know the one. "Is anyone in?" he asked the camera. "Hello, can you hear this? I think something's wrong. I . . ."

Billy's face moved right up to the camera, then beyond it, out of frame. The rustle of the bush as he clambered over it to look through the window, into the living room.

You could hear it. The very moment he spotted Jet, lying there, head bleeding and undone. There was a click in his throat, too mechanical to really sound human, something breaking that might not be so easy to fix. Metal screws and wire mesh wouldn't do.

"Oh my god, Jet, no! Jet!"

Knuckles on glass. Over and over. The dog screeching louder.

"Jet!" Billy screamed. "Jet—can you hear me?! Oh my god!"

That break in his voice, raw and grating, like earlier when he walked away from the house and thought Jet couldn't hear him, crying down the street.

Billy darted back into the frame, past the camera, his jaw set as he eyed the front door.

"I'm coming, Jet!"

He backed up and kicked out at the lock. The door buckled but didn't break.

Billy doubled back, five, then six steps, then he charged at the door, shoulder first.

The wood splintered and the door crashed in, Billy rolling in after it, leaving it wide and gaping.

"Jet! No, no, no! Can you hear me?! Jet!"

The video ended, cutting out his screams.

The next was fifteen minutes later, the paramedics arriving, spiraling red lights on the ambulance. Jet dragged the cursor, speeding through it. She'd watched this one most. One cop car, then two, black and white and red and blue. Jack Finney, removing his hat and holding it over his heart, the chief of police tripping on the front step as he hurried inside.

Fast-forward.

The paramedics coming out again, squeaky wheels as they rolled a stretcher onto the drive.

Jet on top of it, some kind of orange brace around her broken head.

A lifeless arm falling as they turned, finger trailing in the dirt.

"I'm going with her!" Billy screamed, and Jet mouthed his lines with him, memorized after the sixth time. He reemerged, coming out different too. His white-and-brown-check shirt stained red instead, his own glistening handprint over his chest, a smear under one eye. "She can't be alone!" they said together: Billy yelling, Jet whispering. "I'm coming too! So is the dog! No, no, Dad. I'm not leaving him. Jet wouldn't want that!"

Jet smiled sadly, pressing pause, freezing them all in that moment of chaos.

She turned to her notebook, wrote: DNA *probably fucked from the rescue, so many people in and out.*

Jet shifted, and so did Reggie, the empty chocolate packet crinkling under her elbow.

"Enough," Jet told herself. If she knew it off by heart, then she knew it too well, had watched it too many times. Watching wouldn't undo it, wouldn't bring her back to life, and she had a job to do.

There were other motion alerts, earlier that day. Probably nothing

important, but Jet thought she should check them at least; it all happened on the day she was murdered.

One at 8:33 p.m.—when they were out at the fair. Jet settled back and
pressed play.

Five dark figures. Misshapen and inhuman. Teenagers. Three
witches, a werewolf, and a skeleton, ambling up the drive, elbowing each
other and giggling.

"Look at the size of this fucking house!" the skeleton said, exposed
jaw dropping open.

"It's the Masons' house," a witch said, switching her broom to the
other hand. "My mom doesn't like them. Says they flaunt it."

Jet snorted. The witch wasn't wrong.

"How do you afford a house like this?" said Skeleton. "Is he a cartel
leader or something?"

"Stop watching *Ozark,* James, it's becoming your entire personality.
And no. He tears down houses and builds giant new ones, like this.
Mom thinks it's ugly."

Jet liked this one.

It was as though the girl had heard the thought, through time and
through the lens. She turned, staring strangely right at Jet.

"Dave, what are y—"

It appeared faster than Jet could blink, filling the entire screen.

Empty black eyes. A warped white plastic face.

Jet jumped, recoiled from the screen, head slamming into the back-
board of her bed.

A searing jolt of pain in her skull.

"Fuck you," Jet hissed at the screen, at the image of Ghostface from
Scream, smirking into the camera.

"Trick-or-treat, bitches," the boy said, rattly and deep, enjoying himself too much. He must have hidden behind his friends, snuck around to
jump-scare the camera. Little prick.

"They're not in," Sassy Witch replied, as Ghostface moved back,
clearing the view. "Look, it says take one."

The werewolf picked up the bucket and upturned it, emptying the entire thing into his open tote bag. "What?" he sniffed. "I think they can probably afford it."

"They have a doorbell camera looking right at us, you idiot!"

They all turned to look at the camera, at Jet, sheepish and ghoulish.

"Run!" Skeleton yelled, laughing as they all bolted back down the drive and into the night, Werewolf howling at the invisible moon.

"Fuckers," Jet said as the video ended. "I wanted some of that."

A video twenty-two minutes before that, Jet leaving the house for the fair, one hour and eleven minutes after she'd promised Mom she would, calling "Bye!" to Reggie.

3:42 p.m.—Jet driving home, parking her truck, returning after a walk with Reggie. It had been a long one, around Billings Park, and again, because she'd been thinking about that app idea.

3:29 p.m. Sophia leaving the house, baby Cameron balanced on her hip, walking back to her blue Range Rover parked where Jet's truck normally lived. Must have been on her way out after dropping those Halloween cookies off, leaving them on the kitchen counter with a little note: *Love, Sophia xx.*

3:24 p.m.—Five minutes before that, a blue Range Rover pulled up into the drive. Sophia emerged, getting baby Cameron from the backseat, holding him against her chest as she approached the door, pulling out a set of keys.

Wait a minute.

Jet paused the video, rewound it. Blinked and watched again.

Where was the plate of cookies? Sophia wasn't carrying anything other than the baby. So, where the fuck had those cookies come from? She went in and four minutes later she came out, no cookies in either video.

Jet reached for her pen, scribbled: *Cookies???*

2:21 p.m.—What?! It was Sophia again, leaving the house for the second time—no, the first time actually, because Jet was watching this all in reverse. What was she doing? She'd come to the house two separate times on Friday, just over an hour apart. Why? And where were those damn cookies?

2:14 p.m. The hulking blue Range Rover pulled up again. Sophia stepped out, went to the backseat. Picked Cameron up, resting him on her hip. Reached in for something else, holding it in one hand. Ah. The plate of cookies, bats and pumpkins sliding around as she tried to balance everything and get the door open.

"Cameron, don't fidget," she said, flustered.

Cookie mystery solved, then. Because if Jet had been murdered over some fucking magic Halloween cookies, she would have been furious. Still, why did Sophia come back an hour after dropping them off? Did she forget the note, thought it was important enough to come back? Jet didn't know—she didn't understand how Sophia's mind worked anymore.

1:59 p.m.—Jet leaving for her walk, hoisting Reggie up into the cab of her truck, shutting the door as he yipped in excitement.

12:00 p.m.—Mom and Dad leaving on the dot, literally, to go help with the setup for the fair.

"You got the sign?" Mom said, walking out, hands full of plastic bags.

Dad grunted, struggling with it.

"Scott, honestly," she tutted. "We need to take you to the doctor. You're getting worse."

"I'm fine."

And that was it. No other motion detected on Halloween, the day she'd died. And no sign of the killer hanging around before.

Jet looked over at her notebook. Crossed out the *Cookies???* Nothing. A camera out front recording everyone who came and went, and it had given her nothing.

Jet sighed, blew out her lips. Reggie didn't like the sound, grumbling to tell her so.

She'd have to sleep too, wouldn't she? But sleeping felt like a waste of time, and she didn't have time to waste.

On the Ring dashboard, Jet clicked out of *History* into the live image the camera was recording now, right now. The nighttime driveway. Jet's powder-blue truck out of place against all that darkness, lit only by a sickly orange tinge from the porch lights. Nothing moved except the wind in the leaves.

Time ticked by, but the world didn't show it, not from this view.

Past midnight and into a new day. The next day. One day closer to dying.

Dying.

She shouldn't think about that.

She couldn't help it.

Would they come for her again, the killer? To finish her off?

Jet studied the live footage, searched every corner for a sign.

Why bother?

Time and that little bone fragment would finish her off for them.

Her curse, their gift.

Her eyes felt strange, a ghostly sheen, like there was another layer she had to see through now. It was probably from staring at the screen too hard. Probably just tired.

Jet hesitated.

Brought up a new tab.

Google.

Symptoms of a brain aneurysm, she typed.

Pressed enter.

The page of results loaded.

"No, don't."

Jet slammed the lid, shoved her laptop away.

She didn't want to see that.

Her eyes were just tired, that was all.

Jet shuffled down, pulling the comforter up to her chin. She wanted to stare at the ceiling, to search for answers there, but there was too much pain to put any pressure on the back of her head, on her Franken-stein skull. She pressed the right side of her head into the pillow. She never slept this way, ever, facing her bathroom door instead of her win-dow. But it was the only way that didn't hurt.

Jet forced her eyes shut, because if they were tired, she must have been too.

Wouldn't open them. Lay there and waited for sleep.

Not counting sheep. Counting the hours she had left before she died, moving on to the minutes.

Monday
November 3

SEVEN

"What's all this?"

Jet rubbed her eyes, following the noise of dinging plates and low voices, into the dining room.

Luke and Sophia were here, sitting at the table, Cameron's high chair tucked in at the end. Something green and swampish wiped around the baby's mouth.

Mom was serving from a platter of scrambled eggs, bacon on every plate except Dad's. Too much sodium.

"Finally," Luke said, glancing up at her. "You're awake." Like he was annoyed about it somehow.

Not as annoyed as Jet. Couldn't sleep for hours, worried about running out of time, then slept in till eleven, forgot to set an alarm. Didn't forget, actually. Didn't have her phone.

Her parents could have woken her. Actually, it was very out of character that Mom hadn't.

"What are you doing here?" Jet asked her brother.

"Come sit down, Jet," Mom said, handing out pieces of toast. "I asked them over, thought we could have a nice family breakfast." Emphasis on the *nice.*

"Jet, hi," Sophia said, a tremble in her bottom lip. "I'm just . . . just so sorry . . ."

"Why?" Jet pulled out a chair. "The eggs aren't that bad, are they?"

The last thing she wanted right now was a family breakfast, for people to ask stupid questions, like whether she was OK or whether she'd slept well.

"Did you sleep well?" Sophia asked.

"Like the dead." Jet took a bite of buttered toast.

Dad picked up his coffee, inhaled it, hiding his face in the oversized mug.

Luke shoveled eggs into his face, picking up a piece of crispy bacon with his fingers, taking a bite. The crunch of the bacon, not a world away from the crunch of a human skull.

"Luke, slow down," Mom told him, like he was a teenager again.

"Gotta get to work," he spoke through his mouthful.

Mom banged her elbows on the table, put her fingers by her temples. "You can be here for your sister, Luke," she said, suddenly tearful.

Luke slowed down.

Paused to pick up his knife too. That's when Jet noticed it, the graze on his knuckles, both of them actually. Freshly scabbed, the surface cracking when he tightened his grip on the cutlery.

"What happened to your hands?" Jet asked him.

Luke coughed. Banged his chest until the eggs went down.

"Sorry, wrong way." He held his hands in front of him, fingers outstretched, flexing. "Oh, this? I was visiting one of our sites on Friday morning. Tripped over one of the foundation trenches, banged them up a little, catching myself. Just a scrape, it's nothing."

"I hope you were wearing a hard hat, if you were on site?" Dad said, the mug echoing his voice back.

"'Course," Luke answered. "I know what I'm doing, Dad."

Dad tried to smile. "So, you won't be falling in any trenches again?"

Luke chewed his cheek.

Sophia piped up now, resting a hand on Luke's back. "I think it's going to be Mason Homes' best project yet."

"Mason Construction," Dad corrected her.

Sophia's cheeks reddened and Luke shrugged off her hand.

"No, I know," she said, speaking across the table to her father-in-law. "But Luke's been thinking, he might change the name, wh-when he takes over. Thinks it sounds more, well, homey."

Dad had another sip of coffee, finished it with a shrug. "It's been called 'Construction' for forty years, since I set it up. Don't think there's anything wrong with the name."

There wasn't any meanness in his voice—Dad didn't know how to *do* mean—but the color drained from Sophia's face.

"No, of course there's nothing wrong with it."

"I gotta pee," Luke said, chair scraping as he pushed back from the table, disappearing into the hall. Jet was the one dying, and yet somehow Luke had managed to make it all about him. He was good at that.

"Sophia," Jet said now, trapping her with her eyes. "I wanted to ask you something, about Halloween."

"Sure." She still looked pale.

"You came over to the house when we were out. Twice." Leaving the question between the lines.

Sophia nodded, too many nods, cartoon-quick. "Yeah, to drop off those cookies I baked. Don't know if you saw them, pumpkins and bats."

"Saw them," she said. "Ate two of them, before . . ."

"Oh," Sophia said.

"They were fine. A little dry." Jet straightened in her chair. "But you came over twice. First to drop the cookies, and then again an hour later."

"Did I?"

"Yes, you did. The doorbell camera recorded you. I can show you the video if you don't—"

"—Oh, sorry," Sophia laughed, too much breath behind it. "I remember now. I left my phone here. Thought it was in my pocket, but I must have put it down somewhere. Came back to get it when I realized."

Jet's turn to nod. That made sense, the phone thing. But she was enjoying watching Sophia squirm; she was normally so rigid. She didn't use to be like this, when they were teenagers. Sometimes Sophia had even been the funny one. "Which room did you leave it in?"

"The kitchen." Sophia was ready with the answer. "Got baby brain at the moment, don't I, hun?" She looked up at Luke, who was back in the room.

"Huh?" He wasn't listening.

"Jet was just telling us about the doorbell camera footage, from that night."

Luke glanced across the table, locked onto Jet's eyes. "Does it show what time it happened? When exactly it . . ."

"Not exactly," she replied. "But my Apple Watch told us. 10:46 p.m. That's when someone whacked me over the head." Jet spread jelly over a second piece of toast. "Say, Luke, where were you at 10:46 p.m. on October thirty-first?"

"You joking?" he laughed.

"Kinda." Jet shrugged. "But, actually, I do want to know. I need to know where everyone was. And if you don't answer, then everyone's going to think you murdered your own sister." She showed him the inside of her mouth: the sticky, munched-up toast.

"Jet." Mom pressed her temples harder.

Luke threw a corner of bacon at Jet, and the baby squealed in delight.

"I was at home, like I told the cops," he said, half sullen, half smiling. "Me and Sophia got home around 10:15 and put Cameron to bed. Then we watched some TV."

"Which show?" Jet asked, eating the small bacon projectile that had landed in her lap.

"*Friends*," Luke said. "Sophia loves *Friends*."

"Then we went to bed," Sophia added, wiping the green goo from Cameron's face.

"So you two were together all night?" Jet pointed her fork at them. "And, Mom and Dad, you were together, driving stuff from the fair back to storage at the MC offices?" She clapped her hands. "Well, it looks like you all have alibis, then." Jet turned to the baby, accused him with her knife. "Cameron, what about you?"

He blew a bubble.

"Don't we know who it is already, Jet?" Dad said, dragging his fork through his untouched eggs. "They've just got to find him."

"Who?" Luke demanded.

"JJ."

Luke turned to Jet. "It was JJ?" The rage undisguised in his voice, or in his fists, gripping the table too hard.

"No, we don't know," Jet said. "He's just skipped town, won't answer his phone."

"And the text," Dad said. "The *Sorry* text."

"I'll kill him." Luke slammed one hand on the table, making the cutlery jump and the baby flinch.

"Luke, please," Sophia said. "Not in front of Cam."

"No one is killing anybody," Mom said, voice rising, taking charge. "I don't know why we're talking about any of this, wasting time. You all know why you're here."

Did they? Jet looked around at her family. Why *were* they here?

"Jet." Mom twisted in her chair, knees pointed this way, her voice soft and hard at the same time. "It's our last chance. Dr. Lee said it would be too late once the aneurysm forms. If we want to save you, we need to take you back to the hospital now, right now. This morning. Right now. Please. The whole family agrees."

Jet's stomach twisted, the toast suddenly tasteless in her mouth.

"Do you, *whole family*?" Jet announced across the table. "You think I don't get to make decisions about my life, about my death? That you know better than me? You can't understand for one fucking second what it's like to have to make a choice like that. Fuck. And Sophia, I swear to god if you say anything about my language . . ."

None of them would look at her, except Mom, and the baby.

"I'm not choosing to die on the operating table. The answer is no. Sorry, *whole family*." The answer was no, and the other answer was that pain above her right eye—new this morning—which might mean it was too late anyway, the choice out of her hands. Certainly out of her mom's hands.

"Fine." The chair screeched on the oak floor as Mom stood up, marched over to the sideboard.

"I went to the funeral home this morning, picked these up."

She came back to the table, dropped two brochures in front of Jet with a slap.

Jet looked down at them.

One for caskets, every shade of wood, varnished and shining.

The other for urns.

"What the fu—" Jet began.

"—Mom." Luke buried his face in his hands. "You can't do th—"

"—Go on," Mom cut him off, pointing to the catalogs. "Make a decision, Jet. That's what you care about, your choices? So make another choice. Go on. What's it going to be? Burial or cremation? Pick one."

"Mom, there is something really fucking wrong with you." Jet shoved the brochures away, a plate sliding off the table, shattering on the floor.

Cameron started to cry.

"This is what you're doing to me!" Mom screamed, hysterical now, tears merging with lines of snot. "Why won't you listen? I can't lose you—I can't bury another child, Jet. I won't do it. It's not fair."

"Not fair?" Jet asked, incredulous. "I'm twenty-seven. I'm the one who has to die before I've even had a chance to live."

"So don't!" Mom pleaded. "Don't die, Jet, please! I know you think I'm being the bad guy, and I don't care—if it saves your life then I'll do anything! Please, Jet, don't do this!"

"It's already done, Mom!"

"I can't do this." Mom's face folded, came undone, hand pressed over her mouth to hold it together. She hurried out of the room, blindly, bawling into her hands, crying so hard she couldn't breathe, coughing around them. Up the stairs, a thunder that shook the whole house.

Dad sighed, got to his feet. "Now you've upset your mother," he said, eyes downcast.

"Hold on." Jet rounded on him. "*I've* upset *her*? Unbelievable. She put a fucking catalog of coffins in front of me, Dad. For fuck's sake! For once, I wish you would just pick a fucking side, the right side."

"Luke, let's go," Sophia whispered, picking Cameron out of his high chair.

"No, no, no," Jet said. "You stay, enjoy your *nice* family breakfast. I'll go. I'm going." She sniffed, wiped her nose on her sleeve. "I'm leaving. Can't live here anymore."

"Jet, don't say that." Dad stepped toward her, arms open. Eyes kind, but his *kind* wasn't good enough now.

"I mean it, I'm not doing it. I have six days until I die, and I'm not doing that here, like this. I'm going!"

Jet was out of the room before any of them could call her back, not that calling would have made a difference. Her mind was made up. She had something important to do, the last thing she would ever do, and she couldn't do it in this house. It was hard enough.

In her room, she grabbed two backpacks and headed to the drawers. Hey, at least she didn't have to take too many clothes, right? Like packing for a week's vacation. Less than. She grabbed a handful of underwear, a couple bras. A few T-shirts. Sweatpants and jeans, stuffed them in. Into the bathroom to grab her hairbrush, her toothbrush. Her makeup bag—would she even need that? Did the walking dead need concealer? Left the white bottle of Lotrel, the pills she took every day for high blood pressure, for her kidneys, because what was the fucking point now? Didn't need them anymore.

Grabbed her notebook from the bed, and the pen she'd stolen from Jack Finney, put them in the second backpack, along with her MacBook. She went to the socket to pull out the—the—the—what's that fucking word, the white wire thing that gave it more battery. Never mind. She grabbed it, unplugged it, shoved it in the top of the bag. Hoisted both up onto her shoulders, still wearing her pajamas.

Downstairs, she slipped on her shoes and her jacket.

"Bye, Reggie. Love you." She bent to kiss the top of the dog's head. Not even her dog, really. Her parents' empty-nest dog, when Jet left for college. But he was her dog now, and they all knew it. Reggie most of all.

"Jet." Dad came around the corner. "You're not really going."

"I *am* really going."

"Don't," he said. "Your mom wouldn't want this."

"It's not always about what she wants, Dad. I have to go. I'm going."

He reached for her backpack, held on to one strap. "But, Jet, you can't . . . you're not—"

"—Not what, Dad? Responsible? I can do this on my own. I can."

Just then, the mail slot crashed open, a handful of letters scattering to the *Welcome* mat. Footsteps on the drive, doubling, the mailman hurrying away from the yelling inside.

Reggie rushed toward the mail, but Jet beat him to it.

"Look, see, Dad," Jet sniffed, hysterical too now, in her quieter, flippant way. "Here I am picking up my mail. Ah, see, two letters for *Margaret Mason*. Picking up my mail like a responsible fucking adult." She stuffed the letters in the open backpack, ripping it away from Dad's hands. "Might even be able to wipe my own ass soon."

Cameron wailed, Luke and Sophia coming to stand in the hall.

"Don't worry, you'll get there too, bud."

Jet grabbed her keys and her wallet from the wooden bowl on the side table.

"Where are you going?" Luke asked, because he felt like he had to. Jet knew her brother.

"Literally anywhere that isn't this fucking house! I'm not going to die in here again. Tell Mom she can choose the casket. I really won't care, I'll be dead."

Jet opened the front door and struggled through, flipping off the doorbell camera as she passed. Unlocked her truck and climbed inside, starting the engine, hitting the steering wheel just once, with the heel of her hand. Fuck, that hurt; she wouldn't do that again.

She checked her mirrors and backed out, waving to Dad and Luke and Sophia in the open doorway.

A curtain twitched in the upstairs window just as she reached the street.

Mom's blotchy face pressed to the glass, watching her leave.

JET KNOCKED. THREE times. Waited two seconds. Knocked again. Waited. But she'd waited long enough, sitting in her truck, wondering what the fuck she should do, where the fuck she should go. She really only had one answer, only one person in this whole fucking town, so she knocked again and again and again. He'd forgive her for the hostility; he always did.

A click and the door swung inward, Billy's confused face in the crack.

"Jet." He pulled the door the whole way. His eyes looked swollen, hiding underneath those dark curls.

"I asked at the bar downstairs, they told me you lived in 1B," Jet explained.

"You OK? Sorry, sorry, I didn't mean that. Stupid question."

His gaze settled on her bags, another question forming on his lips, skirting his teeth.

"Yeah, so," Jet said, sucking in a breath. "I was wondering . . . can I stay with you? Here? In your apartment?"

Billy's mouth didn't move but his eyes did, tracking across her face, a flash of his old light behind them.

"Probably won't be much of a roommate," she laughed. "I definitely won't be paying any rent, might keep some strange hours, eat your food. And I know I come with baggage." She gestured to the backpacks on the floor, but they both knew that's not what she meant. "But it's not like it'll put you out *that* much, 'cause, you know, um, like, I'll be dead by the end of the week."

Billy swallowed.

"Is that a yes?"

EIGHT

"Billy, really, it's fine. Don't worry."

Jet raised her legs from the coffee table, so he could get past with the vacuum cleaner.

"I've put the sheets in the wash," Billy said, over the whir, the crackle, as the machine found a stash of crumbs. "You take the bed, I'll have the sofa."

"I'm not kicking you out of your bed, Billy." Jet's eyes returned to her screen, to the Google Street View of River Street, clicking up and down, hunting, a digital stalker. As though she might somehow find her phone there, hiding in the past, in the grass or the dirt.

"I like the sofa. Sometimes I sleep there anyway."

Billy Finney was the worst liar. And this sofa was a piece of crap, lumps of springs digging into Jet's thighs already.

He disappeared with the vacuum into the bedroom, kept it running as he reached for a can of deodorant, spraying it around the room, into every newly tidied corner. Coughing as he inhaled the fumes.

Jet smiled, kept her teeth to herself, started back at the top of River Street again.

More cursing from the bedroom, more rustling.

"Billy, stop worrying." Again. It was hard to concentrate with all the worrying.

He reemerged, a small box in his hands. "Got this for Christmas last year. Never opened it."

He opened it now, a green candle in a glass jar. A scent described as *Cedar Delight*. Billy placed it on the coffee table, grabbed a lighter from a kitchen drawer, and bent low to light the wick, the baby fire reflected in his glassy blue eyes.

"Lovely." Jet grinned up at him. "I can see myself living here, for the rest of my life."

Billy retracted his thumb, gave her a look.

"What? That's funny." Jet gave a gruff laugh, if he wouldn't. Billy normally laughed at all of her jokes.

"I'll just grab this," he muttered, reaching for the photo frame that lived in the middle of the coffee table. It had been blocked by Jet's screen before, but she saw it now as he picked it up. A woman with dark curly hair and glittering eyes, an ice cream melting over her fingers. Billy's mom. Mrs. Finney. Beth. Three names for the same person. There was a boy in the photo too, same hair, same ice cream, same cool blue eyes. The Billy Jet knew best, about twelve years old. Billy averted his eyes and Jet averted hers too, pretending she hadn't noticed, watching out the side of her eye as Billy took the photo and shut it away, on the top shelf in the closet.

"You don't have to put everything away just because I'm here."

"Oh," he said, remembering something else to worry about. "I keep a spare key under the mat outside the front door. You should have it. I'll get it for you."

He got it for her, almost breathless when he arrived back at her side, putting the key down on the table, between her feet. His eyes caught her screen, mirrored it back.

"That's the street where your phone was turned off?"

Jet nodded, craned to look at him, towering above her. "You know anyone who lives there?"

Billy chewed his lip. "Don't think so. You think that's where they live?"

"Well, they went straight there, after the attack," Jet said. "Turned my phone off in this spot." She pointed to the street view, where River Street passed North Street.

Billy thought about it. "Could have been on their way home, then realized it was a bad idea to do that with your phone still on. Doesn't mean they live exactly there, right? Just that it was on the way."

"Maybe." Jet nodded. "So maybe they live north of town."

That was a lot of *maybe*.

"What else do you have?"

Jet glanced at the scribbles in her open notebook, Billy following her eyes.

"Not a lot. The police think it's JJ, I can tell."

Billy bent lower, leaning on the back of the sofa, his head hovering over her shoulder.

"Do *you* think it's JJ?"

"No. JJ's not like that. But I'm trying to keep an open mind." She paused. "Well . . . someone bashed it open for me."

That one *almost* got a smile out of him, a lopsided twitch in his cheek. His eyes still didn't look right, though: haunted, but also busy somehow, ever moving, too much going on behind them. He was the one who'd seen her dead—well, almost dead. Maybe that took a while to go away. Jet hadn't had to see it, hadn't had to live it after those first few seconds, but she wondered if her eyes looked haunted too. Felt like it, that deep pain behind her right eye, the dull ache and itch beneath the bandages. Not dull enough; she should take more codeine. At least Dr. Lee gave her the good stuff.

She winced.

"What's wrong?" He bent even lower, to meet her eyes. "You need your painkillers? Food? I can make you something, anything you want."

"Billy, it's OK. Stop doing stuff for me."

"I like doing stuff for you."

He always had.

Billy was nine months older than her. Jet didn't know a world he didn't exist in. Always right there, next door.

Hey Billy, wanna ride bikes? I'll race ya. Hey, did you let me win because I'm younger and smaller? Don't let me win, Billy.

Hi Mrs. Mason, is Jet in? I found a frog and I need to show her. Jet loves frogs.

Only stopped when Jet turned fourteen, when Sophia became her best friend instead, took all Jet's time and attention, because Billy couldn't come over if Sophia was already there—that would have been weird, two worlds that didn't mix. Jet and Billy had outgrown each other, no more bike races, no more frogs. Billy was right, though; Jet did love frogs. It was a fucking awesome frog.

A notification pinged up on her screen: low battery.

"Shit," Jet said. "I need my—fuck sake, what's that word? The white wire thingy?"

"Charger?"

"Yes!" Jet clapped him on the shoulder. "Charger, that's it."

"I'll get it." Billy straightened up, because he couldn't *not* do stuff for her. For anyone, really. He was just like that, made like that. Jet was made a different way.

She pointed him toward the red backpack. "In there."

"You got some mail here," Billy said, digging through, pulling the envelopes out to reach the charger.

"Oh yeah. I was proving a point. Let me see."

Jet lowered her feet to the floor, MacBook on the table, and took the letters out of Billy's hands. The first was a red envelope, handwritten address. Jet flipped it over and ripped open the tab, while Billy moved his guitar case so he could reach the wall socket, plugging her ch-ch—white wire thingy in.

"It's a card," Jet said, pulling it out.

A white card, with a vase of flowers drawn on the front, in garish colors. Below the vase and its little shadow were the words: *Get Well Soon.*

"You've got to be kidding me."

She held it up so Billy could see. He winced.

"Who's it from?" he asked.

Jet opened it, scanned the handwriting inside.

"From Gerry Clay."

"The village trustee guy?"

Jet nodded, clearing her throat to read aloud. "*So sorry to hear about your accident.* Accident, Gerry? It's called premeditated murder. *Sending all of our thoughts and prayers.* Well, Gerry, you can shove your thoughts and prayers up your—"

"—What's this one?" Billy asked, picking up the other envelope from her lap. "Looks official."

Jet swapped the card for the letter. It *did* look official, her name and address in a type so neat it looked almost aggressive, through a thin plastic window. *PRIVATE & CONFIDENTIAL* in bold capitals across the top.

She ripped it open, pulled out the folded letter.

"*Late Notice*," she said, reading it out. "Wait, what the fuck?"

"What is it?" Billy sat next to her, the sofa cushion dipping toward him.

"It's from one of those online loan companies, LightFi. *Dear Margaret Mason, you have defaulted on your monthly repayments for the secured loan detailed below.*" Jet scanned the page. "What the fuck? Thirty grand?"

"What did you need thirty grand for?"

"I didn't need thirty grand, Billy," she said, the annoyance shifting to him. "I didn't do this. This wasn't me." She pointed at the letter, to the series of numbers listed after *Bank Account Number.* "This isn't my bank account. I didn't get this money, didn't take out any loan." She read on. "*As the loan was secured against the below personal asset, this will be seized unless we receive repayment* . . . blah, blah, blah . . . *or we will have to proceed with filing a lawsuit* . . . wait, what *asset*?" She scanned lower. "*Vehicle Ford F-150, 1986, registration: HB*—that's my truck!" Jet shook the letter, mouth falling open. "Someone took out a loan against my fucking truck, in *my* name!"

"You sure you didn't—"

"—I think I'd remember getting and spending thirty grand, Billy. How many lattes and avocados do you think I buy?"

He nodded, taking her heat, cooling it down by blowing out his lip. "Then it's identity fraud," he said. "If someone took this out in your name. Spent that money."

Jet slumped back against the sofa, forgetting about her broken head, hissing when the bandage made contact. "Talk about kicking me when

I'm down." She waved the letter, sharp edges carving through the *Cedar Delight*–scented air.

Billy studied her. "Well, it might not . . . might not be a coincidence, Jet."

She sat back up.

"Couldn't this be related to your attack?"

Jet studied him back. "You think?"

"I mean, has this ever happened to you before?"

"No," she agreed. "And I've never been murdered before either."

"Exactly." He stood up. "I think we need to take this to the police. Aren't they looking for a reason someone might have wanted to kill you?"

"Over thirty grand?" Funny, Jet always thought she might be worth more than that. "You're right," she sniffed, getting to her feet, swiping Billy's spare key from the table.

This was *something*. More than clicking up and down River Street on Google Maps. A possible lead.

She grabbed her jacket from the hook by the door, put it on, key in one pocket—where her other keys lived—letter and envelope in the other. Patted her jeans pocket to check she had her phone, remembered that checking was useless; her phone was with her killer.

She slipped her thick socks into her Birkenstock clogs.

"See you later," Jet said, reaching for the door.

"Oh," Billy replied, one arm already inside his fur-lined denim jacket. "I thought . . . no, yeah, that's fine."

Jet faltered in the open doorway. "Oh," she said too. "I just thought you'd be busy, you know. I'm probably imposing enough, right? Don't need to take up any more of your time."

Billy's jacket fell, his face too, catching it with the hook of his little finger. The jacket, that is, not his face. He'd already picked that up, a one-sided smile. "Yeah, no, you're right. I've actually g-got a shift at the bar later anyway, so that's . . . yeah, that's fine. S-see you later."

Later. The meaning different now, shortened to a few hours. Because that's the only kind of *later* Jet had left.

"Yeah, see you later, Billy."

NINE

"And when did this arrive?" Detective Ecker's eyes scanned down the letter again, creasing by his thumbs.

"Came in the mail this morning." Jet sat across the table from Detective Ecker and the chief, tucked into metal chairs that were too small for them. Jack Finney stood against the back wall of the interview room, a file in his hands, hugging it to his chest.

Ecker glanced at the digital clock hanging over Jet's head. She turned to follow his eyes: 4:52 p.m. It had the seconds too, ticking up in angry red digits—red for danger, and blood, and mistakes.

"I didn't open it until this afternoon," she said, answering a question he hadn't asked. "And I sat in re-re-re—the waiting room for over an hour, waiting for you to get here. You know I'm on a bit of a tight deadline, right?"

Ecker didn't answer, even though Jet *had* asked him a question. He studied the letter again, moving his thumbs down, the top half of the page flopping over.

"The loan was taken out two months ago," he said. "And the first repayment was supposed to be made last week."

Jet shrugged. "Guess I've got bigger things to worry about than a bad credit score." She rubbed the spot above her eye, the pain deepening under these bright overhead lights. They never heard of soft lighting? Lamps?

"And you don't recognize this bank account number? The one the money was paid into?"

"Nope, that's not mine."

Ecker clicked his tongue. "OK," he said, "we'll look into it."

"You think it's related? To my murder?"

The detective folded the letter, slid it back inside the envelope. "We're not ruling anything out at this point."

More cop speak.

"Well, you've probably ruled *some* things out. I'm no detective, but it probably wasn't aliens or Taylor Swift. She's very busy."

Chief Lou smiled, hiding it with his hand.

"Let us look into this." Ecker banged the letter against the table and stood up, tiny metal chair screeching, making more noise than it should, to make up for its size.

"Wait." Jet's voice stopped him on his way to the door. "You said you were going up to River Street last night, to speak to the people who live there. You find anything?"

Ecker's fingers stalled on the handle. "Spoke to the neighbors. No one remembers seeing or hearing anything out of the ordinary that night. The house nearest the phone's last known location, number 12, the elderly woman who lives there was already asleep at the time in question. We had some officers on a grid search this morning. Nothing's turned up so far. I'll let you know if it does."

Jet nodded, but she didn't entirely trust that he would.

"Oh, and you can tell the pricks at LightFi that they will be seizing that truck over my dead body."

Crickets. Jet hadn't even meant to do that one. Death was every-where, linguistically speaking; she hadn't really noticed until she was dying.

Ecker opened the door, and the chief followed him out, dipping his head toward Jet as he did, replacing his cap. The door closed behind them, and the clock shifted upward another minute. Counting up, but counting down really.

Jack came alive then, pushing off the wall and into one of the abandoned chairs, too small for him too. He put the file down on the table and stretched his fingers.

"We had a call into the station a couple of hours ago," he said, holding her eyes. "Your mom, trying to file a missing persons report."

Jet sighed, the air heavier on the way out. "I'm not missing."

"I know," Jack said gently. "It's just her way, Jet."

"I wish it wasn't."

"She said you left home this morning. She's very worried about you . . . in your condition."

"I'm fine." Jet sniffed. "I'm staying with Billy."

Jack nodded, left his chin up. "I assumed. I'll let her know, when she calls back."

Silence, also heavier than it was before.

"Will you get in trouble?" Jet said, head jerking toward the door. "Because I asked for you to be in here too?"

"Don't remember you *asking.*" Jack smiled. "More like *demanding.*"

Jet smirked. "Sorry. It's just, I don't *know* them. I don't trust them." She played with her hands, slotted them together. "And they don't know me either. I know they don't really care, beyond closing a case. But I *do* know you, and I know you'll tell me anything I need to know. It's next-door-neighbor code."

Another smile.

"So . . . is there anything I need to know?" Jet prompted. "Anything turn up from processing the crime scene?"

The metal chair creaked as Jack shifted his weight. "Well, I should probably wait for Detective Ecker to—"

"—Please, Mr. Finney." Jet leaned forward, catching his flailing eyes. "I don't have a lot of time."

He sighed, checking over his shoulder, watching the door for a few seconds, time ticking away. The clock was silent, but Jet could hear it all the same.

"OK," Jack said quickly, rubbing his nose with one hand, sliding the file over with the other. "We did find something interesting."

"Interesting?"

Jack opened the file, flicking through pages and photographs, those yellow numbered markers from the scene. Jet tried to catch all the words, failed because they moved too fast, upside down.

"Here." Jack stopped at a large photograph, slid it out and held it up.

A gloved hand at the top of the frame, two fingers pinching a clear baggie in front of a white surface, sealed at the top. And inside the plastic baggie was a hair. Jet squinted, leaned closer. The hair looked red, straight, about five inches long.

Jack handed the photo over and Jet studied it closer.

"That hair was found at the scene. More specifically, it was found where you were lying, after the attack. And this hair was on the wooden floor, underneath the main pool of blood. The hair was there first, and you bled over it; the techs can tell things like that."

Jet lowered the photo, looked back at him. She thought she knew what that meant, but she wanted him to say it.

Jack nodded. "Which means it wasn't left there by any of the first responders or police officers, or Billy finding you, when the scene was contaminated. This hair was under the blood. It was left there either before, or during . . ."

He didn't finish his sentence, didn't need to.

"So it was left by the killer?" Jet asked, eyes returning to the photo, running her finger along the zoomed-in strand of hair. Did Jet even know any redheads? Sophia's hair was dark brown, but sometimes looked a little red under the right lighting.

Jet swallowed. "DNA?" But she already knew. Knew that movies and TV lied about that stuff, fast-tracked it. Knew that it could take weeks to get any results back from the lab. Jet didn't have weeks, and she wasn't in a movie.

Jack shook his head. "No need," he said quietly. "It's not human."

Jet narrowed her eyes.

"It's synthetic," he said. "Plastic."

Jet looked back at the hair. "You mean a wig?"

"I mean a wig." Jack reached forward, took the photograph from her, replaced it in the file, another look over his shoulder. "You know anyone who was wearing a red wig at the Halloween Fair?" But he'd asked it like he already knew the answer, like this wasn't really a question at all. Which was why Detective Ecker hadn't needed to ask it.

Jet exhaled. "JJ," she said, her hands finding each other again, gripping on.

Jack pressed his lips together, closed the file.

JJ couldn't have done this, right? He'd hardly raised his voice the whole time Jet had been with him; in fact, maybe yelling would have showed that he cared more. But JJ was missing. JJ sent her a *Sorry* text after the time of the attack. JJ was wearing a red wig with straight hair on Halloween, on the night Jet was killed.

Jet could see it in Mr. Finney's eyes, could count them one by one.

Three strikes against JJ.

TEN

The inside of the truck smelled like salt and grease, stronger somehow, the colder the fries got. Maybe Jet hadn't needed four whole boxes—large, of course—as well as a double cheeseburger. But she hadn't eaten fries in years, to save her kidneys, and what had been the damn point?

She finished off the last three fries from her second pack, eating with spite more than anything else—because she could now, so she would. They weren't as good as she remembered, and now her tongue stung from the salt.

It was coming up again. The location.

Jet lightened the pressure in her right foot and the truck slowed to a crawl.

River Street.

Right here, where the road met North Street, continuing straight on ahead, where her headlights couldn't reach.

It had been three nights now, since her phone was brought here by her killer, turned off in this exact spot.

What did this place mean to them? Where were they going?

If JJ was the prime suspect, then how did this tie into the police's theory? JJ had never mentioned knowing anyone on this street either, so why would he have come here after killing her? And—scratch that—why would he have killed her in the first place? They used to make each other laugh . . . a lot. Although, now Jet thought about it, maybe the laughter had been mostly one-sided. His. At work, catching stolen moments in the gym staff room, before they realized there were cameras in there. They'd been good together, but good hadn't been good enough for Jet. You had to aim for something better than good, something bigger, and Jet had her whole life in front of her . . . back then, at least. She'd done it nicely, even quit her job at the gym so it wouldn't be awkward for either of them. That wasn't a reason to kill somebody, right?

It was Jet's fourth time driving the street tonight, and she still had no answers, no sign. Apart from that yellow sign over there. *SLOW: Children,* it said. Jet *was* going slow, but not because some sign told her to. So slow that the truck came to a stop, sighing, settling back on its wheels.

Jet sighed too.

Maybe she should get out of the truck, walk the street instead of driving it, swap the smell of congealing fries for the crisp night air. Maybe she'd see it from a different perspective, in a new light. She pulled off onto the grass alongside someone's pristine white fence. Pulled the handbrake but didn't turn off the engine, not yet. The clock on the dashboard was her only way to keep track of time, without a phone, without a watch. It read 10:55. Which meant that, in one minute, it would be the exact same time as well as the exact same spot. The time and place the killer was when they turned off her phone.

Jet pulled the key from the ignition, got out, locked the door. Then she turned, one hand resting on the truck, and she watched the street. The middle of the road, where the last blue blip of her phone had floated, its final stamp on the world. It had guided her here and now she was lost.

Nothing happened. She counted to sixty, and still nothing happened. Just the wind whistling in the burnt-orange trees. Well, what had she expected exactly?

Jet kept going, following River Street, leaving her truck behind. Head spinning as she looked at the houses on either side: that white one there, with the triangular porch and the red car outside, must have been the house Ecker mentioned, where the elderly woman lived. Asleep and useless to Jet.

Her shoes slapped the pavement, the only sound on this too-quiet street. No more streetlamps beyond this point, just the faint glow of the moon hovering over her.

Her killer must have known someone who lived down this way, right? Or why drive straight here after breaking Jet's head open? Could she ask the police for a list of all the owners' names, Mrs. Red Shutters and Mr. American Flag?

Not just a flag outside that house, though, a jack-o'-lantern too, carved into the face of a skull. The bottom looked a little soggy, but it wasn't rotting yet. It shared its death stare with Jet, and she shared hers back.

At this rate, all the pumpkins would outlive Jet.

The houses petered out again, making way for the cemetery. Strange shapes skulking in the dark, crosses and headstones like wonky rows of teeth, an angel weeping over them all. Jet kept walking, didn't want to think about it too hard. This wasn't the only cemetery in town; she might not end up here. But Emily was buried here, and there was something in that, wasn't there? Sisters, together again. Jet much older than her older sister ever got to be. And, look, there was a fresh corner of grass, a patch waiting to be filled. There you go: Jet had thought about it anyway. Would anyone leave flowers for her? Jet liked sunflowers best.

The cemetery ended and the houses came back. More shutters, more dormer windows, and Jet skulking below. She came to a crossroads, four ways to choose. River Street continued if she picked the road ahead; she'd only just reached the halfway point, but her legs felt a little un-steady. Tired, just tired. She was allowed to get tired; it didn't mean any-thing else. And the back of her head throbbed, a wet kind of pain. Jet had left those painkillers behind at Billy's, hadn't realized she'd be out so long.

She picked the road that branched off to the left, back toward town. She'd come all this way, might as well loop around to go pick up her truck. Better than having to walk back past the cemetery again anyway.

The world darkened as she followed the road, the moon blocked out, trees pressing in on either side of her. The bridge waited up ahead in an orange glow, flickering in and out from a faulty streetlamp. Middle Covered Bridge, the one all the tourists stopped to take a photo of, because it was *so Vermont*. That was during the day; at night it looked like something from a horror movie, like you wouldn't step inside unless the plot forced you to.

But no one was forcing Jet. She continued toward the wooden walkway that ran alongside the bridge, her steps echoing around the whole structure, reverberating in her aching head.

Jet stopped.

A rustle in the trees behind her, something moving, following.

She looked over her shoulder, couldn't see anything.

Probably just a fox.

And that was when Jet realized: she wasn't afraid. She *should* be afraid: it was night, it was dark, she was alone, walking, without her phone or any way to call for help. But she wasn't afraid, or her heart hadn't noticed those things, forgot to drum out any warning.

And her heart was right: what was the point being afraid anymore? The worst had already happened—the thing from your nightmares, the reason you didn't go out alone in the dark or held your keys in your knuckles if you had to. Jet couldn't get any more dead; it had already happened.

Was this what it felt like to be a man? Walking on this creepy dark bridge, not scared for a second that she wouldn't make it out the other side, because it didn't really make a difference whether she did or not. The night belonged to her now too.

A dead woman walking. And dead women had no use for fear.

JET PUSHED THE door open with her hip. "Want some fries, Billy? They're cold."

Billy stood three feet away, eyes wide and unblinking, phone in his hand.

"Where have you been?" he said, breathless, though he hadn't moved.

Jet passed him the two leftover boxes of fries. He held them to his chest, almost dropping one.

"From that burger place on Route 4. Near the police station. Haven't eaten fries in about four years and it was a bit of an anticlimax, if I'm being honest. Maybe I should have found a McDonald's."

"It's late." Billy put the boxes on the table, one pack overturning, fries cascading over the edge. "I was worried. Tried to call but you don't have a phone. What were you doing?"

"I went to the police station, then I went to the burger place on Route 4, then I drove up and down River Street for a while, eating fries, looking for my killer. Walked it too. Pointless, didn't find anything."

Billy blinked, eyes coming back even wider.

"I could have come with you. It's dark, it's not safe."

"I wasn't scared. What's going to happen, Billy? I'll get murdered again?"

"Maybe."

"So, why does it matter?"

"It matters," he said, scooping up the floor-fries, wiping the grease from his hands. That look in his eyes was bigger than worry. It was fear. Jet thought men weren't scared of the night, but Billy was made different. And now she felt guilty, for some reason.

"I said I might keep strange hours," she said, not really an apology, not even close. "I've got a murder to solve."

Billy sniffed, reluctantly took a sagging fry, held it to his lips. "What did the detective say? About the loan thing?" He folded the fry and stuffed it in.

"They're going to look into it. *Not ruling anything out* apparently."

"That's good." He chewed. "Yeah, these fries are shit. I'll get you some good ones before—" He cut himself off, a flush in his cheeks.

Jet helped him out, pretending she hadn't heard, hanging up her jacket. "I got something from your dad, after Ecker and the chief left the room."

Billy raised his eyebrows, going for another fry.

"Really? He never tells me anything. All we have is football and the weather," he sniffed.

"Showed me a photograph," Jet said. "Of a hair found at the scene. It was under the blood, so either it was there before, or it came from the killer."

"How long does it take to do a DNA test?"

"It's a wig hair." Jet sat down, pulling her notebook across the sofa, opening the page. "A red costume wig hair." She looked up at Billy. "And we all know who was wearing a red wig for Halloween."

"Yeah." He sucked in a breath.

"JJ—"

"—Andrew Smith," Billy said at the same time.

They stared, pointed at each other.

Spoke at the same time again.

"JJ had one—?"

"—Andrew Smith was wearing a red wig?" Jet's eyes narrowed, voice lowered.

"He was a clown, Jet."

Jet searched her memory. "I remember the painted red nose. He had a wig on too?"

"One hundred percent." Billy dropped down on the sofa next to her.

Jet closed her eyes to peel back the time, to see the scene playing out before her.

"Yeah, but clowns have rainbow-colored hair, don't they? And it's curly, like, coiled? This hair at the scene was straight, like five inches long."

Billy closed his eyes too, trying the same trick. Jet watched him, blew on his face when he took too long.

"You know, you haven't changed much since you were eleven," he said.

"Neither have you." She prodded the side of his head, through to his memory. "Anything?"

Billy nodded. "It was definitely a red wig, just red, and I'm pretty sure the hairs were straight. Fluffy red. Like the clown from *It*."

Jet clicked her pen at him. "You sure?"

"No," Billy said, crumbling under the pressure of the pen. "But we could go ask him. He lives literally three steps from my front door, in the other apartment." Billy rose up from the sofa. "We can just—"

"—No, we can just not." Jet pulled him back down, their legs colliding. "We can't go around and ask him about a wig. If he's a suspect, that will give him time to get rid of it, destroy it. No one can know about the hair at the scene; your dad wasn't even supposed to tell me. You're bad at murders, Billy, god."

"It's my first time!" He surrendered, palms up. "How are we going to confirm what wig he was wearing, though? It's important. Takes you from one suspect to two."

"Possibly more," Jet thought aloud. "Almost everyone was in costume. There could have been more red wigs wandering around that fair."

Billy shrugged, deflating. "I didn't take any photos."

Jet didn't need to close her eyes this time, the memory burrowing its way to the front, riding that tunnel of pain behind her eye. "No, but someone else did." She clicked her fingers. "Gerry Clay's son, I think his name is Owen. He was taking the official photos at the fair, with a fancy-ass camera. He's got photos. *A lot* of photos."

Jet grinned, and Billy mirrored it back.

"Come on." She jumped up, heading for her jacket.

Billy coughed. "You're not going now, are you? It's eleven-thirty."

"I'm kinda on the clock here."

Billy hesitated.

"I think you'll get a better reception if you go in the morning. And you look tired."

"Tired is fine, Billy. Not-dying people get tired too." She slipped one arm into her jacket.

"There's something else," Billy said, dropping his eyes, like his gaze was suddenly an intrusion. "You're . . . you're leaking. Through the bandage at the back."

Jet stopped, the jacket clattering to the floor, her hand moving to the back of her head. A sharp pain when she pushed, warm and sticky. She winced.

"I'm supposed to change the dressing every day." But how? She couldn't see, couldn't reach.

"I can do it," Billy offered, before Jet had to ask for help. He'd known her all her life; maybe he knew those hidden parts of her too, that she couldn't ask for help because it was the same as feeling useless.

"If you really want," Jet sniffed. Besides, she knew some hidden parts of Billy too: that he always had to help, whoever it was. So this wasn't even really about her.

"Yeah, come on, sit down." He patted the sofa, like this was no big deal, a Band-Aid on a grazed knee. He'd probably done that for her at some point too, when they were kids. "I've got a first aid kit. Got some gauze pads, and some of that tape. Antiseptic cream."

"Not sure we need to bother with the cream." She was going to rot either way.

Billy opened the closet door, beside the TV. The framed photo of his mom peeking out from the top shelf, her eyes watching Jet as she flinched from another throb of pain beneath the bandage. On the shelf below were a tool kit and a little blue first aid box.

"Presents from Dad," Billy said, "when I moved out. Never used either of them."

He unzipped the first aid kit and pulled out some plastic-wrapped pads, a little roll of tape.

"OK, look forward. We'll do the back first, then the one at the side." He rested his elbows on the back of the sofa, kneeling, so his head was at the same height as hers. "I'm going to go slow, OK?"

"Just do it."

Jet gritted her teeth, waiting for the pain. Billy's breath was warm against the back of her neck. And then it wasn't; he was holding it, concentrating. His fingers soft against her head as he pulled at the old dressing, the tape lifting away, pulling at her skin and the weeping wound.

Jet winced, gripped the sofa cushion.

"Sorry, sorry. Oh god."

"Are you going to faint, Billy?"

"Not if I can help it. There. Done."

He lifted the bandage away, the air cool against the exposed back of her head. Too cool.

"Did they shave my head, Billy?"

"Um," he answered. "It's . . . it's not your best angle. Bit crusty. Little bit bald. Let's get this covered up, nice and clean."

The sound of ripping plastic behind her ears.

"Here we go. I'm just going to place this on, very carefully, then tape it down. OK?"

Jet waited for him to get close. Closer.

"AH!" she cried suddenly, making Billy jump out of his skin, falling back into it and off his knees.

"Jet, that's not funny!"

She cackled, deep and gravelly. Because it was, actually. And so was the look on his face.

"Don't do that again."

JET TURNED OFF the bathroom light, closed the door behind her as she stepped into the darkened living room.

Billy was already tucked up on the sofa, his head against one of the patterned cushions, using the matching throw as a blanket. It wasn't long enough, and neither was the sofa, Billy's bare feet dangling over the end. Eyes glowing as they watched her approach.

"I'm done in there now, thanks for the toothpaste," she said.

"No problem."

Jet picked her way past the sofa, toward the bedroom, the small lamp glowing inside. She hesitated, turned back.

"You can come with me," she said to the darkness. "In the morning, to talk to Owen Clay. If you want?"

Only because she knew Billy wanted to. Then at least she didn't have to worry about him worrying, or hear about it after.

"I'll be there," his voice found her, across the dark room.

Jet slipped inside the bedroom, the bed ready and made, a glass of water on the nightstand that Billy must have just put there.

"Night, Jet."

"Night, Billy."

Tuesday
November 4

ELEVEN

Jet pressed the doorbell, holding on just longer than was polite.

Number 19, Pleasant Street. *Pleasant* was the right word: a big house with yellow wooden siding and sleek gray shutters. This must have been a Mason Construction project; it had that look.

Jet reached for the bell again.

"Give them a minute," Billy said, behind her on the steps.

"I'm running out of minutes." She ignored him, pressed the bell again, three short bursts.

The door swung inward, Gerry Clay's face appearing in the crack, his dark skin wrinkling as he blinked them in. Recognized them a second later, the wrinkles becoming smile lines.

"Oh, hello Jet. Nice to see you so *early.*"

"Hi Gerry." She arranged a smile to match his. "Got your card. Really *thoughtful,* thanks."

Gerry's smile faltered, eyes trailing to the bandage at the side of her head.

"Do they know who—"

"—Not yet," Jet cut him off. "We're working on it. Actually, that's why we're here. I remember your son was taking photos at the Halloween Fair. It would be really useful to see those. Is he in?"

Gerry stuttered, trying to take that all in. "Uh, y-yes, he's here. In the yard, actually, flying his drone. He—he does that a lot."

"Better than meth." Jet took another step forward, forcing Gerry's hand.

"Do you want to come in?" he asked, moving back, holding the door open.

Of course that's what she wanted. "Thanks," she said instead, passing him, stepping down the hall, Billy on her heels.

"Come through to the kitchen," Gerry's voice sailed past them, the front door clicking shut.

A rectangular mirror was mounted on the far wall of the hallway. Jet watched as their reflections approached, real people meeting mirror people: Jet too small that only the top half of her face showed, Billy too tall that his head was cut off at the top, only one swinging arm of Gerry visible behind.

Jet paused for one second, caught her eye. The right eye. She'd noticed it in the bathroom mirror when she woke up, and it hadn't gone away. The pupil on this side was dilated, huge, a black hole, not much space for the orbit of hazel around.

"You OK?" Billy asked, catching up. If he'd noticed it too, he hadn't said anything yet.

"Fine." Jet dropped her own gaze and turned, following the hall into the bright kitchen at the back, sage-green cabinets and white marble counters. There was a faint high-pitched whine coming from somewhere.

Gerry circled past them, headed for the glass doors into the backyard.

"I need to get to work, but Owen will help you out with those photos." He rapped his knuckles on the glass.

A teenager was standing in the backyard, lost inside a baggy hoodie, some kind of remote clutched in his hands. He glanced up as Gerry knocked again, beckoning him in with a curt spin of his hand.

The sharp whining grew louder, angry and waspish, as the drone lowered into view, landing in the grass by Owen's feet. He picked it up and hurried toward the door.

"I'm off to work," Gerry announced as Owen shut the door behind him, placing the drone down carefully on the kitchen table. "This is Dianne Mason's daughter. You help her out, OK?"

He didn't give his son a chance to respond. "I'll give my best to your mom, Jet," he said with a wave, heading back to the hallway and the front door. It thudded shut behind him.

Owen stood there, shrinking inside his hoodie, blinking at them.

"I'm Jet," she said. "This is Billy. You're Owen."

He swallowed, studying his own feet. Painfully awkward—the kind you maybe didn't grow out of.

Jet didn't have time for awkward.

"We're here to see the photos you took at the Halloween Fair."

Owen shuffled, one foot nuzzling the other. "They're not fully edited yet."

"That's really OK. We're under a bit of time pressure."

Owen glanced up from his feet, an unasked question on his face.

Jet exhaled. "On Halloween, someone hit me over the head, and now I'm going to die in five days, so it would be really great to look at those photos so we can figure out who killed me. Or we can all stare at our feet some more."

"Oh, that's you," Owen said, a little more life in his voice.

"Yeah, that's me."

Owen's eyes shifted behind Jet, to Billy, trailing up all six feet, two inches of him, across those wide shoulders. He shrank inside his hoodie even more, like he had any reason to.

"I'm just Billy," Billy said.

He forgot the *poor* and *sweet*.

"OK, THESE ARE all the files. Six hundred and twenty-eight in total."

They were in the teenager's bedroom, Owen sitting at his desk in his spinning chair, two large curved monitors glaring over him, Jet and Billy hovering behind.

"Did you get any drone footage that night too?" Billy asked.

Owen shook his head. "Just photos. Didn't take her out that night."

Her. Urgh.

"OK great, we'll have a look through these, thank you so much." Jet gestured toward the door.

Owen didn't budge, hand still cupped around the wireless mouse.

"OK, Owen, that's great," Jet said, harder. "We'll have a look at these now. You can go back to playing with your girlfriend in the backyard."

"I don't have a— Oh."

"Yeah," Jet said. "Up you get."

Owen got reluctantly to his feet.

"OK," he sniffed. "Well, don't delete anything."

"Won't, I promise." Jet took his chair, eyeballed him until he left his bedroom, disappearing down the stairs.

"He's definitely got some kind of weird porn downloaded on this computer," Jet said, turning to the monitor, fingers finding the mouse.

"Stop traumatizing teenage boys." Billy leaned his elbows on the desk beside her.

"I do not traumatize teenage boys."

"You did."

She double-clicked on the first file, and the photo opened full screen. A jack-o'-lantern, glowing eyes and an eerie too-human smile. Jet pressed the arrow, through many more artsy overexposed shots of the pumpkin, until they reached the fair, the sun setting, early darkness, before Jet had even got there.

Kids at the face-painting stall, missing teeth and gummy smiles for the camera. A vampire carrying two pies in foil dishes. Gerry Clay in his full cat costume, holding up two furry peace signs for the camera.

A lot of knockoff superheroes at the costume contest, a shitty plastic gold medal for the winner: Spider-ish-Man.

Jet paused. A photo of Mom and Dad at their stall, grinning behind a huge pile of bagged-up candy corn. Mom's smile was tight, and Dad's was pained, his skin a little yellow in the flash, too shiny across the forehead.

"Your dad doing OK?" Billy asked, noticing it too.

Jet dipped her head. "His kidneys are starting to fail. It was always going to happen, once he reached sixty. Might have to think about dialysis or a transplant soon." She pressed her lips together and clicked on. "Shame my kidneys are no good either."

"There, stop!" Billy leaned forward, his hand over hers on the mouse. "That's JJ."

Yes, it was. Hardly recognizable in his striped shirt and denim overalls, thick black scars painted across his face. A brassy red wig on his head, the hairs static-straight, about five inches long. He was standing with his arm slung around his little brother, Henry, matching smiles they'd both inherited from their Malaysian dad, but not much else because he'd skipped out when they were kids. Henry was wearing a pirate hat, emblazoned with a skull and crossbones, a gold plastic hook for a hand. JJ was resting his head on his brother's shoulder: younger but taller.

"Does that match the hair from the scene?" Billy asked.

"Think so. Same color, the right length."

Jet dragged the photo across onto the second monitor, left it there waiting, the Lim brothers staring at them as they kept going.

"Jesus Christ," Jet hissed as she clicked onto a zoomed-in picture of herself, a photo she didn't know had been taken, *clearly:* her eyes glowing red from the flash, nose crisscrossed into a maze as she bit into a candy apple, caramel smears on her cheeks. "I'm deleting that one," she said, clicking on the icon, the photo shrinking down, dropping into the trash, where it belonged.

"Jet," Billy scolded her.

"I'm dying," she reminded him, a catch-all defense.

She skipped through more photos. A group shot: three witches, a skeleton, a werewolf, and Ghostface. The same kids from the doorbell cam, who stole all the Masons' candy. That one witch was flipping off the camera, and Jet liked her even more now.

More photos.

"That kid's wearing a red wig." Billy pointed at the screen, a girl grinning with a creepy-doll smile, standing between two men, one of them dressed as a cop, because it was Lou Jankowski, Chief of Police. "Does actually look like the same wig." Billy looked back and forth, from JJ to the kid.

"Yeah, it does," Jet said, sucking her teeth. "But an eleven-year-old girl is probably the one person who isn't taller than me. Rules her out. Off the suspect list."

"Agreed." Billy smiled.

Jet clicked on.

"Aw," Billy said as a photo of Luke and Sophia popped up, Luke holding baby Cameron in his pumpkin costume.

A puff of air out of Jet's nose, before she could hold it in.

Billy knew what that meant.

"You and Sophia used to be best friends," he said, tentatively.

"*You and I* used to be best friends too, Billy."

"*We* were kids. You and Sophia were really close. What happened?"

Jet snorted. "Not me. She's the one who never replied to my texts when I went to college. Dropped me and made a beeline for my brother instead. Luke's too stupid."

Billy nudged her. "You were maid of honor at their wedding."

"Yeah. Maybe Sophia thought that might make up for her abandoning me. It didn't. Ugly dress too. Bet she did it on purpose."

"Well. Cameron's cute."

Jet shrugged. "Kinda boring."

"Jet, you can't call babies boring."

"Babies are boring, and people who've just had babies are even more boring."

"Jet!" But he was laughing too.

"Wait," Jet hissed, eyes drawing her back to the screen, pulling at something in her head. Not Sophia, something about her brother.

Luke was holding the baby up for the camera, hands gripped around the rotund pumpkin costume—both hands, knuckles out, ridges in the thin skin. Jet reached for the screen, swiped her finger across Luke's clean hands.

"What?" Billy asked.

"Luke lied to me," Jet said, her finger coming away, Luke's knuckles still unmarked, not a trick of the light. "The fucker."

"What?"

"His hands. They're all cut up, grazes on his knuckles. They were like that when I woke up." Jet stared into her brother's eyes, her own reflected back in the dark screen. "I asked him about it, and he said it happened at a work site, Friday morning. That he tripped. But this is Friday evening and . . ."

"There's nothing wrong with his hands." Billy finished the thought for her.

"Something must have happened, after this," Jet said. "Why would he lie to me about it?"

"Maybe he meant Saturday morning," Billy offered.

"He was already with me at the hospital by then," Jet countered.

"You're not thinking that Luke could have anything to do with . . ." Billy trailed off, unable to finish.

"He and Sophia were together at the time of the attack." So they said. But if Luke had already lied once . . . Jet couldn't finish the thought either. "Well, he's not wearing a red wig, so . . ."

Jet moved on, spooling through more photos, searching for any flash of red hair, the reason they'd come. They hadn't come for Luke.

"Wait, stop!" Billy said.

Jet clicked one back.

A photo of Gerry Clay, with his human head now, grinning, bookended by two cops, his cat arms looped around Chief Lou and Jack Finney. All smiles for the camera.

In the background, in the far left, Jet could see herself, face frozen mid-frown as she looked up at Billy. But in the right side of the frame, behind Billy's dad, was Andrew Smith, heading toward them, beer bottle paused on the way to his mouth. Blurred in the background, in motion, but still clear enough. A smear of red painted across his nose, black lines down his eyes, and on his head was a red wig. Billy was right: straight hairs, static almost, fluffy, the same length as JJ's.

"That's it, isn't it?" Billy watched as Jet dragged that photo to the second monitor too, lining the photos up side by side, zooming in. "They're wearing the exact same wig, aren't they?"

Same burnt-red color, same texture, same length. And both looked like a match for that singular hair dropped at the scene, by Jet's killer.

Jet nodded. "Probably bought it from the same place."

"Amazon," they said, accidental unison.

"So." Billy drew back to his full height. "JJ and Andrew Smith."

"JJ or Andrew Smith," Jet corrected.

"You really think Andrew is a suspect?"

"He was drunk that night. He was mad." Jet stared at the screen, at the stumbling clown. "You heard what he said at the fair. That he hates all the Masons, death to all Masons—"

"—Not quite what he said," Billy cut her off. "So what do we do?"

Jet stood up, stumbling, one leg still asleep. Billy held her arm, steadied her.

"Well, JJ isn't here for us to talk to," she said. "But Andrew is."

Billy nodded, lips disappearing in a grim line. "I think I know where to find him."

"Come on."

Jet walked out of Owen's bedroom and straight into Owen, who was hovering by the open door. He darted away with a yelp, pressing up against the wall, making himself as small as possible.

"Hey." Jet's eyes burned into him. "You better not have been eavesdropping."

"I wasn't, I swear!"

"Tell anyone, and I'll let your dad know about your freaky little porn collection."

Owen whimpered.

OUTSIDE, JET MARCHED across the street to where they'd parked her truck, powder-blue paint gleaming in the morning sun, not out of place on Pleasant Street. But something was out of place: a plastic sleeve, stuck to her windshield.

"You've got to be fucking kidding me," Jet said, ripping it off, holding it up so Billy could see. "A ticket? We were only here for like forty-five minutes. These new parking meters, I swear . . ."

But she didn't have to swear, and she didn't have to do anything. She'd be dead in five days, so this little ticket right here in her hands, it meant nothing. Not a thing. Jet pulled the paper out from the sleeve, ripped it in half—Billy's mouth dropped—ripped it in half again—Billy's mouth dropped farther, almost twitching into a smile.

Jet let go, the shredded pieces fluttering to the ground like fallen moths, sticking in the mud.

"I'm not fucking paying that."

TWELVE

"Told you he'd be in here."

Billy held the door for her, up the steps into Dr. Mandrake's Dive Bar. Jet always thought of it as Billy's Bar instead, where he worked, his apartment right upstairs. Not that she ever came here.

Mahogany panels and striped navy walls, glass shelves full of bottles behind the wooden bar, an assortment of different lamps around the room, the stranger the better, lighting the darker corners. In the darkest one sat Andrew Smith, at a table, beer bottle in his cupped hands.

"It's only noon," Jet said, eyes circling the hunched-over man. No more red wig, just a stubby graying ponytail at the back of his head.

"He's always down here when we open."

Jet looked up at Billy. "And who thought it was a good idea for an alcoholic to live above a bar?"

"*He* did," Billy answered. "It's OK, that's probably his first."

"We should speak to him before he orders his second."

Billy crossed to the bar to say hello to his boss, and Jet went the other way, past a pair of upside-down legs, black and white striped, bursting from the floor. A lightbulb balanced between its ruby slippers, cord running to the closest socket. Definitely not in Kansas anymore.

There was only one chair at Andrew's table, and he was sitting in it. Jet picked up another, dragged it over, a squeal that made Andrew wince, cover his ears.

"You mind?" he said, gruffly.

"Yeah, I do." Jet dropped into the chair, steepling her hands, elbows on the sticky table.

"I'm trying to drink here." He finally looked up, eyes not too faraway, not enough that he wouldn't recognize her.

"I can see that."

Billy had come over too now, placing a chair next to Jet's, facing the wrong way, straddling it.

Andrew sniffed in his direction, gaze returning to Jet.

"What happened to your head?" He pointed at the bandages with his beer bottle.

Jet glanced at Billy, and he glanced back.

"You haven't heard?" Jet studied Andrew's eyes, his puffy red hands. "I was attacked, on Halloween."

Andrew grunted, shook his head. "No, I never touched you. I just yelled."

"Not at the fair," Jet said. "After. In my house. I didn't see who it was."

Andrew shrugged. "I don't know nothing about that."

Jet wasn't convinced; of course the killer would say that, pretend to know nothing about it. Didn't alcoholics have to get good at pretending? Until they stopped caring, that was, like this man in front of her.

Andrew picked up his beer, took a swig. Jet clocked which hand he'd used.

"You're right-handed," she said.

"So's everyone." A fair point.

"Sergeant Finney escorted you home from the fair, walked you back to your apartment upstairs." Jet glanced up through the ceiling. "What time did he leave, after getting you home?"

Andrew sniffed. "I don't think Jack Finney woulda done that to you. He's a cop."

Jet leaned forward, said in an almost-whisper: "I'm not asking about Jack Finney."

"Me?" Andrew laughed, an uneasy wheezing sound. He looked at Billy. "She thinks it was me? I was passed out all night."

"So you won't mind answering what time my dad left you in your apartment?" Billy's way was softer, but it seemed to work.

"You should ask him. I was drunk, don't remember." Andrew put his beer down with a thunk. "But I do remember texting a friend, right *after* he left. Hold on." He reached behind him into his pocket, came back with a phone.

His face lit up with a silver under-glow, strange upward shadows playing on his forehead as he tapped at the screen.

"Yeah. I sent that text at 10:29. Mr. Finney must have left just before that."

Seventeen minutes until the first strike hit Jet's head. It only took ten minutes to walk to the Masons' house from here, less if you ran—plenty of time for Andrew to make it through their back door. Jet memorized the time, would write it in her notebook later, fingers twitching in her lap.

"And then you were alone?" Jet pressed.

"Yes, sweetheart." That eerie whistling laugh again. "Cop escorting me home is a pretty solid alibi, I'd say."

"It's not an alibi," Jet corrected him, "if you were alone and have no witnesses to co-cor-co—back you up, by the way."

"Why? What time were you attacked?"

"I'm asking the questions here," she said. She didn't want to tell him that they knew the exact time. It seemed smarter to keep that back. Also smart to hold on to the fact that Jet was dead, if he didn't know that already, if he thought they were just talking about an assault. The word *murder* might make him panic, make him stop talking and start planning. Better to let him think he failed—if it *was* Andrew.

"Don't know why you care so much," he said, returning to his beer. "Number of times I've woken up with a bloody head and a black eye, and don't know who did it."

"Because someone tried to kill me."

"But they didn't."

Jet caught Billy's eye, gave him a tiny shake of her head. She looked around the room, searching her mind for another way in, eyes idling across the bar, skipping over beer tap logos and a pinned-up flyer with a picture of a guitar and a microphone. *Live music tonight,* it said.

"Why do you hate my family so much?" Jet turned back to Andrew, treading carefully around any accusation. "At the fair, you said we destroy everything. What did you mean?"

Andrew snorted, the sound echoing in his beer bottle, almost empty. He didn't follow it up, didn't speak.

"I thought our families used to be close," Jet continued. "You and my parents have known each other forever. My sister—Emily—and Nina . . ."

Andrew winced at the sound of his daughter's name.

"They were best friends. I was only young, but I remember Nina at our house all the time, in the pool, sleeping over. Your wife too, when she came to pick her up, used to get stuck chatting with my mom. Emily and Nina were inseparable, weren't they?"

"And where are they both now?" Andrew spat, a flash of something darker in his eyes. "Don't speak about my daughter to me."

"I'm sorry," Jet said. "I know it must have been really hard, when she—"

"—Shot herself in the head?" He laughed, empty and vicious, ripping a strip from the bottle's label. "Yeah, it was *really hard.* Even harder knowing whose fault it was."

Jet blinked. She knew she was close to something, didn't want to push too hard, push him over the edge. "Who—" she began.

"—Dianne." Not a name, but a rumble in the back of his throat.

"My mom?"

Andrew rubbed his hands through his hair, down his face. His movements erratic, unpredictable. The hairs rose up the back of Jet's neck, her heart picking up, warning her.

"Even after everything we've been through, sh-she . . ."

"What are you talking about?" Jet pressed.

"She's the reason Nina killed herself. The last straw. Got her fired from her job at the hotel. Nina loved that job. She was doing so well."

Too many questions; Jet didn't know which one to go for.

"How do you know—"

"—Because Nina told me. She said that Dianne had it out for her, that she just got fired and knew who was behind it. Your mom pulled some strings, and she's got many strings, doesn't she? With her seat on the trustee board, running this town. She did that, Nina knew, and then two days later Nina . . ."

Jet gripped the chair beneath her, her hand grazing Billy's on the way. He grazed hers back, like she'd done it on purpose, like their hands had a secret conversation of their own.

"Why would my mom get Nina fired?"

Andrew coughed, a wet, gravelly sound. "I don't know, ask her. Nina never got the chance to tell me." His face cracked then, struggling against it, trying not to break, not to cry. He fought hard and only one tear managed to get through. "It wasn't just the job. She'd had a hard life, Nina. Losing her best friend so suddenly like that, only sixteen. Then her mom getting sick and passing away, when Nina needed her most. She didn't want me to sell the house, said she'd always imagined living there, raising kids of her own, that it had too many memories. But I did, and I shouldn't have. I shouldn't have sold it. It broke her heart. But they were offering too much money."

"Who?" Jet asked.

"*You!*" Andrew's voice whistled. "Your family. Luke. Came to me with an offer. They already had the property next door, wanted mine too. It was way over what the asking price would have been. What was I going to say? *No, Luke, you keep all that money.* He knew exactly how to convince me to do it, made it seem like a favor almost, a kindness. Of course I sold it." He hiccupped. "Though where all that money has gone, I couldn't tell you."

He glanced over at the bar, at the bottles behind, like he knew exactly where all that money had gone. Down the drain, down his throat.

"Said they were going to renovate and resell it. I used to walk by, see what they were doing to it, especially after Nina . . ." He sniffed. "There was some holdup in the construction, think they changed their mind. They've knocked it down now. My old house, and the one next door. Think they're going to combine the lots, build one giant McMansion for some rich asshole. Nina would have been devastated, to know the house she grew up in is completely gone. It's gone, all gone. I checked last week. Digging foundations where our home used to be."

Jet nodded, because she had her answer now: *Why do you hate my family so much?* But none of that had been her. It was Luke, it was Mom. Or maybe that was why he chose Jet—taking Dianne's daughter, like he thought she'd taken his?

"I'm sorry my brother knocked down your house, but—"

Andrew laughed over her, ripping his beer label clear off. "*He's* not. I'm sure he'll make a nice big profit off it. Show his daddy who the big man is now." He laughed again, harder, almost frantic, like it hurt his ribs to do it. "You know what's funny, though?"

Jet didn't.

Andrew rubbed his nose. "Luke thinks it's gonna be him next, doesn't he? That he's going to be *the* Mason, your dad retiring, leaving the company to him. Well, I know something you don't. Man, I'd love to be the one to tell him."

"Tell him what?" Jet said, losing track. "What do you know?"

"Your daddy's not leaving the company to little Luke." His breath whistled through his teeth. "He's going to sell it. To Nell Jankowski."

Jet narrowed her eyes and Andrew licked his lips. Must have enjoyed the confusion on her face, ate it up, a substitute for her brother. This couldn't be true, could it? Andrew was making shit up; he was a drunk, maybe even a murderer.

"How do you know this?" Billy asked, stepping in.

"She told me herself. Nell."

"The chief's wife?" Billy asked.

Andrew nodded. "She's got a construction business too, out of town. Makes sense she'd want to expand here, in Woodstock, now they live here, now he's running the police. She's going to buy Mason Construction— they've already started talking, she and your daddy."

Jet blinked, coming through the shock, recovering just enough to ask: "Why wouldn't my dad leave the company to Luke?"

Andrew inhaled the air from his beer bottle, long empty. "Nell said Scott doesn't think it would be fair, to give the company to one of you, when he has two kids. Well, two kids still alive."

And now Jet did almost believe him, because that sounded exactly like something Dad would say. He was all about *fair.* But this wasn't fair: Jet would never want the company—she'd wanted to do her own thing, something big to prove that she could, and Luke was dying to take over. Dad knew that—*everyone* knew that, even this drunk fuck sitting across from her.

"I don't believe you," she said, a lie of her own.

"You're not the first to say that." Andrew grinned.

"What do you mean?" Billy piped up. "Who else have you told about this?"

Andrew shrugged. "I'm not good with secrets. Never tell a drunk your business plans. I like Nell, she's nice." He rolled the empty bottle away from him. "I need another drink."

Jet stood up, righting the bottle, slamming it down with a thud. She'd had enough of his face, of his wheezing laugh, of collecting reasons why this man might have killed her.

"Come on, Billy," she said, walking away, past those stripey legs that came from another world.

Billy came, caught her by a lamp with the body of an ostrich, shade covering its head.

"What are you thinking?" He lowered his voice, eyes on Andrew at the bar.

"I'm thinking he has no alibi for the time of my murder, and he has motive. A few to choose from, actually." Jet sniffed. "Blames my family for losing his house, for his daughter's death. Maybe he thought it was Mom's head he was bashing in, I don't know, got me by accident."

Jet glanced back at Andrew. He'd ordered a harder drink this time, whiskey, nursing it on the way back to his table.

"He's going to be drinking down here for a while," Jet said. "We could just go upstairs, break down his door, search for my iPhone in his apartment, prove it that way."

That should have got more of a reaction from Billy, more alarm, but he must have been distracted, eyes spooling through some unknown thought.

"What?" Jet demanded the thought from him.

"Just thinking. If he brought the phone home with him, why did it last ping on River Street? That's nowhere near here, and definitely not on the way from your house. What's the connection?"

Now Jet was distracted by Billy's thought too. It was a good point.

"Fine," she said, marching back over to Andrew's table, not taking a seat this time.

"You're back," he laughed, choking on the amber liquid.

"One more thing," Jet said, sharpening her voice, aiming for the back of his head. "River Street. You know anyone who lives there?"

"River Street?" he repeated, spinning in his chair to glance up at her. "Yeah, I know people. Used to be my neighbors."

"What?" Jet said, too breathy, forced out by her quickening heart.

"I used to live over there. My old house, it was on North Street. Just off River Street, the only way to get to the house."

Jet's head snapped to the side, finding Billy's eyes. Now the alarm was there, where it belonged, a coating over that watery blue. Probably a matching look in hers.

"You're saying there's a Mason Construction site on North Street?" Jet asked the back of Andrew's head, still intact. "Your old house?"

"It's *your* family's company." Andrew took a large gulp. "Down the end. They're only just starting the new building now." Another. "Why you asking me about River Street?"

Because it had been the wrong question, and the wrong street.

North Street.

That blue dot hanging in the road right on the corner, where River met North, and Jet had been chasing down the wrong one.

She hooked her arm through Billy's, dragged him away.

"We were looking at the wrong street," she hissed, heading for the exit. "Maybe Andr—th-the killer turned the phone off, then headed down North toward the construction site. Didn't continue along River like we thought."

"You think it *is* Andrew, then?"

"Well, he's connected to that location." Jet glanced back at the man, sitting in shadows, seeing off his glass of whiskey. "Probably doesn't know we have the phone data, that we can see it was turned off there, the idiot."

"And if it's not Andrew?"

Jet gave Billy his arm back. "If it's not Andrew, if someone else killed me, then maybe it's not about the killer's connection to that site. Maybe it's about *mine*."

Billy stopped by the door, a glint in his eye as he paused to ask: "To North Street?"

"To fucking North Street," she answered.

THIRTEEN

H ere it was. Fucking North Street.

The road stopped abruptly in front of them, choked up with vans, some white, some branded with the *Mason Construction* logo. A low growl of heavy machinery, shaking the ground and Jet's truck with it, as a yellow digger rolled up the hill toward all that mud. A rickety wire gate pushed off to the side, two signs attached to it: *CAUTION: Construction Area* and *DANGER: Hard Hat Area.*

They couldn't get any closer than this, parking behind a tree less than fifty feet away from her phone's last known location. Jet cut the engine and the truck sighed as she stepped out, Billy on the other side. The sound of their slamming doors was lost in the uproar of clanging metal.

Jet picked their way through the vans and sleeping machinery, heading toward the site, through the open gate.

"There used to be two houses up here?" Jet asked Billy, eyes ahead.

"Apparently."

Now it was just a field of mud and men in silly yellow hats.

They moved past a cement mixer, spinning and churning, being fed by the spadeful, one man doing all the work, another just watching.

"This must be Luke's big project," Billy said, scanning the chaos, avoiding a track of the sloppiest mud. "Sophia was telling me about it at the fair. His first project that's all him, not your dad. That's why he's so stressed about it, needs it to go well."

Jet shrugged. "Luke's always stressed." The same thing she'd said to Sophia at the fair, shrugging her off too.

"Well, this one's important, Sophia said. Apparently, construction was already delayed a while back, a floor collapsed or something, so Luke had to change his plans. Decided to demolish, start again. I guess combining it with the lot next door. I get the impression that this is his baby."

Jet wrinkled her nose; it didn't look like much. An outline of wooden trenches carved out of the mud, buttressed by planks. The new foundations. Fucking hell, Luke, this was going to be a stupidly big house, look at the size of that. Most of it was just an empty track right now, only one small section at the front filled with concrete. Looked like they were getting ready to fill the rest.

"Maybe that's why he was being extra assholey at the fair," Jet said.

"Yeah, Sophia said he was nervous because they were starting on the foundations—no going back now."

"And yet, according to Andrew Smith, Dad isn't even going to let Luke have the company."

Billy chewed his lip. "Well, I don't think Luke knows that."

No, he definitely didn't. And it probably wasn't even true.

"Hey!" a voice cut through all the noise. Uh oh, they'd been spotted.

A man was hurrying toward them, in a neon jacket that clashed with his hard hat, waving his arms. It wasn't a hello, but Jet made it one, waving back with a grin.

"What are you doing here?" the man yelled, catching up to them. "You can't be here. This is a construction area."

"Yeah, I saw the signs," Jet told him.

The man pushed up his hard hat, falling into his meaty eyes.

"I'm going to have to ask you to leave. This is private property, and it isn't safe."

He pointed them back toward the road, a hand on Jet's back.

"I'm going to have to ask you to stop asking us to leave," Jet countered, pulling away. "Scott Mason is my dad."

The man hesitated. "And Luke, he's—"

"—My brother, yeah," Jet said.

The man nodded, retracted his arm. "He's not here right now."

"That's OK." Jet smiled. "It's you I came to see."

His mouth folded down, merging with his chin. "M-me?"

"What's your name, sir?"

He pointed to his own chest, a silent question. Jet nodded.

"It's Jimmy."

"Hi, yes, Jimmy," she said. "Just the man I was looking for. You're the foreman, right?"

"Right?"

"Great," she said, moving toward the outline of the new house, through the mud. Her poor Birkenstocks. "I'm just here to ask you a couple of questions about the site. It's a company policy thing."

"But I—"

"—That gate across the road." She pointed. "I assume that's shut and locked at night?"

"I—Of course."

"But it's not like there's a fence around it, so even if nobody can drive through, you could easily walk around, onto the site."

"Yes, well, Luke didn't think we needed a fence, as these are the only properties up here and it's not a through road. No one ever comes up here."

Jet pursed her lips. "But *if* they did, you guys got any cameras set up here? You know, for security?"

A blank look on Jimmy's face. "Why would we need cameras?"

"A great question. Billy, my associate, will write that down."

Billy's face stirred, taken aback.

"He's new," Jet said to Jimmy, in a loud whisper behind her hand.

"If you're on site, you really should be wearing hard hats. It's the rule."

Jimmy doubled back to an open van, grabbing two yellow hard hats from the pile.

"Your associate?" Billy whispered out the side of his mouth, watching Jimmy return.

"Don't talk back to your boss."

"Here." Jimmy passed one to Billy, one to Jet. "Accidents happen all the time on site. We had a floor collapse here a while ago, brought some of the roof down with it, some guy still working inside. I wasn't here then, wouldn't have happened if I was here. But my point is, anything can happen. Gotta protect those heads." He knocked against his own hard hat.

Billy blew out his cheeks, something he did when he was uncomfortable, hadn't grown out of it yet. He rammed the hard hat onto his head, avoided Jet's eyes.

Jet dropped hers in the mud. "I'm not putting this on, Jimmy, because, quite honestly, it doesn't match my outfit. And I don't see any roofs that might collapse anytime soon—doesn't even have foundations yet."

And there was no way she was forcing that hat over her bandages, to press against the pain, magnify it. There was only so much the codeine could do.

"Speaking of the foundations," Jet continued, breezing past the horrified look on Jimmy's face, "when did you start pouring the concrete? It's already set here, on this front part."

The point closest to the road and what Jet imagined would be the future driveway, about fifteen feet across, blockaded at the corners by more wood.

"Yeah, that's the garage we started on," Jimmy answered, but that's not what she had asked.

"When did the concrete go in, Jimmy?"

Because what if it was—

"—Saturday morning, I think," Jimmy said, speaking over her thoughts. "Finished the trenches Friday afternoon. We started on this"—he pointed to the channel of hardened concrete—"Saturday morning. Would have finished too, but the boss wanted to be here, and he had to take a couple of days, for personal reasons."

"Hi," Jet said, "I'm Personal Reasons."

Jimmy narrowed his eyes, clearly had no idea what she was talking about and didn't want to know. "We're only just back today, really," he said, for something to say. "I can make up the time, don't worry."

"What time did you start work on Saturday—start pouring the concrete?"

Jimmy shrugged. "Probably about eight a.m."

"Great," Jet said, grin widening with the word, trying to cover for her eyes, for her quickening heart. This was something, she knew it. "And it's just mud underneath, right? You'd already dug the trenches, so you wouldn't have known if there was anything in the mud?"

Jimmy stared at her, confused. "Did you lose something?"

"Only my mind. Could you give me and my associate two minutes, please, Jimmy? Yeah, you go just over there, that's great."

"Jet?" Billy looked down at her.

"You thinking what I'm thinking?" she hissed.

"Probably not."

"That concrete was poured, what, like nine hours after my murder? And we know the killer was here with my phone. Like, right there." She pointed beyond her truck, to the street. "If you knew that was going to happen, that the foundations were going in the next morning, wouldn't this be the perfect place to hide it?"

"Hide the phone?" Billy eyed the concrete.

"And the other thing missing from the scene," Jet said. "The murder weapon. If they're under concrete, in the foundations of a house, who would ever find them?"

"Ah, shit." Billy fiddled with his hair, tucked it under his hard hat. "Should we call the cops?"

"And let them have all the fun?"

Jet winked and Billy swallowed, her eyes tracking the movement, the lump in his throat, up and down.

"Why are you smiling like that? You can't be serious?" he hissed.

"Dead serious," she said, and not just to make him nervous, though that was fun too. "The police would have to wait, apply for warrants or something. Could take days. Longer." She patted Billy on the shoulder. "I don't have time for paperwork, bud. Sorry."

Billy's head dropped back, blinking at the sky. "You're not sorry, though, are you?"

"Hey Jimmy!" Jet called, mud squelching, soaking into her socks as she ran over to the man. "How deep does that concrete go?"

Jimmy looked even more confused now. "About three feet deep. Why?"

"Three feet," Jet muttered to herself, studying the new foundations. "That's doable. OK, guys!" she called, cupping her hands to send her voice farther. "Break time! Everyone take five. Or . . . a few fives. Hey, shut that digger off!"

"You can't tell them to do that," Jimmy said, his confusion thawing, melting into something like anger.

"I just did. You're working too hard, Jimmy. Go grab a coffee, or go take a piss, I don't care. Hey you!"

Jet stopped a young-looking guy who was walking toward one of the vans, a sledgehammer in his hands.

He widened his eyes, deer in her headlights.

"Hey," Jet said. "You mind if I borrow that?"

He didn't say anything. Passed it over and skittered away, into the safety of his van.

The sledgehammer was heavy.

Jet held it with two hands, the handle sleek and orange, rubber grips at the end. The dense metal end was well used, marked with scratches and dents.

"I guess I'm really doing this," Jet said to Billy and to herself, carrying the sledgehammer over toward the new foundations. She climbed down and over the trench, standing in the footprint of the garage-to-be.

"What are you doing over there? Get out!"

"Sorry, Jimmy," she called back, raising the sledgehammer. "I don't think you and me are going to be friends."

She brought the hammer down, double-handed, into the center of the concrete channel. It cracked, the pressure locking her wrists, riding up her arms, the thud ringing in her ears.

A large chunk came loose, a crater where it used to be.

"What are you doing?!" Jimmy screamed, voice finding a new octave. "Stop that!"

He barreled toward Jet, sliding in the mud, hands out to reach across the trench and grab her.

"No!" Billy got there first, stood in front of Jet, blocking Jimmy's way. A barricade made of arms, flexing his shoulders. "You leave her alone," Billy said, straightening up to his full height, leaning over a red-faced Jimmy. "Please."

"But she's—"

"—I know she is," Billy said, calmly. "But neither you or me are going to stop her. Believe me, she can't be stopped."

Jet swung again, another thwack, another slice of concrete, the size of her hand.

"Please." Billy doubled down, too damn nice sometimes, should have just told Jimmy to go fuck himself. Give Jet a second to catch her breath and she'd do it herself.

Jimmy growled and Jet glanced up, ready to swing at him if he dared to hit Billy. But he wasn't, he didn't. He spun on his boots, walking away, pulling a phone out of his back pocket.

"He's gone," Billy said, the last word lost as Jet swung again, widening the hole, fault lines cracking, spidering along the once-smooth surface.

"I love it when you fight over me, honey," Jet told him, already breathless. "You got some balls now, huh, Billy Finney?"

"And you've got a death wish."

"Billy, I'm not even going to comment on that one."

Jet swung again. She guessed she was really doing this. She had to—she was dead in five days and she had a murder to solve. And . . . well, she'd kind of always wanted to just smash shit up.

And shit was smashing. The middle of that hole might have already been two feet down.

Billy was watching her, his teeth out, pressing little moons into his bottom lip.

Jet shifted, aiming closer, trying to break the crater into a cross section. She'd need to check the entire trench; it could have been anywhere along it.

"I get it, Billy," she said, feeling his eyes. "You're stuck because you want to help, because helping is what you do. But you can't help me now." Jet wiped her sleeve across her face, beads of sweat prickling her nose. "You still have to think about consequences. But I don't. It's OK. You cover me. Save me from more angry builders."

She swung again.

Again.

Stopped to remove her jacket—too hot already—and swung again.

Billy wasn't there when she glanced up; he was gone.

Jet sniffed, letting go of the sledgehammer, dropping to her knees to clear some of the debris, chucking it behind her, out of the way.

She stood up and started again, digging toward the outer boundary now.

Swung.

Thud.

Looked up.

Billy was back.

Crossing the trench, a blue sledgehammer gripped in his hands.

He came to stand beside her, didn't look at her, looked down instead.

"Only you," he said.

He raised the sledgehammer above his head and brought it down, the sound so loud it shook the world beneath Jet's feet, a huge pit where he'd struck the concrete.

"Always getting me in trouble," he muttered, swinging again.

"I am not!"

She waited for Billy to go again, then took a turn.

"What about the time you made us put red food dye in your parents' pool because you wanted to make a shark movie?"

Jet removed a huge slab of concrete, dragging it out of Billy's way.

"Let's not talk about the pool," she grunted. "Actually, let's not talk at all. This is fucking hard work."

Jet swung, made a dent, then Billy swung, his dent twice the size of hers.

"Hey," she said, "your sledgehammer's better than mine. Switch."

It wasn't the sledgehammer.

Billy took a turn, and then Jet, one strike then two, while the other reared up, ready. Like a broken clock, the ticking uneven, too slow then too fast, counting down to something, seconds and minutes Jet would never get back.

"Stand back, Jet. Let me do a few."

Billy smashed, once, twice, and again, concrete breaking up, springing free. "We're at the bottom here," Billy panted, dropping the hammer to move the rubble.

They'd done it: cleared a jagged passage in the middle, about three feet wide and three feet down to the soil underneath.

"Let's check it," Jet said, dropping her hammer, standing directly over the channel, one foot on the concrete either side. "Billy, grab that spade over there."

He handed it to her and Jet raked the spade through the exposed mud, driving the tip in and loosening the soil. "Nothing here. Let's keep going."

"Let's open it out this way." Billy pointed with one hand, wiped the sweat from his forehead with the other, adding a smear of mud. "Closer to the road, to where the killer would have approached from."

"OK," Jet said, following his lead.

The builders were all watching them now, sitting and standing around in an amphitheater of their making, paper cups in hands, following each rise and fall of the hammers with their stupid yellow plastic heads. Jimmy at the front, arms folded over his belly.

They found their rhythm again, the heat creeping up Jet's chest, sweat creeping down, trickling, following that dip between her ribs. The same in her lower back. No, lower than that. Lower. OK, yes, fine, her ass was sweating too.

They cleared another three feet of width, a little easier now that they could chip away at it from the side. Checked the mud underneath, moved on.

Billy paused to take off his hard hat, throwing it over his shoulder. Then his jacket five minutes later, then his shirt five minutes after that, down to just the white T-shirt underneath, a see-through ring of sweat around his neck, the muscles in his bare arms straining and twisting as he struck the concrete.

Jet watched him for a moment, taking a break, catching her breath, but she caught something else instead: movement. Someone jumping out of a car, short buzzed hair, heading straight toward them.

It was Luke, breaking into a run now. Any chance he hadn't seen her yet?

"Jet Fucking Mason, what the fuck are you doing?!" Luke screamed across the site.

Jet brought the hammer down, an island of concrete breaking free, falling to the bottom of the trench.

"Jet, what are you doing?" Luke yelled, voice pitching up, near-hysterical.

"Construction!" she yelled back. "Decided to go into the family business after all!"

"Why are you smashing up my foundations?!"

Jet stole a breath; the air didn't want to give itself up, her throat too tight.

"Because they weren't good enough—you need to start again!"

Billy looked at Jet. She nodded and he kept going.

Jet swung again.

"Jet, stop!" Luke roared, pushing past the rows of watching builders. "Why are you doing this?!"

"Because I have to, Luke! Fuck sake, it is hard to do this and talk! God, my head hurts. God, I'm thirsty. This is what dying must feel like."

Luke had almost reached them. "Give me that hammer!" he roared, approaching the trench, fury staining his face red. "Now!"

"Come any closer and Billy will hit you with a sledgehammer!"

"I'm not going to hit you with a sledgehammer, Luke," Billy clarified, the only one not yelling. "What she means is that we can't stop, and we're very sorry."

"Jet!"

"Luke!" she screamed back. "It is important! And stop making me talk or you're going to kill me off early!"

Luke's hands balled into fists, scabs pockmarked across his knuckles. The scabs he didn't get from tripping at a work site Friday morning, the ones he must have got sometime after the Halloween Fair, and then lied about.

"I'm calling Dad!" he shouted, unclenching one hand, pulling out his phone.

"Fine, call him!"

"And I'm calling the cops!"

"No, Luke, *don't* call them!"

"They're already on their way," a voice pitched in from across the site.

"You're such a fucking rat, Jimmy!"

Jet channeled it, taking it out on the concrete. One hit, two, three, a huge slab cracking and falling away, revealing the dark dirt underneath. She bent to pick it up, double-handed, wrenching her back to haul it out.

Luke was off the phone already, more yelling.

"Why did you let her pick up a sledgehammer, Jimmy? You let anyone just walk in off the street and pick up your tools? Who are these people now?"

Jet glanced up. *These people,* ones without yellow helmets, standing by the open gate, watching. Probably neighbors from River Street, being nosy, drawn here by all the fuss Luke was making.

"Stand back, Jet. Let me clear this part."

Billy moved into position, standing wide across the trench, slamming down, again and again, a trail of sweat escaping down his temple, blinked into his eye. He didn't stop to wipe it, not until his sledgehammer found soil instead.

He dropped down to remove the rubble, his hands dusty and scratched. "Here, cleared another section. Let's check it."

Jet had been leaning on her hammer, using it as a crutch. She dropped it now, swapped it for the spade. Raked it, blade down, over the new section of mud. Dug the tip in to overturn the surface, moving from back to fro—

The spade found something.

Flipped it out of the soil.

A corner of material, filthy and sodden.

"There's something here," Jet said, breathless, jumping down into the trench to get closer.

She used the tip of the spade to loosen the mud, brush it away. A corner became a flap, and Jet could see a pattern printed into the material now, underneath all that dirt. A pattern she recognized: little cartoon oranges, freckled, green leaves out the top like hair.

"Oh my god," she whispered.

"What?"

"This is one of our dish towels, from the kitchen," Jet said, the hair rising up the back of her neck, a thousand cold fingers tracing her spine. "Mom has a set of three. Didn't realize one was missing."

She brushed more dirt away with the spade, carefully, even more carefully, revealing the rest of the grimy, folded dish towel. Lumpy, because it was wrapped around something.

"Shit, I need gloves."

"Work gloves?" Billy suggested, pointing at the row of watching builders.

"No." Jet shook her head, eyes following his outstretched finger. "Plastic gloves, like the police use. It—"

Her eyes snagged on something else, in one of the builders' hands. Not gloves, but lunch: a clear plastic bag, resealable at the top, a triangular sandwich inside. One was already half eaten, balanced in his mouth.

"That will do," Jet muttered, scrambling out of the hole toward him. He froze when he saw her approaching. It was the same guy as before, eyes petrified and wide, or maybe that was how he always looked.

Luke grabbed her arm, got in her way.

"Jet, can you tell me what—"

"—Not now, Luke. I'm a little busy."

"This is *my* site. Mine." His fingers dug in. "I'm in charge here, and you're not allowed to just—"

"—Man, Luke, you are going to feel real stupid in about thirty seconds. We found it."

"Found *what*?"

Jet shrugged him off, an extra jab with her elbow.

"Hi, Creepy Eyes. Me again. Thanks for the sledgehammer. Can I just—"

Jet took the sandwich bag out of his hand. She upturned it, the other sandwich falling to the mud-churned ground, flapping open.

"PB and J, dude? You twelve?"

"It's my dessert sandwich," he said, weakly, recoiling back.

Jet walked away, sliding her hand inside the clear bag, avoiding a large smear of peanut butter. The plastic formed a glove around her fingers, awkward and misshapen and sticky on the inside.

Back into the trench, Billy taking her arm, helping her down.

Jet dropped to her knees beside the dish towel, not too close.

Her breath loud, but there was a new sound too, echoing through the late-afternoon sky, growing, a high-pitched wail, blaring up and down.

"That's the cops," Billy said, "coming down the street."

Jet reached over, fingers outstretched in their clear bag.

She pinched the corner of the dish towel, just the very corner, and flicked it open.

Clumps of mud and soil rained over her, scattering around her knees. Jet blinked.

There it was, lying against the white inside of the towel, almost clean. Her iPhone.

The screen shattered, glass split into delicate little fronds.

The frame buckled, under the weight of all that concrete.

And next to the phone, tucked up against it, was a hammer.

Black handle.

Metal head.

Flecks of brown on the blunt end that might have been dirt or—

"That's—" Billy began.

"—The murder weapon," Jet finished.

This little thing, right here. No more than sixteen inches long. Head like a metal bird, a few strands of blond hair caught in its mouth.

This was it. This was what killed her. The thing that had broken open her head, shattered her skull, left a sliver of bone where it shouldn't be.

This, right here.

The thing that took Jet's life before she'd even lived it, stole her future, all of her *laters* and all of her *tomorrows*, leaving her with just a handful. Leftovers. Scraps.

It wasn't even very big.

The siren was almost on top of them now, splitting the sky, the clouds roiling above to mend the cracks.

Billy was on his knees too, right here in the dirt with her. He placed his hand on her back.

"Jet," he said softly, from another world, the one that belonged to the living.

The touch of his fingers brought her back, warm and clammy against her shoulder.

"Your phone," she sniffed, dropping the sandwich bag to hold out her hand. Grime was caked under her fingernails, dirt and concrete dust staining her palm gray.

Billy didn't hesitate, placed his phone face up in her filthy hand.

Jet swiped for the camera and leaned forward, over the hammer.

She held her breath, the siren screaming in her head and her head screaming back.

Took a photo. Hand closer. Took another, and another, moving from its head to the claw, down its black spine, rubber ridges for better grip. Stopping over the logo at the bottom. A yellow circle with pointed ends, the brand name *Coleby* printed inside. Took a photo. Tapped the screen to make it focus, took another.

The siren cut off, leaving just a phantom in Jet's ears.

Three doors slammed.

"What the hell is going on here?!"

THEY WERE ALL behind the gate now, yellow hats replaced with dark police caps, officers securing the scene, waiting for the forensic teams to turn up. More black-and-yellow tape—*CRIME SCENE—DO NOT ENTER*—being spooled across the flimsy gate.

"You think you can get DNA from it?" Jet asked Detective Ecker, knowing she didn't have time for DNA. "Fingerprints?"

Ecker's eyes flashed, mouth set in a grim line.

"You should have called us." His voice was gruff, an edge of impatience. "You're lucky we turned up when we did. You've heard of chain of custody, right?" He tapped his pen against his notebook. "Some lawyer hears about the stunt you pulled here, they might be able to get that evidence thrown out in court."

"That's a strange way of saying, 'Thanks for finding the murder weapon for us.'"

"Jet, please," he sighed. "You can't do this."

"Do what?"

"Get in the way of the investigation like this."

Jet cracked her fingers, her back warm and aching. "*In the way?* I've made more progress than you have."

"Jet—"

"—I'm running out of time. And I'm not afraid to get my hands dirty. See."

She held them up for him, crusted with dirt and dust.

"Jet—"

"—I know you think it's JJ, but doesn't this change things?" She gestured at the site. "Finding my phone and the murder weapon here. JJ has no connection to this place. But someone else does. Andrew Smith. This was his old house. He's been watching the work, could have known the concrete was going in the morning after. He was wearing the exact same red wig as JJ on Halloween, so the hair at the scene could have come from him too."

Ecker faltered, chewing the air. "How do you know about the hair at the scene?"

Jet blinked. "I . . . guessed?"

Ecker glanced over his shoulder, back at Jack Finney in his uniform, standing over there with Luke, Billy, and Jet's parents. Shit. Sorry, Jack. Now he really would be in trouble.

"But *if* there was a red wig hair found at the scene," Jet continued, "that makes Andrew Smith just as much a suspect as JJ. And don't just tell me you're not ruling anything out, again."

"I'm not ruling anything out, suspects either. And the red hair doesn't limit us to just two options."

"Well, the other matching red wig was on an eleven-year-old girl, so I think—"

"—Hairs can transfer, Jet. Synthetic ones too." His mouth twitched, watching Jet's eyes spin, like he was scoring points, firing back. "Just because this wig hair was at the scene, doesn't mean the perpetrator had to be wearing the wig. All it could mean is that they had contact with somebody wearing that wig, that a hair transferred to them, and then to the scene."

"Oh," was all Jet could say. And all she could think was: *You stupid fuck, thinking you were good at this.*

"You said you spoke to JJ at the fair, when he was wearing that wig?" Ecker asked, taking aim again. "Did you have any physical contact with him?"

Jet shrugged. "He might have touched my arm. I can't remember."

"Right." Ecker nodded, the winning shot, eyes softening, but smug all the same. "So the hair might have transferred from JJ to you, and you're the one who transferred it to the scene."

Jet didn't like this, being on the receiving end. She wanted to be the smug one, and now she felt . . . flat, the win snatched from her, arms too tired to snatch it back.

"So, you're saying the killer could be anyone who had contact with either JJ or Andrew Smith at the fair. Or if the hair was transferred from JJ to me, then the killer could be . . . well, anyone?"

Ecker exhaled, put his notebook away.

"Please don't get in the way of the investigation again," he said.

"Cool." Jet blew out her lip. "Good talk. Always a pleasure."

She sidled over to her family.

"Oh, Jet, look at you, sweetie," Mom said. The past day must have been hard on her, her face grayer and gaunter somehow. "You're filthy."

"Yep." Jet's arms slapped down to her sides.

"Why don't you come home? I'll run you a nice bath."

"No." Jet sniffed, sleeve to her nose, rubbing more dirt on than off. "I don't have time for a *nice bath* and I'm not coming home. I'm not giving up, not this time, Mom. I can do this. I'm *doing* it, see. I just found the murder weapon. Not the police, *me*. I have to do this. I'm supposed to do this."

"But, Jet—"

"—It's supposed to be hard," Jet said, trying to convince herself too. A lot harder now, her suspect pool shifting, opening up from two to . . . anyone. No, not anyone. Someone who had a connection to this construction site, who knew that the concrete was going in the morning after, that this would be a perfect place to hide the phone and the weapon. That narrowed it down a bit. Maybe a lot.

"Dad." Jet turned to him. "Can you get me a list of all Mason Construction employees? All contractors and subcontractors, anyone who could have known about this site?"

He nodded, hand pressed to his side, knuckles white. Jet knew what that meant, knew the unrelenting pain.

"Luke can get that for you, honey," Dad said.

Jet turned to her brother, eyebrows raised. "As quick as you can, Luke."

He sniffed. "This project was already delayed, and now it's shut down. Now it's a crime scene."

"It's not a crime scene because I smashed up your foundations, Luke. It's a crime scene because the killer came here to bury the evidence, probably someone you know or someone you employ. Be mad at them, not me."

"Luke's not mad at anyone," Dad said. Because Dad had no idea. None at all.

"Sergeant Finney!" Ecker called. "A word?" Beckoning him over.

Jet pursed her lips, shot Jack a look, said *sorry* with her eyes as he wandered away.

She pulled out Billy's phone, still in her pocket, swiped into the photo reel.

"This is the hammer, Dad." She showed him. "See the brand. Coleby. Is that one you use at work, that your employees have?"

Dad took the phone from her for a closer look, squinting at the screen.

"No, it's not the kind we usually order in." He cleared his throat. "But contractors will often use their own tools."

"Know anyone who uses this type?"

Dad's chin dipped, moving side to side. "Sorry, kiddo."

"Luke?" She showed him the screen.

"Not off the top of my head."

"No, it was off the top of *my* head, Luke. The back actually."

"You feeling OK, Jet?" Mom interrupted, stepping between them.

"I feel like I just spent an hour playing with a sledgehammer."

"Billy." Dianne's gaze fixed on him, sudden and surprising. Ah, so she *did* remember his name. The same thought spooled behind Billy's eyes; Jet could tell, the twitch in his parted lips. "Are you making sure she's getting enough rest?"

"Well, I—"

Dianne didn't let him answer.

"—Jet, come home. Please."

"I can't." Jet folded her arms in front of her heart, hiding it, protecting it? "I have to keep going. Come on, Billy."

Billy came on.

"I'll take good care of her, Dianne. I promise," he said.

"And Luke," Jet called, opening the truck door. "That list. ASAP. ASAP meaning I'll be dead in less than five days, got it?"

FOURTEEN

"Oh good, you're back."

Billy stood in the doorway, *his* doorway, plastic bags rustling, five hooked over his fingers.

"Got some more food," he said, shutting the door awkwardly, Billy Bag-Hands, taking them over to the counter. "That chocolate you like. I know it wasn't on the list, but . . . Stopped by the pharmacy too, got better bandages."

Jet was sitting on the floor, legs crossed, her laptop open on the table, eyes back to the screen. The web page spliced, doubled, but Jet hadn't touched anything; she swore she hadn't. She rubbed her eyes, blinked, and the image fused together again, back to normal.

"OK, so I've done more research on this hammer," she said, over Billy's rustling. "Turns out you can't actually buy the hammer on its own. It's only sold as part of a set. Comes with a sixty-piece set in this black tool kit." She clicked through the images. "Various screwdrivers, lots of different fittings, a file, this little wrenchy thing, measuring tape, a knife, a little saw, pliers or something. You get the picture. So the killer has to have this full set somewhere. Or once had it."

"OK," Billy said, putting a carton of milk in the fridge.

"And the other thing I found out," Jet continued, "is that this set is only sold in North America, various retailers like Home Depot, Lowe's, Amazon, so that . . . well, I mean, that doesn't really help us at all."

Billy pulled out a loaf of bread. "And we now think it's someone connected to your dad's company, who might have known about the project on North Street, and when the foundations were going in."

"Correct," Jet said. "They had to. Just waiting on that list from Luke, then I can figure out who knew about the North Street site, then go ask them what their favorite brand of hammer is." Jet stared at it on-screen. The clean, shiny new version of the thing that killed her. "Maybe we got a little too excited about the red wig hair, but it still could be Andrew—he has that connection."

Jet glanced through the front door, re-creating the space beyond it, that narrow hall that split toward two apartments: 1A through there, and here 1B. Fancy that—living about twenty feet away from one of your murder suspects.

"OK." Billy balled up the empty grocery bags, quickly, the swishing sound of their whispered secrets. "I better get down to the bar." He turned to check his reflection in the mounted microwave, fixing his hair, one stubborn curl that wouldn't let itself be fixed.

Jet slumped against the sofa. "You working tonight?" she asked, watching Billy as he crossed to the far wall, picked up his guitar case.

He shrugged, hiding his face from her. "Kinda," he said. "It's th-that live music thing I told you about. I—I'm the music. And I'm . . . live," he added.

"Oh," Jet said. "That's tonight?"

"Yeah. Tuesday is the only day Allison will let me do it."

"When's it start?"

Billy glanced back at the microwave, at the little clock. "Literally ten minutes. I should already be down there, setting up. People are waiting." He finally looked at her, resting the case on the tops of his shoes. "But I can cancel it, I can stay, if you—"

"—No, no," Jet cut him off. "You go. Wouldn't want you to get in trouble with Allison. I'm fine."

Billy hoisted the guitar case on his back, his eyebrows furrowing. Maybe his arms were sore too: Jet's were killing her. OK, OK, she heard it.

"I mean," Billy said, quieter now, unsure, "you could come down, i-if you want. It's not far." He attempted a smile, but it didn't reach his pale eyes. "You've been staring at that hammer for hours already. A quick break might, I don't know, do you good."

Jet opened her mouth, but she couldn't find an excuse in time. *Busy* was already out the window, she knew it, and Billy knew it too. She couldn't say *later*, or *next time*, because those weren't options either, not anymore.

Billy watched her, jumped in to fill the silence. "Your mom told me to make sure you're getting enough rest and . . . she terrifies me." He laughed, catching it in his closed fist. "I'm not . . . I'm not terrible, if that's what you're worried about."

"I didn't think you were terrible." Lie.

Billy smiled, like he knew it. Ah, fuck sake, Billy Finney, looking at her with those sad blue eyes, a tug of warm guilt in her chest, sliding down to her belly.

"Yeah, OK," Jet said. "Maybe I'll see you down there."

Billy's eyes lit up, a different blue somehow, trading ice for a summer sky.

"OK," he said, a lopsided smile. "See you down there."

The front door closed behind him.

"Fuck sake, Billy," Jet muttered, closing the lid of her laptop. She pushed herself up from the floor, the muscles down the backs of her arms complaining. An ache they didn't forget as she headed into the bedroom. Well, she couldn't go down to the bar in her sweats, could she? And her clothes from today were basically ruined.

She slipped on the clean pair of jeans, searched her backpack for a shirt. Hmm, see, this was why you didn't pack in a hurry, or when you were mad as fuck. She hadn't packed anything bar-appropriate. Her eyes scanned up to Billy's closet, pulled it open. Flannel shirts of almost every color combination, checked and striped and checked again. Billy was a Country Boy and he knew it. And he probably wouldn't mind if Jet borrowed one. Probably. Jet pulled one out—navy and cream—and buttoned it up.

In the bathroom, Jet sprayed some of Billy's deodorant, pulled out her makeup bag, and studied her face.

Her hair was a mess. Should she try to wash it sometime, around the wounds? Was there even a point? Jet tried to get a brush through; it was still matted around the bandages, but it would have to do.

Next, her face. Her skin was a little blue, a little swollen, by her temple, the bruise creeping out from under the bandage there. A bit of foundation covered that, and the circles under her eyes. Blush on her cheeks and a little on her nose. Eyebrow gel to stick them up the way she liked them. A pale pink on her lips, up and down the sharp lines of her cupid's bow.

Jet leaned closer to the mirror, mascara wand in hand. She blinked. The pupil on the right was still dilated, a dark abyss in the middle of her eye, mismatched from the other. There wasn't much the mascara could do about it. But, hey, for a dying girl, she could have looked worse.

JET HAD HER own table, the one by the upside-down-witch-legs lamp, hands cupped around a cold bottle of beer, stinging the raw scrubbed-clean skin of her palms.

The bar was busy, surprisingly busy, maybe forty people in here, shuffling feet and chatter crammed into the small space. A completely different world from earlier, when it had just been Jet and Billy and Andrew Smith.

The crowd started to cheer, bursts of clapping, and Jet watched as Billy emerged from the door behind the bar, his hand around the neck of his guitar. He jogged toward the makeshift stage, the microphone on a stand waiting for him. More applause, whoops from a group of middle-aged women, a wolf whistle from a burly man at the back.

"Thank you," Billy said into the microphone, a screech of feedback. "Thanks Steve."

Jet gripped the underside of the table, too nervous for him, crossed her legs because she couldn't sit still.

"I'm Billy, and it is my pleasure to play for you tonight," he said, strumming one chord, hooking the guitar strap over his head. "I'm gonna start off with a song probably none of you have ever heard before."

He started to play, fingers dancing across the strings, and the opening riff drew a laugh from the crowd. More when he started to sing.

That song everyone knew. The one about Vermont and sticks. *Very* popular around here, especially at this time of year, right on the cusp of the season of the sticks.

The crowd quieted and Billy continued the verse, and Jet gripped the table harder and . . . wait a minute. Wait a fucking minute. Billy was good. More than good. He could actually sing, oh my god, he could actually sing. A raspy tone to his voice that wasn't there when he spoke, climbing the notes like it was the easiest thing in the world.

Jet felt the hairs standing up along her aching arms. She hugged them to herself. Billy Fucking Finney, eh? Who would have thought?

Everyone joined in with the chorus, butchering the notes, coming in too late. Jet wanted them to shut up, so she could hear her friend sing.

Billy's eyes scanned the crowd, like he was looking for someone, and then he found her, sitting here at her table, alone.

Jet raised her beer and Billy winked back at her. Moved on to the next verse, but he was smiling so wide out one side of his mouth, it must have been hard to sing through.

"That's my friend," Jet said to a guy at the next table.

"Billy's everyone's friend."

Well, fuck you, sir.

The song ended, another wolf whistle from the back of the room.

Billy grinned into the microphone. "OK, next up: Steve's favorite, because he'll start heckling if I don't."

He cleared his throat and picked at the strings. *Teenage Dirtbag,* another crowd-pleaser, and Steve back there looked more than pleased.

Jet took another sip of her beer, the fizz of the liquid inside her cheeks, a warm glow pressing in from the other side. Well, in one of them; the other cheek felt nothing. Could you normally feel your cheeks? Jet took another sip, finished off the beer. She glanced over to the bar, scouting her path through the crowd. There was a clear way, there, right to one of the bar stools, and a woman sitting on it. Jet recognized her immediately. Her name wasn't Noelle, like Billy was singing now, but it was close. Nell. Jankowski. The chief's wife.

Jet got to her feet, zigzagged her way through, all eyes on Billy.

"Can I have another?" Jet placed the empty bottle down on the bar, standing right next to Nell, hair like bronze, graying at the temples. She was drinking a glass of white wine, the glass sweating, ghostly fingerprints left behind. "Hi," Jet said. "I'm Jet."

Nell glanced at her, eyes that matched her hair, softening as they landed on Jet. "Hi, sweetheart," she said, straightening up. "I know who you are. Lou's told me about . . . He's good, isn't he?" Nell pointed her glass toward Billy.

"The best," Jet answered without a pause. "What has *Lou* told you?"

Nell hesitated, breathing in the wine. "I just wanted to say, I'm so sorry about your situation. It's truly awful, what happened. Are you feeling OK? If there's anything I can do before—"

"—I feel fine," Jet lied. "No different. Turns out dying feels a lot like living."

"I'm sorry." Nell stared into her glass, wincing as the crowd joined in with the chorus.

Jet waited for the sound to die down, then asked: "Is it true? That my dad is planning to sell Mason Construction to you?"

Nell choked on her wine. "He told you?"

"Someone else did."

Nell's chin dipped up, a question in her eyes.

"Andrew Smith," Jet answered. "So it's actually true?"

Nell nodded. "He shouldn't have done that."

"Probably a lot of things Andrew Smith shouldn't have done."

"I pay him to do jobs around the house sometimes," Nell said. "One of the first people I met in town, in here actually." She looked around, but Andrew wasn't here. "I worry he's lonely. We chat sometimes. I didn't think he . . . He shouldn't have told you that. Your dad doesn't want anyone to know yet."

"Are you going to buy it?" Jet asked. "The company."

Nell ran her finger around the rim of her glass. "It makes sense to. I own a home construction business, based in Hartland and Hartford, where we lived before Lou got this job. Now we live in Woodstock, it makes sense to expand here. We're not total out-of-towners, like people think. Lou actually lived here for six months, in his thirties."

"Thank you," Jet said to the guy behind the bar, handing her an open beer.

"I'll get this." Nell jumped in, reaching toward the card machine before Jet had a chance.

"Thanks." Jet took a sip. "It would also make sense for my dad to leave the company to Luke when he retires. He's worked there more than ten years. It's what we all thought would happen."

Nell went back to staring at her wine. "Your dad doesn't want to do that. He has two children. Doesn't think it would be fair on you, to give the company to Luke."

"Well, lucky for Luke, I guess that's not going to be a problem anymore. Dad's only gonna have one kid left by the end of the week." Jet took another sip. "Excuse me—someone's trying to steal my table."

Jet made her way back, eyeballing the man who was reaching for her chair until he backed off.

"Thank you, thank you," Billy said, his breath tickling the mic. "OK, next I'm gonna play one of my own songs." The crowd oohed. "I know, I know. I wrote this song a while back, so you might have heard it already. This one's called *For Her*."

Billy's fingers skipped across the strings, picking out the chords, eyes down on his feet.

"*If you asked my heart how long, it could only say it's been a while,*" he sang. "*And I'd ask you instead: how could you not love that dangerous little smile? She laughs like an old man dying, and I gotta keep it together, I'm really trying. Loved her since the start, since day one, but day one won't ever be one day 'cause . . .*"

He strummed harder, the guitar picking up for the chorus, Billy's voice too, gravelly beneath the notes. He sang:

> *She might not ever love me back,*
> *Wrong place or time or maybe neither.*
> *But she looks at me with those earthy eyes,*

And I'm not sure I can breathe ugh.
Don't think it's in the cards or stars,
Not on the same page or track.
But, hell, I'm gonna play it,
Because I wrote this little song . . . for her.

Billy swallowed, stepped back from the microphone. He looked nervous, Jet could tell, eyes still on the ground.

"Whoooo," Jet called between her cupped hands, clapping them together. "Come on, Billy!"

The crowd joined in.

Billy's smile came back, and so did his eyes, surveying the bar, having fun with it now.

"She's my cup of tea, my bit of me, why yes, I've watched British Love Island *on TV, why do you ask?"*

Jet laughed.

"No, stop asking, we're just friends, stay on task, I've got a verse to sing. She's a queen but I'm no king, I'm just royally fucked, and I'm sorry for swearing."

Everyone laughed, and Jet's cheeks glowed harder. That was *her* friend up there.

"GOT YOU A beer."

Billy took the seat opposite, resting his guitar case against the arm.

"Thanks."

"So," Jet said.

"So?" Billy asked, gripping the bottle, eyebrows up, forcing little folds onto his forehead.

"You're not terrible." She smiled, could only feel it on one side.

Billy laughed. "I told you I wasn't terrible." He took a sip, mouth creased at the corners, almost dribbling his beer, catching it with his sleeve. "I'd never lie to you. Wh-why are you prodding your face like that?"

"I can't feel my cheek," Jet said, driving her finger into it, nail first. "Can you feel your cheek?"

Billy leaned across the table, fingers outstretched.

"No, not *my* cheek, yours. Can you feel anything when you prod it?"

Billy picked up Jet's bottle of beer instead. "How many of these have you had?"

"You're good, Billy," Jet said. "Better than good. Fucking good."

"Stop." He pulled his shirt up, hooking it over his nose, covering his face.

Jet reached over and yanked it down, her fingerprints remaining, creases in the fabric.

"Why have you been hiding that?"

"I didn't hide it," Billy said. "I've invited you like fifty times. You're always busy."

"Always busy," she murmured, a puff of air that was both a sigh and a laugh, it couldn't decide, and neither could Jet. "But, Billy, you could do this, you know. Write songs, play them, get paid to do it."

"Nah," he said, the sound echoing in his beer bottle.

"No, you could, I'm serious," Jet said, seriously. "You just have to be discovered, and then it can all really begin."

"What can begin?"

"Life, Billy." She slapped the table. "I can't believe you've been sitting on this. You've never thought about purs-pur-p—doing this? Doing it properly?"

Billy shrugged. "I don't think I want that. I just write songs because I like to do it, that's all. Makes me happy."

Was he joking?

"But," she said, "what's the point in doing it, if it's not to achieve something big?"

"Maybe there is no point."

Jet felt a flash of annoyance warm up her neck, sitting straighter with it. "But there has to be a point. Otherwise you're just wasting your time."

Billy shrugged. "Is it a waste of time if I love every minute?"

Jet chewed her lip, studied his face. "Yes, Billy. You've literally just described a waste of time."

He laughed into his beer.

"It's not funny," Jet exhaled into hers. "You're lucky you found the thing you're good at. I never did find mine. And I looked *a lot.*"

"What are you talking about, Jet? You got into UPenn, one of the best law schools in the world."

". . . And dropped out after two semesters."

"Then you worked at that fancy bank in Boston."

". . . And quit because the hours were too long, and I never had time to drink enough water, so I kept pissing blood, which is *not* good for you, apparently." She held out her bottle to Billy's on the table, *cheers*-ed it.

Billy's smile turned down at the corners. "I think you're too hard on yourself."

Jet shook her head. "Not hard enough. Yeah, I haven't actually finished anything I've started . . . ever." She rubbed her eye with her sleeve—Billy's sleeve—came back with a grin, used it as a shield. "Actually, that's not true. When I was ten, I did come first in the regional spelling bee, beat all the teenagers."

Billy's eyes flickered. "Wasn't that the same day that—"

"—Emily drowned, yeah. Forgot you were there that day."

"I didn't forget." Billy abandoned his beer, chewed his thumb instead. Could he still hear her mom's screams too, if he searched his memories far enough?

Jet cleared her throat. "You know, I was never allowed to have my hair long after that day. Mom forced me to cut it short, even though I hated it. Guess it kind of stuck with me." Jet fiddled with the ends of her hair, skimming her shoulders.

"I remember," Billy said. "No one was allowed to go in your pool unless there were two adults there, constantly watching. And no swimming under the surface ever, especially anywhere near the drain."

Jet sniffed. Looked into Billy's watery eyes. She could just tell him. She'd never told anyone before—not Luke, not Sophia, not JJ—and if she didn't now, it would probably die with her.

"You know, I . . ." She stopped herself, false start. Pushed herself to try again. "My mom, she blames me for Emily's death. Said it was my fault."

Billy blinked. "What are you talking about? You weren't even there."

"Exactly," Jet said. "It was my fault both my parents were out that afternoon, watching me at the competition. If I hadn't reached the final, Mom and Dad would have been at home, and Emily wouldn't have died." Jet dropped her chin, hiding it behind Billy's collar. "I overheard Mom saying it to Dad, right after the funeral. That it was *my* fault Emily died."

Billy shuffled, his shoes pressing against hers. "That's crazy."

"She blames your dad too," Jet sniffed. "It always has to be someone's fault."

"My dad?"

"Yeah. Apparently they passed him on the way to the competition, and my mom asked your dad if he could check in on Luke and Emily in a couple of hours. Emily was sixteen, Luke was thirteen, and *man* did they fight all the time. I guess she was worried about them killing each other while they were out. And I guess your dad never did go check."

Billy shook his head. "Emily's death was a freak accident; it wasn't anyone's fault her hair got stuck in the—"

"—I know," Jet interrupted him. "But my mom doesn't know that. I think she's punished me for it ever since."

Jet tapped her foot, nudging against Billy's. Something else she'd never told anyone: "Those were all Emily's plans, you know. She was the one who wanted to go to Dartmouth, then UPenn for law school. I tried, but . . ." Had she really tried, though? Survived Dartmouth—never felt at home there, never made any lasting friends to fill the hole Sophia left— just buckled down, eyes on her shiny future. And then it was there, Jet had it, just as shiny as she'd imagined, and she'd given up law school as soon as she found any reason to, like she'd been waiting for a way out. Why was that? "You remember what Emily was like, don't you? So cool, so sure, so smart, she didn't even have to try. Effortless. I wanted to be just like her. She won that same spelling bee, you know, when she was ten too. Being Emily, it just came so easy to her. But it wasn't easy for me. Guess I never really filled those shoes, huh?"

Billy pressed his toes against hers, a half-smile. "You've only got little feet."

Jet snorted, kicked him away.

"I know your mom is hard on you," he said, dropping the smile. "But she does it because she cares."

"Really?"

"Well, she didn't up and leave when you were eighteen, sent two birthday cards then forgot the rest, no phone call ever, no explanation, no idea where she is." Billy ran his hands through his hair, finger tracks breaking up the curls. "That's a mom who doesn't care, Jet."

Jet caught his eye, a warm creep of guilt stirring in her gut.

"I'm sorry about your mom, Billy."

"And I'm sorry about yours. Moms, huh?"

"Moms."

They clinked beer bottles.

"Right, let's stop being depressing," Jet said. "Acting like somebody died over here."

"You're doing that on purpose now, Jet."

"Let's go back to talking about you becoming a famous singer."

"Let's not."

"Is that a Tile tracker on your guitar case?" She pointed.

"Yeah." Billy traced it with his fingers. "It's my baby."

"Oh please," she snorted again.

"Don't *Oh please* me, you're the same way with your truck."

"That truck *is* my baby," she said. "You're never allowed to drive it."

"And you're not allowed to play my guitar," he said.

"Fine."

"Finer."

"Sooooo." Jet leaned across the table to prod Billy in the arm. "That song you wrote, it's about a girl you like, huh?" She leaned even closer, whispered: "Who is she?"

Billy tipped back in his chair. "No one. It's not about anybody, I made it up."

"Oh, come on," Jet said. "You can tell me. I've known you forever. Who could be a better wingwoman? Let me help—it's my dying wish. Does she work at the bar?"

Billy fiddled his fingers, stared down at them too hard, acting strange and un-Billy-like. Which was all the *yes* Jet needed.

"She does, doesn't she?" she hissed. "Is it Allison? It's Allison, isn't it? You wrote the song about her?"

"No," he coughed. "It's not. The song isn't about anybody. It's just a song."

WEDNESDAY
NOVEMBER 5

FIFTEEN

"So, I guess you really don't know the meaning of ASAP?" Jet raised her voice over the sound of the screaming baby, banging his little fists against his high chair.

Luke didn't react, scooting past Billy to the cupboard over the sink.

Billy stuck his tongue out at Cameron, tried to make him laugh; didn't work.

"Luke?!" Jet said.

"I heard you," he snapped, a muscle ticking in his jaw, something alive beneath the skin.

"I need that list."

"I'm in the office later, I'll send it to you then."

Jet folded her arms. "Why can't you go now? Where's Sophia?"

Luke closed the cupboard, harder than he needed to, snatched open the one beside it. "Sophia has Pilates on Wednesday mornings so I have Cameron."

Jet turned to look at the baby, face reddening, his awful screeches reverberating inside her skull, finding all the cracks.

"What's wrong with him?" she asked.

"He's teething."

"Well, can you turn him down?"

Luke tensed. "That's what I'm trying to do, it's— Ah, here it is."

He pulled a red box down from the highest shelf. Infants' Tylenol. Opened the flap to pull out the glass bottle and little plastic syringe. "OK, it's coming, Cam. Shh-shh," he said, which made absolutely no difference at all.

Jet's head ached, pushing back against the sound, returning fire.

"Shit, I don't know how much." Luke narrowed his eyes at the tiny syringe. "Jet, can you check my phone? Sophia texted about it the other day. There, on the table. Should say the amount."

Jet sighed, tapped the darkened phone screen. "Code?" She repeated the phone's demand.

"213024," Luke said, unscrewing the medicine as Jet tapped the code in.

She pressed the *Messages* icon, opened Luke's thread with Sophia.

"What am I looking for?" she asked, scrolling up.

"Tylenol," Luke said through gritted teeth, like the sound had made its way inside his head too.

"OK." Jet clicked her tongue, scanning the screen. "Is it normal to talk about your baby's poop this much?"

"Jet!"

"Found it. *Just called doctor,*" she read from the screen. "*He says try Tylenol instead of Advil when he's bad. 3ml.*"

"Three," Luke repeated. "Perfect." He dipped the syringe into the bottle, but Jet's eyes strayed back to Luke's phone screen, to that message from Sophia.

It was sent on Friday, at 3:06 p.m. But wait . . . Jet shifted. Wasn't that in the time span between the Sophia sightings on the doorbell camera, when she said she'd left her phone at the Masons'? How was Sophia texting from a phone she'd left behind?

Maybe Jet was wrong; she'd have to check the times in her notebook.

But there was something else too, a few messages below.

A text from Sophia to Luke.

Call me.

That's all it said. Jet swiped to the left and the screen told her it had been sent at 10:52 p.m. that Friday night. Six minutes after Jet's head was split open. When Luke and Sophia were supposed to be here, together, in this house. That was what they'd said in their police statements. But Sophia wouldn't have texted *Call me* if they were here, together, watching *Friends*. So . . . one of them wasn't in the house, and both of them had lied about it.

Jet narrowed her eyes. Billy caught her, widening his in response. She shook her head. Not here, not now.

"There we go," Luke said, oblivious, his back turned, pressing the plunger of pink liquid into Cameron's open mouth.

The baby swallowed and the screaming stopped, Jet's ears ringing with relief. Cameron clacked his tongue, poked it through his lips. Then his little mouth bared again, a silent scream, revving up, followed by a not-silent one.

"He's still screaming," Jet said, hands to her ears.

"It doesn't work immediately." Luke threw her a look, rinsing the plunger.

"OK, I need to leave." Jet crossed the kitchen, heading for the hall. "Send me that list of employees, Luke. As soon as you get to the office. Or I'll ask Dad instead."

"I'll do it," Luke said, head over the sink, the loud splatter of the water joining in with the screams, an assault of sound.

Jet ran away from it, to the front door, Billy on her heels.

"What was that face for?" he asked her, closing the front door behind them, shutting away all that noise. They headed to her truck, parked in front of the double garage. "What did you see on Luke's phone?"

"Luke and Sophia lied." Jet opened her door, slid inside. "One of them wasn't at home around the time of the attack, like they said. Sophia lied twice, actually. Said she left her phone at my parents' house that afternoon, but I'm pretty sure she was texting Luke at that time. I'll have to show you the doorbell footage."

Billy clicked in his seatbelt. "So, what are we going to do now?"

Jet slotted the keys into the ignition.

"I needed that list, fucking Luke," she said, looking over her shoulder to scowl at his house. "I wanted to interview those employees this morning. After Andrew Smith, that's our strongest lead: someone who works at the company, would have known about the foundations on the North Street project, might own a hammer like that."

"We could go back to the site, ask some of the builders there?" he suggested.

"It's been shut down; it's a crime scene now. Won't be anyone there."

Billy sat back. "I don't know what to suggest."

Jet started the engine. "I do," she said. "I know someone who works for the company, whose name will be on that list. Maybe he can help us."

"JJ'S BROTHER?"

Billy closed the truck door, staring across at the small, two-bedroom house: gable roof and once-white panels. Tiny yard along the road and a broken fence. It wasn't broken the last time Jet had been here.

"Yeah. Henry," she said. "He works for Mason Construction. Or . . . he did, before his accident."

"What accident?" Billy asked, still sizing up the house.

"Like seven, eight months ago. Henry got stupid drunk and fell off a wall, fell like a whole story. Shattered his kneecap, had to have surgery. Also fell right on a nail or something, went through his eye."

Billy winced.

"Doctors couldn't do anything about that, though. He's blind in that eye now. JJ was so mad at him for being so fucking stupid. He won't admit it, but his little brother is his world. They come as a pair." Jet copied Billy, stared at the little house. There would have been space for her in that pair too, if she'd wanted it. "Anyway, obviously Henry couldn't walk, so he couldn't work, but he can now, so maybe he's back. Might be able to tell us about other employees or contractors who worked on North Street, anyone who might seem, I don't know . . . murdery. Anyone with reason to hate me, or my family."

Jet started to move but Billy stepped backward, blocking her way to the front door.

"JJ lives here too?" he asked.

"He's not here." Jet sidled past him. "We know that. He skipped town. Billy, stop worrying, there's no danger here."

Jet walked up the path, gravel crunching under her mud-caked shoes. She reached the front door and balled her fist, knocked three times.

They waited.

Billy glanced down at Jet and she up at him.

"Thanks again," she said, "for helping me wash my hair."

"No problem again."

Except it had been—a problem, that is. Jet bent over the kitchen sink, Billy pouring lukewarm cups of water over her head, the sting when the shampoo found the wounds, clinging to the clumps and clots.

They'd waited long enough; Jet knocked again, three more times.

A dog started barking, down the street.

"I don't think he's home," Billy said.

Jet put her ear to the door, closed her eyes to focus. Behind the glass, down the hall, there was a faint rumble of voices, and the tinny laugh of a studio audience.

"TV is on," she said. "Someone's home."

Jet knocked again, knuckles on wood, then the backside of her fist, door juddering in its frame.

The door wrenched open and Jet's hand couldn't stop in time, crossing the threshold. Her eyes next.

A gun, pointed straight at her face.

Finger on the trigger.

SIXTEEN

Jet stumbled back, falling into Billy.

"Don't shoot!" Billy shouted.

"Henry, what the fuck!"

The gun lowered, hand shaking, Henry's terrified face behind it.

"Shit, Jet." He fumbled the gun, hid it behind his back. "Sorry, I thought you were someone else."

Jet straightened up. "Someone else? Who were you planning to point a gun at, Henry?"

"No one," he sniffed. "Doesn't matter." He doubled back inside, put the gun down on the shelf above the radiator, barrel pointed away from them, same place JJ always used to leave his keys. Jet studied his hands, still shaking, as he stuffed them in the pockets of his jeans. He'd held the gun in his right hand. Right-handed.

"Since when do you have a gun?" Jet's voice was still frantic, heart in full agreement, dancing against her ribs. Billy could probably feel it too, her back still pressed against him, his panicked breath in her hair.

"I got it the other day." Henry avoided her eyes. "It's registered. Don't worry."

"Don't worry?! You just almost shot me—don't fucking worry!"

"I said sorry."

Jet studied his face, now the shock was sinking away, slipping into the uneasiness in her gut. There was a graze on his cheekbone, right below one eye, a ring of bruise around it, a wine-dark purple. Recent.

"Does JJ know you bought a gun?"

Henry shook his head. "He's not replying to my messages, picking up the phone."

"Do you know where he is?"

"No, I don't know, just like I told the cops." Henry stepped toward the threshold again, peered around the corner, face rearranging, the fear back in his eyes, the smell of it too, like stale sweat.

"Anyone with you?" He eyed the street behind them.

"No, it's just me and Billy."

Henry moved back, hissing when his step landed, doubling over to press his hand against his ribs.

"Who are you scared of?" Jet asked, clocking the ribs too.

"Nobody. I just wanted a gun."

"JJ?" Billy added.

"Who is this guy?" Henry sniffed. "I'm not scared of my brother."

"I'm Just Billy."

"Why did JJ leave?" Jet cut in. "He left Friday night, same night I was attacked."

Henry shook his head, finally meeting her eyes. "You think he did that to you?"

"Well, the police do," Jet snapped back. "Doesn't look great, him disappearing the same exact night. If he had nothing to do with it, why doesn't he come back and explain himself?"

"I don't know where he went, or why. He was just gone, after the fair. Some clothes missing. But you know he wouldn't do that, assault you." Henry eyed Jet's bandages, his left eye a little filmy, a little behind.

"It wasn't just assault," Jet said, darkly. "In four days' time it will be murder."

Henry's mouth dropped open, teeth visible again, and a cut on the underside of his lip. "What are you talking about?"

"Fuck sake, you too?" Jet said, sharing a look with Billy. "Why do the cops keep only half telling the story? I'm going to die, Henry. There's a piece of my skull where it shouldn't be, a brain aneurysm that will be fatal when it ruptures. So yeah, there's that."

Henry's lip shook; his head too. "That can't be true."

"Well, it is," Jet said. "Medical anomaly over here." Pointing her thumb to her chest.

Henry wiped his nose on his sleeve. "Does JJ know?"

"I assume not," Jet said. "If no one can get hold of him."

"He needs to know," Henry said. "He'll want to see you, before . . . God, Jet. I can't believe it. Can't believe that you won't be . . ." He couldn't finish, but Jet didn't need him to, that was enough, said it all.

"I know."

"I've missed it, you know. Having you around the house. JJ does too. He won't say it, but I know."

Jet knew that too.

"If there's anything I can do."

Jet jumped on that. "Actually, there is, Henry. We didn't come over to talk about JJ. I came to ask you some questions."

"Me?" Henry shuffled, glanced back at his gun. "You gonna ask me where I was on Halloween between ten and eleven p.m.?"

"No." Jet hesitated. "Do I need to?"

Henry shrugged. "Cops already did. I was here. Alone."

"No, I wanted to ask you about Mason Construction actually."

A shadow crossed Henry's face, eyebrows lowered. "Wh-why?" he asked.

Jet turned to Billy, reached into his jacket pocket like it was her own, pulled out his phone. Billy didn't mind.

"Do you recognize this hammer? Know anyone who uses one like this, anyone who works for my dad's company?"

Jet held the photo up for Henry, the clean picture from Amazon, not the one flecked with her blood and bone.

Henry stared at the screen. "Not mine," he said. "My tools are red and black."

"But do you remember if anyone else at Mason Construction had this Coleby set? Anyone who was on that project over on North Street?"

Henry swallowed, transferring his eyes from the screen to Jet, something unfamiliar behind them. "Why would I know that? I've never worked for Mason Construction."

Jet's arm dropped, and so did her stomach, the phone skimming her side. "What are you talking about, Henry? I *know* that you did. I practically used to live here with you. Used to give you rides to go pick up a van."

"I don't know what you're talking about," he murmured.

"No," Jet raised her voice. "I don't know what *you're* talking about."

"Sorry that I can't help you." Henry stepped forward into the morning light, the sun finding new colors in that bruise under his eye. His hand snaked around the door, knuckles out, hinges creaking, like he was trying to push it shut without them noticing. A pang in the back of Jet's head and the world split: two Henrys, two of his hands, two doors, and two guns, spliced over each other.

"What happened to your eye?" Jet said, stopping him. And what was happening to hers? Everything still doubled, two Jets, two Billys behind.

Henry blinked. "I can't see so well anymore. The other eye was injured too, during my accident. Blunt trauma, they said. I had to have an operation a couple months ago, to stop the retina from detaching. It . . . well, it didn't work. I need another surgery, or they say I'll lose the sight in that eye too." He blinked again.

"I was actually talking about the bruise," Jet said, trying to read his face. "But doctors are usually right. You should get that surgery ASAP."

He sniffed. "Can't afford it."

"You don't need to *afford* it," Jet said. "That's what health insurance is for. Just ask Luke about it, he deals with all the finance and employee stuff."

"Doesn't help me." Henry's hand tightened on the door. "I've never worked for Mason Construction."

Jet stopped the door with her foot. Two doors, four feet. "Henry, why are you lying? What's going on?"

"You must be confusing me with someone else."

"No, I must not be." Frustrated, trying to hide it in her voice, trying to hide the panic on her face because they'd all fractured, multiplied, and she was the only one who could see it. "Did someone attack you, Henry?

The bruise, your lip, the ribs. Is that why you bought a gun? You can tell me, you know. I can kinda relate. You help me and I can help you. What's going on?"

"You have to go." He pushed the door and Jet was too unsteady, a replica of herself with no clear edges, stumbling back over the threshold. "I have . . . stuff. You need to go."

The door slammed shut in their faces.

And maybe it was the slam that did it, because Jet blinked and the world righted again. One door, one set of hands in front of her face, one Billy staring down at her, holding her elbow, concern darkening his pale blue eyes, a gale blowing through that calm lake.

"I'M FINE," JET said, dropping her jacket to the floor, angry hiss of the zipper dragging across, still attached to one arm. "It's just a headache."

"I don't know, Jet." Billy pulled her jacket the rest of the way off, placed it on the hook. "I wouldn't describe that as the best driving I've ever seen."

"Just tired, just a headache," she said, narrowing her eyes so the world didn't split again, holding it together. "This whole thing is giving me a headache. Sophia's lied twice, Luke lied, maybe he's lying to cover for Sophia. Because we *know* Sophia knew about the foundations, because she told *you* about them. But now Henry's lying too, and I can't figure out why. It's all just too confusing and, yeah, my head hurts, but I bet yours does too. Whoa."

Jet's legs buckled beneath her, catching the arm of the couch, gripping on.

Billy swooped forward, wrapped his arm around her waist. "I've got you."

"I don't need to be *got*," she said, wiping the sweat from her upper lip. "I think I just need to lie down. Yeah. Just like twenty minutes. A nap. Wake me up in twenty minutes, Billy. I can spare twenty minutes. And then we're gonna work out why Sophia lied about leaving her phone, and what she was really doing at my house on Halloween. OK, deal?"

"OK, deal," Billy answered, guiding her toward his bedroom.

"And Luke should have sent the list by then; we don't need Henry anyway. We have time. Twenty minutes."

"Twenty minutes," Billy promised, delivering Jet to the bed.

She sat down, kicked off her shoes. Lay back, head on the pillow, facing out. Billy pulled the comforter up over her shoulders, his eyes still troubled, dark and stormy.

"Twenty m-minutes," Jet muttered, the drumbeat back in her head, eyes fluttering shut, locking her inside with it.

A SOFT RAP on the door.

Jet sniffed.

"Jet?" Billy's voice, soft too.

She opened her eyes, slowly. Phew. Nothing was doubled, everything looked right, looked normal. Her head ached, but she was getting used to that now, a new normal.

"Has it been twenty minutes?" she croaked.

"It's actually been forty. You wouldn't wake up."

"No, Billy." Jet sat up, suddenly awake, suddenly angry. "We said twenty minutes. I don't have time to—"

She tried to throw the blanket off.

Tried.

But her arm wouldn't move.

Her right arm.

She stared down at it and it still wouldn't move. Not at all.

Jet's heart fell to her gut, curdled there, swimming in the acid.

No, no, no.

Her left arm would listen, shifting with her as Jet threw the comforter off.

She tried again.

Tried to twitch the fingers in her right hand.

Nothing.

Jet pressed her working fingers to her right arm. Pressed harder. Harder. Half-moon imprints from her nails in the skin.

She felt nothing. Just a hunk of meat, attached to her shoulder.

"Billy!" she screamed, voice grating in her throat. "Billy, help!"

The door was open before she could scream again.

"What?" Billy rushed in, eyes wide and circling. "What's wrong?"

"My arm." Jet picked it up with her other hand, too heavy. It fell back to the mattress. "I can't move it. I can't feel it. Something's wrong."

Billy crashed to his knees beside the bed.

He slotted his fingers between hers, held her hand.

Gave it a squeeze.

"Feel this?" he asked.

Jet shook her head, her heart coming back to her throat, bringing the acid up with it.

"I can't," she said. "I can't feel it. It's all gone. It's—"

Her throat constricted around her heart, no space for any more words around it.

"Come on," Billy said, dropping her hand, hooking his arm under her shoulder instead. "We need to get you to the hospital."

Jet got to her feet, testing her legs before she trusted them.

"I can walk," she said, letting Billy go ahead of her, through the bedroom door.

Arm swaying uselessly by her side, weighing her down.

"I can't move my fucking arm, Billy."

He turned back, tried to hide the panic in his eyes, but Jet caught it before he could, feeding her own. He looked just as scared as she was, maybe more.

"It's going to be OK," he said, lying, even though Billy didn't lie. "We're going to the hospital."

Jet reached for her keys from the table, where she'd dropped them. No. She thought about reaching for her keys, but nothing happened. Her arm just hung there.

She grabbed them with her left hand instead.

"Billy," she said, looking down at the keys, her hand balling into a fist around the sharp metal, because it could, because it still worked. "I can't drive."

Billy's eyes hooked onto hers. Blue and hazel and fear.

"I know how much you love that truck."

He stretched out his arm, opened his hand, palm up.

Jet took a breath, held it.

No other choice.

She dropped her keys into his waiting hand.

SEVENTEEN

"Sorry about the wait."

Dr. Lee strolled into the room, letting the door swing shut behind her, heels clipping the polished floor, the smell of bleach hanging low in the air.

Jet straightened up, her hospital gown bunching around her knees, right arm dangling lifeless off the bed. Was Dr. Lee really sorry about the wait, or was she sorry about something else?

Billy had been sitting beside Jet, the thin mattress sighing now as he stood up, bowed his head.

"I've had a look at the images from your CT scan, with the radiologist," Dr. Lee said, a file gripped in her hands. "And." She stopped, cleared her throat.

"Can I see?" Jet asked.

The doctor nodded, eyes heavy, mouth set.

She opened her file and pulled out a thin sheet of plastic, walked around the bed to hold it up against the light streaming in through the window.

Another grid of pale blue images, the inside of Jet's head. She'd been conscious this time, aware of every second as she was fed into that giant metal circle, the machine whirring around her, dissecting her brain.

There was something new this time.

"You see this white mass here," Dr. Lee said, circling it with her finger.

"Is that the aneurysm?"

"That's the aneurysm."

Jet swallowed, too tacky in her dried-out throat, gouges her heart had left behind.

"Guess you were right, doc."

What, had Jet seriously thought there was any chance the doctor could have been wrong, that she wouldn't die after all? Stop asking like that, because—because maybe she'd started to, just a little bit, last night in the bar with Billy, when she forgot for a few minutes, forgot that she was dying because she'd been distracted by living. Before, it had just been a *what if,* a theoretical time bomb ticking away, and here it was, made real and tangible, a white shape against the gray mass of her brain. Jet swallowed again, her very last bit of hope.

"Looks big," she said instead.

Dr. Lee nodded. "It's a large aneurysm. Twenty-three millimeters across. Just two away from being classified a giant aneurysm."

"Well, that's good, I guess." Jet sniffed. "At least it's a high-achieving aneurysm."

Dr. Lee didn't smile. Neither did Billy, his eyes swimming.

"The other symptoms you've described—the headaches, the pain above your eye, the double vision, that dilated pupil," Dr. Lee said, "those are all typical symptoms of an unruptured aneurysm of this size. You may experience others, such as weakness, loss of balance, difficulty concentrating, numbness in one side of your face."

Jet looked at Billy; she'd forgotten to mention her cheek. Another one checked off the list.

"And her arm?" Billy asked, staring at it, like he could bring it back to life with his eyes.

Dr. Lee hesitated.

"What is it?" Jet ran her fingers down her bare arm, felt nothing, like it belonged to someone else, not even someone close—a stranger.

"The scan shows us that the aneurysm is leaking." Dr. Lee tapped the scan, the plastic crinkling. "We call this a sentinel bleed. A possible side effect is that this internal bleed is putting pressure on one of your nerves, interrupting the signals, which would explain the loss of function in your arm."

"Will it come back?" Billy asked.

Dr. Lee's face was answer enough: no, it would not.

"I'm sorry, Jet."

Not sorry about the wait at all. Sorry about the rest of it, and that she had to be the one to say it, again.

"Why is it leaking?" Jet asked. "What does that mean?"

Dr. Lee nodded, like she'd expected the question. Or maybe like she wanted to delay answering.

"A sentinel bleed is also known as a warning bleed. It will normally occur just a few days before a significant rupture."

Jet sighed, letting out that tiny last sliver of hope she should never have had in the first place, watched it disappear in the bleach-heavy air.

"So you were right, about all of it," she said to the doctor. "I had a week, and I've used half of it already."

Half. Halftime. Halfway dead. No return. No taking it back. No un-doing her choice.

"I'm so sorry, Jet."

Billy dropped into the chair, grabbed Jet's hand, the one she could feel. He held on tight and Jet held back.

Her gut churned, laying claim to her heart again, sinking, her chest empty without it.

"Wh-what will it feel like?" She looked up at the doctor. "When it ruptures? When I die?"

Dr. Lee hugged the file, holding it over her heart.

"Patients who have survived a ruptured brain aneurysm describe it as the worst headache of your life. Like a thunderclap, all of a sudden." She looked into Jet's eyes, like she felt she owed her that, eye contact, while describing her death. "Other symptoms will come on suddenly, because of the rapid bleeding inside the brain. Your neck might feel stiff, nausea, sudden weakness in the limbs. You might have a seizure as the electrical activity surges in your brain. You'll start slipping in and out of consciousness as the blood starts to starve the brain cells of oxygen. And then . . ."

"And then," Jet repeated. They all knew what came after.

Billy stroked his thumb across the back of Jet's hand, his skin hard where hers was soft.

"I'll give you two a minute alone."

The door swung shut behind Dr. Lee, shushing as it did. It didn't need to; the room was silent anyway.

Jet took her hand back, used it to push up from the bed, bare feet on the cold tiles.

"Come on," she said, heading to the chair in the corner, and her pile of folded clothes.

"Jet." Billy's voice was small, far too small for him. "We can talk about it, if you—"

"—We don't need to talk about it," she cut him off. "We already knew all that. Nothing's changed."

She picked up her jeans with her left hand, gripped the waistband, and shook them to open up the leg holes. Stepped her right leg inside and almost tripped.

"Do you want my help?" Billy asked, tentative. Like he knew she was going to snap:

"I can do it with one hand. I'm not useless."

Jet stepped the other leg through, found the floor. Pulled the jeans up to her knees, left hand moving from one side to the other, wriggling as she yanked them up over her thighs, breathless with the effort. The ass was the hardest part, but she would *not* ask Billy for help—she didn't need his help, she could do this, she would not be useless. She tucked the hospital gown up and yanked the jeans the rest of the way, knocking into her dead arm, making it sway.

"There," she exhaled. "I did it."

She glanced down at her waistband, the zipper gaping open.

Fuck.

"I can't," she started. "I can't . . . Can you—"

"—Do the button?"

"Yeah," she said, her voice now smaller than his.

Billy stepped forward and Jet averted her eyes as he reached down, pulled the zipper up for her, fastened the button, his fingers grazing the flesh of her belly, her heart not hiding in her gut anymore, but in her ears, burning.

"Done," he said, not waiting for a thanks. Which was good, because Jet wasn't giving it. But if she had to be useless in front of someone, maybe she would have chosen Billy Finney anyway. She didn't use to mind, when she banged her knee falling off her bike, and he would fix it for her.

Jet sighed, picked up her bra, avoiding Billy's eyes, and he hers.

Now *that* was too far.

She stuffed it into her jacket pocket instead, along with her T-shirt, and draped her jacket over one shoulder. The hospital probably had enough of these gowns anyway. And what were they going to do about it: arrest her for theft?

"Jet, are you OK?" Billy asked, still looking away.

"Fine," she said. "Like I said, nothing has changed. I was always dying. I always had a week. Come on, we better get going. My murder isn't going to solve itself."

JET STOPPED AT the top of the steps, left hand to the wall. Right swinging by her side.

"What are you all doing here?" she asked, narrowing her eyes at the group of people standing outside Billy's apartment, too many voices, clogging up the hall.

Detective Ecker, Jack Finney, the chief, and Jet's parents.

"There you are," her mom said, breathy with relief. "We're looking for you. Where have you been?"

"At the hospital," Billy answered from the step behind, before Jet could intervene. She would have preferred her mom not know that, because she was only going to—

"—The hospital?" Dianne snapped, eyes wide. "Why—what's happened?"

Yep, she was only going to make a big deal out of it. Thanks, Billy.

"Nothing," Jet said, nudging Billy with her elbow, the one that worked. "The aneurysm has started to leak, and I can't move my arm anymore."

Jet pointed to the arm in question, limp at her side in the jacket sleeve.

"What do you mean you can't move your arm?" Dianne's voice pitched higher. "Show me."

Jet blinked. "I can't show you—that's the point. It looks like an arm that can't move, Mom. Not much to see."

"Did the doctors give you anything for it?"

Jet pursed her lips. "Yeah, some magical pills to grow another arm."

"I should have been there, Jet. You never ask the right questions—"

"—What are you all doing here?" That was the right question now, Jet's eyes moving to the cops instead, to Billy's dad, because she knew his face best, searched it for answers.

Detective Ecker was the one to step forward. "We need to talk to you. Can we come inside?"

"The spare key's not under the mat anymore," Jack said over Jet's head, looking at Billy.

"Jet's got it." Billy fished his keys out of his pocket, winding his way through everyone to the door of 1B.

He unlocked it and held the door open, guiding everyone through.

His dad hesitated, rested a hand on Billy's shoulder as he passed.

"Patriots game on Sunday," Jack said stiffly, hand still there. "It's supposed to rain, though. You gonna watch it?"

"I don't know, Dad," Billy said, voice quiet, finding Jet's eyes in the hall. Because Billy didn't really like watching football, only pretended for his dad, so he had someone to watch it with after Billy's mom left. Or because that Patriots game was scheduled for the day Jet would die.

But Jack must not have gotten all of that from Billy's eyes, couldn't read them like Jet. He cleared his throat, dropped his hand, and walked on through.

Jet's mom fussed over her as they crossed the threshold, touching the limp arm on purpose, like she was checking, waiting for a reaction.

Too many people inside this small apartment, boxed in, nudging shoulders.

"Sit down, Jet," Mom said, guiding Jet to the couch, settling in beside her, almost on top of her. Dad took the other end, leaving her a bit more breathing space.

"Does anyone want a coffee or . . ." Billy offered, hovering by the kitchen.

"Not now, Billy," Dianne hushed him. "The detective has important news."

Ecker had taken the seat opposite, the chief and Jack arranged behind him, a tableau of cop, their mouths set, eyes serious.

"Who died?" Jet said, trying to lighten the mood. Didn't work, only got heavier, pressing down on her chest.

Ecker steepled his fingers, two pointing up, pressed them to his lips, like a gun made of flesh and bone.

"Jet," he said, voice too loud, echoing between her ears. "We've arrested JJ Lim for your assault."

Jet sat forward, Mom clinging to her, rubbing her back.

"JJ?" she said. "You found him?"

"He came back to town a few hours ago." Ecker dismantled his finger gun, hands dropping to his lap. "He says his brother texted him, explained about your situation. That's why he came back."

"You've spoken to him? JJ?"

"We've interviewed him once already, after his arrest, yes."

"And?" Jet lowered her voice. "What's he saying?"

Ecker swallowed. "Well, he's denying everything at the moment. But we had enough evidence for an arrest warrant."

"Evidence?" Jet asked.

Ecker nodded. "The red synthetic hair at the scene was a match for the wig JJ wore at Halloween."

"Right, but you said it could have transferred?"

"There's his *Sorry* text to you, after the time of the attack. And that he has no alibi and left town in a hurry that night."

"But why would JJ want to kill me? You don't know him like I do."

"There's more," Ecker said. "We have a theory on motive. We are told you turned down his proposal a few months ago."

"Yeah," Jet sniffed. "Because we weren't right for each other. That's not enough of a reason for—"

"—Men have hurt women for far less," Ecker spoke over her. "And that's not our only potential motive." He pulled something out of his pocket, the letter Jet had given him, from that loan company. "This loan for thirty thousand dollars, taken out in your name, secured against your truck. The bank account it was paid into belongs to JJ."

Jet's breath stalled, caught in her throat.

"It was JJ?" she said, more to herself.

"He committed identity fraud, cashed the money in your name. He'd already taken out several loans in his own name previously, tanked his credit score. Then he couldn't afford the monthly repayments on this loan." Ecker shook the page. "Defaulted on them. Our theory is that he panicked when he realized you were going to find out what he did, that he felt he had no other choice but to . . ."

"Kill me?"

Ecker didn't answer, not directly. "The prosecutor wants us to hold him a little longer, see if we can get a confession. But this is a strong circumstantial case, Jet, enough to proceed with charges."

Jet didn't know what to say. Looked like, maybe, her murder *had* just solved itself. So, what the fuck was she supposed to do now?

"I want to reassure you," Ecker continued, "that the charges . . . after you . . . when you—"

"—When I die," she finished for him.

Ecker inclined his head. "The charges against JJ will be amended to first-degree murder. I know it was important to you, to have the answer before . . . well, now you do."

Something tightened in Jet's gut, twisted. *She* was supposed to find her killer, not the police. That was the whole point. She needed this, her final chance to actually *do* something, see it through to the end. And now they were sitting over there, telling her the end was already here? Offering her the easy way out. Jet had always taken the easy way out, quit when things got too hard. But it was supposed to be different this time—she wasn't supposed to give up. And for some reason, accepting it was JJ felt like giving up, didn't feel right. Her gut agreed, and so did her broken head.

"What about the hammer?" She leaned forward. "Does JJ own the rest of that Coleby tool set? It's a sixty-piece set. Are the other fifty-nine tools at his house?"

Jack cleared his throat. "We've conducted a search of JJ's residence. Nothing has turned up yet."

"Well, it's a small house," Jet said. "It's not going to turn up if you didn't find it already. So how do you know he owned that hammer?"

"Well, we don't," Ecker said. "In a case like this, you aren't always able to tie up all the loose ends."

"Well, excuse me for being picky, but if I'm going to die, I'd kind of like all those ends to be tied up. Real fucking tight."

"As I said, we are hoping to press JJ for a confe—"

"—What about the foundations on North Street?" Jet said, staring down that easy way out, right there, in between the cops, taking no steps toward it. "How could JJ have known the concrete was being poured the next morning? He had no connection to that place. Are you telling me he just got lucky?"

"He might have passed that way when leaving town. Spotted the construction and took a chance."

"So, what?" Jet's voice rose now. "You're done? You aren't investigating anymore?"

Ecker shook his head. "We are investigating. We will be shoring up the case against JJ so the prosecutor—"

"—And if it wasn't JJ?"

"Dad," Billy spoke up. "I think you should listen to—"

"—Jet," Mom interrupted, turning to her, face too close. "It was JJ. They wouldn't have arrested him if they didn't have a reason to. It's over, sweetie."

It wasn't over. Not for Jet. She still had time, and she was not going to let it go to waste. She'd wasted enough already, her whole life. This was a test, and she wasn't going to fail, not this time, not even with one work-ing arm.

"OK, sure," she said bluntly. "Thanks so much for your service, offi-cers. Give JJ my best."

"I know this is hard for you, Jet," Jack said, running a finger over his stubble. "But now we've got him, at least you can enjoy the time you have left."

"Terrific." Jet grinned, too many teeth. "Yeah, I think I might rewatch *Stranger Things*. Maybe knit a scarf. Try get some abs?"

"Jet, please come home." Mom sniffed. "We should be together, as a family."

Jet could go home. She'd done it before when things got too hard, the last time her body turned against her. She could, you know. She could.

But she'd made one hard choice, and now she made another.

"Sorry, I can't," Jet said. "There's just too much to do. And I need to enjoy the time I have left. Cops' orders."

Mom's lip twitched.

"We'll leave you to it, then," Detective Ecker said, chair creaking as he stood. "Let us know if you have any questions. And we'll inform you when JJ has been officially charged."

Jet nodded, following him with her eyes.

Ecker paused, turned to Jet's dad. "Scott, are you able to meet us back at the site on North Street? We have a few more questions to run through."

Jet's dad clapped his hands to his knees. "Sure," he said. "We'll be right behind you. Dianne?"

Mom stood up, stopped herself. Bent down to place one kiss to the top of Jet's head. It hurt, everywhere hurt. But that knot in her gut had loosened, finally let go.

The chief nodded by the door, and Jack left with a sad smile, first for Jet, then for Billy. Ecker was the last to leave, behind Jet's parents, closing the door with a click.

Billy followed, peered through the peephole, watching them all leave, voices fading down the stairs.

He turned back, a new glint in his eye, saved just for her.

"We don't think it was JJ, do we?" he said, head back against the door, voice hovering somewhere between resigned and excited.

Jet smiled, a real one, just the right amount of teeth. "No, we don't," she agreed. "I'm not saying it's *not* JJ, but I want to have answers to all of my questions before I can die happy. I'm not half-assing this one, Billy. I'm not dying a half-asser, you know that," she said. "Did JJ have access to that hammer brand, and where are the rest of the tools, then? How could he have known about the concrete going in on North Street, if he did? Who else had contact with JJ and Andrew at the fair, could have transferred that red hair? Could it have been Andrew Smith? Why is JJ's brother pretending he never worked for Mason Construction? And why are people in my family lying to me about the day I died?" She cracked her neck. "Let's start with Sophia."

Billy nodded, a sideways smile. "You never even thought about stopping, did you?"

"Maybe for a second," Jet said, meeting his eyes. "But I need to do this. I've got like three and a half days to live, and I need to be the one to find my killer. Anyway, do *you* want to stop? Smashing shit with sledgehammers, pissing Luke off, being an asshole because I'm dying and I'm allowed to be, having guns waved in our faces. I'm having fun, aren't you?"

EIGHTEEN

Jet tried to point at the screen, almost felt herself doing it, stared down at her lifeless arm. A phantom that moved in her head but not from the couch. OK, left hand then.

"See, look," she said. "Now Sophia comes back and it's 3:24. She's in the house for about five minutes before leaving again."

Billy nodded, watching Sophia on-screen, pulling up in her blue Range Rover.

"And this is just over an hour after she already dropped those cookies off?"

"Correct," Jet said as Sophia approached the front door, Cameron on her hip. "And when I asked her about it, she said she accidentally left her phone in the house, came back to get it."

"But she texted Luke at—"

"—3:06 p.m.," Jet finished for him, glancing at her notebook on the coffee table, at her handwritten times. The glance became a stare. Her handwriting. Such a small thing. The way her zeros slanted, the way her ds had no tail. She'd never write anything again, one small death already, a prelude to the main event. Jet swallowed, a slow sinking in her gut, a small blip of grief, tucked away with that other one: that she'd never drive her truck again either.

"But she told you she'd left her phone at your house between 2:21 p.m. and now." Billy paused as Sophia closed the front door behind her. "3:24."

"Yeah, so she lied." Jet turned to him. "I told you it was weird. On the day I'm murdered, she lies about not having her phone, about the reason she came back to the house. And then there's that *Call me* text at 10:52, when she and Luke were supposed to be together at the house, watching TV."

"What do you think that means?" Billy paused the video.

"I don't know." Jet chewed her thumb. Felt strange doing it on this side. "Maybe it was a *Call me because I just bashed your sister's head in six minutes ago.*" She pitched her voice higher, like Sophia's. "*And I've got her iPhone and I'm about to turn it off and dump it in the foundations on that North Street project because I know you're doing the concrete tomorrow morning, could you come and give me a hand? Oh, and how's the baby doing?*"

Billy tried not to smile at her impression. Was spot on, though; how had Jet not discovered this before?

"You really think Sophia could have killed you?"

"Maybe she doesn't like me much either." Sinking back to her normal voice, deep and ragged. "But there's clearly something going on. Something secret she was doing in the house on Halloween, that she doesn't want me or the police to know about."

"Connected to your attack?" Billy chewed his lip.

"Maybe."

"Oh," he said suddenly, eyes widening. Jet watched them in the darkened laptop screen. "Maybe she did forget something, but it wasn't her phone. It was something she was supposed to do, to get ready."

"Like what?" Jet held the reflection of his eyes. "Hide the hammer?"

"No, I was thinking about the door. Wasn't the back door unlocked? That's how the police think the killer got inside. What if someone made sure it was unlocked earlier in the day?" He stroked his fingers on the trackpad, awakening the laptop, pressing play. Sophia came back to life again, leaving the Masons' house without a glance at the camera, head down, eyes locked ahead, Cameron sucking on his pacifier.

"For herself?" Jet said, playing the scenario through in her head, reversing Sophia's steps, rewinding her into the kitchen, then the laundry room, flipping the latch to unlock the back door.

"Or someone else?" Billy suggested with a shrug.

Jet wrinkled her nose. "Like a hit man? Do we even have hit men in Woodstock? Hit women. Hit people."

"I don't think hit men use hammers," Billy said, backing down from the idea. "OK, let's think this through. I know it's the same day you were attacked, but could this just be a coincidence? I mean"—he gestured to the screen again—"has she ever done something like this before? Bake cookies, drop them off when you and your parents are out?"

Jet leaned forward, dropped her chin into her left hand, finger to her temple, thinking back. Did thinking make her head hurt more? Did remembering? That constant ache, simmering away, like a little fire. But it wasn't fire; it was blood, a slow leak.

"Yeah," Jet sniffed. "Maybe she has." Definitely not the first time Sophia had baked; it had happened enough times to start to piss Jet off. But when? "I think she made a cake for Mom's birthday. Yeah, she did. And she dropped it off during the day too. Said she didn't want to bring it to the restaurant we were meeting at later. And it was a fucking carrot cake. Vegetables in cakes."

"When?" Billy asked, finger on the trackpad, clicking back to the Ring dashboard.

"August thirtieth, Mom's birthday. Me and Mom and Dad were out during the day, visiting my aunt Laura. Came back to find the cake. *Isn't Sophia so thoughtful?*" Jet said, an impression of Mom now.

"Does it save data from that far back?" Billy checked the screen.

"Yeah, goes back one hundred and eighty days. Let me." Jet shoved Billy out of the way with her elbow, her left hand to the trackpad, finding the correct date on the dashboard. "Here. This must be Sophia."

She clicked on the video for *Motion Detected* at 12:07 p.m. that day.

Blue Range Rover pulling up on the driveway, parking.

The car door opened and Sophia stepped out, headed toward the backseat. She pulled out a different baby. Cameron from two months ago, a quarter of his life stripped back, you could tell: the size of him, less hair, pinker-faced, Sophia not struggling so much as she balanced him in one arm and a frosted cake in the other. In a plastic-topped container.

She put the container down on the front step as she pulled a set of keys out of the pocket of her denim shorts. Opened the door, eyes meeting the camera for just a second, alighting on Billy and Jet two months in the future. She took the cake inside and shut the door.

Jet skipped to the next *Motion Detected,* four minutes later: Sophia leaving, without the cake.

"OK," Billy said. "And does she—"

"—I think she does come back," Jet cut him off, clicking on the next video. "We didn't get back till like four that day, and this is 1:33 p.m. Yeah, look, it's her."

The blue Range Rover pulled up again. The same routine, minus the cake. Sophia in and out with Cameron, only inside for three minutes.

Billy leaned even closer to the screen. "What the hell is she doing?"

"Tell you what she's *not* doing," Jet answered. "She's *not* forgetting her phone. Here." Jet reached for her notebook and the pen resting on top, passed them to Billy. "Can you write the dates and times down? I—I can't anymore. Yeah, there's good. No, neater than that, Billy. You write like a four-year-old."

"Any other time you can think of?" He turned to her, pressed the pen to the corner of his mouth. "Any other baked goods that turned up when you were all out?"

"Yeah, actually," Jet said, finger on the trackpad, finding the date just as she said it. "Fourth of July. My parents had a cookout in the yard that evening. I remember Sophia dropped off some cookies, little American flags. Would have been when we were out at the store, buying Woodstock out of burgers. Which was weird, because Luke and Sophia were coming to the cookout, so I remember thinking: why didn't she just bring them then?"

Jet clicked play, *Motion Detected* at 10:47 a.m. that day. "Oh, OK, this is us leaving," Jet said, watching her parents walk out the front door, Mom cupping her eyes against the morning summer sun, buds and flowers where there were none now.

"Jet, hurry up!" Mom called back into the house. "We have a lot to do today."

"We have plenty of time," Summer Jet said, rushing out of the house, wearing the same Birkenstock clogs, not caked in mud. Both arms moving, hands in her hair, tying it into a stubby ponytail, so alive, so unaware that in four months' time she wouldn't be.

"Is JJ coming tonight?" Dad asked her. "We should get another pack of burgers, Dianne."

That Jet scratched her head. "I think he's busy. Maybe next time."

This Jet skipped ahead to the next time the camera detected motion.

"This is literally two minutes after we drove away from the house," Jet said, watching as Sophia's blue Range Rover peeled into the drive once more.

"Weird," Billy muttered. "Almost like she was close by, waiting for you guys to leave."

"Almost," Jet agreed.

Sophia got out of the car, wearing a denim jacket and a pale blue summer dress. She went to the back, pulled out a different baby again— even smaller, pinker, balder. Leaned farther in and emerged with a plate of red, white, and blue cookies, Saran-wrapped.

Cameron was fussing by the time she reached the door, grumbling through his pacifier.

"I know," Sophia cooed at him. "We'll just be a few minutes, I promise."

She opened the front door, took the baby and the cookies inside with her.

Jet started the next video, four minutes later.

The front door opened and Sophia walked out, both hands around the baby, the cookies gone, left inside.

Sophia checked her footing on the front step just as Cameron spat out his pacifier, bouncing off the ground.

He started to cry, now his mouth was unplugged.

"Oh no," Sophia said. "Mommy will get it, don't worry."

She bent forward, reaching for the green-and-white pacifier on the front path, and as she did, something fell out of her jacket pocket. Rattled loudly as it hit the ground.

"Whoopsie." Sophia's voice squeaked as she scrabbled for the white object rolling away from her, quickly stuffing it back in her pocket, a bulge in the denim. Then she grabbed the pacifier and walked to the car, Cameron's screams building.

"Wait." Jet rewound the video, dragging it back to the moment the white object hit the ground, too fast, too blurry. Jet paused, swiped her fingers on the trackpad to zoom in.

"What is that?" Billy asked, craning forward too. "A pill bottle?"

"Yes." Jet zoomed even closer. The object too tiny, too pixelated, but she recognized that band of pale blue across the bottom, the illegible blurred black writing and orange numbers near the top. "Lotrel," she said, her heart picking up, echoing the word back. "Five ten. Amlodipine besylate. One hundred capsules."

"How the hell can you read that?" Billy looked at her, impressed.

"I can't," she said. "I don't need to, I know it. Those are mine."

"What?" The look in his eyes changed, a tiny storm in the blue again.

"Those are my pills," Jet said, more sure now. "Lotrel. I recognize the bottle. It's for high blood pressure. I have to take one every day for my kidneys. Those are mine." She zoomed out again. "Why is Sophia stealing my pills?"

Billy blinked, but it didn't shake the storm. "Were they ever missing?"

"No," Jet said. "I would have noticed. I take one every morning. They're in the cabinet in my bathroom. Take it after I brush my teeth."

Billy returned to the screen. "Did she come back this time too?"

Another *Motion Detected* at 11:51 a.m. that day. Billy pressed play before Jet could.

Blue Range Rover.

Open door.

Sophia.

Blue dress and denim jacket.

Baby Cameron on her hip, a clean red pacifier in his mouth now.

Nothing in Sophia's hands this time. But there was something in her pocket, the same-shaped lump the pill bottle had made just over an hour before.

Jet pointed.

"She has the pills in her pocket still."

"Is she bringing them back?" Billy asked the screen as the front door closed behind Sophia. He clicked on the next video, recorded three minutes later.

Sophia time-jumped, walked back out of the house with Cameron, turned to shut the door behind her. The pocket of her denim jacket was flattened, the lump gone, which meant—

"—The pills are gone," Billy said.

"She must have put them back."

They turned to each other, eyes hooking on.

"Is that what she was doing all of these times? Mom's birthday? Halloween. Coming in to take my pills and then bring them back?"

Billy swallowed. "You think she's doing something to them?"

Jet reached forward, slammed the laptop shut, the sound echoing in her chest. Because what the fuck else could Sophia have been doing?

"Only one way to know for sure. Come on. I left the pills at home. Mom and Dad are at the North Street site—we need to go now, while they're out. Can you . . . can you help me with my jacket?"

NINETEEN

Jet waved to the doorbell camera, waved to her laptop back at Billy's apartment, waved to whoever might watch this footage after the end of this week, waved beyond the grave and even farther than that.

She slotted her keys in and pushed open the front door. It still smelled too clean in here, a chemical bite to the air even after three days. Billy coughed behind her.

A skittering of claws on the polished wood and Reggie rounded the corner.

He yipped when he saw Jet, speaking to her, yelling. Something like: *Where the fuck have you been, hi, hi, hi, I forgive you already.*

He jumped up, scrabbled at her legs.

"Hello handsome Sir Reginald the Woof." Jet dropped to her knees, left hand scratching behind Reggie's ear. "Who's a good boy, huh?"

His tail wagged his whole body, climbing up on her thighs to reach her face, nudging her lifeless arm with his nose.

"I can't do the double scritches anymore, bud, I'm sorry." Jet scratched even harder with one hand, Reggie leaning his head into it, eyes hooked on hers, almost the same shade of hazel. "You'll have to ask Billy very nicely." The dog squeaked. "But Billy is nice, so he'll say yes."

Reggie looked up at Billy, tail smacking Jet as he rested his head on her shoulder. She hugged the dog with one arm.

"It's better this way," she said quietly, resting her chin on the dog's fur. "I thought I was going to have to watch you die someday, after I stole you from Mom and Dad, obviously. Now I'll be the one checking out first. Sorry, bud. I would've missed you, and I know you'll miss me."

Billy bent over them, cupped both hands behind Reggie's ears and scratched away, his knuckles grazing Jet's neck.

Reggie closed his eyes and groaned.

"Yeah." Jet smiled. "That's the good stuff, huh? Told you Billy will look after you. He's good at that, huh? Better than me?"

"Could never be better than you." Billy smiled too, drew back.

"OK." Jet's knees cracked as she straightened up, Reggie circling between their legs. "Come on, Reg. We're on a mission, to see if my sister-in-law has been poisoning me for months."

She headed toward the stairs, Billy and Reggie following closely behind.

"You really think Sophia's been trying to kill you?" Billy asked, still taller than her, even though Jet was two steps up.

"Well, *someone* tried to kill me." Jet gestured to her messed-up head. "Maybe there was a first plan, to do it slowly. Then it got ex-exp-ex—fuck. You know that word, when something needs to happen sooner."

"Sped up?" he guessed.

"No, smarter than that."

"Accelerated?"

Jet pursed her lips, reached the landing. "No, but that will do. Then the plan got accelerated, swapped pills for a hammer."

Jet paused outside her bedroom, the door shut. It was never normally shut.

"But why would Sophia want to kill you?"

Jet grabbed the handle. No, *thought* about grabbing the handle, with the arm that no longer worked, still dominant even though it was gone. Used her left hand instead, overriding instinct, scolding herself.

"I can think of a reason," Jet said darkly, ushering the two boys into her bedroom. "Sophia cares about money, always has. When you're fifteen, you tell each other everything; she grew up with parents who couldn't afford much, always argued about money, and she said she would never live like that. She wanted to be like us, the Masons. I always thought that's why she really went for Luke. But, hey, I'm no romantic." She paused. "Maybe Sophia found out that Dad wasn't going to leave the company to Luke, because it wasn't fair on me. Well, if you get rid of me, you get rid of that problem."

"That's dark," Billy said, looking around.

"I think motives for murder usually are pretty dark. But it *is* my first time."

"Looks different in here." Billy gestured toward the bed, and the walls. Plain walls with dark baseboards, light cotton sheets, and neutral-patterned cushions.

"Yeah." Jet followed his eyes. "I guess you haven't been in here in like—"

"—Fourteen years," Billy finished.

"No more frog wallpaper." Jet clicked her tongue. "And the green bed is gone."

"Don't tell me you got rid of Mr. Rabbitson, the Fifth Earl of Wood-stock?"

"I'm not a monster," Jet scoffed, heading for the bathroom. "He's in the closet. One of his arms fell off, though. Ooh, foreshadowing."

Jet pushed the bathroom door open with her shoe, flicked on the light.

"OK. They're in here."

She approached the mirrored cabinet above the sink, her reflection drawing closer, that strange dilated eye, like it was lost in terror, always ready in fight-or-flight. Billy watched her face too, not his own—she caught him.

Jet opened the cabinet and banished both of them, reaching for the white pill bottle on the bottom shelf, her left arm getting tired, doing all this extra work.

"Here we go."

The pill bottle rattled as she carried it over to the toilet. She flipped the lid closed and sat on the floor, resting her elbows on top of the closed toilet.

Billy joined her, sitting on the opposite side, his knees grazing hers around the toilet bowl.

Reggie settled himself across the threshold, giving them some space, standing guard . . . lying guard. Facing the wrong way, actually.

Jet clenched the pill bottle in her fist, stared down at the childproof top. A push-down-and-twist kind of lid. She blew out her cheeks.

"Need me to open it?" Billy asked.

"Kind of feels anti-feminist if I let you do that."

"No one's watching."

"Apart from Reggie."

"He won't tell," Billy said, leaning forward, placing one hand over Jet's on the bottle, the other on the lid, pressing down and twisting it off. "There, you did most of the work. I just finished it off."

"Don't humor me." Jet looked inside the bottle.

"Yeah, you humor yourself too much already."

Jet tipped the bottle and poured the contents out against the white toilet lid. Little yellow capsules rolled everywhere, a small mountain gathering together in the center. Tiny black writing printed on each one: *Lotrel 2260.*

"What do these pills actually do?" Billy asked, picking one up to study it.

Jet did the same, pinching it in her left hand.

"It's a *calcium-channel blocker,*" Jet said, quoting from the packaging, long ago memorized from the times she'd forgotten to bring her phone to the bathroom with her, had to find something else to read. Shampoo bottle also worked in a pinch. "Treats high blood pressure, a side effect of PKD, which can make our kidneys worse, me and my dad. That's why we gotta take these. See anything strange?" Jet brought the capsule closer to her eye, picked up another one instead. They both looked normal, no dents, the top half aligned with the bottom.

"Not really," Billy said. "But you're the one who's taken them every day for years. You see anything strange?"

"Not really," Jet repeated him. "Can you open one up, pour out the powder?"

Billy screwed one of the small capsules between his fingers, working one end away from the other, splitting it into two halves, the powder sitting inside the bottom part. He bent forward and tapped the white powder out onto the toilet seat.

"Is that what it's supposed to look like?" Billy asked, his breath tickling the powder, scattering some.

Jet lowered her head, bringing her eyes down to the level of the powder, studied it. "Don't know," she whispered. "I've never opened one before. What does it taste like?"

Jet licked her left index finger and pressed it to the pile, the powder clinging to her damp skin. She stuck out her tongue and swiped her finger across, tasting it.

Her mouth filled with saliva to wash out the sharp taste.

"Not good?" Billy watched her face, tasting some too.

"I don't know," Jet said. "Tastes chemically. Chalky. Tastes like medicine, really."

"So maybe they aren't tampered with?" Billy pulled the same face, retracting his tongue.

"Well, I don't actually know what poison tastes like either. Probably chemically and chalky too."

"They don't look tampered with." Billy picked up another one. He unscrewed the two halves and then tucked them back together into a whole. "See, it doesn't look perfect now. There's a dent there, and that line isn't exactly aligned. It's hard to make it right again without denting it more." He tried. "I think we'd be able to tell if she'd opened every one and replaced the medicine with something else."

He held out the evidence to Jet and she picked up the slightly deformed capsule. He wasn't wrong.

"But we literally *saw* her taking my pills away, then coming back to plant them an hour later. What was she—" Jet's mind got there before her words did, not even a close race. At least that part of her brain still worked. "Not *my* pills," she hissed, scattering more powder, capsules rolling away from her. "My dad takes the same ones. It was *his* pills Sophia took. Come on. Can you—?"

Jet gestured to the mess on the toilet seat.

Billy understood perfectly, scooping the capsules with both hands, sliding them into the open bottle. He blew to clear away the last of the powder, re-screwing the lid and handing the bottle to Jet. Wrong hand. He blushed. Jet didn't.

"Come on."

Jet rattled as she left the bathroom, pill bottle swaying at her side, stepping over Reggie. He got up to follow immediately as they headed out of Jet's room, down the hallway toward her parents' bedroom.

The bed was immaculately made, always was. Old hardcover books on the wall-mounted shelves that weren't actually for reading, display only. The large French double doors leading to the balcony that looked out over the garden, over the pool.

Jet veered left, toward their en suite bathroom.

"His and hers sinks," Billy muttered. "Nice."

Jet smirked at him, through the ornate art deco mirror hanging in the center. She approached the sink on the left—*his*—placed her pill bottle on the counter, and reached up to open the wooden cabinet above. Her fingers closed around the matching bottle of Lotrel, and she turned to hand it to Billy, no speaking this time, no need to.

Billy pushed down and twisted the bottle open with a clack that echoed around the tiles.

"Here," Jet said, clearing space on her mom's dark oak vanity, pushing away bottles of perfume and makeup brushes.

Billy followed her over, tipped the pill bottle, and let the yellow capsules tumble out. More than had been in Jet's bottle, almost a full pack. Dad must have picked up his prescription last week sometime.

Jet pinched one carefully, raised it to her eye. There was a small dent in the capsule shell where one half met the other. The two white bands against the yellow background didn't quite line up as she rolled it between her thumb and finger.

"Shit," Billy said, studying a different pill, noticing the same thing. "These don't look like yours did. They look—"

"—Tampered with," Jet agreed, picking up a few more to be sure. "Open one, Billy."

He was already doing it, unscrewing a capsule, the job easier this time, like it had already been done once before.

He tapped the open capsule out, white powder trickling down against the dark wooden surface. It had a different texture than hers, the grains of white a little larger, a little shinier, like tiny crystals.

"That looks different," Billy commented, putting the empty shell down.

"That *is* different," Jet agreed. She dipped her finger into the powder.

"The taste test might not be useful." Billy watched Jet's finger move toward her mouth. "If she swapped it out with another medication, how would you be able to tell?"

Jet flicked her tongue out, pressed it to the powder.

It soaked through, disappearing in her mouth, the taste immediate and bitter.

Jet coughed. "I know exactly what that is. It's salt." Her eyes met Billy's. "Table salt. Try some."

Billy took a pinch, placed it inside his mouth. Swallowed. "Yep. Definitely salt." Like it stung his eyes too.

"Salt," Jet gasped, the taste sinking in, and the meaning behind it.

"What?"

"That's, like, the worst thing you could give someone with PKD," she said. "Open some more, check them."

Billy did.

"Salt," he said. "Salt again. And here. They're all salt, Jet."

Her gut twisted, made a break for her spine, hairs reacting, standing up.

"We're supposed to follow low-sodium diets," she said. "Can't even have the good fucking cheese. Salt increases your blood pressure, and if Dad hasn't actually been taking Lotrel for months, but a whole bunch of salt instead . . . oh my god." Jet leaned against the wall, hand slipping on the tiles. "You've seen him. That's why he's det-de-d—got so much worse this year. His kidneys have started to fail, doctors talking about transplant or dialysis soon." She took a breath, hardened her voice, coming out of shock, finding rage on the way. "Because Sophia has been poisoning him. She's been killing him."

"Fuck," Billy hissed, tucking his hands under his armpits. "Fuck." Because no other word would do.

"Fuck," Jet said too, kicking out at the legs of the vanity, making the yellow pills judder and roll. "Seems there was more than one murder going on in the same fucking house. And if Sophia is willing to kill one *in-law*, then . . ." Jet pointed to herself, thumb screwing into her chest.

Billy gestured to the pills. "What should we do? Take these to the police?"

"Fuck the police. No offense to your dad." She sniffed. "They're convinced it's JJ. I don't have time to wait around un-convincing them. This is for me, not them. I will deal with Sophia. And I don't want my dad taking any more of these."

Jet scooped up as many pills as she could in her left hand.

"Grab the rest," she told Billy, heading toward the toilet.

She dropped the yellow capsules in, floating and twirling in the waiting water, keeping just one, sliding it into her back pocket.

Billy followed her, double-handed, with the rest.

Jet flushed and the pills disappeared in a rushing whirlwind, Billy's hand skimming hers as they watched, side by side.

"To Sophia's house?" he asked.

Jet cracked her neck, bit down on her back teeth.

"There's going to be a lot of yelling, isn't there?"

"I'll go in alone," Jet said. "I'll get more out of her alone. You wait down the street."

"But—"

"—Don't worry, I won't turn my back on her, in case she has any more hammers lying around. I want to see her face when she realizes that I know. That she's been killing my dad. Should have just kept you as my best friend, huh, Billy? You're not the poisoning type."

Billy sniffed. "Yeah, you should've."

"One more thing."

Jet walked back to her dad's sink, picked up her bottle of Lotrel pills, untampered with. She placed them in her dad's cabinet, in the exact same spot where his had lived, closed the door.

Her final gift to him. Jet didn't need the pills anymore. And maybe it wasn't too late for her dad.

She caught herself in the mirror again, the fire behind both eyes, filling that endless black pit and whatever lay underneath, held together with screws and wire mesh.

"To Sophia's," Jet said. "I am going to . . . fuck . . . her . . . u—"

TWENTY

"Up?" Sophia asked, singsong high, looking down at the baby, both his arms raised. "You want *up* out of the high chair?"

At least Cameron wasn't still screaming, like this morning.

He changed his mind, lowering his arms, shoving another tiny floret of broccoli into his mouth, mashing it around.

"Sorry, Jet." Sophia ruffled Cameron's hair. "Right in the middle of dinnertime. What were you saying?"

"How was Pilates this morning?"

Sophia pursed her lips. "Um, it was good. Why?"

"Just checking in with you, sister. Having a chitchat, see how your day's been." Jet leaned against the doorway, only half in the kitchen. "Mine's been a bit shit, thanks for asking. Been to the hospital, can't move my right arm anymore, so that's an interesting development on top of the whole only-having-three-and-a-half-days-left-to-live thing. But I'm glad Pilates was good."

Jet crossed the threshold into the room, spotting something on the counter. "Stop it," she almost laughed. "More baking?" She pointed to the cake on the side, white icing, blue edging. "Aren't you just the perfect housewife?"

"Oh." Sophia handed Cameron a piece of shredded chicken. "That's for Cameron's best friend, Noah. It's his first birthday tomorrow, having a little party."

"You're too much, Sophia," Jet said darkly, staring down at the cake. "Make the rest of us look bad."

"Haven't finished it yet." Sophia stepped closer, throwing a dish towel over her shoulder. "Need to do the writing."

Jet nodded. "Where's that going? In the middle, here?" Jet pointed down at the cake, pretended to write with her finger. "*Happy First Birthday Noah.*" But her finger kept going, an indent in the icing, then a hole, then right the way through, grabbing an entire handful right out the middle.

"Jet!" Sophia shrieked. "What are you doing? You've ruined it!"

"Just tasting it." Jet brought the handful to her mouth, took a huge bite. Cloying and sweet, sticking to her tongue.

Cameron giggled.

"Jet!"

"Hold on," Jet said, mouth full of cake, stuffing the rest in, chewing. She pulled a face. "My god, Sophia. Waaaaay too much salt. What are you trying to do, poison these kids?"

Sophia's eyes widened, feet rooted to the spot. Had she caught that? Jet hoped she'd caught that.

"You've got icing on your face," Sophia said, sharpening the letters, letting them hiss.

"I know," Jet said. "And Cameron's got broccoli on his. Excuse me."

Jet walked right over to Sophia, too close, looking up into her eyes as she wiped the clumps of cake and icing off on the dish towel, getting some on Sophia's clothes, sucking the rest off her fingers, wiping again.

"What has gotten into you?" Sophia lowered her voice to a whisper.

"An aneurysm, apparently." Jet stepped back. "You should listen to what I said about the salt. Can be really dangerous to eat too much, especially for someone who has PKD."

"I have no idea what you're talking about." Sophia hadn't moved.

"Oh, really? No idea?"

"No." Sophia dropped the dish towel into the sink. "You can't just come in here and—"

Jet placed the little yellow capsule down on the counter.

Sophia's eyes snapped to it.

"Is this where you'd do it?" Jet gestured around with one arm. "The kitchen? Pour the medicine down the sink, fill each one with salt instead, put them back together. That's fiddly work." Jet flexed her chin, like she was impressed. "One hundred pills in each bottle. No wonder it took you over an hour each time."

"I don't know what you're—"

"—Yes, you do. Don't be boring, Sophia, I don't have time for it." Jet folded her arms. "The doorbell camera has footage of you taking the pills out of the house. Coming back an hour later to put them back, after you'd replaced each one with salt. You thought no one would figure it out? Fourth of July. Mom's birthday. Halloween. It's been going on at least four months, maybe longer."

Sophia pressed her lips together, a tight line.

"Oh good, no more denials," Jet said. "Guess we're being grown-ups now, huh?" She wiped her face on her sleeve, more clumps of crystalline icing. "Honestly, I thought it was me at first, the one you were poisoning. Got excited, seeing as I'm looking for who murdered me. But, no, it's Dad. You've been poisoning him for months, Sophia. Killing him."

Sophia's mouth opened with a pop of saliva.

"Don't be so dramatic, Jet. I wasn't trying to *kill* him."

"You were poisoning him. Every day. With salt. The man with the dodgy kidneys. They're starting to fail. He'll need dialysis or a transplant soon or he'll die. You did that to him. That sure looks a lot like killing somebody to me—"

"—not to *kill* him." Sophia shook her head like the idea was ridiculous, and so was Jet. "I was going to stop as soon as . . . I just wanted him to get a little sicker, just for a little while."

"Why the fuck—"

"—So that he'd realize it was time to retire, time to take his health seriously."

"Seriously?" Jet snapped, stealing Sophia's word, changing it.

"Oh, come on, Jet, I thought we were being grown-ups." Sophia sniffed. "We all know he was supposed to have retired by now. It's been two years since he said he would. Luke has been waiting for so long. I was just trying to . . . speed that process along. Give Scott a little push, make him finally let go of the company. I was not trying to *kill* him," she spat the word.

"Ah, sure," Jet laughed, deep and empty. "Poisoning someone so they retire early is completely different from poisoning someone so they die early. One is definitely morally justified, Sophia, you're right. I shouldn't have questioned your fucking principles."

"Shut up, Jet. We all do what we have to do."

Jet clutched her right arm at the elbow, edged her way toward another question, studying Sophia's eyes for a reaction. "And you think Dad is going to leave Mason Construction to Luke?"

"Yes, of course he will, eventually," Sophia said, no change in her eyes.

Jet's heart kicked up, reacting instead. Sophia must not have known about Dad's plan to sell the company to Nell Jankowski. And did that mean Sophia no longer had a motive to bash Jet's head in with a hammer? Killing one Mason, but not the other?

Sophia was still talking. "He just has to retire first. He wants to, your dad, he's tired, he's ready. I'm not just doing this for me. This is for all of us."

"Yeah, you're such a fucking saint, Sophia. Thank god you married into the family."

"You're so ungrateful, Jet. Always have been. That's why you never got anywhere."

"Oh, and you went somewhere?" Jet rounded on her. "'Cause it looks to me like the only place you went is my brother's bed."

"Ah, she finally says it."

"Says what?"

Sophia flashed her eyes. "I've always known you were unhappy that I married Luke!"

"I'm more unhappy that you've been slowly murdering my dad so you and Luke can take his company, actually!"

A muscle twitched in Sophia's jaw. "Luke has worked really hard. The company came close to going under last year, and Luke is the one who turned everything around. He deserves this!" Her voice faltered, came back weaker. "Why do you hate me so much, Jet?"

Jet widened her eyes, gestured to the small yellow pill.

"No," Sophia sniffed. "Before this. Before Luke. What did I ever do to you?"

"Are you joking?" Jet got stronger as Sophia weakened, shrank back. "You abandoned me, Sophia. I used to think of you as a sister; we spent every day together. Then I go away to college, and everything is scary and new and I don't really belong, and I needed you and you stopped answering! You weren't there!"

Sophia shook her head. "Funny," she said. "'Cause that's not how I remember it. You're the one who stopped responding to me, Jet. I didn't have anybody when you left Woodstock. You were my everything, and then you were gone, so focused on Dartmouth, on trying to be Emily, that you forgot to be yourself."

That stung, Jet felt it behind the eyes. "No!" she barked. "You never met Emily. You don't get to talk about her like you know anything. You stopped responding first."

"I remember it differently."

"You remember it wrong!"

"Fine!" Sophia snapped, coming back. "You can hate me as much as you want, but I did this for Luke. I'd do anything for him, for the people I care about."

"Poisoning your father-in-law seems a step too far, if you ask me," Jet said. "Why couldn't you just wait until Dad was ready to retire?"

"Luke can't wait," Sophia said, tensing like she'd accidentally said too much.

"Why?" Jet stepped closer. "Why can't Luke wait? Has he done something?"

"No, no, no," Sophia said, two *nos* too many. "He's just waited too long already, that's all."

"Sophia," Jet growled. "Tell me."

"There's nothing to tell!"

"Where were you when I was being murdered?" She stepped forward again, squishing a piece of cake into the floor. "10:46 p.m. on Halloween.

I know you and Luke weren't here together, like you said. One of you was out. Was it you? Was it him?"

Sophia blinked. "I don't know what you're talking ab—"

"—Not this again," Jet cut her off. "Yes, you do. You lied to me. You texted Luke, saying *Call me* at 10:52 that night. Look, go get your phone, if you want to keep playing dumb. One of you was not in the house like you said. Was it you, Sophia? Where were you?"

Sophia blinked. "I was here," she said, voice deflating.

"So it was Luke?" Jet pressed. "Luke went somewhere?"

"No."

"Sophia, tell me!"

"I can't tell you anything! Luke was here with me!"

"You're lying!"

"I'm not!"

"What about those cuts on his hands?" Jet pressed even harder. "Did he come home with those?"

"Luke didn't leave home!"

"Oh, fuck off, Sophia."

"Not everything is about you, Jet," she shouted. "The world doesn't revolve around you, you know!"

"Well, I'm the one dying this week, so it can revolve around me just a little bit, 'kay? Temporarily."

Jet drew back, a phantom itch at the back of her neck, heat just below the surface. She pointed to the Lotrel capsule.

"Does Luke know? About you poisoning Dad? Did you plan this togeth—"

"—No, he doesn't know." Sophia sniffed, a wet sucking sound, though there weren't any tears. "And, Jet, you can't tell him. You have to promise me you won't tell him."

Jet folded her lip, scoffed in Sophia's desperate face. "I'm not promising you shit."

Sophia grabbed Jet's arm. Her right arm. Jet only knew because she watched her do it, couldn't feel a thing. Sophia could squeeze as tight as she wanted, dig those nails right in, and Jet wouldn't flinch. Not a bit.

"No, Jet. You can't tell Luke about this."

Jet narrowed her eyes, took aim, right up through Sophia's head. "I can do whatever I want. I've got three days to live. No consequences, Sophia."

She shoved Sophia away.

Walked past Cameron—happily picking away at the rest of his broccoli—toward the hallway.

"You've been spending a lot of time with Billy Finney this week, haven't you?" Sophia called after her, breathless between the words, forcing them out.

Jet ignored her, kept going for the front door.

"Does Billy know?" she called. "What you did to him? How you ruined his life?"

Jet's feet faltered, stopping her on the welcome mat. She pressed her teeth together, swallowed the guilt back where it belonged. Deep down. Farther than that.

"If you tell Luke about the pills, Jet, I'll tell Billy about his mom!"

Jet's heart followed the guilt, down into her gut, hissing in the acid.

"Fuck you, Sophia!"

"Fuck you, Jet!"

"Don't fucking swear in front of the fucking baby!" Jet yelled, wrenching the front door open.

Dark outside, the moon hanging low in the sky.

She slammed the door behind her.

They still had a jack-o'-lantern on the front porch, uneven toothy smile that was closer to a smirk, like Sophia's, upside-down triangle eyes, just starting to soften and sag.

Jet let it take over, the rage, starting in her gut, chewing on her doubled-up heart, clawing behind her eyes. She smashed her heel down onto the jack-o'-lantern and the pumpkin exploded, orange innards everywhere. She stamped again, and again, until it was flat, just chunks and the little stringy goo that held them together.

It helped, actually, to pretend it was Sophia.

The rage burned itself out, but Jet suddenly lit up, here on the porch. A spotlight—no, two. Covering her eyes against the glare.

Headlights.

A car pulling up on the drive, parking beside the blue Range Rover. It was Luke, coming home from work.

Jet scraped the pumpkin guts from the sole of her shoe—these Birkenstocks, man, been through a lot this week—and hurried down the steps, reaching the car before Luke had even switched the engine off.

Left hand. She grabbed the passenger door handle and opened it, dropping inside, shutting them in together.

"Um, hi." Luke stared across at her, keys clutched in his hand. Scabs starting to peel off his knuckles.

"Yeah, um, hi," Jet replied.

"Did you just smash our pumpkin?" He looked through the window beyond her.

"Yeah, I was mad," Jet said, no hesitation. "Where's my list?"

"What?"

"The list of Mason Construction employees, Luke."

Luke pinched his nose, sighed. "Fuck, Jet, I forgot."

"You forgot?" Jet leaned closer, a new glimmer of rage with a different face. This one lived in her chest. "Not like this is life-or-death or anything, Luke."

"I'm sorry." His eyes flashed, catching the moonlight, reflecting it back at her. "Work has been crazy, with the North Street site shutting down and—"

"—Is there a reason you don't want me to see it?" Jet said, knowing there must be, that there was something more here. "Because you've sure been stalling a lot."

"I just forgot, sorry." He looked down.

"I don't think you would forget. You know I have three days to live, how important this is to me. What's going on, Luke?"

"Huh?"

"Just tell me. I know something's going on."

"There's nothing going on."

"You didn't kill me, did you, Luke?" Jet laughed but it was cold, empty, not quite sure of itself.

His jaw tensed, chewing on the stale air inside the car.

"You seriously asking me that?"

"You weren't here, at home, during the time when I was attacked. I know you lied about that."

He sniffed. "Yes, I was. Me and Sophia—"

"—Sophia just told me," Jet said, a lie of her own. But she was pretty sure she was right, that Sophia had been home, and Luke hadn't. "Those grazes on your hands, you didn't get them Friday morning. There's photos of you at the fair, Luke, I've seen them. Your hands are fine. You must have hurt them after, sometime Friday night."

"While I was smashing your head in with a hammer?" he asked, a laugh, just as empty.

"I'm just asking."

"Well, don't." Luke wiped his face, stubble hissing against his fingers. "You know it wasn't me. You're my sister, why would I want to kill you?"

Jet sat back. She could think of only one reason: if Luke knew about Dad's plan to sell to Nell Jankowski, if getting rid of Jet was his only option.

Silence, too heavy, pressing down on Jet's shoulders as she watched her brother, scoring his fingernail along the metal of his keys.

"Is . . ." Jet faltered, tried again. "Is getting Dad's company really that important to you?"

Luke laughed, pressed the keys into his palm, little teeth leaving indents behind, marking him. "The most important. It's literally the only thing that matters."

"Really?" Jet asked, trying to find his eyes. "Like you've spent your whole life fixated on this one goal, on achieving this one thing to prove to everyone that you can. And when you have—when you finally get it—life can actually, really begin, and you'll finally be happy? Like that?"

"Yeah." Luke stared ahead. "Something like that."

"But do you think it will?" Jet looked out the windshield too. "Make you happy?"

Luke thought about it, sucking in all the air, leaving none for Jet. Pushed it back out.

"Yes, I do," he said. "It has to." He glanced over. "Why?"

Jet shrugged. "Just been thinking. About you and me, how we grew up. If we really understand what *happy* is supposed to look like. Because of Emily, because of what happened. Always being compared to her, the things she was going to do. Happened so much that I wonder if we think that life is just about constantly comparing ourselves. To Emily, to each other, to everyone else. To prove something, to Dad, to Mom especially. Like we can be good enough too. But is that right? Is that what it's all supposed to be about or . . ." Jet trailed off. She didn't know where that was going either, what came after the *or,* what other choice there was. It was a stupid thought, blood leaking into her brain, making her think stupid things.

"No, I don't think about that," Luke said, shutting her down, unbuckling his seatbelt, like he was finished with this conversation.

But Jet wasn't, and the world revolved around her this week.

"You know," she said, raising her voice, bringing him back in. "You know you've always said you would give Dad one of your kidneys?"

Luke nodded, something new in his eyes, shifting. "I would have given you one too."

Jet smiled, too wide. "Lucky it's my brain that's killing me, because you really can only give away *one* kidney, Luke."

"Right."

"Well," Jet said, "you might have to do that, for Dad, sooner rather than later. You can thank your wife for that."

"What are you talking about?" He looked across at her.

"Tell Sophia Jet said to ask about the Lotrel and the salt." She smiled. "Make sure you do—it's a pretty funny story, actually."

Jet leaned her left arm across herself, reaching for the door handle. "My right arm doesn't work anymore," she explained, catching the confusion on Luke's face, opening the door. "Aneurysm's leaking. Means it'll only be a few days, so . . ."

Jet stared out the open door, the wind picking up, howling as it trespassed inside the car.

She swung one leg out, hesitated, turned back.

"Luke?"

"Jet?"

If Luke knew about Dad's plan to sell the company to Nell Jankowski, then that gave him motive, and Jet couldn't write him off. Even though he was her brother, even though they grew up together, even though he was supposed to be her ally, even though no one had truly felt like an ally inside the war zone of 10 College Hill Road, after Emily died.

His reaction would tell Jet everything she needed to know.

"I found something out," she said, choosing her words carefully. "And I think I should tell you, because it's you, and it's me."

Luke shifted in his seat, facing her. "What?"

Jet swallowed. Luke could never hide his temper, never, so if it came out, then didn't that clear him?

"Dad isn't planning to leave the company to you," she said, quickly, before she lost her nerve. "I know that's what we all thought his plan was, when he retired. But . . ."

A shadow crossed Luke's eyes, face shifting, crowding the corners of his mouth.

". . . He's planning to sell the company, to Nell Jankowski," Jet continued, studying Luke, watching the shadow spread farther, bringing a flush of angry red out in his cheeks, creeping down his neck. "She owns a big home construction business, wants to expand here in Woodstock. Dad's planning to sell to her, because he doesn't think it's fair to give you the company when he has two kids. Even though I would have never wanted it, Luke, you know that."

His bottom lip dropped open, teeth bared.

"Is this true?" he said, voice just a dark whisper, holding it all back. "Or are you trying to hurt me?"

"It's true," Jet said. "I spoke to Nell."

Luke exploded, came apart at the seams, his eyes empty black holes, mouth one too. "Fuck!" he roared, strings of saliva binding his teeth, just about holding his face together. "FUCK!"

He punched the steering wheel.

Screamed.

Punched it again with the other hand, opening the scabs on his knuckles, a trickle of blood across his wedding ring.

"Fuck!" Luke screeched, taken over by his temper, possessed by it, hitting the steering wheel over and over.

The horn rang out as his fist connected.

And again.

Kept going, bloody knuckles, like the noise fueled him somehow. The soundtrack to his fury.

"FUCK!"

Jet stepped out of the car, left the door open, left her brother behind. She walked down the darkened street.

Luke's screams and the staccato of the wailing horn followed her all the way.

TWENTY-ONE

A car beeped outside on Central Street, the sound rattling the windows in Billy's apartment, breaking up the silence.

Then Billy broke it again.

"I'm sorry, we're going to *what*?"

He stared at her, sandwich clutched between his hands, open-mouthed, matching the bite mark in the bread.

"We're going to break into Mason Construction," Jet said, pulling her jacket zipper all the way to the top, one-handed. She could do it now, if Billy started it off for her, pulled the two halves together, up a few inches. "You really should listen the first time."

"I did listen, I was just giving you a chance to reconsider." He abandoned the sandwich.

"I've considered," Jet said. "Reconsidered." Grunting as she stepped into her shoes again. "And re-reconsidered. Luke is hiding something. There's a reason he doesn't want me to have that list of employees; he's not *that* forgetful. What's the time now?"

Billy tapped his phone screen. "Nine-forty."

"Perfect," Jet said. "No one will be there. All ours."

"And what will we be looking for?" Billy folded his arms, hugged them over his chest, wearing the same shirt Jet had borrowed last night at the bar.

"That damn list," Jet hissed. "And the reason Luke is being so cagey about it. He didn't know about Nell Jankowski, but there's something going on at Mason Construction, I'm sure of it. Why Sophia felt she had to poison my dad to make him retire sooner, stop him poking around. She said Luke couldn't wait. And I want to know why. Because maybe it's the same reason someone took a hammer to my head five days ago. It's all connected to the company, so that's where we're going."

She moved toward the closet, her dead arm catching on the back of the couch, making her stumble. Or maybe it was the fact that everything had doubled again, her eyes tripping over the interwoven edges, Jet trying to find her way through, somewhere down the middle.

"You got a flashlight?"

"Er, yeah." Billy pointed. "Should be in that closet, maybe on top of the tool kit."

"Duct tape?" Jet asked, pulling the closet door open, missing the handle the first time, scrabbling to its left.

"Why do we need duct tape?"

"Billy."

"In one of those side pockets, I think."

Jet found the flashlight resting on top, the tape just on the shelf beside. Struggled to hold them both in one hand as she avoided Mrs. Finney's eyes in the framed photo above.

"And you've got the flashlight on your ph-phone." She nodded toward it, on the counter. The nodding unbalanced her.

"You going to eat anything before we go?" Billy asked. "The sandwich I made you?"

"Not hungry." She leaned against the wall, tried to blink the world back together. Blink. Stitch it. Glue it. Hell, duct tape it. Blink.

"Jet." Billy softened his voice, already cloud-soft. And what was softer than a cloud? "You sure you're OK to do this? You don't look—"

"—I'm not dead yet," she sniffed, wiping her nose on her sleeve.

"No," Billy whispered.

"Not quite." Jet forced out her old man laugh, gruff and breathy, stopped because it hurt her head. "You ready?"

"To break and enter? To commit a crime?"

"*I'm* committing the crime, Billy." She hooked her good arm through his. "You're just the getaway driver. And the get-there driver. You're my Emotional Support Billy."

"Physical support too, huh?" he said, arm tensing, holding Jet up, taking half her weight.

"Just for the stairs. I'll be good in a minute."

"Can't believe we're really doing this." He scooped up Jet's truck keys from the counter, and his phone.

"Best week of your life, huh, Billy?"

"You said it, Jet."

THE TREES LOOMED over them, thickening the darkness, hiding the moon. They shook their leaves, some kind of ancient warning, snatches of sugary red and fiery orange in the headlights. One perfect leaf dropped onto the windshield, making Billy swerve.

"Nervous?" Jet said.

"Nope," he answered too quickly.

They were on Hartland Hill Road, the road out of town, not quite out of it yet, and they never would be, because Dad's offices were coming up on the left.

"Pull up over here." Jet pointed through the windshield. "Don't go down the drive. There's a camera on the gate."

Billy pulled off the road, tires scraping gravel, coming to a sudden stop in the grass, his foot clumsy on the brake.

"Careful!" Jet said.

"We've already had this discussion." Billy pulled up the parking brake. "If I'm driving, you're not allowed to criticize."

"Actually, we said I was allowed to criticize twice per trip. I got one more left."

"Not my fault anyway," Billy said. "Brakes are too sensitive."

Jet gasped, placed her left hand on the dashboard, leaned forward to whisper: "He didn't mean that, baby."

"So what's the plan?" Billy turned to her, across the darkness, whites of his eyes and whites of his teeth.

"I'll go inside, cover the cameras, turn off the security alarm." Jet swallowed. "Go find some incriminating spreadsheet or something, which explains Luke's behavior, points right to my killer, and we solve my murder and go home and get a large beer. Easy-peasy."

"No problemo," Billy answered.

"Keep the change, ya filthy animal."

"Yippee ki-yay," Billy said, leaving the best bit for Jet:

"Motherfucker."

"OK, let's go." Billy opened his door, stepped out.

"You're coming in?" Jet got out. "I thought you were staying in the truck?"

Billy smirked. "And let you have all the fun?"

"Ah, so you *are* having fun? It kinda suits you."

Billy's smile deepened, pushing out one side.

"But wait, really." Jet grabbed his arm, wearing the duct tape like an oversized bracelet. "You know you can still get in trouble, right? I've got a get-out-of-jail-free card. It's called dying. You don't."

Billy looked down, gently pressed Jet's bandage, one corner that was peeling off.

"I'm obviously coming in with you," he said. "I go where you go. Best friend shit, yeah?"

Thank fuck, because Jet really hadn't wanted to go in alone. Not that she was scared—no, remember, she couldn't get scared anymore. But it was just nice, to have a Billy again. She grinned at him, her gut unclenching, heart spinning, both at home when Billy was right here beside her. How had she forgotten, for so many years, this easy feeling she only had around him? Nothing to prove, and no reason to try.

"Yeah," she agreed. "We'll make up a handshake later."

Billy flared his nostrils. "You've forgotten our handshake?"

"Come on."

Billy hesitated, glancing back at the powder-blue truck.

"Won't someone spot the truck, driving past? Not exactly subtle."

Jet shrugged. "Nah. They'll probably think it's just two teenagers, screwing around, because his parents are religious and hers are light sleepers."

"Your mind," Billy muttered, shaking his head, following her down the drive.

"I know," she said. "You can keep it, when I'm gone. Pickle it, in a jar."

"Jet, stop."

She did stop, because the gate was right up ahead.

Jet grabbed a handful of Billy's shirt, dragging him off the drive and into the tree line.

"Camera faces this way." She didn't let go of him. "We can sneak up behind it, cover the lens with tape."

"Have you done this before?" Billy whispered.

"What?"

"Crimes?"

"No," Jet snorted. "But I've watched TV, so . . ."

They walked slowly, together, skirting the thick undergrowth that lined the drive, eyes on the gate, the big white-and-blue sign that read: *Mason Construction.* A little boxy logo of a house, two windows and a roof.

Jet pointed out the small white camera, mounted on one of the posts.

They approached it from behind, hidden in the shadows, in its blind spot.

"I'm too small," Jet said. "And one-armed. Can you . . . ?"

Billy took the duct tape from her wrist, pulled a section free—hissing like a trapped wasp—and tore it off with his teeth. He reached up and around, pressing the tape over the front of the camera, adding another piece to be sure.

Jet walked over to the gate, stepped in front of the taped-up camera, and flipped it off. She'd only said it as a joke, but maybe she really was having fun. Billy too, joining her in front of the blind camera, raising his shirt up, flashing the pale flesh of his tight belly, even giving it a nipple.

Jet laughed, crashing into him.

Billy held her up, pointing to the keypad in the middle of the gate.

"You know the code?"

"Yeah." Jet clicked on the flashlight, pointing the beam at the metal keypad, trying to ignore that she saw two beams where there should be one. "I came to work here, actually, for a couple months, after I left Boston. Had to leave because Luke was too annoying about it, thought he'd start pissing in all the corners, claiming his territory. I didn't want to be here anyway."

She handed Billy the flashlight, freeing up her hand.

Pressed her finger to the buttons, the metal cold, stinging her skin.

"022492," she said aloud as she punched it in. "Emily's birthday."

The gate buzzed, grating in her ears as it swung open, letting them through.

"Breaking and entering," Billy muttered, following Jet as she turned the corner, the brick-and-metal building sitting there, waiting for them against the dark sky.

"Just entering for now," Jet corrected. "Haven't broken anything. Yet."

They passed a parking lot, regimented rows of white vans with the *Mason Construction* logo emblazoned on the side. A small army, Woodstock's own.

"There's a camera on the main entrance too." Jet pointed, Billy's flashlight following her finger. "Careful," she hissed, "don't let it see the light. If you hide behind the wall and reach over, you should be able to get the tape on it."

"Yeah, I can do that," Billy said, sizing it up. "You wait here."

He passed the flashlight back, fingers grazing hers, and hurried over to the wall, using it as cover. He tore off a long bit of tape, dropped the roll into his pocket, and pressed his back to the wall, pausing to shoot two thumbs up at Jet.

She shot one back, just one, all she had.

Billy sidled over to the corner, peered around, his hand following his eyes, reaching. Reaching harder.

"Two inches up," Jet said.

He found it, pressing the tape over the lens, winding the spare around the back of the camera.

"Nailed it," Jet said, patting him on the back.

"They don't record sound, right?"

"Just picture."

"They're gonna know someone was here, though." Billy glanced over his shoulder, wincing as the wind rattled the trees, throwing whispers at them. "That the cameras were tampered with."

"Nah, I doubt Dad even checks them," Jet said. "Unless he has reason to."

Billy nodded. "Let's not give him a reason to, then."

"Yep," Jet agreed. "We'll leave everything as we find it. Don't worry, they'll never know."

Billy pointed to the lock on the front door, the building pitch black behind the glass.

"Got the key?" he asked.

Jet pressed her lips together. "Not exactly."

"Did TV teach you how to pick a lock, Jet?" Billy shot her a look.

"Don't need to. There's a lockbox." She pointed to the little black box mounted against the wall, behind a plant pot, a combination lock across its face. "But I love your faith in me as a master criminal. Let's keep that energy going."

She shuffled the pot out a few inches, bent down, started sliding the numbers of the lock.

"Emily's birthday again?" Billy asked.

"No." Jet strained, the plant tickling her face. "It's actually just *zero-zero- zero- zero*. Kept telling Dad that wasn't very secure. Got it."

She pulled the front of the lockbox open, scrabbled inside for the key. Passed it to Billy, who slid it into the lock.

"OK, don't freak out," Jet warned him. "The alarm will start to beep. But it's fine, I know the code to disable it before it goes off. And that *is* Emily's birthday again."

"Won't freak out." Billy twisted the key and pushed open the heavy door.

The alarm woke up, started to chirp, ushering them through into the darkness inside.

Billy held the door for Jet, his hand on her back, closed it behind her.

"OK." She approached the alarm, eye height on the inside wall, its screen illuminated, counting down. *57 seconds, 56. System armed*, it said. *Enter code?*

Yes, she was going to. Pressed the rubber buttons: *022492 enter.*

The alarm beeped at her, in between the chirps.

Code attempt 1 of 3, it said.

Jet's heart made a break for it, thrumming in the base of her throat.

"Fuck." She smacked her fist against the wall. "They've changed the code."

"OK." Billy's voice behind her, breathy and panicked. "Now I'm freaking out. Try something else? Another birthday?"

40 seconds. 39.

Jet tried Luke's next: *051695 enter.*

The keypad beeped again, angrier now.

Code attempt 2 of 3.

"Fuck," Jet hissed. "Not Luke's."

"Jet."

22 seconds. 21. 20.

One last attempt, one final chance.

Jet pressed the buttons: *120597.* Her birthday, exactly one month away. She hadn't noticed that, hadn't registered the date. Would never make it to twenty-eight.

11 seconds.

10.

9.

"Jet."

She pressed enter.

A high-pitch tone erupted, clashing with the chirps, and then . . .

Silence.

Just the ringing in Jet's ears, a ghostly echo trapped inside her skull.

Code entered. System disarmed.

"Oh thank god," Billy said, dropping his head, chin to his chest.

"Well, would you look at that." She turned to him. "*My* birthday. Guess Dad really is all about being fair. One dead daughter for the gate, another dead daughter for the alarm."

Billy bent forward, blew out two chipmunk cheeks of air.

"You'll live, Billy," Jet said, giving his shoulder a squeeze. "Come on, the office part is upstairs."

"Lights?" Billy asked, pointing to the switch.

Jet steadied her flashlight instead. "Let's keep them off—someone might spot them from the road."

"Right." Billy pulled out his phone, swiped the screen to bring up the flashlight.

They walked through the warehouse, several towers of pallets wrapped in clear plastic, piles of shimmering blue bathroom tiles stacked inside. Beyond them, rows of huge wooden timber beams, long enough to mock the trees they came from. Twenty years ago, Jet would have tried to balance-beam on those, but Luke and Emily could always stay on longer. Not the kind of siblings who ever let her win.

"This way."

Through the show kitchen at the back of the warehouse that Jet always found creepy: a kitchen where no kitchen should be, stools at the breakfast bar where only ghosts ever sat.

Through the door, down the corridor to the base of the metal stairs.

Their steps hollow and too loud as they walked up, two beams carving through the darkness. Well, actually, four beams and double darkness, but don't tell Billy that.

Jet shouldered the door at the top, metal becoming carpet underfoot.

She swung the flashlight across the open-plan office space, the beam reflecting off the windows and sleeping computer screens, winking back at them.

"How many people work up here?" Billy asked, trying to count the desks.

"Think there's about fifteen full-time in this office." Jet ventured forward, checking her path with the light. "Dad has his own separate office down the hall, next to the kitchen." She showed Billy with the beam. "Luke doesn't have his own office, but Dad let him have a partition. This way."

She led Billy through the office to the back right corner. Luke's corner. A folded screen made of white-painted wood and thin glass, to separate his desk from the others. Not quite his own office, but all he was going to get.

Jet dropped into Luke's chair, way too high, her feet dangling above the ground. It squeaked as she took it for a spin, hand on the desk to catch herself.

Luke's MacBook screen caught the flashlight, held it there, open on the desk, connected by HDMI to a larger external monitor.

"OK," Jet said, wiggling the mouse, clicking to wake the computer up.

It blinked into life. The lock screen was a family photo of Luke, Sophia, and Cameron taken on the Fourth of July, sprinkles of fireworks dripping onto their shoulders from the background. A gray box blocking out the baby's eyes, asking Jet for the password.

"I'm guessing this can't be Emily's birthday too?" Billy said, deflating, kneeling beside Jet, head almost as high as hers.

"No." Jet stretched the fingers of her left hand. "But there's a high chance it's the same password he uses on his iPhone."

"And you know that?"

"You know it too." Jet sniffed. "He told us this morning, about thirteen hours ago, when I unlocked his phone to check his messages with Sophia."

Billy's mouth dropped open, a twinkle in his eyes. Impressed. "You remember that?"

"I'm good at remembering numbers and all other kinds of useless shit, Billy," Jet said, pressing *213024* on the keyboard. "That's how I passed all my exams. Must have had a good math teacher."

She regretted it almost instantly, wincing, the guilt reacting to the sudden change in heat, simmering away.

Billy blinked. "Better math teacher than she was a mom."

Jet hesitated. Should she say something; did Billy want her to? "That's not true, Billy."

"Shitty math teacher too?"

"No, she was a good mom. You used to talk about her all the time. I actually used to get a little jealous."

"Yeah," he sniffed, voice hollow. "She was. Probably my best friend after you found Sophia instead. Until she decided to leave me and Dad with no explanation."

Jet didn't know how to respond, so she didn't. She pressed enter and crossed her fingers . . . not literally, had no fingers to spare.

The home screen jumped out at them, icons and files covering every inch of the desktop.

"It worked," Jet hissed, catching Billy's eyes across the darkness.

She picked up the mouse and guided the on-screen arrow, double-clicking on *Finder* to bring up Luke's files.

"Doesn't take two of us to go through one computer." Billy straightened up. "I should keep looking. Does he have files in his desk or . . . ?" He opened a couple of drawers; just pens, a calculator, a tangled yarn ball of cords with different-shaped heads and metal teeth.

"There's a whole room of filing cabinets." Jet turned to him. "I think Dad's old-school, likes to keep hard copies of invoices and whatever. It's the little room, beyond the kitchen. That way." She pointed with her flashlight.

"OK, I'll go look in there."

Billy walked away, then came right back, the flashlight on his phone pointed up at his face, distorting it with strange upward shadows.

"Um," he said. "What am I looking for?"

"Anything," Jet replied, unhelpfully.

"Anything. Yeah, cool. Got it," Billy muttered to himself, walking away and out of sight, the darkness claiming him.

"Yell if you find anything," Jet called to him.

"Yeah, you too," his voice floated back, Jet smiling as she caught it.

She turned back to the screen. Where first? She clicked on *Documents* and about fifty blue file icons filled the page. Hmm, this could take a while.

Instead, Jet clicked on the little magnifying glass to bring up the search bar.

Coleby hammer, she typed into it, frustrated at how slow it was, typing with one hand, and her weaker hand at that.

Pressed enter.

No results.

Just *Coleby,* deleting *hammer.*

No results.

Fuck it, fine, wasn't going to be that easy. Not a document that said, *Oh hey, Jet, I see you're looking for your murder weapon. Here's a handy little order form with the exact employee who owns that tool kit.*

The hard way, then.

She clicked on a folder named *Important Work Files,* then *Finances,* then *2025,* then kept going, clicking through an entire Russian doll of folders, each one eaten by the last.

Eventually she found an Excel spreadsheet called *October 2025 Payroll,* last edited a few days ago. Double-clicked to open it up, dragged it over to the larger monitor.

She rubbed one eye and then the other with her left hand, tried to read the screen, even though every letter and number had more edges than they should.

It helped when she squinted, sharpened it a little.

A list of employees' names down the left-hand side, starting with those who worked full-time in the office, Scott Mason and Luke Mason at the very top, moving down through names Jet recognized to ones she didn't: the contractors. Their salary or pay rate. Hours worked. Any overtime. Then a highlighted column for *Gross Pay,* the total amount at the bottom.

Jet scanned the list of names for Henry Lim. He wasn't on here. But there was another name missing too, nagging at the back of Jet's mind, she was sure. No, she wasn't. She went back over the list of names, those who worked in the office, these desks right in front of her, these people she knew, many since she was a kid. Under her dad and her brother, there was Carl, yes, Maria, yes, Amal, yes. Jet's eyes skipped ahead. Wait, where was Angie? Angie Rice? She'd worked at the company for over twenty years. Had she retired and Jet missed it? Her name wasn't here.

Jet used her elbow, rolled away from the desk, pushed herself to her feet.

She grabbed her flashlight and stumbled out of Luke's corner, crashing into Carl's desk with the arm she couldn't feel, searching. Scanning the desks with her eyes and her light.

Not that one.

No, that's Amal's.

Didn't know this person, must be new.

Here.

The flashlight reflected off the dead computer screen, and then off something else. A photo frame propped up on the desk, beside a pot of pens.

Jet put the flashlight in her mouth, between her teeth, and picked up the frame.

It was Angie Rice, grinning at the camera, her arms around her two grandkids.

"Knew it," Jet whispered to herself, awkward with her teeth gritted around the flashlight. She put the frame back, the light catching something else.

A Post-it note, stuck to the monitor screen: *Angie—can you get back to Reid about the new designs on Maple?*

Angie Rice *did* still work here; this was her desk. So why was her name not on the payroll last month?

Jet hurried back to Luke's desk, back to the screen. She studied the list of names again, going through them all, pressing her finger to each cell of the spreadsheet, checking them off.

"No Angie."

Back to the files, Jet opened the payroll from September. Scanned again. No Angie, no Henry. August. The same: no Angie or Henry. July, June. Nope. May, April. Nothing. All the way back to March, then February. Back when Jet was still with JJ, when she knew Henry was working for Mason Construction. But the spreadsheet called her a liar, because his name still wasn't here. And neither was Angie's.

Something cold danced up her spine, spider-leg fast, setting off the pain in her head.

She grunted, pressed her palm to her eye, to the invisible knife behind it.

Why were their names missing? Was it just an error—Luke forgot to type them into the spreadsheet?

Jet clicked the back arrow on the files, again and again. Came out of *Payroll* and into a folder named *Tax Filings,* then *Payroll Taxes,* then *FICA.*

She clicked on a file, opening a 941 form for October's tax return.

She studied it, made her head hurt more. Thought this was supposed to be fun.

It matched. The numbers matched those on the spreadsheet.

And for September, August, July.

So, if it was an error, then Luke had made the same one here. And people like Luke didn't make errors on something as important as federal taxes.

Jet clicked out of taxes into a folder called *Insurance,* then *Workers' Compensation Insurance.* Clicked the document for the most recent filing, the premiums Mason Construction was paying to the insurer. The records matched; it detailed the same number of employees as listed in the payroll, the number that didn't include Henry or Angie.

"Did you call me?" Billy's voice sailed through the dark office, making Jet jump, the arrow careering off the screen.

"No," she said, watching as he came around the corner, a small pile of papers clutched in his hand.

"Oh." Billy flexed his lip, lighting Jet up with his phone. "Thought I heard something. You found anything?" He gestured to the screen.

"Maybe," Jet said. "Did you find anything?"

"Maybe."

"You go first." Jet spun in her chair to face him.

"OK, so I was looking through the files at random." Billy leaned against Luke's desk. "Really boring, by the way. And then I found a folder for a project labeled *19 Pleasant Street.*"

"19 Pleasant Street," Jet repeated. "That's Gerry Clay's house."

"That's what I thought." Billy saluted her with his papers. "Most of it looks fine. They were doing a front extension about twelve months ago, remodeling the front of the house and fitting a new kitchen, right?"

"Right."

"And then, for the kitchen stuff, I found this invoice here, a client invoice, so this one was for Gerry, from Mason Construction." He held up one of the sheets of paper.

Jet pretended to scan the page, but her eyes tripped up over themselves, not just doubled, doubled on top of doubled, a tangled mess of black lines. Didn't help that Billy couldn't hold it still.

"So here"—he pointed—"they charged Gerry twelve thousand dollars for *White Calacatta Marble,* for the countertops. Sixty square feet. For materials alone, right?"

"Right."

"But." Billy held on to the word, switching to the sheet of paper below. "This here is an order confirmation form, from a place called Imperial Marble. And the order was for sixty square feet, right, but it was for *Standard Italian White Marble.* And it cost seven thousand dollars."

Jet swallowed, felt it slide all the way to her gut.

"That's . . . different," she said.

"Five thousand bucks different," Billy added, holding up the two pages side by side.

"Invoice fraud?" Jet said in a small voice. "Has Luke been committing invoice fraud? Pocketing the difference?"

"This is the only example I found, but I can keep looking." Billy sniffed, shuffling his papers. "But I think you'll want to see this first. You know Henry Lim was acting strange, told us he didn't ever work for the company when you know he did?"

"Yeah," Jet said, turning to the screen, "about that—"

"—Well, I found a folder that had a lot of paperwork for the project on North Street."

Jet turned back. "You did?"

"Haven't been through it all yet, but look."

He handed her a sheet of paper. Jet laid it on the desk, picked up her flashlight.

"It's a delivery notice, from a scaffolding rental company, to North Street. Look who signed it off, who accepted the delivery."

Jet could read this one, big looping writing in the box that said, *Sign here.*

"Henry Lim," she said, reading out his signature. "I knew it. And he was on the North Street project too. When was this from?"

Billy prodded his finger against the top of the page. "Third of March, this year," he said.

But Henry hadn't been on the March payroll. What the fuck was going on here?

"March," Jet said. "That must have been right before his accide . . ." she trailed off, abandoning the word, her mind busy with other words, *what ifs* and *maybes*.

"Jet—"

"—Shh, thinking."

She looked back at the screen, the pieces slotting into place, not a puzzle but a house, four walls but no roof, and somehow there was space for it inside her busted-open head.

"Oh my god, Luke," she whispered.

"What?" Billy dropped to his knees again, eye to eye.

"It's not just invoice fraud," Jet said, voice coming back to her, bringing her heart up to her throat with it. "It's tax fraud too. Luke is the one who does the payroll, the taxes. There are employees and contractors who are missing from the payroll, and the tax filings. There's Henry but there's also Angie Rice, and I know she works here because her desk is right over fucking there." She pointed. "That's only two of them, but there must be more we don't know about. Luke must be paying them, but not on the books. Under the table. Maybe cash. Maybe from his own money, I don't know. Then he doesn't have to file payroll taxes for them—he saves that money for the company. Federal taxes, Medicare, Social Security, he wouldn't have to pay any of it if their wages aren't reported. He's been doing this for months, maybe even years, since he took over all the finance stuff." She swallowed, pointing to the screen. "Insurance fraud too. Because he's misreporting the number of employees to their workers' comp insurance provider. And if one of those unreported employees doesn't have workers' comp, it means that if something happened at work, if they got injured, they wouldn't have access to healthcare or salary compensation."

"Wait," Billy said, catching on, building a picture of his own.

"Remember that prick Jimmy, the foreman?" Jet said. "He mentioned there was an accident on North Street. That a roof collapsed, injuring the worker who was still inside. And the project was delayed and Luke had to change his plans."

"Do you think that worker was—"

"—I think that was Henry." Jet nodded. "I don't think he got drunk and fell off a wall in March, blinding himself in one eye and shattering his kneecap. I think it happened while he was at work, for Mason Construction, working on Andrew Smith's old house when a roof collapsed on him."

"Fuck," Billy said, his mouth staying open, long after the word.

"And Henry would have been fucked," Jet said. "He would have had to pay for all of it himself, the hospital stay, the surgeries, the treatments. That could have cost, like, tens of thousands of dollars."

"Maybe more," Billy said. "And remember, he said he needed another surgery now, to save his other eye, but he couldn't afford it."

Jet nodded, adding that to the picture as well. "Luke would be fucked too, the one actually committing the crime here. If Henry ever told anyone, if anyone found out what Luke . . ." She swallowed, and by the look in Billy's eyes, she could tell his mind had gone to the same dark place.

"Does this mean—" he started. "Would this give Henry a motive? If Luke did this to him, if he hated him for it, could he have—"

"—killed me, to hurt Luke, or send him a warning, or blackmail him for the money he desperately needs?" Jet completed their shared thought. "I don't know."

"And he worked on the North Street site," Billy thought aloud. "Maybe he kept track of the work after—maybe he knew about the foundations going in the morning after Halloween. Fuck."

"Fuck," Jet agreed, standing up, the chair spinning a full circle without her. "I should email these files to myself. The payroll, tax returns. You go back to the files, see if you can find—"

Jet choked on air as it erupted with sound.

A sharp wailing noise, screeching ear to ear, and between them too, inside, Jet's skull vibrating with it.

She clapped one hand over one ear, Billy covering both of his.

"What the fuck?" Jet screamed over the two-tone high-pitched whine. "I disabled the security alarm! You saw it, it said *disarmed*!"

Billy stared across at her, his phone and its silver light pressed against his face, making his watery eyes glow in the dark.

They shifted, something new in them, shock giving way to something worse.

"I don't think that's the security alarm!" Billy screamed back. "Jet, do you smell smoke?!"

TWENTY-TWO

Jet didn't need to smell it; she could see it now, dancing in the beam of her flashlight. Smoke creeping out of the carpet beneath their feet and up, gathering into a dark cloud against the ceiling, skulking over them.

"The building's on fire!" Billy screamed. "We need to leave!"

Jet's feet wouldn't move, rooted there, the floor growing warm through the soles of her shoes, warmer, into hot. They needed to leave, yes, she knew that, but for some reason she couldn't make herself move, her brain left behind, back twenty seconds ago when it was still quiet, her heart seized in her chest, so fast, like it wasn't even beating at all, erased by the blare of that alarm.

The building was on fire? How was the fucking building on fire? Her mind stuck on that part first.

"Jet!" Billy screamed over the alarm, in her face now. He grabbed her working arm, pulled her back into life. "Run!"

She finally moved, brain back in her body, moving with her, fear taking over.

"Wait!" Jet snatched her arm from Billy, doubled back toward Luke's desk. "We need these!"

She grabbed the pile of papers Billy had found, scrunching them around the flashlight, holding it all in one hand.

"Jet, let's go!"

"Right behind you!"

She ran to catch up.

"No, you go first, I've got you!"

Billy caught her, pushed her ahead, his hand pressed to her back, the smoke thickening the darkness around them.

They moved together, past Angie Rice's desk.

Darting around another.

Steps faster than the repeating pattern of the alarm, racing it to the door.

Billy crashed into it first, grabbed the handle, hauled it open.

A wall of heat slammed into them, clawing at Jet's eyes, too hot, too bright.

"Oh my god," she said—not that she could hear herself, over the alarm or the growl of the flames.

It was all gone. Nothing but fire, licking up the walls, hungry, crackling, an angry laugh as it destroyed everything, screamed for more. Everywhere. Reaching up toward them, claiming half the staircase. The metal steps screeched as they buckled and bent in the heat.

Not a corridor anymore, just a tunnel of flame, building, growing stronger as it bent around toward the warehouse. The deepest reds and the blackest smoke spilling out in a firestorm, faster, hungrier. Not a warehouse anymore, it was hell broken open, raging right beneath the office.

Jet coughed, the thick black smoke reaching them first, claiming them. But it wasn't just smoke she could smell. There was something sharper, more acrid.

Gas.

Billy grabbed Jet by the shoulders, pulled her back, kicking the door shut.

The smoke found other ways in, through the cracks, through the floor.

"Is there another way down?" Billy screamed, scrabbling at Jet's neck, pulling her shirt up over her nose. He coughed, then covered his own.

"Another staircase at the back!" Jet yelled through the fabric, holding it with her one hand, flashlight and papers still gripped in her fingers.

"Go!"

Billy pushed her ahead, back through the office. The smoke hovered lower now, eye level, blinding them, stealing everything but each other.

Jet crashed into a desk, a sharp pain above her knee. Kept going.

She couldn't see, she couldn't see, the flashlight only found more whirls of smoke, lighting it from within. She wanted to take Billy's hand, but she couldn't see it, had no hands to spare.

Couldn't see, couldn't see.

She planted her foot and the floor cracked beside it, a fault line of bright glowing orange that she could see.

Could see.

The floor crumbled away, down, an earthquake groan as it ruptured, melting into the inferno below.

Jet stumbled away from the hole, that widening mouth, falling back, crashing down.

She watched as it happened. She could see now, too much, the flames finding their way up here, clambering out of that hole down into hell.

With another groan, one of the desks tipped, lost its legs. It slid into that gaping mouth, lost to the flames below. Angie Rice's desk, the photo frame tumbling in first.

Jet could see Billy now, on the other side of hell.

"No, don't!" she screamed, too late.

Billy jumped clean over the chasm, crashing to his knees beside her.

He wrapped his arms under hers, dragged her to her feet.

"This way!"

They ran the other side, away from the flames chasing behind them, eating up the carpet in widening rings. Finding more to consume. The desks. The walls.

Heat like nothing Jet had ever felt before, bearing down against her skin, pushing from behind, a sharp stab of it against her fingers.

Jet glanced down.

She screamed.

The papers clutched in her hand were on fire.

She dropped them.

The flashlight falling too.

A little white glowing triangle, abandoned behind her.

The floor gave way and ate that too.

"Run!" she screamed as she and Billy barreled into the hall beyond, past Dad's office and the filing room, past the kitchen on the left.

Jet's dead arm thrashed as she sprinted, a puppet arm without a string, unbalancing her, throwing her off.

"That door, down the end!"

They were almost there, and Jet could hear herself now. The alarm wasn't blaring anymore; must have burned, melted away with everything else.

They reached the door together, Billy slamming down on the handle.

"No!" he screamed. "It's stuck!" Tried again, double-handed, rattling the handle up and down. "I'll get this open. Stand back!"

Jet did, clearing the way, choking on the smoke, covering her nose to breathe her own air instead, watching as Billy backed up from the door.

He kicked off his heels and bounded toward the door in three fast strides.

Rammed his shoulder into it, hard.

It jolted but didn't open.

Billy drew back, three steps, threw himself at the door again.

It buckled, gave him a few inches, not enough.

Billy backed up again and Jet blinked and they weren't here anymore, on the brink of hell, the world crumbling around them. Jet was behind a computer and Billy was on-screen, breaking down another door, ramming it with his shoulder. Screaming her name like if he screamed hard enough, it could bring her back to life.

"Jet!" The same scream now.

Jet blinked, brought herself back to hell.

Billy had done it, tumbling through the open door into the stairwell.

No smoke swarming in this way, the stairs clear.

They were out.

Jet took a step forward and it all came undone.

The floor split in front of her with a deafening roar, a gorge opening up.

The wall, the one separating them from the office, folded over, caved in. Shrieking as it fell to the flames, plugging the hole, bringing some of the roof down with it.

Jet looked up, could see the stars, before the smoke stole them away.

She couldn't see Billy anymore, on the other side of all that rubble.

But she heard him.

"Jet!" he screamed. "Jet, are you OK?!"

Jet coughed, a hacking sound against her hand.

"Billy, go!" she yelled. "You're out! Go!"

"No, Jet! I'm not leaving without you!"

"You have to!"

"No!"

Jet stepped back, the ground groaning beneath her.

"Billy! Go, now! The whole thing is going to come down!"

"Not without you!"

Jet's throat seized, a fist around her heart.

"Go, Billy! You have to leave! You have to live!"

She stepped back again.

"Not going without you!"

"Yes you are!" she screamed, voice fighting the flames, the sigh of the dying building. "I have three days left! I'm already dead, Billy! You're not, you have to live!"

"No!"

"Billy, you go! You leave or I will never fucking forgive you!" Her voice cracked, not the ground. "And I will die hating you, I swear. Go! Please, Billy! For me!"

His voice wasn't there anymore, just the sound of boots striking the metal steps, doubled up, like a heartbeat.

Good, he was gone, he was safe.

Billy had to live.

But so did she.

Jet's body absorbed the heat, used it, lit a fire in her gut.

Yes, she only had three days left to live. But those three days were hers, and she was not going to let hell take them from her. They were hers, and she was going to fucking live them, every small moment, stretch each minute into a lifetime.

Jet had to live.

And the other side of that too, came crashing in, her breath shuddering with it.

She didn't want to die.

She did not want to die.

Her heart screamed it and her head too, guiding her feet back.

She was scared to die.

She would not die.

All that fear she thought she'd lost, because the dying didn't need fear but the living did, it all came rushing back, wearing her skin, roaring in her ears.

Jet flinched, jumping out of the way of a burning ceiling panel, and she ran.

Back down the corridor, charging through the door into her dad's office.

Shutting the door like it could stand between her and hell, keep it at bay.

To the window at the back.

Jet slammed into it, staring down through the glass, blinking away the smoke.

Yes, she was right.

About ten feet below the window was the tilted roof of a long, narrow lean-to. A covered storage area against the wall down there. Better than jumping out the second story of a burning building and hoping for the best, and that was Option B.

She just had to get the window open. A sash window, only two panes of glass between her and living.

Jet reached up, undid the catch in the middle, the smoke gathering around her, forcing its way into her throat.

She coughed.

She choked.

She grabbed the handle on the lower half of the window and she pulled.

It didn't move.

No, no, why wouldn't it move?

The window was stuck, or her left arm was too weak.

She needed both arms, needed two hands. Fuck.

Jet pulled again, straining, through her fingers all the way up through her neck, screaming with the effort.

"I am not going to die!" she yelled at the window, at her own ghostly reflection.

She lifted one foot, drove it into the windowsill to give her left arm more power, and she pulled.

The window didn't move.

"Fuck you!" Jet coughed.

Smash the glass, smash the glass, she needed something to smash the glass.

Not going to die, not going to die.

The computer on Dad's desk? That was heavy. No, too heavy, Jet couldn't pick it up with one hand. Something else, something else.

A large gold pot in the corner with a sad-looking palm plant inside, too green among all this smoke.

Jet picked it up and ran, ramming it into the window, the plant still inside.

The pot shattered but the window did not, dirt and leaves scattering over her feet.

"Fuck!" she roared.

The door behind her was on fire now, the wall too, the flames finding her, closing in.

Trapped inside her dad's office.

Not going to die here; she was not going to die.

Something else.

On the desk, beside the computer, was a large photo frame. It looked heavy, the frame made of marble or something close to it.

A photo of the Masons. Jet just a squinting red-faced kid, probably thinking about frogs. Mom, Dad, Emily, Luke. That final summer, before five Masons became four.

Jet grabbed it because she was not going to die.

She stumbled through the smoke, back to the window, raised her good arm, and struck.

The corner of the stone frame smacked into the window. Glass broke, not from the window, from the photo, one shard still covering Luke, the rest breaking away, glitters of glass catching in the folds of Jet's jacket.

She struck again, harder, and the window cracked, a spiderweb in a split second, spreading, anchoring itself.

Jet pulled back, aimed for the middle of the web.

She drove the corner through and the window shattered, giving way to the outside world.

Air.

It rushed inside and Jet sucked at it, the cold breeze finding her red-raw face.

The smoke pushed her out of the way, rolling out to claim the sky.

The carpet on fire behind her.

No time, no time to breathe.

Jet smashed the rest of the glass, punching it out with the frame, clearing the bottom ledge.

Then she dropped the photo, wrapped her left hand around the sill.

Pulled herself up onto the ledge, one leg, then two, sitting on the edge.

No time for second thoughts, not even first thoughts.

Jet rolled forward and let go.

She fell, long enough to think, *I'm falling.*

Hit the roof of the lean-to feetfirst, then her back, winded, all the air forced out of her, the smoke too.

She was still moving, rolling.

Going to roll right off the edge, she couldn't stop herself, not with one arm and—

Two hands caught her, appearing out of the dark night, strong against the shoulder she could feel, and the one she couldn't.

Billy pulled her to her feet, standing on the roof of the lean-to, his face dirty from ash, a cut on his neck, trickle of blood, even brighter against the grime.

"You came back," Jet said, voice ragged.

"You got out," Billy said, wiping his eyes. "Don't make me do that again, OK?" The words shook in his throat. "Don't make me leave you. I was going up inside that window if you didn't come out of it. That's not fair, Jet. Not fair."

A thunderous creak behind them as something collapsed inside the building, whining, crying, feeding the fire.

"Got to get out of here." Billy took her good hand, led her along the lean-to. "There's a dumpster over here with pallets inside, that's how I climbed up."

Billy went first, jumping down. Then he turned back, standing on the edge of the yellow dumpster.

"Sit on the edge and drop down. I can catch you."

He did catch her, but he lost his footing, stepping back on the shifting pallets, falling over. Jet landed on Billy, head on his chest, rolled off, a corner of a wooden pallet sticking into her lower back.

She didn't move. Billy didn't either.

They lay there for a stolen moment, staring up at the burning building.

At the window Jet had just come out of, angry flames licking at the frame, escaping outside and up the bricks.

"We almost died," Billy said quietly.

"We're alive," Jet said instead.

"I smelled gas."

"Me too." Jet coughed. "Someone set fire to it."

"While we were inside," Billy added.

Jet looked over at him. "*Because* we were inside?"

A new sound joined the roar of the flames, fighting it, not winning yet, too far away. A high-pitched whine, keening up and down.

"Sirens." Jet sat up. "We need to go before they get here."

She groaned, picking herself up from the pallets one-handed, jumping down to the grass, Billy behind her.

Through the parking lot, around the vans, a loud crash behind them as half a wall caved in, scattering bricks, dragging a section of the upper floor down with it. Sparks as it landed, a snowfall of dark ash.

Billy pressed his lips together.

"We weren't supposed to break anything."

"*We* didn't," Jet told him.

They walked back through the main gate, the sensor opening it for them, sirens getting louder, closer, a werewolf howl at a not-full moon.

"Should we uncover the security cameras?" Billy asked, pointing to the taped-up camera, the one they'd danced in front of only an hour ago.

"Hmm, I think they'll probably be able to tell someone's been here," Jet said, another crash behind, another wall collapsing.

They followed the drive around, Jet's blue truck there, waiting for them.

Jet hesitated, looked back.

Mason Construction was gone—everything her dad had built. Didn't look like a building anymore, folding in around the inferno. Its death throes were loud, almost human, the hiss of things burning not far from a scream. The moon above blocked out by a roiling column of black smoke.

Something else hovered in the sky too, near the smoke: a little red light winking, a dark mechanical shadow against the darker sky.

"Is that . . . is that a drone over there?" Jet squinted.

"Come on." Billy opened the truck door. "They're almost here. We have to go."

Jet could see them now too, red and blue flashes in the trees, right the way down the dark road, speeding toward them.

She opened the passenger door, dropped inside as Billy started the engine.

"Go, go, go!"

JET DIPPED HER head under the stream of water. Reached out, turned the shower colder, colder still. Her skin felt too hot, like the fire had infected her, made itself at home, reminding her how close she'd come, a bit of hell that stayed behind.

The water soaked through her bandages, but she didn't care. Needed that smell of smoke out of her hair.

A burn on her left index finger that she could feel.

A burn on her right arm that she couldn't. A big one, above the elbow, bits of melted fabric from her jacket stuck in the wound, fused with it.

A cut on her knee, a nebula of bruised skin already forming around it.

A gash on her left palm, from the broken window.

But the worst of it was this feeling in her chest. Too tight, squeezing her heart out of place, into the base of her throat.

And those words she still couldn't let go of, even though the danger had passed.

Her lip quivered and her eyes stung.

She pressed them shut and wished it away, this feeling. It couldn't help her.

Turned the shower even colder, her skin ridging with goosebumps.

Her chest tightened, the more she pretended to ignore it, couldn't swallow past her stupid heart.

Jet turned the shower off, had been in here long enough, and the water couldn't wash that feeling away.

Pushed the door open with her good elbow.

Grabbed the towel with her good hand.

How could you . . . how could you wrap a towel around you with only one hand?

Fuck.

That almost did it, broke her in half, but Jet held herself together, even though she only had one hand to do it.

She stood there, naked, dripping, a puddle on the tiles.

Pinched her dead arm, because how dare it leave her to die like that?

Tried something else.

Stuffed one corner of the towel in the gap in the radiator, enough to hold it firm.

Bent down and tried to wrap herself into it, holding the other side.

The towel came free, dropped to the floor.

A frustrated growl that made Jet's eyes sting harder, made them swim.

She blinked them back, tried again.

Stuffed the corner in farther, so it wouldn't tug free. Held the other side in her left hand, wrapped herself inside it, knees bent, spinning, awkward. She just about made it, catching the other corner half a second before it made a break for it.

Both corners in one hand.

She tightened her fist, holding the towel together under her right armpit, covering herself.

She turned.

Stopped.

Stared at the closed bathroom door, no hands to open it.

That almost did it too, pressing her lips together to stop them from shaking, her chin buckling, ready to go, to take her down with it.

No. Jet refused. She raised her foot, pressed her toes against the metal handle, pushed down.

The door opened and she stumbled out.

Billy was sitting on the couch, Jet's notebook open in his lap.

"Oh good, you're out." He glanced up, then back down at the page. "So, I've been thinking. If we think the person who started the fire did it because they were trying to kill you, and it's likely the same person who attacked you on Halloween, then that means we—"

Something about Billy's face did it, took Jet all the way down, no hope of coming back up, of stopping it.

She started to cry.

The tears hot and fast, chest seizing around them.

Billy's eyes stretched too wide, hurting to see her hurt. He put the notebook down, stood up.

"What's wrong?" he said, voice soft. Not prying, just asking. Poor, sweet Billy.

Jet sniffed, tears pooling at the crack in her lips as they parted.

"I . . . I can't hold my towel up with one hand," she cried.

Billy stepped closer.

"Is that really why?" he asked, even softer.

"No." Jet shook her head, snatching her breath between, building up to it. Those words. "Billy," she said, little more than a wet whisper. "I don't want to die."

That did it, broke her all the way.

Not just tears anymore, a howl in the back of her throat, breaking into sad little couplets as she tried to breathe through it. She couldn't. The air couldn't get past her heart.

"I don't want to die."

Billy closed the distance between them in two strides, wrapping his arms around a wet and shivering Jet.

He took the towel ends out of Jet's hand, and she let him.

He crossed his arms around her back and held the towel up for her.

"I'm scared," Jet cried, her arm free, hand pressing up against Billy's chest, her forehead joining it, the tip of her nose. "I don't want to die."

She cried.

Her wet hair dripped and her nose streamed, and the tears doubled up, chasing each other but there were no winners, all soaking into Billy. Her sobs shook both of them, but Billy stood firm, his hands strong and warm against her damp, exposed back.

Jet cried, balling her fist, a handful of his shirt.

Billy bent down, resting his chin against the top of her broken head.

Then his nose.

Then his lips, pressing one kiss into her hair, staying there, his hot breath down her cold neck.

Jet cried.

And Billy stood there and took them all, holding up her towel.

THURSDAY
NOVEMBER 6

Jet knocked, just twice.

Bent down to call through the mail slot into the little house.

"Henry, it's Jet," she shouted. "Try not to almost shoot me this time."

Billy's breath rattled, sucked through his teeth.

"Don't think we should be here," he said again, jittery and nervous. "If Henry's our prime suspect for the person who tried to kill you on Halloween, and the person who tried to burn you to death last night to stop you from discovering *why* he tried to kill you in the first place, what's to stop him trying a third time? And he has a gun and—"

The door opened and Billy swallowed the rest of it, an actual gulp, as Henry's face appeared in the crack. The bruise beneath his eye greener than yesterday.

"Hi," Jet said, with a fake smile. "Us again."

Henry stood back, let the door open fully. No gun.

"They arrested JJ," he sniffed, fiddling with his hands. "Yesterday. He came back, and they took him away in handcuffs."

"I know," Jet said.

"He just wanted to see you," Henry said, quietly. "It wasn't him, Jet. JJ didn't do this to you, I promise."

"How could you know that?" Jet pressed him, keeping her voice light so he didn't realize he was being pressed.

"I just . . ." he trailed off, no answer.

Jet would have to press harder, then, more like a push.

"Hey, maybe you can invite us in this time?" She stepped forward, one foot up over the doorstep, crossing the threshold without permission.

"Um, OK." Henry blinked, beckoned them inside. "It's all a bit messed up, from when the police searched it."

"What were they searching for?" Jet followed Henry down the hall, Billy closing the front door behind them.

"Took the clothes he was wearing on Halloween. Some of his mail too."

Henry gestured them into the living room, no messier than she remembered it.

Jet sat down in her old spot, on the corner of the faded red couch, Billy slotting in beside her, too close, his hands balled into fists on his knees.

Henry took the armchair. That was where JJ normally sat.

Jet cleared her throat, still raw from the smoke, or maybe from the crying. "The police say they have enough to charge JJ," she said. "When I die, Henry—and I *am* going to die—that will be a first-degree murder charge. JJ won't ever get out of prison, if they convict him. You get that, right?"

Henry stared down at his own lap. "He didn't do it."

"If that's true, then you have to help me, Henry. To help JJ."

He chewed the inside of his cheek. "I don't know how to help you, I don't—"

"—I'm going to tell you a few things I've learned since yesterday." She leaned forward. "Stop me if I go wrong anywhere. You *did* work for Mason Construction. And I don't know when it started, but Luke arranged to pay you off the books, probably in cash. Knowing Luke, he probably sold it to you as a good thing, for both of you."

Henry's nostrils flared, just for a second.

"And that was fine, you were working on the project over on North Street, in March, signed for some scaffolding rental. And then your accident happened. But you didn't get stupid drunk and fall off a wall like you told everyone, did you? Something went wrong at the construction site, and the roof collapsed on top of you. That's how you shattered your knee, lost sight in one eye, injured the other."

Henry closed his eyes, like he was hiding them, couldn't trust them not to give him away.

"But the thing is, if you weren't an *official* employee of Mason Construction, it meant you didn't have access to workers' comp or health insurance. You haven't stopped me so far, Henry; am I on the right track?"

He opened his eyes.

"And that means you would have had to pay the hospital for all of it, all the surgeries, the treatment, the overnight stay. And I can imagine that was an unpleasant surprise. A lot of money. And maybe it was only then that you realized just how much Luke Mason had screwed you over. That would make anyone angry, Henry. Angry enough to want revenge. You still haven't stopped me."

Henry shook his head, wouldn't look at her. "No, I don't know what you—"

"—I guess you want your brother to die in prison, Henry?" Jet's voice dropped even deeper, sharpening the edges of the words. "Thought he was your best bud. That's cold."

Henry glanced at the cupboard to his right, then back to his lap, squeezing his own hand, so tight it must have hurt.

His eyes danced from Jet to the ceiling, chest rising, filling, too much, too far, his shoulders rising with it.

He let it all go. His hand. His breath.

"Luke said it was just temporary," he said quietly. "While he was sorting something out with the company." Henry wiped his nose on his sleeve. "He said it was legal. I didn't really realize what it meant until . . . until it was too late."

Jet's heart kicked up, back in her chest where it belonged.

"So I'm right, about all of it?"

"Yeah," Henry croaked. "It happened at that house, on North Street. Luke drove me to the hospital after."

"Why didn't you tell anyone, Henry?"

"Because Luke didn't want me to." He glanced at the cupboard again. "He said he would pay me, that he would cover all the medical costs as long as I never told anyone. He's been transferring money to me every month, so I can pay off my debt to the hospital, but it's not enough, never enough. I told him I needed more. A lot more."

Jet swallowed. "Did JJ know, about all of this?"

"No. No." Leaning hard on that second *no*. "Luke meant it when he said I couldn't tell anyone. JJ still believes the drunk-wall story. But he knows I have to pay the hospital back. He's been helping me pay it off. I don't know what I would have done without him. He's been taking on more clients, working extra shifts at the gym, just working, all the damn time, for me." Henry's eyes went back to his lap, to his empty hands. "He borrowed money until they wouldn't let him borrow any more, because we couldn't pay it back, because it was all going to the hospital, and it still wasn't enough."

"Jet," Billy said, voice vibrating through the back of the couch, turning to her. "The loan JJ took out in your name. This is why he did it."

"What?" Henry sniffed.

"You didn't know about that?" Jet asked. "It's part of the police's case against him. He took out thirty grand in my name. Defaulted on the first monthly repayment. The police think that gives him motive for my murder."

Henry's eyes widened.

"I didn't know," he said, little more than a whisper. "I'm sorry, Jet. JJ wouldn't . . . he wouldn't have done anything like that if I hadn't . . . we're just desperate. Only got worse after that other eye surgery. And it didn't work. We need to find another eleven thousand or I'll go blind, but we can't—we can't, we're out of options." The words chased each other out, moving faster than his darting eyes. "Already in so much debt. Can't pay our rent anymore. They're gonna kick us out soon. And now JJ's been arrested, and I can't do anything for him. He took care of me, our whole lives, and I can't do anything for him. Don't have the money to bail him out of jail, if it comes to that. To pay for a lawyer. It's all fucked. This is all my fault."

He dropped his head into his hands, pressing his fingers into his eyes.

"It's not, though, is it?" Jet said, treading carefully. Because Henry had talked himself out onto the edge, and he had a gun. He knew where it was, and they didn't. "It's Luke's fault. He did this to you, put you in this position. You got injured on *his* work site. And now he's the one paying you to keep quiet about it."

Henry raised his head a few inches.

Jet kept going.

"It's Luke's fault, Henry, not yours. He did this."

Henry straightened up, looked at her eye to eye, though neither of them could see too well anymore.

"Do you hate him, Henry?" she said. "For doing this to you, putting you in this position."

He didn't answer.

"Did you want to do something about it? Punish him?"

Henry sniffed. "No, no, it wasn't about that. I just wanted the money. I don't want to go blind, Jet. I'm scared. I just wanted the money. That's why."

Jet's gut twisted, bile rising in her throat. Was that a confession? Had she . . . had she done it? Had she really just solved her own murder?

"You thought attacking me would make Luke pay up? Did you mean for it to go that far—did you mean for me to die?"

"Wait." Henry's face darkened. "What are you talking about? It wasn't me, Jet. I didn't hurt you, I would never—"

"—Where were you on Halloween, at 10:46 p.m.?"

She stood up.

"I was here."

Henry stood up too.

So did Billy, straightening to his full height, shoulders wide.

"Alone?" Jet said. "You know *alone* doesn't count as an alibi, don't you?"

"I—I—" Henry stuttered, shrinking back. "I wasn't alone."

Jet tilted her head, surprised by that. "But you told the police that you were . . . Who—who was here, Henry? Who was here with you?"

Henry swallowed, taking the name with him.

But Jet didn't need him to say it. She got there on her own, new pieces clicking into place, filling in the gaps.

"Luke," she said. "Was Luke here?"

Henry nodded, barely, the smallest movement up and down.

Jet's chin dipped, creating more space for her head as it all came together. "Sophia texted Luke at 10:52 p.m. asking him to call her, because he wasn't at home, he was here," Jet said, looking at Henry but speaking to Billy. She glanced down at her own knuckles, a Band-Aid across the palm of her left hand. "They lied to the police, said Luke was at home too, to give him an alibi. But not an alibi for my murder, for something else." Jet shifted, tried to catch Henry's eyes. "Because he was here, beating the shit out of you, wasn't he?" Jet didn't wait for an answer. She pointed with her good hand. "Black eye, cut lip, bruised ribs—that happened to you on Halloween night, Henry. And Luke had matching grazes on his knuckles from that same night, and he lied about how he got them. Because he was here, wasn't he? And he did that to you?"

"Yeah," Henry sniffed, another check over his shoulder to that same cupboard.

"Why?" Jet pressed, her voice softening, now she no longer thought she was speaking to her own killer.

Henry shrugged. "I just wanted the money, that's all. Was desperate. I messaged Luke, told him that if he couldn't get me the money, then I'd have to speak to your dad, see if he could help me out. The company is his, and I thought that maybe he could—I don't know . . . I didn't threaten to tell the cops or anything. It was just your dad. Luke saw me trying to talk to him at the Halloween Fair. He intercepted, stopped me. Then he came over to the house and . . ." Henry swallowed, eyes faraway. "He wanted to make sure I'd never do something like that again, never try to tell anyone."

The silence was thick, too thick, burrowing into Jet's ears.

"Is that why you bought the gun?" Billy said gently, not quite breaking the silence, skirting just below it. "Were you scared of Luke coming back?"

Henry blinked. "Luke can be scary."

Jet sniffed. Luke wasn't scary, he was just Luke. To her at least. But the Luke she knew wasn't all of him. Not Sophia's Luke. Not Henry's.

"What time was Luke here?" Jet asked Henry.

"I remember when he left," he answered. "I looked at my phone right after, wondered if I should call 911. That was 10:56." Henry held Jet's gaze, returned it. "He was here less than ten minutes."

Jet looked at Billy instead, finding the same strange look behind his eyes as she must have in hers.

"So you didn't kill me, Henry," she said, barely more than a whisper. "You had an alibi."

"And so does Luke," Billy said darkly, like he'd really thought it possible, even for a moment, that Jet's brother could have been the one to kill her.

Two suspects, canceling each other out. And where did that leave them now? So many questions answered, just not the one that truly mattered.

But someone had tried to kill Jet again, twelve hours ago, and even though the theory was neat, made most sense, it might not have been the same person who took a hammer to her head five days before.

"Did you burn down Mason Construction last night, Henry?" she said. "You have more reason to hate the company than most. Did you set fire to it?"

Henry's eyes narrowed. "It burned down?"

"Where were you last night?"

"I was here."

"Alone?"

"Alone," he answered.

Jet sighed. "You know *alone* is not an alibi."

"I was alone," Henry said, more power behind his voice.

"OK."

Jet glanced at the cupboard that Henry kept looking at, pointed to it.

"Hey, Henry, can I borrow your gun?"

"What?!" That was Billy, not Henry, though Henry parroted him half a second later.

"Someone tried to kill me on Halloween, and again last night," she said. "I think I'd feel better having a gun around, if they try a third time."

Henry didn't move.

"And if I die before figuring this out, then JJ will probably spend his whole life in prison for my murder."

That did it.

Henry shuffled over, bending to open the cupboard door.

He reached inside and pulled out the gun.

Stopped.

Stared at it, turning the black pistol around in his hands, a muscle twitching in his jaw.

Jet watched him, those words still ringing in her ears: *Luke can be scary.*

"You won't have to worry about Luke," she said. "I'll deal with him, OK, Henry?"

"OK."

Henry turned the gun one last time, then held it out by the barrel, aiming back through his own chest.

Jet reached out, wrapped her left hand around the grip, the gun heavier than she expected.

"Safety's on. It's loaded," Henry sniffed.

"Thanks." Jet lowered it to her side. "You can have it back when I'm—"

"—Yeah," Henry said, so she didn't have to finish. "Bye, Jet."

Jet turned to go, catching Billy's face, beckoning him with her eyes. He wasn't happy, she could tell by the set of his mouth.

"Do you even know how to use a gun?" he asked as they crossed the doorstep, shutting the front door behind them.

"Yeah, it's just point and shoot," Jet replied, hiding the gun against her leg.

Billy opened the passenger-side door for her, hand folded over the top as she climbed in the truck.

"I can point and shoot." Jet looked up at him, the gun resting in her lap. "Even with my left hand. It's not rocket science, Billy."

He closed the truck door, jogged around to the driver's side.

Jet leaned forward to open the glove compartment, shoved some of the papers aside to make room for the gun.

"It can live in there," she said, closing the compartment as Billy sat down, clicking in his seatbelt. The gun out of sight but not out of mind, either of theirs.

"Jet, I don't know about this—"

"—It's just a precaution," she cut him off, tempering it with a small smile. "Someone also tried to kill you last night, Billy, or didn't care if you were col-coll-co—"

"—Collateral?" he guessed.

"Right." Jet nodded. "And you're not dying anyway, like me. You're alive, have to keep on living. It's just a precaution." She patted the glove compartment.

"Oh shit," Billy said, his phone in his hands, scrolling through. "I've got loads of missed calls. From your parents. And my dad. Hold on." He tapped the screen, raised the phone to his ear. "There's a voicemail."

He listened, the low buzz of a voice rattling from the speakers, words too fast and too fuzzy for Jet to understand. But she understood that look in Billy's eyes as he turned to her, lowering the phone.

"It's Dad. He says they need to speak to you at the station. It's urgent."

TWENTY-FOUR

"It burned down?"

Jet's voice pitched up, joining her widened eyes in feigned surprise.

"It's all gone." Jack Finney sat across the table from her, Chief Jankowski beside him, squeezed into those too-small metal chairs.

"We're still waiting on the full report from the fire department," the chief said, his chair creaking, sighing, as he leaned forward to rest his elbows on the table. "But this is a clear case of arson. An accelerant was used. The whole place would have gone up in minutes."

The whole place *did* go up in minutes; Jet knew, she'd been there, stood on the very edge of hell, its heat still prickling in the burn on her hand. Jet eyed it, dropped the hand into her lap, hiding it under the table.

"Acc-acce—" she began, couldn't find the word the chief had used, one she'd lost out the hole in her head.

"—Gas," Jack said, helping her. "Someone poured gas all over the first floor, set fire to it."

"That's terrible." Jet swallowed. "Who would want to burn my dad's company down?"

"That's what we wanted to talk to you about," the chief said.

Jet met his gaze. "Do you think it's related to my murder? That it was the same person who burned down Mason Construction? But JJ is in custody, so that means—"

"—We're just considering if there's a connection," the chief cut her off. "Nothing concrete yet. We wondered if you knew anything that might help us?"

Jet pressed her lips together. "No, sorry. I don't know who would want to do that."

"And where were you last night, Jet?" The chief opened the file on the table, clicked his pen as it hovered over a blank page.

Her chest tightened, heart reacting to the question before she could.

"I've asked a lot of people a similar question the past couple days."

Not an answer, and not a lie.

The chief clicked his pen twice more. "So, you understand why we have to ask it, don't you?"

"Sure," Jet said. Now she had no choice but to lie. She kept her face blank and her reddened hand in her lap. "I was home. Billy's apartment, I mean. That's where I'm staying."

The chief wrote something down.

"Alone?"

"No, with Billy."

"Billy Finney?"

Jack coughed into his hand.

"Yes sir," Jet answered.

"All night?"

"All night."

The chief glanced over at Jack for a moment, then closed the file.

"OK. If there's nothing else you think we should know?"

"Is there nothing else you think *I* should know?" Jet countered.

The chief stared blankly at her.

"About *my* case," she said. "I have about two days to live. Did you forget that?"

"I didn't forget, Jet." He held the file against his chest. "There's nothing new. JJ Lim has been arrested."

Jet's turn to lean forward, only one elbow on the table, the other hanging lifeless by her side. "Are you going to charge him? Doesn't the fire change things?"

Jack answered instead.

"Detective Ecker is interviewing him again now. He hasn't confessed yet, but we believe the prosecutor will move forward without a confession." His eyes hooked onto hers. "We will get him, don't worry. I made you a promise."

"Thank you, Sergeant Finney," the chief said, standing up. Not a real thank you, a warning disguised as one.

The chief gestured toward the exit and Jet took the hint, getting to her feet. But she blinked and the door doubled before her eyes, another world intruding over theirs, Jack's hand—twice—grasping the handle, holding it open for her, two ways to go, one of them not real.

"Thank you," Jet said to him, not a warning, just a thanks as she stumbled through.

Outside in the rec-rece-re-re—ah, fuck off, the waiting room, Billy and Jet's parents sat, well, waiting. Another doubled man behind them all too: Gerry Clay.

Billy jumped up, but Mom reached Jet first, folding her into a hug that Jet couldn't return, because her arms were pinned down, and one didn't work anyway.

"It's just awful, isn't it," Dianne said, voice breathy in Jet's hair before she pulled away. "We wanted to be the ones to tell you."

"I'm sorry, Dad." Jet's eyes found him, struggling up from his chair, hand pressed to his side, to his kidneys, a wince of deep pain on his face. "Must be hard for you. You spent your whole life building that place."

"We're insured," he said, hiding the pain in his voice. "We can come back from this. I'm just glad nobody got hurt."

Jet found Billy's eyes and she found his. Hazel and blue. One blink and a thousand silent words.

"Does Luke know?" Jet asked, looking between her parents.

"He was the one who called me, in the middle of the night," Dad said, a yellow tinge to his skin but gray under the eyes, betraying his lack of sleep. "He won't leave the scene. Been there all night. Your mom took him some breakfast, but he won't leave. Just staring at it."

"Don't know why," Dianne sniffed, a self-conscious glance back at Billy and Gerry, at the non-Masons in earshot.

"I do," Jet said, taking Luke's side, even though she couldn't remember the last time he took hers. "All his dreams, gone up in smoke. Literally."

Jet studied her dad's face for any sign of the truth. Because the company was never going to be Luke's anyway, whether it burned down or not.

He didn't react, only Dianne did, pressing her fingers to her temples. "I've got such a headache."

Jet rolled her eyes. "I'm sure it's worse than mine too."

"What did they ask you?" Dad hissed, hand to his kidneys again. "Is it related? Was it something to do with JJ? He has a brother, doesn't he? Do you think—"

"—I don't know anything," Jet cut across him. "Maybe it was the same person who killed me, maybe it was someone else."

"Well, Gerry might be able to help with that," Dianne said curtly, bringing him in.

Gerry rose to his feet, Jet's eyes snapping to him. "What do you mean?" she asked the room, waiting for the answer, because it was a waiting room after all.

"Don't know about that." Gerry shuffled over. "It's just Owen. He was flying his drone last night. Heard the sirens, got curious."

Fuck, it *had* been a drone Jet saw, against the whirling column of smoke. But had the drone seen them back? Jet caught Billy again, over Gerry's shoulder.

"Oh," she said, that mock-surprise back in her eyes, plastered over the shock. "Did he manage to record anything?"

Gerry inhaled. "The building was already collapsed by the time he got it there, only just beat the fire department. Couldn't see a lot through the smoke." He paused. "We've watched it a few times, can't see anything important, nobody coming or going. But maybe the police will spot something we can't see. I've got the footage, thought it might be helpful."

Too fucking helpful, fuck sake, Gerry.

"Thank you," Jet said, clearing her throat. "But the footage doesn't show anybody, right? Who might have started the fire?"

"Not that I can see."

So, Billy and Jet were in the clear, but so was whoever tried to burn them to death, and no leads as to who it could have been. Only JJ was ruled out, and the two of them.

"I know," Gerry said. He must have read her face as disappointment. "But I think I know who did this."

Everyone in the room turned to him, waiting again.

Jet and Billy waited a little harder.

"Yes?" Jet snapped, spooling her left hand impatiently.

Gerry glanced over at Dianne.

"Dianne, did you tell the cops? About the cat thing?"

Dianne sparked back into life, running a hand through her hair, taking her right arm for granted.

"Don't be ridiculous," she said, almost a laugh, but it hissed too much around the edges. "Nothing to do with that."

"You sure?" Gerry asked. "Someone says they hate Mason Construction, and your family. Threatens you. And now the premises get burned down."

"That was a long time ago, Gerry. It was just a prank. It's not relevant."

"What's he talking about?" Jet's eyes zeroed in on her mom. "Mom?"

"Oh, it's nothing, Jet."

"Doesn't sound like nothing. If there's someone who hates the company, hates our family, that means they could be a suspect not just for the fire, but the person who killed me."

Dianne blinked. "JJ is the one who—"

"—What's the cat thing?"

"It doesn't matter, Jet." Mom doubled down, already taking up two outlines, splitting into more.

"Gerry!" Jet pressed him instead. "What's the cat thing? And remember, I only have two days to live so it'd be really great if we could stop wasting time."

Gerry swallowed, the lump in his throat moving up and down with it.

"It was—" he began.

"—It was nothing," Dianne cut him off. "Just a harmless prank by someone who hijacked one of our Town Hall meetings, during citizens' comments."

Jet pushed out her chin. "Dressed as a cat?" she asked.

"No," Mom said. "The meetings are online, on Zoom."

"It was a filter thing," Gerry added. "To hide his identity. And he distorted his voice too. Was actually kind of creepy. That was my Halloween costume this year. Doesn't seem so funny anymore, if he's the one who set the fire."

"You never told me about this," Dad said, finding his voice.

"Because it's not relevant," Mom replied. "It was a harmless prank and we've all forgotten about it."

Apart from Gerry. Apart from her mom too, hands tucked behind her back, balled into fists, telltale knuckles pushing through the skin.

"When was this?" Jet asked both of them, either of them.

Gerry looked up, searched the ceiling and his mind for the answer. "Maybe a year ago. Or less."

"Thank you, Gerry," Dianne clipped.

"Do you still have the recording of the meeting?"

"Well, yes," Gerry said. "Everyone does. All the village trustee Zoom recordings are posted online on the town website, along with a transcript of the minutes—"

"—Yes, thank you, Gerry," Dianne shot him down.

Gerry continued mumbling, something about "transparency of democracy."

Dianne turned away. "Look, there's Sergeant Finney now. Jack," she called, "Gerry has something he needs to show you. About the fire."

Gerry's shoulders slumped. Just wait until he finds out how much Luke ripped him off over marble countertops. Maybe he'd be happy that someone else already burned it down.

He shuffled away, dismissed, clearing the path between Billy and Jet. Another thousand words in the blink of an eye.

And a new lead.

For someone who might have started the fire.

Someone who might have smashed Jet's head in with a hammer.

"Come on," Jet said to him, but he was already coming, truck keys trailing from his finger, his liquid eyes on her. Jet's heart picked up, not in the bad way, not fight-or-flight, actually just flying, side by side with Billy, a new electricity thrumming under her skin, sidestepping her right arm.

Somehow, Billy could tell. "Are you excited?" He smiled down at her.

"Aren't you?" she whispered.

"Where are you going?" Dianne called just before they reached the door.

Jet turned back. "Home," she said. "Billy's."

Mom released her balled-up hands. "C-come home for dinner?" She shrank as she said it, eyes heavy and swimming. "We won't have many more chances, for the family to be together and . . ."

Jet softened, an ache in her chest that hurt her in small ways, not like the one inside her head.

"Tomorrow," she said. "I promise." And she meant it.

Mom brightened, almost a smile, not quite making it. "Tomorrow," she said, accepting Jet's promise . . . just. "Why, what are you doing to-night?"

"Watching cat videos."

TWENTY-FIVE

"Fuck me, I'm so bored."

Jet held one eye open, staring at the laptop screen on the coffee table in front of her, cross-legged on the floor.

"Is it possible to die of boredom?"

"Don't try it," Billy said, stretched out beside her, straight-legged, his hand splayed on the rug, pressed against her right knee.

The video kept playing, full-screen, a Zoom recording split into two halves. One side was labeled *Village Trustees,* a meeting room inside Town Hall, harsh overhead lighting and a long U-shaped table. The five village trustees sat at the far end: Jet's mom, Gerry Clay, and the others. Lou Jankowski was in his uniform, sitting on the right, and a handful of other municipal employees along the left, notebooks and pens at the ready.

On the other side of the split screen was a *Ms. Duffy,* sitting too close to the camera, ruddy cheeks and sagging skin in the unforgiving light of her computer screen.

"Thank you for joining us for citizens' comments *again,* Ms. Duffy," Gerry said, cheerfully. "Are you here to talk about something other than your neighbor's solar lights?"

"Yes, actually," Ms. Duffy said, voice old and crusty, annoyed before she even started. "I want to talk about those new parking meters over on Pleasant Street. It is absolutely ridiculous. My daughter lives there and I've already gotten six tickets. I'm not paying them."

"I hear you, dude." Jet scrolled the cursor, fast-forwarding the angry woman. No other faces appeared on the split screen, just Ms. Duffy; then back to the Town Hall meeting, stretching to take over the full screen again.

"Is there anyone else in the Zoom waiting room, Milly?" Gerry asked someone off camera.

"No, that's all," replied the disembodied voice.

"Great, let's move on," he said. "Any additions or deletions to the posted agenda? No? OK, so let's discuss this financial report, starting with the police revenue."

Papers and people shuffled.

"Next," Jet said.

Billy leaned forward, finger on the trackpad, exiting out of the video, back to TownOfWoodstock.org to the page called *Village Trustee Meeting Uploads*.

"OK, so this next video takes us back to January this year," Billy said, double-clicking it. They'd started in March to be sure, and this was their fifth video already.

Billy pressed play.

Jet held her eye open again.

The same people, in the exact same positions, wearing different clothes, apart from Lou Jankowski in his uniform. Jet eyed her mom, in the middle, hair swinging around her bare neck.

"We're good?" Gerry Clay asked, looking off camera, then back to the room. "OK, everyone, I'm Chair Gerry Clay, and I call to order this meeting of the Board of Trustees for the Village of Woodstock. It is 6:30 p.m., January fourteenth, and I want to wish you all a happy new year for our first meeting of 2025. Present is myself, Dianne Mason, David Dale, Florence Chu, Richie Collins." He reeled off the rest of the names. "And introducing our new chief of police, who was elected by the trustees in a secret ballot at the end of last year: Police Chief Lou Jankowski."

Lou dipped his head as there was a polite spattering of applause, a tight smile on Jet's mom's face, the first to stop clapping.

"OK, Milly," Gerry said. "Do we have anyone in the Zoom waiting room for citizens' comments?"

"No one today."

"Perfect." Gerry grinned. "Let's get to the agenda."

Jet leaned forward this time, pausing the video, freezing them all.

"Next?" Billy asked.

But it was something else.

"I just realized something," Jet said, mind aching as it reeled back, her eyes fixed on Mom's pixelated face, staring across at the new chief. "The vote for the police chief, it's a secret ballot, right? At the Halloween Fair, I heard Gerry telling your dad that he voted for him, not Lou. And obviously David Dale would have voted for your dad, he and Jack and Luke play golf together, like, every weekend."

"Right?" Billy said, bending it into a question.

"Well, for Lou to have won, that means my mom must have voted for Lou, not your dad. There are five trustees."

"Oh." Billy turned back to the screen.

"Why would my mom vote for Lou Jankowski?" she said. "She probably didn't even know Lou before, and she's known your dad for over thirty years, been neighbors all that time. I just assumed it was Mom and David for your dad and the others voted against him. Why would Mom vote for Lou instead?"

Billy shrugged. "Maybe she thought he'd do a better job."

"Seems like a bit of a dick move," Jet said. "They're friends. Anyway, not relevant—we're looking for a cat."

Jet exited the video, on to the next.

"Doesn't look like they had a meeting in December, so we're into November 2024 and—"

Gerry Clay spoke over her, from the speakers.

"—This is Chair Gerry Clay, calling to order this Village of Woodstock Board of Trustees meeting. It is 6:30, November twelfth, and present we have . . ." Jet skipped ahead, dragging the cursor to the end of the names.

Lou Jankowski was gone, replaced with the old police chief. Much older, in fact, hair snow white and so thin it almost looked like it was floating above his uncovered head.

Jet circled his face with the on-screen arrow, poking him in the eyes. "Can't wait to retire," she said, putting on an old man voice. "These meetings are so fucking boring."

"Yeah," Billy joined in. "Can't wait to do all that old people shit. Puzzles. Gardening."

"Bang so many bitches," Jet added. "That *I used to be a police chief* line works every damn time."

"Gonna eat so much ham."

"Ham?" Jet's old man asked Billy's old man.

"Yeah. I really like ham." Billy's accent had slipped, somewhere between surfer and stoner.

Gerry stopped the fun, as usual.

"OK, let's get this meeting started," he said.

"Milly, do we have any citizen comments today?" Jet asked before Gerry could, parroting her a few seconds later.

Milly's disembodied voice floated through the speakers. "Yes, there's someone in the waiting room. I don't actually have a name; their screen name says *Anon.* Shall I let them through?"

Jet leaned forward, holding her breath. Billy too, right beside her.

"Yes, let them through." Gerry waved his pixelated hand.

The screen fractured into two, and not because of Jet's eyes this time. Town Hall halved, shrinking all the people inside it.

On the right-hand side was a darkened room, no lights, just a pale glow from a window in the background. In front of it, lit from the silver of the computer screen, was a cat.

Not a real cat, not even a full cat. Some kind of filter: a digital ginger-and-white cat face plastered over the human one below, moving with it, blinking bright green, uncanny eyes. The cat wore a dark hoodie zipped up to cover their neck. Pointed cat ears out the top of their head, just a sliver of visible dark hair, but their human ears showed beyond the orange fur.

It tilted its head, cat face moving with it, staring right at Jet, almost an entire year later.

She felt the hairs stand up on her arm. Just one arm.

Then flinched as a sound erupted from the speakers: Town Hall bursting into laughter.

Gerry Clay hooted.

Jet's mom covered her mouth with her hand, giggled into it.

"Oh dear!" Gerry called over all the commotion, barely able to speak. "Ms. Duffy, is that you?"

"Oh my god." Florence Chu laughed so hard she had to wipe her eyes.

"I'm afraid it looks like you have some kind of filter on," Gerry continued. "Has one of your grandchildren been playing on your computer, Ms. Duffy?" His voice broke, more laughter, high and tuneful before he wiped it away. "Is there anyone there who can help you turn it off?"

The cat blinked slowly.

Opened its mouth, a flash of human teeth.

An awful, inhuman sound rattled against the laptop speakers.

Gerry Clay covered his ears; so did the old chief of police, and Billy.

"I don't want to turn it off," the cat said, its voice terrible and deep, from another world, reverberating on each word. Some kind of voice-changing software. "I don't want you to know who I am."

The hair rose up the back of Jet's neck now. Billy pressed closer.

Gerry lowered his hands, the smile still on his face, flickering at the edges, like he didn't know whether to laugh or . . .

"Who are you?" he said, deciding to go with the smile, but the laughter was gone, almost all trace of it.

Dianne's hand was still in front of her mouth.

"I'm a citizen of Woodstock," the cat answered in its dark and dreadful voice. "And I have a comment. For Dianne Mason."

Jet's mom lowered her hand, uncovering her mouth.

"About Mason Construction," the cat added.

Dianne found her voice, an audible clack from her tongue. "Well, I don't actually work there. That's my husband's company. Do you have a comment about—"

"—I want to know, how you sleep at night?" the cat asked, tilting its head the other way.

"Excuse me?" Dianne's voice rose.

"How do you sleep at night?" the cat repeated, voice growling, filling Town Hall, and Billy's apartment one year later. "Stealing people's homes so you can build mansions and vacation homes for people who don't even live here."

Dianne shook her head, sharing a glance with Gerry.

"Mason Construction does not *steal* homes," Dianne replied. "And if you don't mind, we—"

"—offering too much money to people who are too weak to say no. What's the difference between that and stealing? You're still predators."

"Milly," Gerry called, "I think we should—"

"—Pull out of the sale," the cat barked over him. "You know which one. It's not too late."

Dianne shook her head, almost rolled her eyes too; Jet knew that look. "I don't know what you're talking about," she sniffed.

"Houses aren't just four walls and a roof." The cat flashed its teeth. "They are important to people. And they are not yours to take."

"If you have an issue with Mason Construction, I'm afraid you'll have to take it up with my husband—"

"—I'm taking it up with you," the cat spat, shaking the room. "Because you can do something about it." Tilted its head the other way, blinked its strange, empty eyes. "And because I know your secret."

Dianne went back to laughing, a hollow sound, looking around at her fellow trustees.

"I don't have any secrets," she said. "Other than my apple pie recipe."

A spatter of polite laughter from the others.

"OK," Gerry said, his smile back. "Milly, let's move o—"

"—You do have a secret, Dianne," the cat cut him off. "The one your family doesn't know. Except Emily. She knew."

Dianne's eyes snapped wide, and so did Jet's, behind the screen. A gasp went around the room, because name-dropping Dianne's dead daughter was a step too far, and no one was laughing now, or even pretending to. Jet gripped the edge of the laptop, leaned even closer.

"The fuck," she muttered.

"Milly, get rid of them," Dianne barked.

"I'm trying," came the voice. "Sorry, I . . ."

The cat smiled, its awful human-hybrid smile.

"Do you know that Emily knew?" it asked. "She told me, before she died."

"Milly!" Dianne shouted, pushing up to her feet.

The fast clip of her heels as she ran alongside the table, toward the edge of the frame, her face and the panic in her eyes growing clearer the closer she got to Jet's screen.

"Actually," the cat added, "it was *right* before she died."

"Milly, what are you doing?!"

Dianne disappeared off frame. "Move, Milly. I'll do it myself."

"Make it stop, Dianne," the cat said, an amused half-smile, watching the chaos unfold with those blank eyes. "Or I'll tell—"

The cat disappeared.

Town Hall stretched back out, everyone doubling in size, taking over the whole screen.

"The fuck," Jet said again, watching her mom reappear, walking back to her place at the table, straightening her jacket, running a hand through her mussed-up hair.

She sat, her face cracking, an empty smile that showed too many teeth, didn't reach her troubled eyes. "Teenagers and their pranks," she laughed, picking up her papers, banging them against the table. "Well, that certainly livened up the meeting, didn't it?"

Gerry took her lead, a sigh that stretched into a laugh. But his heart wasn't really in it, echoing strangely around the room. "That was crazy," he said.

"Yes, absolutely ridiculous," Dianne agreed. "Complete nonsense." Doubled down. "OK, everyone ready to discuss banner permits?"

Jet clicked pause, freezing her mom, shoulders too rigid and back too straight.

Billy didn't say anything; neither did Jet. She dragged the cursor back and pressed play again.

"You do have a secret, Dianne." That hellish voice, rattling against the speakers. "The one your family doesn't know. Except Emily. She knew."

"Jet?"

She spooled forward, the cat jerking silently, coming alive again when she stopped.

"She told me before she died."

Yelling, heels rushing on a polished floor, in a race against the pounding of Jet's heart.

"Actually, it was *right* before she died."

"Jet?"

"What?" She paused the video, back in the room.

Billy touched the screen. "Who is this?"

"I don't know."

Jet stared at the cat, into its half-human eyes.

"Is it true?" Billy frowned. "About Emily telling them a secret?"

"Emily died seventeen years ago," Jet replied, not really an answer.

"So this is someone who knew your family back then?"

Jet shrugged, but something else had caught her eye behind the cat. A window visible in the background of the darkened room. Jet swiped her fingers on the trackpad to zoom into it. Zoomed again. A silver glare in the dark, pixelated window, turning it into a mirror.

"That's the reflection of the laptop screen." Jet zoomed in again on the hazy silver shape, her arrow tracing a pinkish blur around it.

"Pink?" Billy said.

"Rose gold," Jet corrected him. "And a black keyboard. Looks like a MacBook Air to me."

"OK." Billy chewed his lip. "And how does that help us identify the cat?"

Jet shot him a look. "I mean, I don't know a *man* who would buy a rose gold MacBook, do you?"

Billy shrugged. "It's a bit of a leap."

"*You're* a bit of a leap," Jet muttered.

"Can we see what's outside the window?" Billy leaned closer, propped his chin up on his knuckles.

"No, it's night outside and the laptop's too bright," Jet said.

Billy thought about that for a moment, chewing his cheek.

"Does the cat ever move in front of the laptop, blocking the screen's reflection? Then maybe we can—"

Jet was already doing it, pressing play on this zoomed-in view, focused on the window.

"Make it stop, Dianne," the cat voice said, just a reflection from this angle, an unknown person. "Or I'll—"

The cat shifted and Jet paused. Its human shoulders blocked the light from the laptop, the silver rectangle gone from the glass of the window, just the darkness beyond and a pinprick of orange.

"Hold on," Jet said.

"Holding."

She turned up her laptop's brightness, and again, shapes emerging in the darkness outside the window.

"That orange thing is a streetlamp." Billy pointed. "So we're on a second floor. A bedroom?"

But Jet was looking at something else behind it. A blurry white square. A house. Faint little lines for the panel siding, the windows arranged almost like a face. A little triangle roof above the front porch and a red car parked outside. Did Jet know that house?

"Do I know that house?" she said aloud this time.

"I don't know, do you?"

She did. Her heart got there first, climbing her ribs, making itself at home in her throat.

"Shit," she hissed. "That's the house on River Street. Right on the corner, where my phone's last known location was."

Billy's eyes widened. "You sure?"

"I saw it a million times on Google Street View, drove past a million times too. I'm sure it's that house. It's River Street."

Billy's eyes darkened, another storm. "But if we can see that corner of River Street from this window, that means we're on—"

"—North Street," Jet finished for him, throat tightening around the words and around her heart, her head not too far behind, filling in the gaps. "We're in Andrew Smith's house. Before it got knocked down. This house, *again*. I swear, if houses could be prime suspects."

Billy glanced over at his front door. "So . . . it's Andrew?" he asked, still a few seconds behind.

"No." Jet lifted Billy's chin so he'd look at her. "It's his daughter."

"Nina?"

"Remember what the cat said." But Jet couldn't remember exactly, so she dragged the cursor back, pressed play, and let it run, that dark demonic voice vibrating the laptop and the table.

"—offering too much money to people who are too weak to say no. What's the difference between that and stealing? You're still predators."

Gerry next: "Milly, I think we should—"

"—Pull out of the sale. You know which one. It's not too late."

Jet paused it.

"Andrew told us Nina was devastated when he sold their family house to Luke. This was her, trying to stop that sale. *Too much money to people who are too weak to say no.* She's talking about her dad." She swallowed. "It was Nina."

Billy nodded, seeing it now. "But Nina, she's . . . when did she—"

"—She shot herself last Christmas, a few weeks after this." Jet zoomed back out, stared at the cat face, into those fake green eyes, trying to picture Nina's real ones beneath, all that pain she was hiding under a filter.

Billy sniffed, deflated. "But Nina's been dead for eleven months, so she can't be the one who burned down Mason Construction last night, or who attacked you on Halloween. So this is a dead end."

"I don't know," Jet said, following a new train of thought, past all the broken bits. "It's *Nina.*" She leaned on the name, as though that explained it. "Nina was Emily's best friend. And what do best friends tell each other?"

"Secrets?" Billy guessed.

"Right." She hooked her arm through his. "And something else Andrew said. That Mom got Nina fired from her job at the hotel. We didn't know why my mom would do that. But now . . ."

She left it open for Billy. He pointed to the cat.

"Dianne figured out that this was Nina, the one threatening her? And then she got her fired to punish her?"

"Or silence her," Jet said. "This was not just a prank, and my mom knew it. Look at her face, Billy. She's scared. And if she really did get Nina fired, that means whatever Nina was threatening to tell, it was true. Doesn't it?"

Billy nodded, eyes ahead, circling little pixelated Dianne.

"And if it was something bad enough for her to do that to Nina . . ." he set Jet up.

"Then maybe it's something bad enough for someone to kill me over, seventeen years later."

"Well, shit." Billy slumped back.

"Well, shit indeed." Jet joined him.

"You think your mom will tell you what it is?"

"I'm not going to give her much choice," Jet said. "She already lied her ass off, tried to stop us finding this video. I'd like more evidence before we go to her so she can't just deny it, like she'll try. It's always someone else's fault with my mom."

"What evidence?"

"Emily's secret," Jet said. "At least some idea of what it could be."

She laughed to herself then—short, just a sniff.

"What?" Billy turned to her.

"Just. I never could get out of Emily's shadow. And now, with this last thing I'll ever do . . . here we are again. Always comes back to her."

Billy clapped his hands, bringing her out of that particular hole.

"So how are we going to figure out Emily's secret?" he said. "A little tricky, considering both people who knew the secret are now gone. Do your parents still have any of Emily's stuff? Her old phone?"

Jet shook her head. "She died seventeen years ago. And as much as they love to bring her up all the time, they also really wanted a big guest bedroom. There's nothing left."

"OK. A little trickier, then." Billy pressed his fingers to his lips, splitting them into little pink quarters. "What year did she die?"

"2008." That date seared into Jet's brain, the day she won the regional spelling bee and life changed forever.

"2008," Billy repeated. "And how would two sixteen-year-old girls have communicated in 2008?"

Jet sat up. "Facebook?" She searched his eyes.

"Facebook," Billy confirmed. "Do you think you could get into Emily's account?"

"I don't think so. Maybe I could find out the email address, but the password? And it's not like we have one of her devices that might still be logged in after all this time. Seventeen years."

Jet followed that thought—her eyes too—over to the front door of Billy's apartment, and beyond. "But Nina died only a year ago . . ." she said, left it hanging there for Billy to pick up. He didn't. "Do you think Andrew still has her belongings? Her phone, or her laptop? Her rose gold MacBook?"

Now Billy picked it up, his eyes shifting, joining hers at the door.

He turned back. "What are you thinking?"

"Oh, come on, Billy." Jet grinned. "You're thinking the same thing."

"No, I am not."

Jet stood up, winked at him.

"What am I thinking, Jet? What are we thinking?"

"Andrew will be downstairs in the bar, won't he?"

"Oh no," Billy said, deflating. "I know what we're thinking."

TWENTY-SIX

"Here," Billy hissed, wide-eyed, standing by the glass door into Dr. Mandrake's Dive Bar, half in, half out.

Jet was waiting outside, hiding from the orange pool of the streetlamp, fading into the darkness.

She hurried toward him, held out her left hand.

Billy dropped a set of keys into it.

"Had to wait for him to go take a leak," he whispered. "Those were in his jacket pocket."

"Good job." Jet closed her fingers around the keys. "Now you've just got to distract him. Make sure he doesn't come upstairs while I'm in there."

"Distract him?" Billy's eyes widened even more, endless pools.

"Be neighborly. Buy him more beer."

"He's an alcoholic," Billy hissed.

Jet shrugged. "So it's the perfect distraction."

Billy groaned, blew out a mouthful of uneasy air.

"Just buy me ten minutes to find the laptop, then I'll meet you in your apartment." She pulled herself out of Billy's eyes, through the open doorway behind him, watching as a hunched figure slumped down at the table in the farthest, darkest corner.

"Andrew's back," she hissed. "Go."

He went, the door swinging shut behind him.

Jet turned the corner and watched Billy through the windows, walking with the same pace, matching each other, one inside, one out. Billy awkwardly stuffed his hands into his pockets as he approached Andrew's table, opening his mouth to say something, anything.

Jet ran out of windows, wished him luck and kept going, to the outdoor stairs just beyond the bar, leading to the apartments above.

She tripped, the steps doubling before her, feet falling between the cracks, a new stab of pain behind her eye. Nothing she couldn't handle, testing her weight on each step to check it was real first, turning left at the top instead of right, toward 1A instead of home.

Jet gripped the key, pushed it into the lock, missed, blinked, tried again, and turned it.

Andrew Smith's front door sighed as it opened for her, like it knew, an apology before Jet could take it all in.

Empty bottles everywhere.

Piles of unfolded clothes.

Balled-up tissues.

Food wrappers.

A couch that was too big for the room, half blocking the door to the bathroom.

The same layout as Billy's apartment, just reversed. And no *Cedar Delight* in here. It smelled musty, too lived in, rebreathed air.

Jet flicked on the lights and that only made it worse.

She let the door shut her in, picked her way through the trash.

There was a framed photograph on the wall, not quite straight. Nina grinned out of it, in a graduation cap and gown, standing between her parents. She and her mom looked so similar, the two of them standing side by side like this, same light brown skin and dark oval eyes. Andrew actually looked happy, a light behind his smile and behind his eyes that was gone now, dulled by the years of drinking. The Andrew in this photograph didn't know anything about what was to come; he just smiled, happy, proud, forever frozen that way. Nina's mom might have already been sick, and none of them knew it. They probably all went

home to their house on North Street after this photograph, had a cele-
bratory dinner. That house was gone now. And so was Andrew's family.

Jet moved past the photo, past the kitchen counter, stacks of used
plates and glasses. Into the bedroom. The curtains shut, like they'd never
been opened, because you couldn't let daylight into a graveyard like this.

She darted through, avoiding the discarded clothes—not that Andrew would be able to tell if anything had been disturbed. It was all
disturbed; that's how he kept it.

She bent down to look beneath the unmade bed. Nothing here, just
some socks that had escaped, found a place to hide.

Jet straightened up. Checked the closet instead. Not much left on the
hangers, or in the drawers. And nothing that looked like it belonged to
Nina. Damn. How long did she have left? Jet thought about Billy downstairs, fought a smile, thinking of the panic in his eyes. Smiled just to
think of him anyway, actually.

Back into the living room, Jet skirted beyond the couch to the same
closet Billy had in his apartment. Pulled one door open with her left
hand, then shuffled back to open the other.

Stuff everywhere. Shelves full of it. Boxes lining the bottom.

Jet's eyes scanned quickly across it all, squinting to try and stitch the
world back into one. They did, just about, settling on a cardboard box
tucked into the farthest corner. *Nina* scribbled across the top, flaps not
quite meeting, too much inside.

"Yes," Jet hissed, leaning forward to drag the box out, her right foot
stepping in when it snagged on another box, helping her left hand to
free it.

It slumped down onto the floor with a thunk.

Jet dropped to her knees in front of it, her thumb tracing across Nina's name, dipping in and out of the ridges of the cardboard. She opened
one flap, then the other.

The first thing she saw was a hoodie, folded neatly, balanced precari-
ously on top. Dark burgundy with a bright yellow logo for Norwich Uni-
versity. The second thing she saw was a pile of loose photographs,
fanning out against the fabric of the hoodie.

Jet scooped up the photos, looked at the first one. Nina and her mom, grinning behind a plate of homemade tacos, too many for a family of three. Shuffled that to the bottom of the pile, looked at the next photo. Nina's clear skin pickling with acne, turning her back into a teenager. Her arm slung around a blond girl grinning at the camera, braces fixed to her teeth. Emily. She must have been about fifteen here, the photo taken on the patio in the Masons' yard. Emily stared back at Jet, with the same brown-green eyes. One sister blinked, the other couldn't. Emily's hair was lighter than Jet's, longer—too long, right down to her waist. So long it had killed her.

Jet placed the photos on the floor beside her, lifted out the hoodie, trying to keep its neat folds even though she only had one hand. Her stomach lurched—heart too—when she saw what was buried in the box beneath it.

A MacBook.

A rose gold MacBook Air, one deep scratch on its case, cutting the *Apple* logo into uneven halves.

"Yes," Jet whispered, taking it out, tucking it under her arm. "Thank you, Nina."

"WELL, I'M GOING to hell," Billy announced, opening the front door, freezing as he spotted Jet by the coffee table, two laptops open in front of her. "You actually found it?"

"Mission accomplished." Jet grinned. "Also, side note: it is very, *very* difficult to open a laptop with just one hand, by the way."

"Ah, but you're a trouper." Billy hurried over.

"I don't give up," Jet said, which wasn't true: she did give up, all the time. But that was the old Jet. "*And* the battery was dead. Of course it was, been sitting in a box for eleven months. So I plugged it in with the ch-char-ch—white wire thingy. It's just waking up now."

The laptop burred, a whirring sound beneath the keyboard as the screen switched from the charging-battery symbol to the lock page. A matching whirring sound inside Jet's head as she leaned forward, clicked the touchpad to enter.

The home screen sprang straight up.

"No password?" Billy asked. And then: "Why do you always have to sit on the floor?" He dropped beside her, legs too long, studying the screen.

Jet jostled, made space for him. "Maybe Nina never had a password. Or maybe Andrew had to get it unlocked after Nina died, documents he needed access to or something." The something could just have been that he missed his daughter, hoped to find some of her still inside this machine. "That's the first obstacle. Now we have to cross our fingers that Facebook is still logged in."

Jet double-clicked on Safari to open the web browser. It was already connected to a WiFi, probably Andrew's router next door. She moved the cursor to the URL box, started typing, one finger to one key at a time. *F a c*

"You're typing like someone called Margaret." Billy smirked.

"Funny." She smirked back, stuck out her elbow.

e b

It auto-filled for her, some ID code at the end of the web address, and Jet pressed enter, crossing the only fingers she had.

The Facebook log-in page.

The username was already filled in: *nina_diaz_smith_92@gmail .com.*

But the password box was blank, waiting.

Jet's heart sank. She clicked into it, to see if it would prompt some password manager to fill it in for her.

Nothing happened.

Except her heart sank farther, dropping into her gut.

"Fuck." She slumped against the couch.

Billy un-slumped her, hand on her back. "Not a total *fuck* yet," he said. "We have her email address, her Gmail, and maybe if she's still logged in to that we can—"

"—reset her Facebook password," Jet hissed, stealing his thunder. He would have given it to her anyway, she knew; he was Billy after all. She gave some back. "Yes, Billy, I love you."

Billy tensed, tensed even more as Jet brushed against him, leaning forward, fingers on the trackpad. She clicked to open a new tab, guided the cursor to the URL. *G m a.* Pressed enter when it auto-filled. Held her breath. Billy had stopped breathing too, a little while ago.

The web page opened, pale blue, lines and lines of emails in Nina's inbox.

"We're in!" Jet laughed, turning to share it with Billy. "You can add shit-hot hacker to your résumé."

He reached over, hugged her awkwardly. Awkward because of the floor-sitting and the one arm.

"Let's do this."

Jet flicked back to the Facebook log-in page, clicked on the *Forgot Password?* button. Let Billy type in Nina's email address: it was faster that way. Clicked *Yes* to send a reset-password link to that account.

Skipped over to the Gmail page. The email wasn't here. Refreshed it. Still not here. Refreshed again.

There it was.

Jet stabbed her finger against the trackpad, opening the email, following the link.

"What password you gonna use?" Billy asked as Jet started to type.

"Emily Mason," she said, reentering the new password to confirm. "Think Nina would have approved."

Password successfully updated, the page told her. It didn't have to tell her twice. Jet flicked back to the log-in page, typed her sister's name into the empty password box. Remembered to breathe and guided the arrow over to the *Log In* button. Pressed it.

The page disappeared, replaced half a second later with a Facebook homepage, blue and white, and all the other colors too, scrolling photos and status updates. A tiny picture of Nina on a sunset beach at the top, arms open like she didn't have a care in the world. But Jet knew she'd had many.

"Can't believe this worked." Billy leaned closer. "There, click into Messenger."

Jet did.

"Probably going to have to scroll really far down," he said.

"Yeah, Emily hasn't replied in seventeen years. She'll be right at the bottom."

Jet sat back, let Billy do the scrolling for her; it was easier with two hands, and they had years to get through.

The page stuttered, reloading each time they reached the bottom, a little spooling circle that started to test Jet's patience.

"OK, last messaged a Mike Fraser in August 2012," Billy read from the screen. "We're getting there. Four more years."

Down, down, down.

The conversations reloading.

The page slowing down, like it got harder the farther back they went, dragging those old messages back into the present.

"We're here, 2008," Billy muttered. "Now where is . . . ah." His hands drew up. "There she is."

Emily Mason.

The second to last name on the screen.

Offline, it said. Yeah, no shit.

Billy sat back, gave Jet some space. She took it, fingers back on the trackpad. She looked at him, held it for another second, then clicked her sister's name, opening a chat box that appeared at the bottom of the screen. A conversation between the dead.

Jet's eyes started reading before she was ready.

Nina's final message to Emily, never opened, never read:

It was your funeral today. I sat with your family, held little Jet's hand. I can't believe you're really gone. I'll miss you forever. When I have a daughter, I'll name her after you. Goodbye Emily.

Billy's breath shuddered. "Hard to read," he said, quietly.

That was June 8, the date of Emily's funeral.

The next message up was from Emily, on Friday, May 30.

"This is the day before she died," Jet said. "*No, I started to,*" she read her sister's message aloud. "*But she had to leave. I'll do it next week.*"

"What was she talking about?" Billy asked, but Jet was already scrolling up, to Nina's message before that.

"*Did you talk to Mrs. Finney yet?*" Jet read, eyes catching Billy's just as his caught hers. A lump in Jet's throat, blocking her heart.

"My mom?" Billy's voice dropped into a whisper.

"She was their math teacher too," Jet said, around the lump. "Probably just school stuff."

"Emily wanted to talk to my mom about something," Billy said, not really a question. "But she never made it to *next week*."

Jet scrolled up again, finding another back-and-forth conversation. "This was two days before that," she said. "Wednesday the twenty-eighth. Emily wrote: *I'll tell you at school tomorrow.*"

"*What?*" Billy said, taking Nina's role.

"*Nina, it happened again. Heard them talking, they didn't know I was awake. Heard something. It's ab-about . . . Luke.*" That pause hadn't been Emily's, it was Jet's, stumbling over the words. She read it again without the gap. "*It's about Luke.*"

Then nothing, no messages until the weekend before, something about Andy White's birthday party.

"Luke," Jet said again, sounding out his name, as though the shape had changed, new angles, that crunch in the middle. The thirty-year-old and the thirteen-year-old that Emily was talking about, and one word that somehow described them both.

"You think that's the secret Nina was talking about?" Billy turned to her. "It's about Luke?"

"It's about Luke," Jet copied him, repeating her long-dead sister, like she'd lost all her own words, and maybe she had, out that black hole in her head or the one in her eye.

"Emily overheard them talking about him." Billy returned to the screen. "She means your parents, right? Talking about Luke. You think this is *the* secret? Nina did say it was right before Emily . . ."

"Fuck sake, Emily," Jet said, words all coming back to her at once. "Why did you have to tell her at school tomorrow? Why couldn't you have just told her right now?"

"Maybe she knew she couldn't," Billy said, "in case someone ever read it. Do you think this is what Emily wanted to speak to my mom about? The thing with Luke?"

"I don't know," Jet sighed, scrolling back down. "We can't tell from this. Could be something totally unrelated. It was a couple days after."

"So, she tells Nina the secret at school, on the Thursday. And then, on the Saturday, Emily . . . dies."

Jet didn't like all the space Billy had left around that word.

"Her death was an accident," she said, sharpening that last word into a point. "The timing is just a coincidence. You were there, Billy, you saw it: Emily was alone and it was just an accident. Nothing to do with this."

"Yeah," Billy said, staring at the screen, a silver reflection on the surface of his watery eyes, the scrolling words of two ghosts imprinted there, rippling when he blinked.

TWENTY-SEVEN

Andrew Smith was slumped over the table in the farthest corner of the bar, head tucked into the crook of his elbow, passed out. People moved around him, talking, laughing, like the drunk man in the corner was invisible to them.

Jet hung back as Billy approached the table to return Andrew's keys, carefully sliding them into the pocket of his jacket, hanging on the chair. Billy didn't come back, not right away; he went to the bar first, grabbed a glass, and filled it with water. Left it there on Andrew's table, for when he woke up. Such a Billy thing to do. Jet smiled to herself, watching him just be Billy, walking back over to her.

He didn't make it again.

"Billy!" Allison called from behind the bar.

Billy made a face just for Jet, then turned, nodding to his boss. "Allison."

"You told me you were sick. That's why you've missed your shifts this week. Don't look sick to me. Saw you buying a beer earlier."

Billy didn't say anything, hid his hands behind his back.

"If I can't rely on you to turn up to work," Allison said, pursing her lips, "then I'll have to hire someone else, you know that."

"Sorry." Billy nodded, eyes like he meant it. "It's just . . . I have something, m-more important."

Allison's hands went to her hips, widening her eyes, a question in them.

Billy didn't answer it, didn't even try.

He walked away, pressing one hand against Jet's back, guiding her toward the door.

"Billy," she whispered, something tightening in her gut. "You shouldn't get in trouble for me. I won't be here—"

"—Maybe it's not for you," he said softly, holding the door open for her, the breeze snatching Jet's hair, throwing it across her eyes.

Billy rounded the corner, following the street, heading for his apartment.

Jet stopped, that thing in her gut pulling her the other way. She caught Billy's arm.

"Can we just . . ." she began, feeling stupid, trying not to feel stupid. "I don't know . . . walk?"

Billy turned, one thumb over his shoulder, pointing toward the stairs. "You don't want to read more of Emily and Nina's messages?"

"We've looked for hours," she replied. "We're not going to find anything. And I don't think learning that Emily's first kiss was with Chris Allen is going to help me solve my murder. I think . . . I want to walk."

"Oh." Billy took a few steps, back to her side. "You want to go talk to your mom now? Ask her what Emily overheard? I guess it's late but—"

"—No." Jet sucked in the air, filled herself with the darkness, breathed it all out. "I think I just want to walk. People do that sometimes, don't they?" She turned, slowly, heading back beyond the bar. "Don't need a reason to, or a place they're going, or a dog to tire out. They just walk . . . for them."

Billy walked beside her, a smile, its edges turned down, both confused and amused. "Yeah, people do do that."

"Doo-doo," Jet snorted, waiting for a car to pass.

"I just thought you'd be worried . . . about not having time."

Jet thought she'd be worried about that too, but her gut had other ideas—her heart too, picking up against her ribs, a different kind of song.

"I have time," she said as they crossed the street.

They walked, just walked. Like people did. Billy on her left side, two of Jet's steps for every one of his, arm nudging against hers. Jet breathed in the night air, spiced with autumn and the first falling leaves, the earthy smell of half-rotting pumpkins on people's doorsteps. Jet looked at the jack-o'-lanterns, but she didn't glare back, didn't feel like it anymore, almost smiled instead.

"This way," she said, following her gut, crossing the street again, toward The Green in the center of the oval road. Patches of grass trampled into mud from the Halloween Fair, six days ago tonight.

They walked under the burnt orange trees, sugar maples, branches shivering but not cold, and not scared, even though it was late and Jet and Billy were the only ones here.

Jet looked up, spotted it just in time. Reached out with her hand, her only hand. The falling leaf whirled, sailing the breeze, round and round and down, falling into Jet's open palm.

She closed her fingers around it, a perfect amber leaf.

Billy grinned. "That's supposed to be good luck," he said.

Jet grinned back. "Then you keep it." She offered it out.

Billy wouldn't take it, shook his head.

So Jet didn't give him the choice. "Please," she said, sliding it into his pocket.

Billy patted his jacket, a silent kind of thank you.

Jet looked up again, beyond the leaves, to the dark sky above. Not really all that dark, actually, little silver pinpricks of stars winking down at her.

"What are you looking at?" Billy craned his neck. "Trying to catch another one?"

"Well, you're gonna need all the luck you can get, Billy, without me here to look out for you." She sniffed. "Actually, I was looking at the stars. People do that too, huh? No reason. Just nice to look at."

"Yeah," Billy said, but he wasn't looking at the stars, he was looking at her.

Jet didn't warn him. She dropped down, sat back, the grass wet through her jeans.

"Whoa, you OK?"

"Yeah." She went all the way, legs out, resting her head back on the grass, not too hard against the bandage and the throbbing inside. "I'm just laying here," she said.

"Why?" Billy said, immediately joining her, his head close to hers, legs pointed the other way. Their own little mismatched triangle.

"Because I wanted to." Jet stared up. Could you always see this many stars here? Jet had never bothered to really look up before, to try counting them, just because.

"I was thinking," Billy said. "Nina said it was a secret that Dianne knew but her family doesn't, so maybe it wasn't your parents Emily over-heard but—"

"—We don't have to talk about it," Jet spoke across him.

"What?"

"*That.*"

"OK." Billy nodded, grass blending with his dark hair, too straight among the curls. "What do you want to talk about?"

"Anything. Anything at all."

Jet counted the stars.

"Why didn't you want to marry JJ?" Billy asked, voice small, barely making it through the darkness.

Jet's chest contracted, ribs closing into a shield. Well, she did say *any-thing.* And this was Billy. She trusted him, with her truck, with her life, and maybe something else too. Her chest opened up and she sighed.

"I used to think JJ was good for me. He pushed me, said I should be the best version of myself, dream even bigger. I think that's who he loved: the best version of me, the one with the big ideas. He would have resented me eventually, when none of it worked out. And nothing ever works out. I give up, so I gave up on him. I think he thought he was *set-tling* with me, and maybe I thought the same too. Because there *had* to be someone better for me, someone perfect—not here, maybe in Boston—once I'd fixed my life, become that better person. And what was the other choice: I marry him and get stuck here in Woodstock for-ever? Become my parents? Or Luke and Sophia?"

Billy pulled out a handful of grass. "You wanted to leave?"

Jet tilted her head, glanced over at him. "Don't you? Don't you ever think about it? Somewhere new? Maybe a lot of somewheres. Not the place that's supposed to be home, but the place that *feels* like home. Find other bars to play your music in, make lots of people smile, because you make everyone smile, Billy. Live out of a truck and have dirty socks and cold beers and sit under new stars every night? Don't plan, or worry about the time. Just . . . be."

Her eyes prickled, a new sheen, made the stars even brighter.

"Yeah," Billy said. "I've thought about leaving, I have." He glanced over at her, Jet saw in the corner of her eye. "But there was always something keeping me here."

Jet sniffed. "Not realistic anyway. Life can't be about that, about wasting time. Has to be about something bigger, doesn't it?"

Billy shrugged, not so easy lying down. "I don't know, I think it might be simpler than that. I think life is about finding your person, your one person." He paused. "And you better make sure that they really love you back, so they don't just pack their bags one night and abandon you. They have to love you back. That's it, I think."

Jet looked over at Billy, hair and grass bunching, tickling her neck. Should she just tell him about his mom? Did she owe Billy that, before the end? But it might change things and Jet didn't want this to change, didn't want Billy to look at her any different, that sparkle behind his pale blue eyes. If Jet had time, she wanted it to be like this. Just this.

"Look." She pointed up at the sky, drawing a shape with the stars. "Do you see it? No, look this way, Billy. Yeah. That's its eye, that's the other one. It's a frog, see?"

Billy laughed. "Of course you see a frog. You love frogs."

"You don't see it?"

Billy breathed out, looked at her. "If it's a frog to you, then it's a frog to me."

"It's a frog."

She dropped her arm to the grass. Turned to smile at Billy.

"Soooo . . . are you cold too?"

"Absolutely freezing," he laughed, teeth chattering. "And I'm soaking wet."

"Me too. Shall we . . . ?"

"Yeah."

Billy stood up, towering over her. He bent down, reached out, offered her his hand.

"Err, Billy," Jet said, dragging her head up, pushing her neck into folds. "Wrong hand."

She waved with the working one.

"Shit, sorry," Billy hissed, switching hands.

Jet snorted, eyes finding Billy's. He snorted too, and that fucking did it.

Jet exploded with laughter, couldn't hold it in, rolling onto her side, ribs against the ground, dead arm somewhere beneath her.

Billy laughed too, hard, harder, weaving in and out of Jet's whistling old man cackle.

"Why are we laughing?" Billy laughed, bent double, tears in his eyes.

"I don't know." Jet struggled to speak, to breathe. "It's not even funny."

But it was, it was the funniest thing in the world and all the stars, and they laughed and they couldn't stop.

Not when Billy found the right hand this time, pulled Jet to her feet.

Not as they stumbled away, crashing into each other, laughing too hard to walk straight.

Jet's stomach ached with it, and she forgot about the worse one in her head.

Billy would try, swallowing the laughter, his after-sigh setting Jet off again, because it was catching, and they both had it.

Red-cheeked and snotty-nosed and scrunched-up eyes.

They walked and they laughed.

This. Just this.

JET LAY IN bed, too awake, staring up at the ceiling. There were no stars here, but they weren't far away.

She was smiling.

Her cheek hurt, just the one side she could feel, because she couldn't stop smiling.

Couldn't fight it, didn't really want to try.

"Good night, Billy," she called first this time, through the half-open door.

"Good night, Jet."

Friday
November 7

TWENTY-EIGHT

"Mom?" Jet called through the empty house.

Not empty.

Reggie scuttled around the corner, launched himself at her.

"Hello, hi, is that the Regmatron?" Jet tickled his ears, one-handed, fingers down his spine to the base of his helicopter tail. "Who's a good boy?" she asked, because she always did. "Who's a good boy?"

Reggie yawned, pattering over to Billy, wagging for him too.

"Of course Mom's out when I need to speak to her." Jet straightened up. "All this talk about *Please come home, Jet,* but she's not even here. And she calls *me* useless."

"She's got to be back sometime." Billy closed the front door. "We can wait."

"We have time," Jet said.

Ms were hard to say now, one side of her mouth too weak to press her lips together, speaking out the other way, smiles cut in half. She only knew because she'd tried to smile at Billy this morning, when he made her pancakes for breakfast. Got up early to do it. Better than fries.

Jet followed the dog, through the doorway into the living room. Here again. No pools of blood or spatter anymore, but Jet knew where they'd been, scrubbed away, painted over.

Billy held his breath, walking through behind her.

He'd seen it that way too.

Held Jet's lifeless body, seen the insides of her undone head. His voice breaking as he screamed her name, breaking something inside Jet too as she'd watched and rewatched the doorbell footage.

Billy shouldn't have ever seen something like that; he was too good for it.

He breathed again when they reached the kitchen.

Reggie pounced on a balled-up sock, discarded beneath the bar stools, grunting as he showed it off to them. His wagging tail disturbed the two dish towels hanging by the stove, made them sway. Marching avocados and lemons, an incomplete set.

Jet kept going, through the laundry room to the side door.

She pulled down on the handle.

It was locked now, lesson learned. Just too late to make a difference.

She flicked the catch and tried again, pushing the door open.

Reggie was first out, barging past, off to dig a hole for his sock and lose it forever.

Then Jet stepped out, then Billy, not one word between them, like they both knew exactly where they were supposed to go without ever needing to say it.

To the pool.

It was covered now, a white plastic cover, creamy against the surrounding ash-wood deck. Wouldn't be uncovered until the summer, or late spring, or whenever Dad decided they'd had two sunny weekends in a row and it was time.

Jet wondered then if they'd ever replaced the water, or if it was still the same water that drowned Emily, hoping the chlorine would take the death out of it.

Her footsteps echoed on the deck, coming to a stop. Billy's too.

"You were here that day." Jet stared at the pool. "Do you remember it?"

Billy chewed his lip. "As much as any eleven-year-old can remember a day like that."

Jet nodded. "Tell me again."

"When we found her?"

"The whole thing."

Billy took a breath, filled himself. "It was a nice day. I was out in the yard with Mom, helping her plant a new flower bed. Sunflower seeds, I think. They still grow there now. Dad was inside cooking, or maybe he was out at the store picking up stuff for a barbecue later. He came back, and he said Luke had been knocking on the door, asking to come play with me. Which was . . ." Billy paused. "Well, Luke never wanted to play with me. He was thirteen, I was eleven. And *you* were mine—m-my best friend. But you were out at that spelling thing, so Dad asked if me and Luke wanted to play soccer outside. We played for a little while. And then . . . see, I was thinking about this last night, after we found what we found. And I thought it was strange at the time, but I haven't thought about it in years."

"What?" Jet looked up from the pool.

"So, we're playing soccer, one on one, and Dad's referee and Mom's still gardening. And Dad throws the ball for us, but it goes right into the bushes at the back of the yard, against the fence. We both go in, me and Luke, to find the ball, because it was really overgrown back there. And I find it, and we come back out. And Luke's arms got all scratched up, and I remember Dad making a big deal out of it, seeing if Luke wanted a Band-Aid, asking Mom to go inside to get some cream. Think he felt responsible. But . . ." Billy locked eyes with her. "I don't know how much you can trust my memory. But the thing is, what I remember—"

"—Billy."

"I think Luke's arms were already scratched up *before* we went into the bushes. He was wearing a T-shirt, and I was sure of that at the time."

Jet studied his stormy eyes. "What kind of scratches?"

"Lots of them," Billy said, "all over both arms. Little ones. The kind you'd get if you climbed through a bush and got scratched up by thorns, or if someone scratched you, like in a fight. The police asked about them later, when we were giving our statements. We all told them about the bushes: me, Mom, Dad, Luke. But . . ." Billy's eyes darkened, lines pulling around them. "Last night, I was thinking, there's something else too. Luke said he hadn't been in the pool at all that day. That's what he told us, and the police after."

"Yeah, I know," Jet said. "He hadn't."

"He said he'd been inside all day, playing PlayStation. Didn't know where Emily was, got bored, came around to see if I was free to play."

"Yeah, that sounds right."

"Except," Billy said, "when we were playing soccer, when I got close, to tackle him, I think I could smell it on him, in his hair."

"What?"

"Chlorine," Billy said, eyes widening, mouth too, a flash of his bottom teeth.

Jet looked back at the covered pool, a switch in her heart, throwing off the pattern.

"Are you sure?" she asked.

"No, I'm not sure. It was so long ago. And maybe it's only because of what we saw in Emily's messages. But I think . . . I don't know. Sorry."

Jet chewed the inside of her cheek, felt nothing, only knew she'd broken the skin when she tasted the metal bite of blood. It was seventeen years ago; Billy was just a kid. Jet couldn't really trust her own memories of that day, so that ruled Billy's out too. Luke *did* go in the pool later, *after*. Billy was probably getting confused.

"What happened next?" she said.

"When we finished playing soccer, Dad was starting the grill and Luke was going home. But then Luke realized he'd forgotten a key and wasn't sure if any of the doors were unlocked at yours. Mom said she'd walk Luke back, make sure he got in OK. I went too. Followed my mom everywhere back then." He sniffed. "We tried the front door first. Knocked. No one answered. We thought Emily had probably gone out. So Mom walked us around the side to try the doors at the back. It was open, that side door." He pointed to it, the one into the laundry room. The same one Jet's killer had walked through. "Me and Mom were just about to leave when Mom looked over here and . . ." He trailed off, eyes flickering over the covered pool.

"You saw Emily," Jet said, not a question.

"You couldn't really see her," Billy said. "Just the colors. The shape. On the bottom of the pool."

Jet swallowed.

"Mom screamed when she realized. Screamed so loud. Luke ran back over. Dad heard, across the road. He came running. So did Mr. Griffin, from next door." Billy closed his eyes, like he could see it all again, unfolding in front of him, seventeen years gone in a blink. "Dad was the one to jump in, right away, all his clothes. He swam down to the bottom. Those were the longest few seconds I can ever remember. He came back up without her. Said that her hair was stuck in the drain and he couldn't pull her up. He told Luke to run inside and find some scissors. Luke did, fastest I'd ever seen him move. He jumped in the pool to get the scissors to Dad. Dad went under. Even longer this time. Came back up with Emily in his arms, hair ragged, half cut away."

Billy moved closer to the pool.

"He got her out, right here." He bent to touch the exact tile. "Luke helped, pushed her legs up. And then Dad started CPR. But . . . she was already blue. I remember thinking that—that it was too late. Mr. Griffin called the ambulance. And Mom, she was hugging Luke. And I watched. Right here." He stepped back and pointed at his feet, where he'd stood as a little boy. "Dad refused to stop, the whole time, even though I think we all knew. The ambulance arrived maybe ten minutes later, took over. And then it was only a couple of minutes, until you got home with your parents."

Billy looked over at her finally, back here and now.

"You were still holding your little trophy." Billy choked up, coughed into his fist. "I'll never forget the sound your mom made, when she saw Emily. People don't scream like that, it . . ."

Jet remembered it too. But people did scream like that. Billy had, when he found Jet.

"So it was your mom who found Emily?"

That pit of guilt opening up in Jet's gut again.

"Yeah," Billy sniffed. "She was the first."

"Did she . . . did she ever talk about Emily after?"

Billy looked at the sky. "We sometimes talked about what happened, about that day. She always got upset."

"But did she ever mention . . . did she know what Emily wanted to tell her, or that she wanted to tell her something?"

"What are you thinking?" Billy asked her.

Jet wasn't sure what she was thinking, hoped she'd figure it out as she was speaking.

"Well, Emily's message said she'd started to tell your mom on that Friday, but then your mom had to leave. So maybe your mom knew something, a part of it, if it wasn't just a school thing, if it was the secret about Luke, what Emily overheard. And, with Emily dying the next day, maybe she would have thought it was more important, I don't know. Told someone what she knew, wrote it down or . . ."

Billy's bottom lip folded up. "She never said anything to me."

"But you were a kid," Jet countered. "Do you . . . do you still have any of her stuff?"

Billy glanced back at Jet's house, his own childhood home hidden behind it.

"Yeah," he said. "Dad wanted to throw most of it out, but I made him keep it. It's all boxed up in the attic. Not her phone or her laptop or anything like that. She took those with her when she left."

"Any of her work stuff, from school?"

"Yeah, I mean there were her work diaries, some calendars, things like that."

"From 2008?" Jet asked, a tiny trickle of hope, filling in that pit in her gut.

"Probably." Billy was still looking toward his house, eyes faraway, farther than that. "Mom liked to keep things like that. Had memory boxes from each year, ticket stubs, pressed flowers—you know, that kind of thing."

"Can we look?" Jet asked, treading carefully. "See if she kept anything, wrote anything down, about Emily?"

"Yeah." Billy turned his back on the pool. "I'm not sure we'll find anything, but we can look while we wait for your mom to come home."

"Reggie!" Jet called, the dog appearing in a flash of orangey fur, now sockless, front paws stained brown from digging. "Come on."

They crossed from deck to grass, through the side door into the laundry room. Jet almost forgot again, went back to lock it.

Through the kitchen and living room to the front door, Reggie leaving a trail of pawprints, only dirt this time.

"Love you," Jet said, opening the door.

"S-sorry?" Billy stuttered.

"Talking to the dog. Bye, Reg. See you later."

They walked out onto the drive, past Jet's truck. Billy had parked it at a strange angle, but Jet wasn't allowed to criticize now, was she? Onto the street and across the road to the fence outside Billy's house, through the little gate.

"Your dad's at work," Jet said, looking at the small driveway to the side of the house, no cars.

"I know you're into your breaking and entering at the moment." Billy smiled at her, pulling out his ring of keys. "But I've actually got a key. Sorry."

Billy unlocked the front door. The entrance opened straight into their living room. Jet had always thought the Finneys' house was more like a home, too much stuff in some corners, too little in others, too plain or too bright, tidy but not neat. A yellow couch with a collection of unmatched cushions, still fluffed, the top corners pointy but inviting. The stairs in the far corner painted periwinkle blue, the paint chipped off in a few places, showing the original white underneath.

"Come on," Billy said, leading her up.

He stopped on the landing, glanced up at the hatch in the ceiling.

"Two seconds."

Billy went over to the big closet, grabbing the pole for the attic. "You always used to hide in this closet," he said, "when we played hide-and-go-seek."

"I was just thinking that. Hey, if we have enough time, I'll rematch you."

Billy raised the pole and slotted it into the catch, turning it to lower the entrance, the ladder sliding down with a metallic hiss. "I'm six foot two now, can't hide anywhere."

"Don't just let me win because I have forty-eight hours to live."

Hours now. Couldn't even count it in days anymore. Billy noticed too, tried to move past it, not let it in. He glanced at the ladder, then back to Jet. "Do you need help?"

Jet scoffed. "I can do a ladder with one arm." She put her foot up on the first step, to prove the point, hooking her left elbow under to take her weight. It was slow—one foot, second foot, then shift her arm—but she was still climbing.

"I'm right behind you if you fall," Billy said.

"I'll crush you."

"I'll catch you."

And Jet was sure he would, actually.

She reached the top, onto the chipboard flooring, and stood up. She didn't even need to duck her head under the low beams, but Billy had to, bending double, flicking on a lamp, yellow and dim.

"Over here," he said, crouching lower, heading toward a collection of cardboard boxes.

It smelled musty up here, old, like if time itself had a smell.

"So . . . this is her stuff." Billy pulled one box off a teetering pile. "That looks like the clothes she left behind."

"She didn't take her clothes?" Jet stepped closer, speaking loudly over the guilt, so Billy couldn't hear it.

"Not all of them, just one suitcase." He sniffed. "Obviously in a real hurry to leave. Took the important stuff, left everything else behind. Us too."

Billy grunted, lifting the box of clothes off the pile, placing it down. But there was something else too, on top of the folded shirts and jeans. A small leather-bound photo album. Jet bent to her knees, behind Billy's back, flicked through it with her working hand while he searched.

The face of the boy she'd known so well, Billy back then. Holding hands with his mom in a pumpkin patch, scribbled words beneath: *Halloween 2006.* More and more, Billy growing older with each turn of the page, cheeks sharpening, halfway smile. Jet stopped at a double page, one side empty, just the corners of tape where the photo used to live. Underneath it said: *Me and Billy eating ice cream Summer 2009.* This must have been the photo Billy had in his apartment, the frame he'd hidden when she moved in.

But that wasn't the only blank page.

Four years later, there was another gap, another missing photo. *Me and Billy testing out our new bikes 2013.* Jet ran her finger over the empty space, closing her eyes to bring the scene to life.

"What are you doing?" Billy interrupted. "Why aren't you helping?"

Jet straightened up, turned the album to face him. "Looks like your mom didn't leave *everything* behind. Took the important stuff," she repeated his words.

Billy hesitated, eyes lighting up as they flicked over the empty page.

"Probably fell out," he muttered, blinking, the light gone again. He took the album from her, dropped it on the floor, didn't want to know.

"Oh, look," he said instead, sliding out the box at the bottom of one of the piles, undoing the tape. "This looks like work stuff. Math textbooks." He pulled some out, grunting at the weight of them. "Some papers." He dug his hand through. "Ah. Here's one of her work planners." He passed it over to Jet. "That's from 2015. The year she left."

Jet turned the little ring-bound notebook around in her hands, opened the front cover. *Beth Finney* was scribbled inside, big fancy writing, the *y* looping over to underline the rest of her name. Jet skipped a few more pages, a little hard to read in this light. Each date had its own page, even the weekends, her scribbles in red or black pen. Notes, reminders, to-do lists with her own drawn checkboxes, uneven little squares with *X*s that didn't stay within the lines. Most were checked off.

Jet read a few.

January 15

Math leadership team meeting at 11.

Order more graph paper.

Extra credit marking.

Speak to Taylor Elliott after class.

Skipped some more pages.

March 7

Email Mr. Elliott.

Order Billy's birthday present.

That one was checked off. Jet wondered what Billy's mom had bought him that year, the year he would have turned eighteen, his last ever present from her.

The knot in her gut pulled tighter.

She sniffed, snapped the notebook shut.

"2008?" she asked.

"I'm looking," Billy grunted, his head almost inside the box. "That's 2013. 2011." He laid them on the floor, carefully, like his mom might need them again someday. "Ah-ha. No, that's 2006, sorry." He buried deeper. "2010. Oh. Here it is—2008."

He reemerged with it clutched between his hands, sitting back on his knees.

"May thirtieth," Jet said. "Find Friday May thirtieth. That's when Emily tried to speak to her. She might have written something down. Your mom wrote things down."

Jet moved closer, leaning over Billy's shoulder as he turned the pages, flicked halfway through the book. *June.* Too far. Flicked back.

"Here it is," he said, running his finger over his mom's writing. "May thirtieth. *Go over practice tests for AP. Lunch with Sarah. Pick Billy up from practice at 4.*" Billy swallowed, glanced up at her. "Sorry Jet. There's nothing here about Emily."

"You sure?" She deflated, resting her arm on his shoulder.

"Yeah." Billy flicked the page, checking the day before and the one after. "Nothing about Emi— Wait."

He settled on the day after, flattened the page.

Saturday, May 31. The day Emily had drowned.

Jet leaned even closer, stared down at the writing, her eyes splitting the words, two layers.

Pick up burgers from store.

Plant flower bed at back of yard.

But that wasn't everything.

Mrs. Finney had written something else on this page, tiny, right at the bottom, not in the lines but sideways across them. The letters slanted, like she'd written them in a hurry, in a panic.

Billy spun the book sideways and they read it together. Silent.

He was already wet. Before.

A shaky line under that *Before.*

Jet's heart doubled, copying her eyes, forcing its way to her ears.

No. Wait. No. Jet couldn't be thinking that. She couldn't. Stop it. Stop.

"He was already wet," she said, barely a whisper.

"Before." Billy finished it, the diary shaking in his hands. His eyes found Jet's, unstable, turbulent. "Luke," he said.

He didn't need to say it, the name was already thundering around Jet's head, throwing itself against the cracks.

She couldn't think it but she was, she had to. Billy's eleven-year-old memories couldn't be trusted alone—but his mom too?

"You were right." Jet sank to her knees beside him, brushing her thumb across Mrs. Finney's writing, to make sure it was really real, not a trick of the light or a trick of her eyes. "You thought Luke smelled like chlorine. Before. Before you all found Emily and Luke jumped in. Your mom noticed it too. He was wet when he came over. He'd been in the pool already. He said he hadn't, but he lied—he must have been in the pool."

"Why would he . . ." Billy didn't finish, left the thought hanging there, settling over the layers of dust.

"Billy, those scratches on Luke's arms. If he . . . could they . . ." She didn't know how to say it, because saying it might make it true. "Did they look like the kind of scratches someone might get, if they were holding someone's head underwater, if that person was fighting for their life?"

Billy blinked and a dark wave crashed behind his eyes.

"It was a lot of scratches."

Jet's knees gave way. She slumped back against the wooden strut.

"Oh my god. Did Luke kill Emily?"

Billy sat back too, his mom's diary still open.

"I don't know," he whispered. "But it looks like, maybe, my mom thought he did."

Jet shook her head, refusing the thought, not letting it settle long enough to take hold, make itself at home. "No. He was only thirteen. I mean, yes, he was bigger than Emily already. Stronger. And they fought all the time, like brothers and sisters do. Luke has a temper, everyone knows he has a temper. But he can't have . . . he can't . . . did he?"

Billy didn't have the answer, and neither did Jet. Billy's mom might have, but she was long gone, ten years gone, and whose fault was that?

Jet shook her head again, the world shifting around her, splitting in half. Everything changed after Emily died, and now it was changing again, coming undone, like Jet's head.

"But her hair was caught in the drain, Billy. You saw it. Your dad had to cut her out. How would a thirteen-year-old know how to do that, to stage it like an accident? To come over here so he had an alibi. He was *thirteen*."

"I don't know."

"Is it possible? Could Luke do something like that? Kill my sister? And if he could kill one sister, could he . . . ?"

"I don't know," Billy said again, like he'd lost all other words out of his own black hole.

"No. He had an alibi. He was with Henry at the time of my attack. He didn't. He didn't kill me."

"That doesn't mean . . ." Billy glanced down at the page again.

"Luke can be scary," Jet said, echoing Henry's words, picturing Luke smashing his fists against the steering wheel, reopening the scabs on his knuckles, blood pooling under his wedding ring.

Jet shook her head. Just kept shaking it, making the aches ache harder.

And a new thought, forcing its way through the cracks, clawing up her tightening throat.

"If it wasn't an accident, if Luke killed Emily . . . then it wasn't my fault."

"Jet." Billy turned to her, the storm settling in his eyes, reaching out to take her hand, holding it in her lap. "It was never your fault."

TWENTY-NINE

"There you are!"

A blue Range Rover was parked outside the Masons' house, too close to Jet's truck, blocking it in.

Sophia slammed the door, marching toward Jet and Billy, meeting them halfway across the drive.

"I was looking for you!" Her cheeks were flushed, eyes swimming.

"Lucky me," Jet muttered, not stopping. "Listen, Sophia, I'd love to stick around and chat, but I need to find my mom and—"

"—You told Luke!" she growled, spit foaming at the corner of her mouth. "I asked you not to tell him, and you did! About the pills. Why would you do that, Jet?!"

Jet's head throbbed, the broken sides crashing together, a spark of rage where they met. Sophia doubled and doubled again, the world splitting apart, time too, all the way back seventeen years. Hot day, cold trophy in her hand.

"You're right, it's *my* fault," Jet spat back. "That you were poisoning your father-in-law so he'd stop going into the office and wouldn't discover all the fraud your husband was committing."

Sophia's eyes snapped wide, nostrils too, looking between Jet and Billy.

"Yeah," Jet said, "we know about that too."

"And about Henry Lim's accident, the hospital bills," Billy added.

"Everything, Sophia."

Sophia didn't blink, like she'd forgotten how.

"Luke did it for us, for all of us! The company was going under, and he's the one who turned it around. He saved it!"

"By scamming people. Not paying taxes." Jet stepped closer, matched Sophia's eyes. "Someone burned the fucking building down, probably because of something Luke did. So I'm not sure he really saved the company. It's gone!"

"Luke's a good person."

"I don't think he is, Sophia!" Jet roared, letting the rage in, letting it win. "Now can you—"

"—Oh, because you are?!" Sophia scoffed, pointing a finger too close to Jet's chest. "Are you a good person, Jet?"

"Sophia, move your fucking car!"

"I told you what I'd do," Sophia lowered her voice, a dangerous whisper. "If you told Luke. I told you what I'd do."

Jet took a breath, met her eyes. "Don't," she said, lower, more dangerous.

Sophia turned to Billy, opened her mouth, stalactites of spit stringing between her teeth.

"Sophia, don't!" Jet pushed her back, one-handed, driving her elbow into Sophia's ribs.

She shoved Jet away, too hard, her back slamming against the Range Rover.

Sophia's eyes found Billy, locked on.

"Do you know?" she asked him.

"Billy, don't listen!" Jet shouted. "Come on, we need to go!"

Billy looked at Jet instead, eyes reacting to the terror in hers, darkening.

"Please don't listen," Jet begged him, the tears prickling her eyes, forced up by the guilt, churning in her stomach. "Let's go."

"Do you know the real reason your mom abandoned you?" Sophia said, almost with a smile.

"Sophia, please stop!" Jet begged her now, caught between the two of them, trapped.

"What do you mean?" Billy said, voice wavering and small.

Jet blinked, memorized the way Billy's eyes brightened just for her, saved it, because they wouldn't anymore, not after this.

"It was Jet's fault," Sophia said, enjoying this. "*She's* the reason your mom left."

"Sophia, stop!" Jet shouted, even though it was far too late; she could tell by Billy's face, that storm in his eyes, that coldness. "Billy." She reached out for his hand.

He didn't take it. His shoulders tensed.

"What did you do?" he whispered, speaking to Jet, looking at Sophia.

"I didn't mean to," Jet said. "I didn't know she'd—"

"—Jet went to her after school, our junior year. Asked Mrs. Finney to cheat for her, to raise her grade on an extra-credit assignment. Guilted her into doing it, manipulated her and—"

"—That's not . . ." Jet cut her off, lost her way, looked at Billy to find it again. "I just, I needed a 3.5 GPA, otherwise I wasn't going to get into Dartmouth. And I had to go to Dartmouth, because that's where Emily . . . I just needed this one assignment in precalculus to be graded higher, that's all."

"We planned it out." Sophia stepped forward. "Me and Jet, what she was going to say to bully your mom into cheating for her. Jet thought using her dead sister was the best way to—"

"—Shut up, Sophia." Jet wiped her face, standing in front of him, making Billy look at her instead. He should hear it from her, not Sophia, who was using her words as a weapon, trying to hurt them both, and doing it with a smile. "I did. I did talk about Emily, told your mom why I had to get into Dartmouth. And then, I repeated that thing I'd overheard my mom say. That she'd asked your dad to check in on Emily and Luke that day. I said I wondered how different life would be, if he had, if Emily was still here. I know it was wrong, it was horrible. I thought that if your mom felt guilty, about Emily, then maybe she'd help me." Jet sniffed. "I didn't realize she'd get so upset. She burst into tears. I went too far, I didn't realize . . . I'm so sorry, Billy. I'm so sorry."

She reached for him again.

Billy stiffened, stepped back. He shook his head, his watery eyes now wet, blinking tears that raced to his chin.

"It was the same day," Sophia said, taking aim again, "that she packed her bags and left you. Jet did that. She's the one who drove your mom out of town. Maybe she wasn't the whole reason, but she was the final straw." Sophia laughed, hollow and cruel. "You've been in love with her since you were a kid, and you never knew she's the one who ruined your life!"

Jet blinked, that one getting her straight through the chest, another black hole.

"I'm so sorry, Billy. I'm so sorry."

Billy's breath shuddered, stepping back from her again, toward the street, tears splitting across his lips as they parted.

"Did she do it?" he asked, not looking at Jet, looking at the sky instead. No stars, just clouds. "Did she change your grade?"

Jet's chin buckled, her bottom lip shaking. "Yes," she whispered. "Billy, I'm—"

"—I can't believe it." Billy ran a hand over his face, catching the rest of his tears. He wasn't shouting, not even now. A hurt too deep for that. "I spent the last ten years of my life wondering why she left us. If I was really that unlovable that my own mother couldn't even . . ." He choked it back, wiped again. "And you just . . . you knew, Jet, and you didn't . . . And it's you. *You!*" he finally shouted, voice breaking in half, Jet's heart with it.

"Billy, I—"

"—I'm sorry, I can't."

He turned, boots scraping against the stone, out of the drive, into the street.

He walked away.

Didn't look back.

"Billy!" Jet called after him, the wind in the trees mocking her, stealing her voice.

"You shouldn't have told Luke," Sophia said, darkly. "No consequences, huh, Jet?"

Jet shoved Sophia, grabbed a handful of her coat.

Wanted to scream in her face, wanted to hit her, wanted to take all her hurt out on her, and Billy's too. But she said something she hoped would cut deeper, carve a hole through Sophia's chest, like she'd done to her.

"I hope you're always this unhappy," she whispered, staring through Sophia's dark eyes, not blinking, so she knew that she meant it too.

Jet let her go and walked away, onto the street. She wouldn't waste any more seconds on Sophia; those seconds, those minutes, those hours were for someone else.

"Billy!" Jet shouted, following him down the street.

He was far up ahead, moving too fast, already on the main road.

"Billy, wait!"

He couldn't hear her, or he didn't want to, moving even faster, losing his edges as Jet's eyes swam, sliced the world into two uneven halves.

Jet wouldn't let it all fall apart. She leaned against a tree, waited for the worst to pass, breathing through it. She lost Billy, couldn't see him anymore, but she was not going to lose him.

She ran, down Church Street, a drumbeat in her head. It couldn't be her heart, because that was gone, wherever that black hole had taken it. The same place as Billy's.

Jet followed him. He must have come this way, past The Green, going home.

Not just Billy's apartment.

Home.

There was an earthquake under the pavement that only Jet could feel, unbalancing her legs, dead arm swaying, weighing her down. She blinked her way through it. Had to catch up to Billy. Find Billy. The only thing that mattered, and this earthquake might slow her down, but it was not going to stop her.

But something else did.

A police squad car pulled up on the driveway in front of her, blocking the sidewalk. A squawk, a short burst of sound as it came to a stop, swimming in and out of Jet's vision.

One door opened, then the other.

The police chief and Billy's dad stepped out.

"Jet," Jack Finney said, shutting his car door. "We need to speak to you."

"Not now," Jet sniffed. She kept moving, doubling around the car, onto the grass. "I have something more important."

"I'm afraid you have no choice," the chief barked, hurrying to catch up to her. He grabbed her arm, the one she couldn't feel, pulled her back. "Margaret Mason, I'm arresting you on suspicion of second-degree arson. You—"

"—What?!" Jet hollowed out, only panic left behind, ugly and hot. "No, no. You've got it wrong. You can't arrest me, I'm running out of time!" She tried to pull away.

"You have the right to remain silent—" the chief continued.

No, Jet had to stop this.

"—You can't! Do you have a wa-wa-w—" FUCK, what was that word, that legal term? She should know this, she had to know this, to put a stop to this. "Did the court issue a wa-wa-war—I need to see it. The wa-warr—"

The chief wasn't listening, his fingers gripped around a set of hand-cuffs, raising them toward Jet's wrist.

Jet couldn't think of the word, and she had nothing else, she couldn't let them take her. It was instinct, a fire that had already started behind her eyes, claiming the rest of her, a new strength.

She shoved the chief back, left hand slamming against his shoulder.

He tripped on the curb, lost his footing, and Jet didn't wait to see what else.

She made a break for it, down the street to the right.

"She's running!" Lou yelled behind her. "Go, Sergeant, go!"

Two doors slammed again, the growl of an engine.

Then a siren, screaming after her.

Jet flew.

Her breath shuddering in and out.

No thoughts; Jet let instinct, or the black hole, take those too. Just run. Run faster.

Shoes hammering the ground, veering this way and that as the world tilted, tried to throw Jet off.

The police car was right behind, chasing her down, hot breath against the backs of her legs.

She turned left, into the parking lot behind the public library, slamming into the hood of a silver truck just pulling out.

The driver beeped.

Jet blinked. She braced and pushed off the truck, stumbling away, disappearing behind it.

Checked back.

The cop car was pulling around the angry truck, following her down the lot, gaining speed.

The siren shrieking, ready to swallow Jet whole.

She pushed harder, sprinting, the end of the parking lot right ahead.

Pinned down between a brick wall and the siren.

Jet sped up, pressed her left hand against the lip of the wall, and vaulted over it. Not clean, caught her foot and rolled in the gravel on the other side, but she was over.

The siren cut out.

Two doors slammed.

"Jet, please stop running!" Jack shouted.

She already was, checking back to see the two cops climbing over the same wall, chasing her on foot now.

They could not catch up to her.

She didn't have time for this. She had less than forty-eight hours to live, and she would not give those up for anyone.

She ran.

Through some trees.

Through a tight alley between two buildings, across the street.

Climbed up onto a parked car to jump over a fence into someone's backyard.

The alarm went off, drawing the cops to her.

Fuck.

She got over, landed on her feet this time. Kept going.

They could not catch her.

Out the house's open garage door, a man yelling "Hey!" after her.

Around the corner, through another parking lot.

Another alley, behind the pharmacy. So close to Central Street. So close to home, to Billy.

The alley grew tighter and tighter, catching her, bricks chewing her up.

Couldn't see much anymore, the world spinning, her legs weakening.

Ribs closing in around her heart, piercing it with their sharp ends.

Jet stopped behind a dumpster to catch her breath, and her heart and her eyes, catch them before she lost them entirely.

Just two seconds, then she'd run again.

Jack Finney appeared at the other side of the alley, a silhouette with a strange-shaped head against the sun and the passing cars.

Jet turned, ready to run back the way she'd come, but the chief was behind her, boxing her in.

"Stop running, Jet!" Jack called.

"No." The word barely came out, no breath to spare.

"Get her!" screamed the chief.

There was a fire escape up the side of the building.

Jet tore over to it, racing both of them.

Grabbed the ladder with her left hand, up with one foot.

If she could climb up, she could break a window, get inside, and—

A fist grabbed her jacket, some of her hair.

Pulled.

Jet crashed back down to the ground, but she didn't fall. She was pushed up against the wall, her mouth and cheek grating on the brick, a hand on the back of her head, where it was broken.

The chief pressed himself against her, wheezing down her neck as he forced her arms together.

The angry hiss of the handcuffs, tightening around her wrists, catching her, too late.

"No. Please."

Her last hope gone, taking with it all the time she had left in this world.

Lost.

Out the hole where her heart used to live.

"Margaret Mason," he said, breathless. "I'm arresting you on suspicion of second-degree arson. You have the right to remain silent. Anything you say can and will be used against you in a court of law."

THIRTY

A lightning flash, hiss and whirr of the camera.
Placard gripped in Jet's left hand.

Name: Margaret Mason
Age: 27
Booking ID: 4669283

"Stop looking down at the slate. Look over here at the camera, please."

She did, blinded by the white light, erasing everything, the room, the booking officer, even Jet, leaving only that unending ache behind her eye.

"Turn to the side."

Another flash.

Time slipping, her mind skipping between snapshots, the ache taking up too much space.

Cuffed to a bench.

Another pat-down search.

"Do you have any weapons on you?"

"No," she said for the second time.

The bench again.

"Place your hand on the glass scanner, fingers apart."

Green light under the glass, a bright line moving up and down, Jet's fingerprints appearing on the computer screen. Black ink, like four dark hooded figures seen from a distance, the crosshatch lines and swirls hidden in her skin.

"Right hand."

"I can't lift it."

"Right hand!"

Pushed into another chair: metal, small. Inside the interview room, the same one Jet had been in before, that digital clock hanging above her, ticking down, close to the end now. Red flickering numbers, the color of blood, a slow trickle through her brain, the color of fire, roaring at her heels.

Jet was cuffed again, the metal imprinting in her wrists. Her working arm tied to her dead arm, dragging both up, elbows on the table.

"Stop looking at the clock, look at me," said the chief, sitting across from her, Sergeant Jack Finney beside him. A dance they'd all danced before, except Jet couldn't leave this time, locks and chains.

"I already told you, I did not fucking burn down Mason Construction," she growled, her voice strange and flat, now the hope was all gone. "It wasn't me."

"This is a very serious offense," the chief said. "A class B felony. You understand that, right, Jet?"

"Yes. And do you understand that I have about thirty-six hours to live because someone murdered me a week ago?" Voice even stranger, flatter. Jet looked at Jack instead, his eyes kinder, more familiar, not quite Billy's, but the closest she'd find in here. "You have to let me go."

"I'm afraid we can't do that," the chief cut in.

"I'm dying!" Jet smacked her left fist on the table, a flash behind her eyes, that fiery edge of hell inside her head now, almost falling in.

"That doesn't make a difference," he sniffed. "The law is the law. We have enough evidence to place you at the—"

"—What evidence?"

The chief sighed, reaching for the file, the file sighing too, against the table.

"You told us you were at Billy Finney's apartment all night on Wednesday, November fifth."

"Yes, I was."

"We know that's a lie, Jet," Jack said, like it hurt to do it, avoiding her eyes.

The chief removed something from the file, a photograph printed on paper. He slid it across and turned it around so Jet could see.

It was a picture of her truck, taken from behind. The world dark around it, lit only by the moon and the flash of the camera. It was parked up on the side of the road, near the entrance to Mason Construction.

Jet didn't react, pushed the photo away. "It's my dad's company, I've been there a lot. This could be any time, doesn't prove anything."

The chief's chair creaked as he shifted forward. "The metadata tells us that this photograph was taken right by the driveway into Mason Construction, at 11:22 p.m. on Wednesday evening."

Fuck.

Jet didn't blink.

"The smoke alarm inside the building was triggered at 11:17 p.m., and the fire department arrived at 11:31 p.m. So, Jet." He steepled his fingers. "Why was your truck parked outside during the time of the fire, if you were at Billy's apartment all night?"

Jet pressed her lips together. Fuck, they had her. Jet needed to get out of here, now—what could she say to make that happen? But another question forced its way in front of that, another glance at the photograph.

"Who took that photo?" she asked it. Because who the fuck was there, taking photos, at 11:22 p.m., while Jet and Billy were almost burning to death inside? She kept that part of the question to herself.

The chief coughed into his fist. "A witness."

"What witness?" She sat up.

"I can't tell you that."

"Why not?"

"Because I can't."

Jet leaned forward, pressed one finger against the photo, dragging her right hand with it, the chain on the handcuffs clattering against the table.

"You didn't think that if this *witness* was at the scene around the time of the fire, maybe they could be your *suspect* instead?"

The chief shook his head.

"This witness had a legitimate reason to be there at that time. You, however, did n—"

"—What legitimate reason? Who is the witness?"

Her chest tightened around her phantom heart. Jet knew she didn't set the fire, so if someone else was there at the same time, this *witness*, it was probably the person who really did it—who tried to kill her the second time. And maybe the first time too. Was this how it ended, how Jet solved her own murder, sitting here in cuffs, accused of something she didn't do?

She just needed the name. "Who?!"

The chief dipped his head. "I can't give you the name, but they aren't a suspect. It was someone who got an alert when the alarm was triggered, went to the scene to investigate. Saw your truck outside and knew it was important to get a photo."

Jet shook her head. "What are you talking about? Got an alert from . . . do you mean my dad?"

The chief didn't answer, didn't move.

That was answer enough, Jet's mind ticking, turning over, working around the ache.

"No." She sniffed. "You mean Luke, don't you? Luke was at the scene before the fire department?"

"The witness saw your truck outside at 11:22 p.m. after the fire started, and took a photo because—"

"—It was Luke." Jet almost laughed, the sound hollow in her chest. "The alarm went off at 11:17 and Luke told you he got all the way over to Mason Construction from his house in five minutes to take that photo? Bullshit. He was already there."

And there was only one reason Luke could have been there already, the last piece sliding into place, held together with metal screws and wire mesh, like the rest of Jet's head.

"Luke handed this photo in to you, did he?" Jet asked, showing half her teeth, a one-sided grimace. "Must have felt real guilty about that, handing you a piece of evidence that pointed to his little sister. What a helpful little *witness*."

The rage dripped down her spine to her gut, caught fire. Jet kicked out, feet catching the table leg, a growl at the back of her throat.

Jack flinched, picked his hands up from the table as it shuddered.

"That fucker," Jet hissed. "It was him. Luke set the fire. And he's trying to fucking pin it on me."

And the other thing Jet couldn't say. That Luke saw her truck, must have known Jet was inside when he doused the place with gas and set it on fire. Her brother tried to kill her, or didn't care if she burned to death with the building. And now he'd gotten her arrested, when he knew she had no time left. That was almost worse. Jet was going to kill him.

"Jet," Jack said, voice firm but calm, "I know this is a stressful situation for you—"

"—Oh, you think?"

"But we need you to tell us what you were doing there."

What was she doing there? She couldn't tell them the truth—that she was the one who'd taped up the security cameras, that disabled the alarm. How would that look? Think. Think.

"You know the code to the gate and the key safe," the chief said, hardening his gaze, moving in for the kill. "That's how you got in."

"Don't know what you're talking about."

"You put tape on the cameras, so they wouldn't record you being there."

True, but not to fucking burn it down.

"Someone taped the cameras?" Jet asked.

"You knew the code to disable the security alarm."

"Are you asking a question or . . . ?"

"It'll be easier if you just confess," the chief said.

"Will it?" She shifted, handcuffs rattling.

"Is that a burn on your hand?" The chief pointed to it.

"I did that cooking."

"What did you cook?"

"Pasta."

"Look, Jet, I get it," the chief sighed.

"Do you?"

"Something awful happened to you, and you're mad. Maybe you thought you'd use the time you had left to take your anger out on someone else. Maybe you're mad at your dad, at your brother, that they weren't there to help you when JJ attacked you. Thought you'd teach them a lesson, burn down the company. Is that it? Talk to us, Jet. We're here to help."

"Like when you solved my murder?" she asked.

"Jet," Jack said, softly.

"I. Did. Not. Burn. That. Building. Down."

The chief banged the table. "Then. What. Were. You. Doing. There?"

"I was in the truck. I just parked there. It's a quiet road."

"Were you alone?"

Jet swallowed. *Alone* didn't count as an alibi. But she would not let any of this fall back on Billy, not that. He was the one who had to live.

"No, I was with someone," she said.

"Who?"

"I can't tell you that," she parroted him.

"Billy?" Jack said quietly, dipped up as a question, but not really. There was no other answer.

Jet didn't say anything.

"And what were you and Billy doing in your truck, on that road, at that time of night?" the chief said, sitting back, like he'd won.

"What do you think?" Jet scoffed, actually just trying to give herself time to think.

"You tell me."

A flash of memory: Billy, his pale eyes wide and troubled, worrying that passersby would spot the truck from the road. Jet telling him not to worry, giving him a reason, actually just trying to make him laugh.

Jet smiled, reused those exact same words now.

"We were screwing, like teenagers."

Jack dropped his eyes to the floor, chair creaking, drawing attention to him just when he was trying to hide from it.

"Sorry," Jet said in his direction, then back to the chief. "I'm dying, and having sex in a truck was on my bucket list, OK? That's why I was there. We didn't even know about the fire. We heard the sirens and got out of there. That's all."

The chief shook his head. "I don't believe you. I know you did this."

"Do you have any evidence that I went inside the building?"

The chief glanced over at Jack, a silent conversation, cop speak for *no*. Jet leaned forward. "Then let me go."

Jack ran a hand over his stubble, like he was torn between his uniform and the man beneath, Jet's neighbor, someone who'd known her since she was born. "We can't," he said. "The judge issued a warrant for your arrest."

Warrant! That was the fucking word.

Jack was still speaking. "The prosecutor has to decide whether to move ahead with charges."

"Fine," she said. "So charge me and let me go—I don't care, it won't matter after tomorrow."

A slight shake of his head. "If you're charged, we have to hold you until morning. You'll go to an arraignment before a judge to enter your plea. You may request bail, and the judge may grant it, but you'll be held in the county jail until it's posted."

"I don't have time for that." Jet's voice rose, but the fire went out, just a trail of smoke from her gut, soot coating the back of her throat, making her cough. "What about now? Can I leave? Is there any way I can leave?"

Another small shake of his head, the other way. "We have to hold you until the prosecutor makes a decision about filing charges."

"How long can you hold me?"

"Forty-eight hours."

Jet's throat closed up the rest of the way, cutting off her breath, the room tilting, doubling, tripling, suffocating her.

She closed her eyes.

"So, this is it," she said. "This is how I die. Alone. In a cell. That's how it ends."

CONCRETE FLOOR, WHITE-PAINTED brick walls that weren't white at the bottom, grimy and gray. A metal toilet in the corner, connected to a drinking fountain, where Jet could refill her plastic cup.

But she'd broken it. Ripped it in half. Then into tiny pieces, scattered around her like snow, like ash.

Sitting on the floor, because it hurt less than the bench. And if Jet stretched out her legs, she could reach the other side of the holding cell. It was tiny, less than Jet squared.

Too cold, a draft blowing in through the black bars from the corridor beyond, the exposed flesh of her arms rippling into small bumps, a shiver up her spine.

Jet was going to die in here.

She was going to die in this tiny cold room with bars instead of a door, and she just had to get used to that, stop crying.

Stop crying now, Jet.

She couldn't.

She blinked and they just kept coming.

It was over.

She failed.

Jet always failed; why had she thought this time would be any different?

So many unanswered questions she was going to die with.

What did Nina Diaz-Smith know about Mom? What was the secret Emily overheard about Luke? Did Luke kill Emily when they were kids, hold her underwater until she drowned? Did Luke mean to kill Jet when he set fire to Mason Construction, to the company he'd worked his whole life to take over? Was he sorry that he sent the cops after Jet to save himself, stealing her final hours? Who owned the Coleby tool kit? Where did the red wig hair come from? Who killed Jet on Halloween and why?

Had she deserved it?

Jet sniffed, wiped her nose on her sleeve.

But there was something worse than all of that put together.

That she was going to die while Billy hated her.

That was worse.

A black hole that spread from her chest, hungry, taking every last bit of her with it.

Leaving her with just Billy's pale eyes.

That frozen, distant look in them as he'd walked away from her. The last time she'd ever see him, and he'd ever see her.

Who would have thought, this time last week, that Billy Finney would be her most important thing?

Not just poor, sweet Billy. So much more than that.

Home.

But this was where she was going to die. Here. In this holding cell. Meant to be temporary, not a tomb.

A door creaked, footsteps, lots of them, echoing down the corridor, getting closer.

Jet sniffed, stood up. She walked to her bars, peered through.

Four men. Two in uniform, two not. One with his hands cuffed behind his back, being escorted through.

"JJ?" Jet said, face pushed up against the bars.

"Jet?" His head snapped in her direction, eyes dark and panicked, brows drawing together, confused. "What are you doing here?"

"Don't speak to her," Detective Ecker growled, tightening his grip on JJ's elbow.

"Doesn't matter," Jet said as the tangle of men passed her cell.

"They're taking me to the judge." JJ tried to stop in front of her, struggling against Ecker and the chief. "They're charging me. It wasn't me, Jet. I didn't do that to you."

"Move!" Ecker barked.

"I know," Jet said.

"I wanted to call you. They wouldn't let me call you."

JJ grunted as the chief shoved him against the wall, moving him on.

Jet pushed her face through the bars, watched them go, JJ pinned between the chief and Ecker, Jack Finney two steps behind, blocking JJ from view.

"I wanted to tell you I was sorry," JJ's voice trailed back, strained, fighting. "About the loan. It was for Henry, I was desperate. I'm sorry."

"I know," Jet said again, head spooling around one of those unanswered questions. Last chance to ask it. "Wait, JJ, did you touch me at the fair?" she called through the bars. "When you were wearing the red wig, did you grab my arm? I can't remember."

"Keep moving."

"No, I didn't—didn't touch you. And I didn't do it! And I'm sorry that you—"

The door crashed shut at the far end, taking JJ away; Jet heard it, couldn't see that far.

"I know," she whispered, because she wasn't the only one who was going to die in a cell.

JJ didn't do it, and Jet didn't either, but she couldn't scream about it anymore, there was nothing left.

Well, there was *something* left.

One set of footsteps, coming back.

It was Billy's dad, stopping in front of her cell, sharing a sad smile.

"I'm sorry about that, Jet." He sniffed. "I said we should have taken him out the back. He shouldn't have spoken to you."

But Jet was glad he had, because she was sticking on something JJ had said, something else left behind that the black hole hadn't gotten to just yet.

"Phone call," Jet said, resting her forehead against the cold bar. "Mr. Finney, don't I get a phone call?"

"Yes. You do."

"Can I . . . can I do it now?"

He glanced through the bars into the cell, the shredded plastic cup around Jet's outline, a phantom version of her, left behind.

"Sure."

He reached into his pocket for the keys, unlocked the cell door. A metallic scream from the hinges as he swung the bars open.

"I'm . . . I'm supposed to cuff you," he said quietly.

"OK."

She couldn't hold her wrists together for him, only one. Mr. Finney had to bring her right arm around, lock her hands together, the cuffs looser than when Chief Jankowski had done it.

"This way."

He led her to the right, down the corridor, through the door, and into an office area. Desks and papers and windows, the fading afternoon light. And a landline phone attached to the wall. Black receiver on a thick metal wire, well-worn buttons.

Mr. Finney led Jet over to it, hand soft on her shoulder.

"You should call your dad," he sniffed. "He can get you the kind of lawyer that might be able to get you out of here, given your circumstances. He can afford that. Call your dad, Jet. He can fix this."

Jet looked up at him, blinked. Call Dad. He could fix this, like he'd fixed things before, get Jet out, give her back her time, time to finish what she'd started. Her head agreed with Mr. Finney, but her heart was back, beating in the base of her throat, pulling her another way. A choice between the two, one or the other.

"I only get one phone call, right?" she asked.

"That's right," he replied.

Jet nodded.

"Then there's only one person I need to call."

She chose.

"What's Billy's number?"

Jack blinked down at her.

"You sure?"

"I'm sure."

He turned to the phone, lifted the receiver, pressing the buttons with his other hand.

"It's ringing," he said, passing it to her.

Jet tried to take it, her dead arm too heavy to raise that high, dragging her other hand down. "I can't."

Jack took her hands, unlocked the cuffs. "Don't tell anyone," he said, placing the receiver in her left hand. "I'll just be over there, give you some privacy."

Jet nodded, raised the phone to her ear.

It rang.

Still ringing.

The sound chiming around her head, through the cracks.

She closed her eyes.

Come on, Billy.

It rang.

Still ringing.

"Pick up, Billy," Jet whispered, barely made a sound. "Pick up, pick up, pick up."

A click.

Jet's eyes snapped open.

"Hello," a robotic voice cut in. "Welcome to Verizon's voicemail service. I'm sorry but *Billy Finney*"—Billy's name in his real voice, Jet's gut reacting to it, flipping over—"is unable to take your call right now. Please leave your message after the tone."

It beeped, too shrill, and Jet wasn't ready, but she had to be.

"Hi, Billy," she said, "it's me. It's Jet. You know, next-door neighbor, childhood best friend." She was nervous, the blood rushing to her face. "Um, yeah, so, I'm at the police station. They've arrested me. They think I'm the one who burned down Mason Construction, which is . . . Anyway, this isn't about that. It's about you." She took a breath, but it didn't work, her voice breaking anyway. "I'm so sorry, Billy. I'm so sorry. You are the last person in the entire world I wanted to hurt. I didn't know what I was doing—I'm not making an excuse. But I think, my whole life, I didn't know what I was doing, just ob-obsessed with this idea, of achieving something big, of proving to my parents that I can be like Emily, I can do what she would have done." She sniffed. "That's why I did it, your mom. And I think . . . I think I've spent so long waiting for it all to begin, for life to really start, that I missed out on what it was really all about. It's not law school, or the big fancy job at the big fancy firm, or solving your own murder because it's your last chance to prove something. It's about all of those small moments I missed while I was waiting. I haven't been able to see it until now. Racing bikes, doesn't matter who wins. Cold beers. Writing songs just because it makes you happy. Laugh-

ing. I haven't laughed so much my whole life as I have the past few days
with you. And that's saying something, because I got murdered a week
ago. Being brave, being useless, and not caring that I'm useless around
you, letting you help me. Sitting on the floor mostly because it bugs you.
Looking up at the stars. It didn't even look like a frog, Billy, not really."
She smiled, tears gathering across her lips, salt on her tongue. "I said I
didn't want to stop because I was having too much fun. I was just being . . .
well, *me*, being an asshole, but I think that, maybe, I accidentally stumbled on it, I just didn't realize. Because, Billy, this past week, I haven't
really been dying. I think, maybe, it's the opposite. I've finally been living. And that's all because of you. You showed me. It's the best thing
anyone's ever done for me, and I'll never forget it. And I wanted you to
know, that it was all you, before it's too late." Her breath stuttered, a wet
sucking sound up her blocked nose. "Gross, sorry. I'm sorry, Billy, and I
hope you listen to this, and you find some way to forgive me. Because
I'm an asshole, and I can't die knowing that you hate me, because I—"

"—You have reached the voicemail limit. To send, please hang up, or
press one to rerecord your message."

Jet swallowed.

Replaced the receiver to hang up.

Wiped her eyes. One eye, then the next.

"You done?" Mr. Finney's voice behind her.

"I'm done," she said.

He didn't put the cuffs back on, just put a hand on her shoulder,
walked her back to the holding cell, silent, pretending he hadn't heard
her one-way conversation with Billy. Jet didn't care that he had; she
meant every word.

Jack pushed the door shut, squealing hinges, mouth in a sad downward line as he locked it, looked at Jet through the bars, face creasing,
sorry.

"Hey, Mr. Finney," Jet sniffed, blinking to try and stitch him back
into one person, the concrete floor unsteady beneath her. "Can I borrow
some more paper? And a pen?"

He glanced over his shoulders, one way, then the other.

"You're not supposed to have anything in there."

"Please," she said, wrapping her hand around a bar, holding herself up. "We both know what's going to happen. I'm probably not going to see anybody again, won't get a chance to say goodbye. But I can write them letters. I have to say goodbye."

Mr. Finney chewed his lip, nodded.

"How many pages do you need?" he asked.

"A lot."

"OK." He nodded again. "I'll be right back."

"Thank you."

Jet sank to her knees, giving in to her legs, sliding back against the wall, feet out in front of her, eyes up. The cell didn't feel quite so small anymore, not as cold.

"Here."

Mr. Finney was back, bending down to slide a small pile of printer paper through the bars, shushing along the concrete. Too clean, too white. He rolled a ballpoint pen through, no cap.

"Sorry, I could only find a red one," he said.

"That's OK." Jet picked up the pen, then the first sheet of paper, laid it on the floor, legs hooked around it, one foot pressed to the corner to hold it in place.

"I'll come check on you in a few hours. Bring you some food."

His footsteps clicked along the corridor, taking him away, through the door at the end that Jet couldn't see.

Couldn't much see the paper in front of her either, her eyes unfocusing, losing their way. But Jet wouldn't lose hers.

She was brave, and she was useless, and that was all fine with her.

She gripped the pen in her left hand, the wrong hand, the hand she never wrote with, wasn't sure she could.

She started. She tried.

D ea r M o m

So slow, the letters squashed and childlike. Red ink crammed together, then spread too far, slipping up and down, out of line, like it was her first time writing, not her last.

It was going to take hours, like this.

But Jet had the time.

She took a breath, steadied herself, anchored herself, looked through her doubled vision, beyond it.

She pressed the pen to the paper and began her goodbyes.

THIRTY-ONE

The hinges screamed and Jet jerked awake, still alive. She knew because the pain came next, head crushed against the wall, knees tucked to her chest.

She blinked at the open bars, at Mr. Finney with his hand on the door.

"I'm not hungry. Thanks," Jet croaked, settling back down on the concrete.

"Jet." He opened the door wider, another creak, an unknown word in the language of metal. "You're free to go."

But those words she understood.

Jet sniffed, sat up, one cheek crushed, the side she could no longer feel, a ring of salt crusted around her eyes.

"Wh-what?" she said.

"You're free to go."

Jet pushed to her feet, one at a time, stumbling, catching herself on the wall.

"Wh-why?" She blinked again, no idea what the time was, or how much she had left.

Jack stepped back, cleared the way.

"We had a witness come in to give a statement," he said. "It corroborated your account. The state attorney wants us to investigate further, before considering charges. Which means . . ." He gestured to the open door. "You're free to go. For now."

"I'm free?" She took a tentative step forward. "Who was the cor-corro-cor—th-the witness?"

Jack pressed his lips together, an almost-smile. "I think you know him. Come on."

Jet's heart picked up, back where it belonged. Home. Her foot nudged something as she shuffled forward.

"Oh, your pen." She bent to pick it up, the world tilting, almost throwing her off. She righted herself, passed the red pen to Jack, then looked back at her cell. Just once.

Patted her jacket pocket to feel them there, to check. Her letters, folded up. Safe. And she might not need them after all.

She was free.

She followed Mr. Finney, holding her breath as she passed by the bars, crossed the threshold, that line, into the corridor beyond.

Through the door she couldn't see, but she could see now, into the waiting room, the bench she'd been cuffed to, the front desk.

The officer who'd booked her was standing behind it. So was the chief, eyeing her as she stumbled past, face creasing—but not because he was sorry, Jet knew.

"I'm free to go," she said, challenging him, eyeing him back, moving her hair out of her face with just one finger. Her middle finger.

The chief didn't say anything, just watched her go, toward the glass-fronted door, the night and the moon waiting beyond.

Mr. Finney opened the door for her.

"Thank you," Jet said. "For the pen."

Jack dipped his head, and Jet walked outside.

The night and the moon weren't the only things waiting for her.

Jet's blue truck, just there, in the parking lot.

Someone leaning against the hood, arms crossed, bunching his checked shirt, protecting his chest.

"I got your voicemail," Billy called.

"You did?" Jet stopped.

"Yeah." He pushed off the truck, crossed one of the headlights, glowing in front of it. "It was pretty long."

"Well, I had a lot to say." Jet cupped her hand over her eyes, to see Billy clearer. The clearest she'd ever seen him.

"You've always got a lot to say." Billy smiled.

"Didn't think I'd ever see you again."

Billy nodded, chewed his lip. "Do you see me now?" Raised his arms.

"Yeah," Jet said, "I see you. Do you see me?"

"I've always seen you, Jet."

Jet nodded, her heart in her throat.

"OK," she called. "Can we stop being weird now?"

"You first."

Jet first.

Time to be brave, time to be useless.

She kicked off the gravel and ran to him, straight into him, hard to stop, both of them colliding into the truck.

Billy's arms wrapped around her, Jet's left hand hooking onto his elbow, holding on as he held her. She pressed her face into his chest, harder, crushing it. Jet couldn't feel it in her cheek, but she felt it somewhere else, felt like wings.

"I'm sorry," she said, voice lost in his shirt.

"It's OK," he said, voice lost in her hair. "I'm sorry too."

"Got nothing to be sorry about."

"I do, Jet." He pulled back so he could look down at her, eyes pale and shining, a summer lake with no end, not even when he blinked. "You talked about having a deadline, one last week, to prove something. And I did too. Something different, something I thought was just as important—the only important thing, actually. And that wasn't fair, on either of us." He breathed out, let something go. "I don't need to prove anything, and you don't either."

Jet thought she knew, what Billy meant. Maybe she'd already known, since she heard his song, maybe even before that too.

"I don't hate you," she said.

"And I don't hate you either." He smiled. "Shall we?"

He stepped back, opened the passenger door for her.

Jet climbed inside, struggling because Billy's guitar was in the foot-well, her legs either side of it.

"What's this doing here?" she asked as Billy dropped into the driver's seat.

"Oh." His cheeks flushed. "Well, I've never got someone out of jail before."

"You thought you could sing me out?"

"No." His dark hair trailed into his eyes. "I was going to find a pawn-shop, sell my guitar, sell your truck too, get money for bail, whatever it took."

Jet gasped, but not really. "You were going to sell my baby?"

Billy ran his hand over the dashboard. "Would have hurt me too. We've bonded."

He shifted, his elbow accidentally bumping the steering wheel, a hic-cup of the horn.

Jet laughed. "She says, *Hands off.*"

"That's fine," Billy said, dropping his eyes. "You can love something without needing it to love you back."

Jet nodded, looking at him as he looked away.

"How did you do it?" she asked. "Get them to let me go?"

Billy's cheeks flushed harder, still not looking. "Don't be mad."

"What?"

"I . . . I said we were together, in the truck."

"Doing what?" Jet pressed, just enjoying this, watching him squirm.

"Screwing like teenagers," they said at the same time, burst into laughter, Billy accidentally hitting the horn again.

"Me too."

Billy sniffed, swallowing the laugh. "Good thing we got our alibi sorted beforehand, huh?"

Jet shifted around the guitar case, felt Billy's gaze on her.

"You know," he said, gripping the wheel with both hands, even though they weren't going anywhere. "I think this has been the worst week of my life, because I'm going to lose you, and I don't want to lose you." He cleared the lump in his throat. "But, it's also been the best week of my life, because I got to spend it with you."

"Me too," she said again. Same words, completely different somehow, another language.

"Good." Billy clicked his tongue. "Glad we agree."

"Yep. Same page."

Billy caught her eye and Jet smiled, just out of one side.

He caught the other half, turned the key in the ignition.

"So. Whaddya want to do tonight?" he asked. "Should we go solve a murder?"

Jet scrunched her nose, glanced down at her nonexistent watch. "I think we have time."

"Where to, Detective?" Billy did up his belt.

"Luke," Jet said, losing the smile. "He's the one who took that photo of my truck, sent the police after me. But if he was there at that time, it means—"

"—He's the one who set the fire," Billy finished. "Tried to kill you the second time. But we know it wasn't him on Halloween, he was with Henry Lim at the same time."

"No." Jet nodded. "Luke didn't murder me. But he might have murdered Emily. I have to know, Billy. My whole life . . . I just have to know, before . . ." She coughed. "Where's your phone?"

Billy pulled it out of his pocket, handed it to her.

Jet scrolled through his contacts, looking for *Luke Mason*.

Found it, just above *Mom*. Pressed the call button.

It rang.

Three times.

A click.

Jet didn't wait for him to speak first.

"Where are you? You at home?"

"Jet?" Luke's voice at the other end, low and gravelly.

"I'm out of jail, by the way. Thanks for that," Jet spat. "Are you at home?"

"No. Not home."

"Where are you?"

Luke hesitated, the cold rattle of his breath.

"I'm at Mason Construction."

Jet nodded, clicked for Billy's attention. "You're at Mason Construction."

Billy started reversing, out of the spot.

"OK, stay there," Jet said into the phone. "Do not move, Luke. I'm coming."

She hung up.

"On it," Billy said, pulling out onto the main road, headlights carving through the darkness.

Jet leaned forward as the night sped past the window, pulled open the glove compartment.

Henry's gun was there, waiting, hiding in the shadows.

Jet reached in, fingers closing around it, its metal shell cold enough to sting. She pulled the gun out, catching Billy's eye as he took another turn, ripples in the lake.

"Just in case," she said. "Luke can be scary."

Jet opened her window, breathed in, filled herself with the darkness, a new shape now. Breathed it out.

They didn't talk.

Jet turned the radio up instead.

"Hey, this is the song you like, Billy."

She turned it up some more.

That song, about Vermont and sticks.

Billy kept driving, started to hum. Jet did too. Then more.

Singing.

Loud.

Louder than that.

Turned the radio up again.

Almost shouting.

Jet making up the words because she didn't know them, Billy laughing at her, singing even louder to make up for it.

Out of tune but not out of time.

Jet cradled the gun in her lap, the night in her hair, closed her eyes and she just fucking sang.

.　.　.

"YOU NEVER HEARD that expression, Luke? About not returning to the scene of the crime?"

Jet walked over to her brother, feet crunching in the fallen leaves.

He didn't move. He was standing just before the gate into Mason Construction, his back to them. The gate locked and padlocked, yellow-and-black tape strung across it in a crisscross. Another crime scene. *DO NOT ENTER.*

The burned-down husk of the building behind it, none of it left standing. Piles of blackened bricks. Bent, curling metal that might once have been the stairs. A collapsed section of the roof, bite mark through the middle. Ash. Soot. All color leaked away except black and gray. The parking lot full of white vans and blue logos looked otherworldly, out of place, still alive, here in this graveyard.

"Luke," Jet called, tearing her eyes from the burned building where she'd almost died, back to her brother. "What are you doing?"

The truck behind Jet and Billy was still running, still breathing, beams on, lighting up their stage. Luke in one spotlight, Jet three steps behind in the other.

"I'm just looking," Luke said, a crack through the middle of his voice. "It's all gone."

Jet sniffed. "Yeah. That tends to happen, Luke, when you cover something in gas and set it on fire."

She took another step forward.

"Did you know we were inside when you burned it down? Were you trying to kill me?"

Luke didn't answer, but one of his shoulders tensed, flinching toward his ear.

"Did you know I was inside?"

Luke sighed.

"You did," Jet said, reading the answer in his silence, the wind howling through it. "You tried to kill me."

"No." Luke found his voice. "I knew you'd have time to get out. I was just trying to stop you."

"Stop me from finding out about the invoice fraud?" Jet said. "The workers' comp insurance, the payroll taxes? What happened with Henry Lim? Well, you didn't stop me. We found them all. You've been busy, Luke."

He turned suddenly, face rearranged around his rage, blinking against the headlight.

"I was saving the company!"

"Someone should have saved it from you!" Jet's left hand was in her pocket, around the gun, her letters folded behind. Luke could be scary, but she wasn't scared. "And you did, by the way, almost kill us. Me and Billy. Me. You probably think it doesn't count, because I'm dying anyway, but it does count, Luke. It matters. Some things are more important than a company."

Luke shook his head.

"They are, Luke." Jet hardened her voice, tightened her grip. "You know, it's because of Emily. Why you're like this."

Luke laughed, a breathy, hollow sound.

"Why does everyone always want to talk about Emily?"

"Why don't you?"

"Because it doesn't matter, it was seventeen years ago. Grow up, Jet."

Jet pressed forward, leaves rustling, whispering under her feet.

"It matters, Luke. Emily dying changed everything. Mom blamed me, you know?" She sniffed. "I overheard her, after the funeral. Said that if I hadn't gotten to the final of that competition, if I hadn't won, she and Dad would have been at home and Emily wouldn't have drowned. Do you know what that did to me?"

Her chest seized, squeezed her heart for just a second, and then she let it go, that guilt, because it wasn't hers anymore.

"But Emily's death wasn't my fault." Jet tilted her head, stared her brother down. "It was yours, Luke."

His face folded up, a scowl, made uglier by the shadows from the beam. "What are you talking about?"

"You drowned Emily, didn't you?"

Luke laughed.

"You've lost your mind."

"No, it's still just about in there, Luke. Tell me the truth. Did you kill her?"

Still laughing.

"Emily's death was an accident, Jet."

It was the laughing that did it.

"Did you kill her?!" Jet screamed.

She pulled the gun out of her pocket, pointed it at Luke, straight through his chest.

Not laughing anymore.

"You have a gun?" he said. "Why the fuck do you have a gun, Jet?"

"Jet," Billy said, behind.

"Tell me!"

"You're not going to shoot me, Jet." He stepped forward, hands raised.

"I have about twenty-four hours to live," she said, gun shaking in her hand. "You think I care about shooting you after everything you just did to me?"

"You won't." Another step.

Jet aimed the gun, pulled the trigger.

A crack that split the night in half.

Luke's eyes snapped wide.

The leaves exploded at his feet.

Jet pulled the gun up again.

"Did you kill Emily?!"

Luke fell to his knees, hands up, the scowl gone, replaced by fear.

"Luke!"

He closed his eyes and screwed his face.

"I didn't mean to!" It started as a shout, ended as a whisper. "I didn't want to, I swear. But once I started, it was already too late, because she'd tell, and I had to just keep going. Just hold her head under, until she stopped struggling."

Jet stepped back, breath heavy in her chest, weighing her down. She'd already known, but now she knew. Bile up her throat, tears too, breaking out of her rubbed-raw eyes.

"She was fighting you," Jet said. "She wanted to live."

"Scratches all up your arms." Billy's voice behind her, standing in the darkness.

Luke slumped, two handfuls of leaves.

"Why, Luke?" Jet said, lowering the gun. "Why would you do that to her?"

He started to cry. "Because she said something. You know Emily could be cruel. It made me mad. I just . . . I lost my temper. Then it was too late to take it back. Couldn't take it back. I wish I could take it back!"

"What did Emily say?" Jet eyed her brother like a cornered animal, not trusting his tears, not all the way.

Luke wiped his face. "All I did was jump in the pool, splash her a little bit. That's all. She didn't need to say that, she didn't need to—"

"—What did she say, Luke?" The gun rattled against her leg.

"She said I wasn't even a Mason anyway. That Dad wasn't my real dad, that I shouldn't even be here." He finally met Jet's eyes. "I just got mad. I thought she made it up, to be mean. I thought that for years, wanted to believe it. But now . . ."

"Now what?" Jet said. "Now you know it's true?"

This was it, wasn't it? The secret Emily had overheard, the one she'd told Nina, the one Nina threatened Mom with and Mom got her back. About Luke. Emily told Luke that day, and she died for it. Luke wasn't really a Mason, and Dad wasn't his dad.

"Is it true, Luke?"

He stared down at the grass, and Jet stared at him, studied her brother, glowing in the spotlight. Hazel eyes, just like Jet. But those came from Mom. Luke was taller than Dad, bigger, stronger, hair shaved short, but when it wasn't, it grew wavy. And something else too.

"There's a fifty percent chance you should have had polycystic kidney disease too," Jet said, working it out as she said it. "But not if Dad isn't your dad. He's not, is he?"

"No," Luke croaked, looking over his shoulder at the burned bones of Mason Construction.

"And you know who it is? Did Emily tell you who?"

Luke didn't look back, eyes lost over there.

"No, she didn't. Didn't have a chance. I only know because he told me."

"When?"

"Wednesday. Before I saw you, before I got home from work that day. Before . . . the fire."

"Who is it?" Jet asked, stepping closer, Luke's voice too quiet, now he was looking the other way. "Luke?"

"I thought he was just nice," he sniffed. "Looked out for me, gave me advice about the company. About anything really. Spoke to me in a way Dad never did. But when he told me, I think I already knew, deep down. I think I always really knew that Emily was telling the truth that day. That I wasn't a Mason, that *this* wasn't supposed to be mine." He pointed, over there, at the ruins.

"Luke?"

"He told me I was his son. He thought I already knew, from that day, with Emily. He told me and he said he was trying to help me. Said that you were going to start looking into the company, and that if I had anything to hide, then I needed to hide it." Luke looked behind him again. "Then I drove home, and you were there, told me that Dad was never going to leave me the company anyway, that he planned to sell it. I just . . . lost my temper."

"Luke!" Jet snapped. "Who is it? Who's your real dad?"

Luke shook his head, his eyes trailing off to the right. "I can't tell you. It doesn't matter."

Jet raised the gun. "Yes, you can—and it does matter!"

"You're not going to shoot me, Jet." He stood up to prove the point.

The gun shook in Jet's hand, too weak to hold it up this long, finger vibrating against the trigger.

"I can't tell you," Luke said. "Not like this, here. The rest of us have to keep on living when you're gone. Don't look at me like that, Jet. I don't want you to be gone, you're my sister. I'll miss you every day. I don't know how we'll be a family without you. No one to make fun of my hair. I always loved arguing with you. I'll make sure JJ never gets out, for doing this to you. You won't shoot me, Jet."

She could.

She stepped forward, pressed the gun right up against Luke's chest, looked up into his eyes, so like her own.

She could.

She would never. Not even after everything Luke had done. Jet wasn't like him.

She lowered the gun and Luke actually smiled.

"Fuck you," she sniffed.

"I know," Luke replied.

"You killed Emily."

"Emily's death was an accident."

"How did you do that?" Jet said, eyes filling again. "You were just thirteen. You were strong, but you were fucking stupid. How did you know how to make it look like an accident, her hair in the drain? Going over to play with Billy, to give yourself an alibi? How did you know how to do that?"

"I didn't."

Jet swallowed. "You didn't? Did somebody help you?"

Luke blinked.

"Was it him?" she said. "Your father?"

Luke ran his hand over his too-short hair, a hissing sound, the wind picking it up, dragging it away.

"He looked out for me."

That was all he said.

Returned to the gate, to watch the burned-down building, the wind howling, screaming through the gaps in the rubble.

Jet turned her back on him, followed her headlight beam back to the truck, opening the passenger door, struggling with the gun.

She got it open, leaned in, put the gun back in the glove compartment. Slammed it, a growl in the back of her throat.

"Jet," Billy said, climbing in the driver's side. "Are you OK?"

She didn't answer.

Her mind was somewhere else, trailing down Billy's guitar case, to the little black square stuck on its neck.

Her eyes circled it, forming an idea.

She reached out, slid her fingernail underneath it, peeled it off.

"Jet, where are you going?"

Back to Luke.

Leaves scattering away from her.

Jet joined him at the gate, side by side. Brother and sister, silhouettes against the blackened ruins.

"I know you didn't kill me, Luke," she said. "But I think you might be the reason I'm dead."

She reached over, touched his arm. Luke could be scary, but he wasn't now, a muscle ticking in his jaw, silent tears. Jet let her hand fall away, moving it down, dropping the little square into Luke's pocket.

"I'm sorry you couldn't change."

She walked away.

Into the truck.

Shut the door.

Another crack that split the night.

Billy released the parking brake.

"Where—" he began.

"—Home," Jet finished.

THIRTY-TWO

"Has he moved yet?"

Jet looked over at Billy, too jittery to sit down, spider legs up her spine, more inside her head, multiplying. An itch behind her eye.

Billy was leaning on the counter, his phone clutched in his hand, staring at the screen.

"No," he said. "Looks like he's still at Mason Construction. Or he found the Tile tracker you put in his pocket and dropped it there."

Jet shook her head. "No, he hasn't found it. This is going to work. It's going to work." She hardened her voice, trying to hear it over her heart, and all those damn spiders. "Luke is going to lead us straight to him, I know it. He's going to go to him. He has to, after what we just talked about. And we're going to follow."

"You're sure Luke's real dad is the person who killed you?" Billy didn't look up.

"I think it's the reason why he killed me."

Jet swallowed. This felt right. It did. They were going to do this; they were actually going to solve her murder. Jet might not have been able to see straight, but she could see the way forward. This was it. Didn't matter that the world was spliced in half, two layers, clashing and filmy, one world closer, the other a little farther back, two Billys, one within reach and one not. Jet rubbed her eye, her hand doubled too, existing in both worlds. She was used to it now, finding the line between.

"And you really don't want to just go ask your mom?" Billy did look up now, four pale blue eyes. "She obviously knows who Luke's real father is."

Jet nodded. Shouldn't do that, almost unbalanced her. "I don't really want to be the one who ruins my dad's life, right before I die. Mom should tell him about Luke, not me. But if we have to . . . We give Luke an hour to lead us to him, or we get it from Mom instead. Luke has an hour to lead us to him."

"An hour," Billy agreed, refreshing his screen. "Who do you think it is? Luke's dad? And don't say Darth Vader again, this is serious."

"Same person as my killer," Jet said, seriously.

"Who?"

"There's two options." She sniffed. "Has to be one of them."

"Andrew Smith?" Billy glanced toward his front door. "If it's him, then Luke would be coming here."

"Andrew is one of them." Jet also stared at the front door, two doors, the truth somewhere in the middle. "I asked JJ at the police station. He says he didn't touch me at the Halloween Fair. And I don't think he did. So it wasn't me who transferred the red wig hair to the crime scene. Which means the killer had to have had contact with Andrew Smith or JJ at the fair. Andrew Smith obviously had contact with Andrew Smith; he was wearing the fucking wig. The construction site on North Street used to be Andrew's house—he could have been watching the work, knew when the foundations were going in, knew to hide the hammer and my phone there. Or maybe he and Luke talked about it. Luke said he gave him advice, about the company."

"Why, though? What could Andrew's motive be?"

"For Luke," Jet said, her words echoing in her chest, heart in her throat, stuck there. "Andrew knew that Dad was going to sell the company to Nell Jankowski, not leave it to Luke, because of me. If you take me out of the equation, then Luke gets the company. That's his motive."

Billy narrowed his eyes, not following. "But why would Andrew want Luke to have the company?"

"Because that's his son. And Andrew has nothing. You don't think he'd want access to all the money that Mason Construction can bring in? He's lost everything. Luke could be his damn meal ticket—his drinking ticket."

Billy chewed his lip. "I don't know. He really seemed to hate Luke when we spoke to him."

"Or that's what he wanted us to think," Jet countered. "Doesn't have to like Luke to want to use him. If he knew about Emily, if he helped Luke get away with it back then, he could threaten to expose that, make Luke give him whatever he wanted when the company was his."

"But he was so angry that he'd lost his house," Billy said. "That he'd sold it to Luke."

"Exactly." Jet slapped one hand on the counter, really just holding herself up, the world tilting again, stomach lurching. "Why would he sell his house to Luke if he didn't really want to, if Nina had begged him not to? He did it to help Luke, knew that project was Luke's chance to prove himself. He did it for Luke. There's something between them, has to be. Andrew hates my family, hates my mom; maybe that's because the relationship ended, because she kept Luke from him, and he blames her for Nina's death too. It's all so messy, but Andrew is connected to all of it, every bit. That fucking house on North Street. It makes sense, why he'd want to kill me."

Billy sighed, conceded, still chewing his lip. "Who's the other option?"

Jet tapped her fingers on the counter, up and down, more spider legs, dragging the name up her throat. "Lou Jankowski."

Billy straightened up. "Really?"

"Let's look at the evidence," Jet said, before she lost her way. "The red wig hair. The chief helped break up the fight when Andrew Smith attacked you at the fair. One of the wig hairs could have transferred to him then. Or maybe it wasn't even Andrew Smith. We saw that photo that Owen Clay took of the little girl in the same wig. She was posing with the chief. The hair could have also come from her, two possibilities. And again, Luke said his real dad has been giving him advice about the company, so maybe that's how Lou could have known about the foundations going in on North Street, where to hide the hammer. And it's this thing, with my mom, that I can't let go. Why would she vote Lou for chief of police when your dad has been our next-door neighbor forever? She had to have known Lou before. He didn't live far, only in Hartland. And remember: Nell told me that Lou lived in Woodstock for six months, in his thirties. That's when the affair could have started, when Luke was conceived. Luke could be his. Why else would my mom vote for a stranger? And, man, he does *not* like me, the chief. He really did not want to let me out of jail, to give me any more time to work this out."

"But what's his motive?"

Jet shrugged. "I don't know. We'll ask him. Probably the same as Andrew's. He wanted Luke to take over the company—probably pays much better than chief of police."

Billy pressed his lips together and Jet's stomach turned over, watching him, a warm buzz in her ears. The same Billy but, somehow, not at all.

"But Lou was going to get the company anyway. Your dad was planning to sell to his wife."

Jet hadn't thought about that, not much space left around the ache in her head and that feeling in her gut, the one with wings. "I don't know," she said. "First, we've got to work out *who*. Then we can ask him *why*, when Luke leads us to him."

"And what do we do, once Luke has led us to him?"

He glanced at his front door again, and Jet missed his eyes. All four of them.

"I don't know. We tie him up, make him tell us how and why. We have the gun, in the truck. We make him confess."

Billy looked back at her, eyes hooked on. Hazel and blue, earth and water, fire hidden somewhere behind.

"And then do what?"

"I don't know," Jet said, and she really didn't. "I haven't thought that far ahead. I wasn't sure we'd get here. I don't know what to do. He killed me. Do I have to kill him?" she asked.

Billy didn't answer, couldn't, the silence ticking on, ticking up. But Jet liked their silences, different with Billy than with anyone else. Not an absence of sound, its own thing. Didn't want to break it. Had to.

"Has Luke moved?" She pointed to his phone.

Billy refreshed the app. "Not yet, still there."

"We should get ready." She sniffed. "Be ready, for when he does move." She pushed off the counter, her feet clumsy beneath her, too heavy, the world pulling at her heels. "Where's that duct tape we took for the security cameras?"

"Why?"

"In case we have to tie someone up."

Jet winked, shot him a half-smile, like that was a normal thing to say, watched Billy fill in the other half, because he liked when she did that. When should Jet tell him? After they were done here, after they found her killer? *Should* she even tell him? Was it fair to tell him, so close to the end? What was best for Billy? He was the one who had to live after this.

"I put the tape back," Billy said. "Closet. Next to the tool kit."

"OK."

Jet stumbled over to it, pulled one door open, then the other, Billy's mom staring down at her.

"Do you have gloves too?" she asked, throwing the question over her shoulder.

"Not even going to ask why," Billy said, abandoning his phone on the counter. "Think I have some in the bedroom. I'll get them."

"Thanks."

He wandered out of the living room, and Jet watched him go, smiled to herself, just for herself, not to share.

She turned back to the closet, reached for the shelf. Patted around. Couldn't feel the duct tape. Where was it? Maybe Billy had put it back inside the tool kit.

Jet wrapped her fingers around the fabric handle, shunted the tool kit toward her, off the shelf. Took its weight in one arm, too heavy, crashing against her chest to keep ahold of it. She bent down and dropped it to the floor with a thump.

Fuck, that was heavy, should have asked for help.

"Jet?" Billy called from the bedroom.

"I'm OK."

She got to her knees beside it and pulled the zipper, undoing the black fabric case.

No duct tape on top.

Jet dug her hand through, moving tools aside, searching for the tape.

It must have been in here.

Jet peered inside, pulled something out that was blocking her search. A set of pliers, handle wide, mouth open.

Black rubber handle with a yellow logo at the bottom.

Wait.

No.

Jet turned the pliers to read the brand name, her heart dropping all the way to her gut, taking the wings with it.

Coleby.

Written in a little yellow circle with pointed ends, against the black.

No, no, no.

Her heart was already there but Jet couldn't follow.

She pulled out more of the tools.

A screwdriver.

A wrench.

Black rubber grips and a little yellow logo.

Coleby.

Coleby.

They were all Coleby.

A measuring tape.

A little knife.

Fuck.

Where was it?

It had to be here.

If the hammer was here, then everything was OK, just a coincidence. Just a strange little coincidence that they would laugh about.

Jet had to find it.

Had to, no choice.

A file.

Another screwdriver.

More pliers.

Where was the hammer? It had to be here.

Jet's hand retreated from the dark folds inside the tool kit. Grabbed its handle instead, flipped it, turned the whole thing over.

The tools clattered onto the floor, Jet shaking the bag until they were all out.

She sank back on her knees, sorting through the chaos of metal and rubber with her one hand, moving the saw, under the screwdriver heads, searching, searching.

It wasn't here.

"No, no, no."

There was no hammer.

"Jet, what are you doing?" Billy said, framed in the doorway.

Jet turned, fell back, the knuckles of her dead arm dragging on the floor as she backed up against the closet.

"It's yours," she said, voice almost gone, joining her heart in the pit of her stomach. "The murder weapon. It's yours, Billy."

She kicked out at the empty tool kit, so he could see the yellow logo stitched on the side.

Billy narrowed his eyes, shook his head.

"Coleby," Jet said, bile rising with the word. "A sixty-piece set. But the hammer isn't here. The murder weapon. It's yours, Billy."

She couldn't breathe, no air here, stuck between these two worlds, two Billys moving toward her.

"It was you."

"What?"

He took another step.

"Don't come any closer!" Jet shouted, pushed herself to her feet, stumbled, tripping over the abandoned tools. "Stay back!"

Billy didn't stay back, he kept coming.

"Jet, what are you talking about?"

"It was you," she said, her head trying to catch up to her heart, pounding, not the trickling of spiders anymore, a drumbeat. "You killed me."

Billy's pale eyes went cold.

Now he stopped.

"No, Jet."

"It was you."

The world went blurry, until she blinked, tears hot and fast, falling into her open mouth. The taste of salt.

"I didn't, Jet!"

Billy kept shaking his head, tendons branching across his throat, eyes wide, full of ice.

"It had to be you. The murder weapon is yours."

"No, Jet. I didn't know about that. I would have told you if I knew. I've never used those!"

"The red hair. It transferred to you from Andrew Smith, when he pushed you at the fair."

"Jet, stop!"

"You had time, if you were running, to take my phone and the hammer. Your hammer, the one you used to kill me. You had time to get over to the site on North Street, then come back to find me, kick down the door."

"Jet, stop!" He was crying now too.

She couldn't stop. One thing led to another, sliding into place. Drums when she blinked, harder, faster.

"You knew about the foundations going in the next morning, because Sophia told you about it at the fair. Told you how important this project was to Luke. You knew about the concrete."

"Please, Jet, you know me," he cried. "I didn't know about that hammer, that it came from here. I swear to you. We can work this out together."

"We already did that, this whole week! And you were probably pushing me to look at anybody else but you!"

"Jet, stop! I would never hurt you, you know that, you do. Why would I hurt you?"

Jet cried, trapped it inside her hand, closed her eyes and listened to the drums.

"Because . . . because you knew my dad wasn't going to leave the company to Luke, if I was alive. You live next door to Andrew; he could have told you about Nell Jankowski anytime. And if Luke had the company, then you could extort him for money—"

"—Jet, stop! None of this is true! You know me. It's me, Billy!"

"Because you knew that Luke killed Emily when we were kids. You're the one who told me about it. You already knew, just pretended you only half remembered. If Luke had the company, you could threaten him about Emily, get whatever you wanted."

"Jet!"

Billy stepped forward and Jet stepped back, toward the coffee table.

"Or maybe you did it because you knew it was me who made your mom go away. Maybe that's why."

"Jet, please!"

"Or maybe it's because I don't—didn't—because I didn't—"

—A thunderclap.

Not in the sky, in her head, out of nowhere, now everywhere.

A pain worse than hellfire and cracking skulls.

Everything else just practice, for this moment here.

A hurt beyond words, beyond nightmares.

Jet screamed.

She screamed.

One hand to her head but what could that do—it was all coming undone.

She screamed.

"Jet!"

She bent double, all that pain, too much to hold up, her neck stiffening.

"No!" she screamed. "It's too soon!"

The world tilted, finally threw her off.

Jet's legs gave way, too weak.

She crashed sideways into the coffee table, caught herself.

Something fell to the floor, smashed. Glass candle. *Cedar Delight.*

"Jet!"

She let go, too weak to hold on.

On the floor.

Billy's face swimming above her, sitting her up, his hands cupping her face.

"Jet!"

"It's happening, Billy."

"No!" Billy was screaming, now she couldn't anymore. "No! We had more time! We need more time!"

Jet shook her head, as much as she could move, the pain moving with it.

"It's happening," she said.

"OK," Billy swallowed, his face folding in half, fighting his tears. Losing. "It's OK, Jet. I'm right here."

"Billy—"

"—You did it. You did it, Jet," he cried. "You solved it. It was me. You're right. You got it right. You did it."

"No, Billy." Couldn't shake her head anymore.

"Yes, Jet. It was me, it was me, it was me." He sobbed. "You did it. It was me."

Jet smiled. Just half, that's all she could do. "No, Billy. I know. It wasn't you."

She knew.

Of course she knew.

Everything was coming undone and still she knew.

This was Billy.

Billy would never hurt her. Never. She didn't know who had, but she did know that. Would bet her whole life on it. And that's what mattered.

This.

Just this.

Her arm jolted out, legs too.

Stiffening.

Seizing.

Couldn't move because everything moved for her, shuddering. Head tilted back, eyes on the ceiling when she wanted to look at Billy, into his eyes. Not ice, just water, and the storm behind them.

He held her, held her until it was over, everything weak again, melting to the floor.

But she wasn't on the floor. She was in Billy's lap, her head in the crook of his arm.

"I'm here, Jet," he cried over her. "You did it, it was me."

"It's OK," Jet said, voice weakening too, forcing it out. "I know, Billy. It wasn't you. It's OK, I don't need it anymore."

It wasn't important.

"But you did it, you solved—"

"—Shut up, Billy," she whispered, reaching for his face, finger finding the dip of his chin.

"OK," he whispered back, his tears falling down her cheeks too, closing the distance.

"Billy," Jet said, while she still could. "There's letters. In my pocket. For everyone."

She blinked.

Everything slowed down.

"Jet?" Billy's voice echoed above her. "Jet. You're back."

"I'm here," she said. "The letters, Billy. You have to make sure everyone gets them. They're in my—my—"

"—They're in your pocket, I know. I'll make sure, I promise."

Jet shifted, body peeling away from her, neck too stiff, made of metal not flesh. But she wanted to see his eyes.

"Billy."

"I'm here."

Here.

Right where they started.

No blood this time; it was all on the inside.

Billy holding her lifeless body. Again.

Nothing had changed.

Except.

Everything had changed.

She blinks.

"Not yet, Jet," Billy is saying. "Not yet."

"I'm here." It's her turn to say it.

"I'll finish this for you, Jet. I promise."

He promises. He presses his warm hand to her face, strokes his thumb across, stealing her tears.

Jet lets him have them.

Blinks.

"Come back, Jet, come back."

She's here. Opens her eyes.

"I'm sorry," Billy cries.

Jet isn't. She's home, because she's here with Billy.

He holds her, tucks her hair out of her face.

Jet smiles up at him, fighting her eyes.

"I love you, Jet."

She knows that too.

"Your letter, Billy," she whispers. He leans closer to hear her. "You have to read my letter."

"I will."

He's trying so hard not to scream again, she can tell, can feel it vibrating under his hot skin, the way he's biting his lip.

"It's OK," she tells him. "Your letter."

"I'll read it."

Another promise.

Another blink.

Slower to come back this time, the other side of that tunnel.

Billy is crying over her, holding her to his chest.

"Bi-lly." Not a word, just two detached sounds, her lips then her tongue.

"Jet."

She knows that when she closes her eyes, she won't come back again. She knows. The tunnel is too far.

Jet stays as long as she can, not wasting a second.

The last thing she wants to see are those eyes, swim in them, and never find the end.

She blinks.

Dear Mom,

I'm sorry I missed dinner.
Think I'm actually
missing it right now.

I wanted to say goodbye
to you, and more too.
So here it is.

I'm sorry that I'm not
Emily. But I was never
supposed to be. Took
me a while to learn
that, and I hope you
can see it too. I spent
my whole life waiting

because I was trying to
live a future that was
never mine. And I did it
because I wanted you to
be proud of me. To just
once say, "Good job, Jet."
I needed it, lived for it,
and I don't think that was
healthy, for either of us.
I'm sorry.
I'll probably die without
once hearing you say
you're proud of me, but
that's ok. I think you'd

have been proud of the person I would have become after this week, because of this week. And even if you aren't proud of her, I am. We've come far, she and I.

You don't have to listen to me, but I hope you do. I think you've spent a lot of your life blaming other people. It's always someone else's fault, when life is unfair or hard. It might make you feel better, just like

it made me feel better to tell myself I always had more time, I always had more "Later."
Sometimes those crutches are the things that are hurting us.

If you can do one thing for me, Mom, I want you to let it all go.

You'll feel so much lighter.

I do.

Love you. And I'm proud of you.

Jet xx

Dear Dad,

I'm not sure where to start so I'll start with this.

You are the kindest man I ever knew.

And I know you probably don't think so—because of our screwed-up kidneys—but I'm so lucky I got to be your daughter.

You are so kind. Sometimes, maybe, to a fault. You always want to be fair, never want to upset people. But I think, sometimes, that makes you choose things that are unfair, on yourself, or the

people around you.
It's OK to take sides.
It's OK to follow your heart
or your gut, not just
what is "fair."
You can get off that fence
sometimes.
Say "no" more.
You'll be OK, I promise.
I'll be watching out for you.
And remember to take those
Lotrel pills — I don't want
you to join me for a long,
long time.
I mean it.
  Love you Dad.
   Jet xx

Dear Reggie,
I know you're a dog, and I know you can't read.
But I ~~~~ couldn't go without answering that one question I always ask you.
Who's a good boy?
It's you, Reg.
You're the good boy.
Take care of Mom and Dad for me.
Love Jet xx

Dear Sophia,

You're a cunt.

Love,

Jet xx

Dear Lukie,

I think we're a lot alike, you and me.

Or we were.

We've spent our whole lives trying to fill Emily's shoes, feeling crushed by her shadow; trying to prove to Mom and Dad that we are good enough too.

For you that turned into one thing: the company. For me, it was many things, and I never saw them through, never completed them, always self-sabotaged. But how were we ever going to win, competing with a ghost?

And what was the point?
I asked you if getting the
company was the thing that would
finally make you happy, that
life could truly begin after you
achieved it. You said that it
was the only thing that would
make you happy, the most
important thing.
  I think you're wrong. Like
I've always been wrong. It
won't make you happy, but
I'm scared it might be too
late for you to hear that.
  Life isn't about proving
something, about waiting for
it all to begin. It already

began, Luke, and you're missing it. But we're different here too. I think I only ever really hurt myself, living that way, but I think you've hurt other people, Luke. I know you have.

I want you to stop, I want you to be better, but I'm not sure you know how.

And I'm sorry I can't be there to help you see.

There are more important things.

Please don't hurt anyone else.

Love,
Jet xx

Dear Billy,

I saved your letter for last, because it's the hardest one to write. Actually, in some ways, it's the easiest, because you're the one person who makes everything feel easy, and Home is wherever you are, Billy.

I already said a lot of what I needed to say to you.

But there's more.

I haven't lived so much in twenty-seven years as I have this past week with you. I wish it could last forever, never end.

I know about the song. I Know you wrote it about me. I know, Billy. And I know you think I could never love you back, that we're not on the same page.

But here's the thing. I don't know if I love you in the same way, not yet, but I think I'm starting to. I think I'm falling, if I know what falling feels like. I know you make me feel safe, I know you make me feel ten feet tall. I know you're my best friend, always have been. And I think, if we'd had more time, we could have got there. We would have got there. But I also think that if I hadn't been dying, if we didn't have this week together, then maybe I never would have seen it. Maybe I would have moved to Boston, forgotten all about you. So I don't know what that means. Maybe it just wasn't in the stars for us.

You're the one who has to live. So live.

But I want you to promise me

something.
Don't be scared to love
someone else, Billy.
And — most important — don't
be scared to be loved back.
Because someone will love you
back, Billy, I promise. And
they'll figure it out much
sooner than I did.
You make sure she's nice to
you, because you're the best
person there is. Tell her I'll
be keeping an eye on her.
So, I think I'm going to
die here, in this cell, and
we still haven't figured
out who killed me.

still haven't solved my murder. Which means we failed. Which means this entire week has just been a waste of time.

But, was it really a waste of time, if I Loved every minute of it?

Love you

(and I do, I really think I do)

Jet xx

The Last Will and Testament
of Margaret "Jet" Mason

Date: 11/07/2025

I, Margaret "Jet" Mason, residing at 10 College Hill Road, Woodstock, Vermont, declare this to be my Will, and I revoke any and all codicils I previously made.

I hereby leave all of the money in my account and all other personal property to Henry Lim, so he can pay for his eye surgery.

And to Billy Finney,
Apartment 1B, 4 Central
Street, Woodstock, Vermont,
I give my Ford F-150 truck.
I know he'll take good
care of it.

Go find new stars, Billy.

Saturday
November 15

EIGHT DAYS LATER

THIRTY-THREE

"Billy, what are you doing here?"

"Hi, Dad."

Billy placed his phone on the side table, screen hidden, watched his dad come down the painted blue stairs, slowing down, unsure.

Still wearing his suit.

Billy wearing his too.

"I thought you'd still be over at the Masons', at the funeral," his dad said, reaching the final step.

Billy sniffed. "Oh, I'm going back. But there's something important I have to do first."

Dad narrowed his eyes, the ghost of something new behind them.

"Why did *you* leave the funeral early, Dad, after the church? Don't think people will notice?"

Dad swallowed; more sure, or less?

"I don't need you to talk," Billy said. "Not really. Stop me, if I go wrong anywhere."

Billy didn't feel brave, but he did when he thought of Jet, her dangerous little smile, used her words instead of his own.

"Luke Mason is your son. You—"

"—I don't know what you're talking about, Billy. Look, this has been a hard day for you. Why don't we—"

"—I said I don't need you to talk." Billy didn't raise his voice, didn't need to. "I know, Dad. While Jet was dying in my arms, Luke came here, to you. Because you're his father. You and Dianne Mason lived right across the street from each other and were having an affair, and it didn't stop when Luke was born. You kept going. Right up until the day that Emily Mason died. Want to know how I know that part?" Billy didn't pause. "Because Mom suspected it. Except she thought it was something else. I've been coming here, reading her work diaries. She'd make little notes in them, Dad. Lists. Observations. Nothing too bad, nothing you'd understand if you just read them, if you didn't know what she was thinking."

"Billy, I—"

"—Times and dates she saw you leaving the Masons' house, when you were supposed to be working late. She didn't pick up on it at all, not until 2008—that's when she started to notice. But here's the thing. I don't think Mom thought you were going over there to see Dianne. She thought it was something else. She thought you were going over there to see Emily. A sixteen-year-old girl."

Dad stepped back, eyes stretching, too much white around them.

"Yeah." Billy sniffed. "That's what Mom was scared of. And then we get to that day, the day Emily Mason drowned. *He was already wet. Before.* That's what Mom wrote. We thought she was talking about Luke, but she was actually talking about you. Mom couldn't be sure, but she was scared that it was really *you*—that you'd killed Emily, then made it look like an accident. She got that wrong, but that's what she thought. She stayed, but she must have been terrified of you. And then, seven years later, Jet goes to her, asks Mom to change her grade on a paper. She talks about Emily, uses that to try make Mom feel guilty, that you were supposed to go check on Emily and Luke. Jet didn't know why it upset Mom so much, but I do now. Whatever Jet said, it confirmed something in Mom's head, what she was already scared of. That you'd killed Emily, that it was your fault. That's why she packed her bags and left that night,

Dad, never looked back." Billy swallowed. "It wasn't about me, it's not because she couldn't love me. It was because of you."

Something healed when he said it, a patch across that hole he'd been carrying around in his heart.

Dad backed up a little more, heels hitting the wooden step.

"But Mom didn't get it all wrong." Billy kept going. Had to keep going. For Jet. "You were wet already when you came back to the house that day, before we all found Emily. Because you *did* go check on Emily and Luke, just like Dianne Mason asked you to. And that's when you saw what Luke had done. Your son, and he'd killed the daughter of the woman you love. Maybe you thought you were doing the right thing, that Luke was just an angry kid, that he didn't really mean it, I don't know. You made it look like Emily drowned by accident. Pulled her to the bottom of the pool, wrapped her hair through that drain. Then you brought Luke over here to give him an alibi. Made us play soccer. Threw that ball into the bushes so you could fabricate a reason Luke had those scratches all up his arms, made a big deal out of it, so me and Mom thought the same. He had the scratches before, Dad. I remembered. And then you sent me and Mom over to the Masons' to find Emily's body. You did that. You did all of that."

Not a ghost behind Dad's eyes anymore, but a sheen of tears. He blinked them back.

"And Dianne blamed you for Emily's death. She blamed other people too, but she blamed you, Dad. Because you didn't go check on her kids when she'd asked you to. Except you had, you could just never tell her. That's when your relationship ended. It must have been going on for fourteen years, maybe longer, but it ended when Emily died. I know, because Mom stopped making notes about you working late in her diaries. She thought it was Emily, and it stopped when she died. I guess she was right in some way."

"Billy," Dad said, just that, but Billy's name sounded strange, out of shape in his mouth. No one said his name quite like Jet had; no one ever would.

"That must have made you feel angry, that the woman you loved stopped loving you, even though you did what she'd asked, that you were just trying to protect her from the truth about Luke. Did you think that was unfair?"

One tear, catching in his dad's stubble, soaking in.

"But you keep in touch with your son, with Luke, as he grows up. You look out for him. Play golf with him, twice a week sometimes. You've never asked me to play golf." Billy sniffed. "He doesn't actually know, all this time, that you're his dad; he just thinks you're being nice. You give him advice about the company. I don't know, maybe it was your idea, when Luke told you the company was going to go under—maybe you gave him ideas of how he could save some money, turn things around. Luke must have told you about his big project on North Street, his chance to prove himself. How the foundations were going in soon, and he must have been nervous to get it right. But why did you care so much about Luke getting the company? Was it about Scott Mason—was it about him? The man you thought had taken everything from you—the woman you love, your son, that big house over there that makes ours look so small. Did you want to take his company from him as some kind of revenge? Did that mean you'd won somehow, if Luke chose you, if Luke was yours and the company was too?"

He didn't wait for his dad to answer, didn't need him to, didn't want to hear his denials or his excuses.

"And now we come to Jet," Billy said, trying to hold his voice straight. He couldn't. It cracked, right down the middle. "To Halloween. The night you killed her."

Dad shook his head.

"Stop!" Billy said, a flash of rage, hand itching at his side. "Don't do that, do not do that, Dad. I know." He swallowed it back, the fire, had to move through it. For Jet. "Jet told me something Gerry Clay said to you both that night. That he'd voted for you for chief of police. You didn't know that before—you couldn't have. You probably assumed both Dianne and David Dale had voted for you, that you'd lost the rest of them to Lou Jankowski. So when Gerry Clay told you he'd voted for you, you must have realized what that meant—that Dianne Mason had voted against you." He searched his dad's flickering eyes, knew he was right.

"Did that feel like another thing that had been stolen from you? You'd wanted that your whole life, to be chief of police, and Dianne, the woman you loved, she didn't want to have to spend any time with you, so she gives it to a stranger over you."

Billy glanced down at the phone on the side table, face down so Dad couldn't see.

"You were already angry. But that wasn't even what tipped you over the edge, was it? Maybe everything could have been OK if it was just that. And then the fight happens, Andrew Smith shoves me and you come over to break it up. That's when one of the red wig hairs transfers to you, Dad. Then, or when you're escorting Andrew home to his apartment, right next door to mine. And at some point, when you're walking him back, or once you've got him inside, Andrew Smith tells you. He thinks it's funny. That Luke Mason isn't going to inherit Mason Construction, because Scott is planning to sell it to someone else. And, what's even worse, he's going to sell it to Nell Jankowski, the wife of our new chief. He stole chief of police from you, and now he was going to steal the company too, your son's company. That's how you saw it, wasn't it? And you realized that Jet was the only person standing in the way. You had time to think it through—it wasn't just the anger of finding out, a spur-of-the-moment thing. You planned it."

Billy shifted, getting there now, cold metal digging in against his flesh, tucked beneath his shirt.

"You let yourself into my apartment after leaving Andrew's, with the key you know I keep under the mat outside. You go to that tool kit you bought me when I moved in. I'd never even used it. You open it and you find what you're looking for, something you can kill a person with. You find the hammer. You get in your car. You drive home, but not to come home, to go to the Masons' house. Out of the car, around the side of the house, so the doorbell camera doesn't catch you. You know that Scott and Dianne will be cleaning up after the fair, that Jet will be home alone. Maybe you try that side door, and if it had been locked, maybe you would have let it go, gone home. But it wasn't locked. Nothing stopped you. You went inside the house and you killed her. Hit her twice in the back of the head. Then, when she was on the ground, one last hit to the side of her head, to really make sure. She was dead—we all thought she was dead, including you." Billy's voice caught, a snag in his throat. "The dog is screaming, making too much noise. Neighbors will hear that. You don't have much time. You take Jet's phone, and you grab a dish towel on the way out, to wrap the hammer in. You drive to North Street, only takes a couple of minutes. You need to hide the phone, because that makes it look like the killer was someone Jet was in regular contact with, maybe her ex-boyfriend. And the murder weapon, because that weapon is a link back to me, which means it's a link back to you. But you know somewhere you can put them, where no one will ever find them, because concrete was going to be poured on top in just a few hours' time. You remember to turn Jet's phone off, just before you get there. You think no one will ever find them at the construction site, that they'll stay buried forever.

"Then you wait in your squad car for the call to come in on the radio. Rushed over to the scene like you were just a cop, doing his job. I bet you didn't expect that I'd be the one to find her. You didn't plan that, did you?"

Tears stung at the corner of Billy's eyes. He'd had to do that twice. Hold the woman he loved in his arms as she lay dying.

"But Jet didn't die. Not yet." Billy's eyes blurred, doubled, the world splitting, just until he blinked and the tears raced to his chin. "It was Jet who figured most of this out, not me. She did it. We just needed a couple more hours, that's all we needed. Then Jet would have known it was you too. She died not knowing." He cried, couldn't stop it now. "I would have let her die thinking it was me, so that she had that. I was going to give her that, I wanted her to have that, I thought she needed it."

But Jet hadn't needed the answer in the end, Billy knew now. She'd found something else, more important. And Billy had learned something too, when he was holding her, when the world was coming to an end, crashing down around them and he confessed because he thought he had to.

He'd finally let something go in that moment.

Not the girl he loved—that would never leave him—but his need to be loved back, to fill the hole his mom had left in his heart.

Billy could be loved, and he had been. He kept Jet's letter close, folded inside his jacket pocket, even now. Especially now, the day she went into the ground, buried forever.

"That's right, isn't it?" He choked. "All of it. Most of it. You killed Jet for Luke, for yourself. Because you were angry, because you felt betrayed by Dianne, because you thought there was this life that had been stolen from you and you wanted to punish Jet's parents for taking it. Punish the woman you loved who now hated you, by taking her other daughter. You chose Luke, because he's the person you care most about in this world. And to do that, you took the person I care most about in this world. Look at me, Dad!"

"Billy, I don't know what to say." He raised his hands. "I think you're grieving, and you're confused."

"You do know what to say!" Billy's voice cracked again, a thousand pieces. "Jet wanted you to confess, so confess!"

He reached behind him, under his shirt, fingers gripped around the cold metal.

Billy pulled out the gun.

Aimed it at his father's chest.

He didn't shake.

The world shook around him, but Billy stood still. So still.

Dad stumbled back, tripping on the stairs, hands raised above his head as he landed, hard.

"Where did you get the gun, Billy?"

"Confess, Dad!"

"Billy, I—"

Billy flicked the safety off, pointed higher, at his head.

"—Confess," he said, didn't need to shout, had no voice left for it. "Did you kill Jet?"

His dad flinched, raised his hands higher, in front of his face, shielding his head. "Yes. Yes, Billy, I did. You're right. Please, put down the gun."

Billy didn't move.

"Are you sorry?"

"Billy."

"Are you sorry, Dad?"

His head slumped, eyes crashing to Billy's feet, more ghosts behind them now, too heavy. "Yes," he said, barely a whisper. "Yes, I am."

"Why?" Billy still didn't shake. "Why are you sorry?"

Dad lowered his hands, pressed them against his chest, crinkling his dark suit.

"It was when we arrived at the construction site, after you'd found the phone, the hammer. I was watching you, Billy. Saw the way you looked at Jet. It's the same way I used to look at Dianne. I didn't know."

"That I loved her? That I'd loved her every single day since I was a little boy? That she was everything to me?"

"I'm sorry." He hung his head, made Billy aim at the gray hair on top.

"Would you have still killed her, if you'd known?"

"I don't know, Billy," he cried. "I don't know why it happened. I was just so angry at everyone, at everything, and I only saw one way out, didn't stop long enough to think it all through. Something else took over, like the day Emily died. I just did what I had to do, to protect Luke. To help my son."

"But I'm your son too!" Billy roared. "I'm yours too! I'm the one who was here, who was always here! And you never even saw me, especially after Mom left!"

"I'm sorry."

"Sorry doesn't bring Jet back. She's gone, Dad. I lost her."

His chest seized, closing in around his heart, hiding it. It belonged to Jet, always would, he thought. But it belonged to Billy now too, shared, one half each.

"Where did you get the gun, Billy?"

"This." Billy flicked his gaze to the gun in his right hand. "It belongs to Henry Lim. He let us borrow it. Doesn't want his brother to go to prison forever, for killing Jet. JJ didn't kill Jet. I know you tried very hard to make it look like he did, wrapped a neat little story around all that circumstantial evidence. Was it hard to convince Detective Ecker, or was he happy to take the easy way out, the simplest explanation?"

"Billy—"

"—I can't live with that, Dad," Billy sniffed, pushing on before he lost his nerve. He wouldn't lose it, because Jet was right here with him, and she was the brave one, dangerous little smile and her old man laugh. "I'm the one who has to live, that's what Jet told me, and I can't live with this. *You,* getting to walk around with her blood on your hands, while JJ goes to prison for the rest of his life for something he didn't do. All for Luke. Why did you do this?!" Billy's voice grated, tearing at his throat. "Why do you care about Luke so much?!"

"Because he's mine!" Dad cried. "And because he's Dianne's. He's ours!"

"And you think Luke would have wanted you to do this? Kill his little sister?"

Dad put his hands up again, eyes dark and urgent.

"He would understand," he said. "I did it for him. I look out for him, always have. He won't have the same life I did, people taking what should have been mine." He shook his head, something stirring in his eyes as he stared down the barrel of the gun.

Billy tightened his grip. "I promised Jet, as she was dying, that I was going to finish this for her. So that's what I'm doing."

"No, Billy, no!" Dad begged. "Don't kill me. Please. Put the gun down!"

"OK." Billy loosened his grip, the gun swinging around his finger. He placed it on the table, beside his phone.

"OK?" Dad was confused, gaze flickering between Billy and the gun.

"I'm not going to kill you, Dad. I hate you, but I'm not like you," Billy said. He picked up his phone instead, tapped the screen. "I got what I came for."

Dad pushed up to his feet, wiped his face. "You were recording me, is that it?" He gestured to Billy's phone, lines of sweat striping his temple. "You think you can take that to the police, that they'll arrest me and you get your ending?" His face tensed, almost a sad smile, not quite making it. "That's not how it works, Billy. A recording like that, it's not evidence, it's not admissible in court, especially as you coerced it out of me, a gun in my face. That's not how this works."

"I know, Dad. I'm not an idiot. I am more than you think I am. Not just poor, sweet Billy." He sniffed, waved his phone. "I wasn't recording you. But someone was listening. Just one person."

The ghosts came back, behind Dad's eyes, mouth dropping open.

"Who?" he whispered.

"Me."

The voice rang out behind them, through the front door Billy had left ajar.

Luke.

Crisp white shirt, a black tie too tight around his reddening neck. His phone in his hand, by his side.

Dad swallowed, the color draining from his face, from his eyes somehow too, graying hair and grayscale skin. "Luke. I can explain. None of that was true. He was pointing a gun at me. I didn't—"

"—You killed Jet," Luke said, voice dark and deep, something ticking by his jaw, beneath the skin.

"No! I just said that because—"

"—I heard everything you said."

"Luke, listen, I—"

Billy cut in now, stepping back, shoulder to shoulder with Luke. Half his brother, half not. This man they shared, shivering before them. "—No, you listen, Dad. I thought this would hurt you most," he said. "This ending. You've lost everything for Luke. And now you just lost him too."

Luke sharpened his eyes, that earthy green, so like Jet's.

Dad shook his head, staring at Luke. The only son he saw.

"I asked you," Luke said, a growl hiding behind his voice. "The night Jet died. I asked you if you had anything to do with it. You swore to me. You said it wasn't you. You lied! You killed her!" The growl didn't hide anymore, splitting his words in half, that temper rearing, up his throat. Billy stepped back from him, half a step.

"Calm down, Luke." Dad raised his hands again. "Let's talk."

"Don't tell me to calm down!" Luke couldn't stand still, vibrating inside his funeral suit. "You killed her!"

"I was just trying to protect you, Luke. I did it for you. All for you."

"Why?!" Luke roared. "So I'd get the company, is that all?!"

"You deserve it—it should be yours!"

Luke balled his hands, knuckles straining through the skin, almost healed. "Why? It won't make me happy. There are more important things. My sister was more important!"

Billy looked at Luke. That was what Jet said to him in her letter, her final goodbye. Luke could be scary, Luke had a temper, but maybe Luke *could* change; maybe he was even changing right now, in front of Billy's eyes. Was this what Jet would have wanted? She never got the chance to tell Billy the ending *she* would have chosen.

"You're right, Dad," Billy spoke up now, standing between them. "A recording wouldn't have been admissible in court. But now there are two witnesses who heard your confession, both your sons. And there's evidence too." He paused, pointed up the stairs. "That Coleby tool kit, I returned it to you, it's in the closet upstairs. The police will find it when they search the house. We'll tell them everything. We'll go to-night, after the funeral, after I say goodbye to the girl I loved. Right, Luke?"

A click in the back of Dad's throat.

"It means nothing," he said. "You coerced it out of me, threatened me with a gun."

Billy pressed his lips together. "I don't see a gun. Do you, Luke?"

He turned back to look at Luke. Jaw still ticking, counting down to something, hands itching at his sides.

"Luke?"

His eyes darkened, neck strained, ridged with tendons, threads pulled too tight.

"I do," Luke said, lunging forward.

Billy didn't have a chance to stop him.

He grabbed the gun from the table.

"Luke, no!"

Luke raised the gun, pointed it at Dad's head, finger on the trigger.

"Dad, run!"

Billy barreled into Luke.

An eruption of sound, cracking the night into two. The before and the after.

Plaster rained down on Billy's head, white dust on his jacket, a bullet hole in the ceiling.

Luke growled. He righted his arm, pointed the gun again, but Dad wasn't there anymore.

He was running.

Past them.

Out the open front door into the night beyond.

Luke didn't hesitate. He shoved Billy back and chased after him, gun at his side.

"Luke, stop!"

Billy's legs flew, and so did his heart, fight-or-flight or something in between.

This wasn't supposed to happen.

Outside, Dad was past the fence, sprinting across the road, toward the Masons' driveway.

Luke on his heels, bearing down on him.

Billy followed. No thoughts. Just Jet. What would Jet do?

Three suits, one gun, stained silver by the same moon.

Up the drive, a dozen cars parked in messy rows.

Dad wound between them, colliding with a blue Range Rover. The alarm went off, a mechanical scream, red lights flashing.

Luke followed him, past the Range Rover, catching up.

Billy chose a different path.

"Luke, no! There's a better way!" he shouted.

Dad had reached the house now, pummeling his fists against the red-painted door.

"Dianne!" he screamed. "Help!"

Luke stopped behind Dad.

Billy behind him.

"Dianne!"

Billy saw her, through the window into the living room. Red-raw face, black dress, peering into the darkness outside the glass, at the chirping car.

Luke raised the gun.

"Luke, don't!"

"Dianne! Help!"

Dad pressed the doorbell instead, that up-and-down song. The camera didn't blink, watching this all happen. Inevitable now.

Luke swung his left arm forward, held the gun with both hands.

"LUKE!"

A thunderclap.

Not inside Billy's head, from Luke's hands.

A flash.

Billy blinked.

Dad fell to his knees.

A spatter on the front door, a darker red, the color of hellfire.

"No," Billy whispered.

Another crack, another burst of white.

Dad fell to the ground.

He didn't move.

Billy blinked.

Not the ending he'd planned, but an ending he could live with. Because he was the one who had to live.

For Jet.

The front door opened.

Dianne and Scott and Sophia.

Someone screamed.

Billy blinked.

FOR HER
(Updated—New verse and chorus)

I won't drag you round in my heart no more,
I'll save one half for me.
Letting go, without ever forgetting, no.
Because you're coming too, get ready.
I'll do what you asked, leaving at last.
Find new stars, OK, I'm going.
Wish me luck in your little blue truck.

One day starts today because—

I loved her and she loved me back,
Same page, same track, not the right story.
Found each other to find ourselves, I'm sorry,
But it's a lesson I'll never forget.
That final week, not quite long enough, not quite dead yet.
But if it's a frog to you, then it's a frog to me too.
And (I swear) I'll always play it (I do),
Because I wrote this little song . . . for Jet.

ACKNOWLEDGMENTS

... And breathe. Sorry, I know that was intense. I still find myself feeling sad for Jet (and I made her up) so I'm sorry for inflicting that trauma on you too. But I hope you don't just remember the sadness. I hope you remember her strength, and channel it when you need to. I certainly have this past year. WWJD (What Would Jet Do). So, my first thank you must go to you, reader. Thank you for letting me live my dream, telling stories for a living. It is bananas—truly—and there are no words for how grateful I am (and I know *lots* of words). But most of all, thank you for trusting me with your time; I hope you loved every minute of it.

My next thanks, as always, must go to the best literary agent in the world, Sam Copeland. This book was really an exercise in trust—for *him*, not me . . . I knew I had this down—as I insisted on writing an entire book, start to finish, while not under contract, much to my agent's dismay. But I wanted this book—and Jet's story—to speak for itself, not to rely solely on those who came before (CC: Pip, Red, and Bel). But the book didn't have to speak for itself, because Sam was there to champion it from day one, sowing seeds and spreading the word before he himself even really knew what it was about. All he had to go on was my vague description: "Woman solves her own murder in seven days, and then it gets a bit *It's a Wonderful Life-y.*" Jet may be one of a kind, and so is Sam. Thank you.

Next, to my other wonderful agent, Emily Hayward-Whitlock, who is the best film/TV agent in the world (see, I can be diplomatic). Thank you, Emily, for being the calm I have so often needed these past couple of years, and for guiding this ship through every high and low. Thank you for dedicating so much time, effort, and care to me as my fictional worlds make their way to the screen. I think we make a jolly good team.

Perhaps my greatest thanks are owed to Dr. Matthew Pitt, without whom this book wouldn't have been possible. Thank you for being so generous with your time and medical expertise, as I detailed exactly what horrors I wanted to put this main character through. Thank you for helping me come up with a scenario that was as realistic and true to life as possible. I did deviate slightly from what we discussed—swapping out a bullet fragment for a sliver of skull—so any medical inaccuracies are mine and mine alone, but I hope you'll forgive me as I hold my hands up and yell: "Poetic license!" Thank you for making this story I was dying to tell possible.

Now, to my incredible publishers. Firstly, the team at Bantam. My amazing editor needs no introduction, but I will do so anyway. Thank you so much to Jennifer Hershey, for adding me to your incredible existing list of authors, and for so expertly taking me and Jet under your wing. I'm so glad we both found our home with you, and I'm so grateful for the time and care you've dedicated to us. Thank you also to Kara Welsh and Kim Hovey, for believing in this book, and in me. Thank you to Taylor Noel in marketing, and Jennifer Garza and Melissa Folds in publicity. Thank you to Scott Biel for my incredible cover. I love it so much, and thank you for your patience as we slowly found our way toward it—ha! In this instance, I really hope people do judge a book by its cover. And thank you to: Loren Noveck, Jenn Backe, Debbie Glasserman, Saige Francis, Pam Alders, Richard Booth, Sarah Feightner, Nicholas LoVecchio, Deborah Bader, Kate Gomer, Julia Henderson, and Bridget Sweet. Thank you all so much for working so hard to take this story and turn it into a real-life book. I'm still convinced it's magic.

And to my and Jet's UK publisher, Michael Joseph. As soon as I met the team—before any of you even really knew what this book was about—I felt completely at home. I knew that not only were you the best team for the job, but that we would also have fun in the meantime— a lesson I also needed to learn, alongside Jet. Thank you so much to my amazing editor Joel Richardson; I'm so grateful that I have you in my corner, with your sharp eye and your boundless enthusiasm. Thank you to Max Hitchcock, Louise Moore, Hannah Smith, and Nalisha Vansia, for being as excited about this book as I am. Thank you to Sriya Varad-harajan and Frankie Banks in publicity, and to Annie Moore and Vicky Photiou in marketing. And thank you to Lee Motley for my amazing UK cover.

Thank you to booksellers across the world who make sure my books actually find their way into readers' hands. I owe you everything.

Thank you to my family, as ever, for always being the first readers of all of my books. But most especially to my little sister, Olivia, who was my very first reader ever. My origin story as an author began at ten years old, when I would write (murder-filled) short stories just for you. Thank you for letting me traumatize you, both back then and forever. And thank you to my parents for not catching on to the above, while I fostered a love for storytelling. Thank you to Joe, who is now *officially* family. Thank you for trusting me to (*unofficially*) marry you and Liv, and to write something different—full of hope and happy endings—for a change. Thank you to Peter and Gaye for your unending support, and to Katie for talking brains and other medical things with me. And to Harry for caring about me and my books more than most. Thank you to Dexter—*you* are actually the good boy, Reggie is just made up, I swear.

And, as ever, the most important thank you belongs to one person. Ben. Unlike most of my book couples so far (oops sorry), we actually are endgame.

ABOUT THE AUTHOR

Holly Jackson is the author of the #1 *New York Times* bestselling series *A Good Girl's Guide to Murder,* an international sensation with millions of copies sold worldwide and a hit Netflix series. She enjoys playing video games and watching true-crime documentaries so she can pretend to be a detective. She lives in London.

Instagram: @hojay92
TikTok: @hojax92

ABOUT THE TYPE

This book was set in Minion, a 1990 Adobe Originals typeface by Robert Slimbach. Minion is inspired by classical, old-style typefaces of the late Renaissance, a period of elegant and beautiful type designs. Created primarily for text setting, Minion combines the aesthetic and functional qualities that make text type highly readable with the versatility of digital technology.